STARGAZY PIE

Also by Laura Lockington:

Capers in the Sauce

STARGAZY PIE

Laura Lockington

CENTURY · LONDON

Published by Century in 2002

1 3 5 7 9 10 8 6 4 2

First published in the United Kingdom in 2002 by Century
The Random House Group Limited
20 Vauxhall Bridge Road, London, SW1V 2SA

Random House Australia (Pty) Limited
20 Alfred Street, Milsons Point, Sydney,
New South Wales 2061, Australia

Random House New Zealand Limited
18 Poland Road, Glenfield
Auckland 10, New Zealand

Random House (Pty) Limited
Endulini, 5a Jubilee Road, Parktown 2193, South Africa

The Random House Group Limited Reg. No. 954009

www.randomhouse.co.uk

A CIP catalogue record for this book
is available from the British Library

Papers used by Random House
are natural, recyclable prod   made from wood grown in
sustainable forests. The manufacturing processes conform to
the environmental regulations of the country of origin

ISBN 0 712 67093 9

Typeset by Deltatype Ltd, Birkenhead, Wirral

Printed and bound in Great Britain by CPD, Wales

For Julie B.

Acknowledgements

With love and a huge amount of thanks to: Iain Mann for providing endless technical support; Andrew Kay, fellow *bon vivant*; Louby Lou for listening; Georgina Capel for being so positive; Kate Elton for a great idea; Peggy Ziolkowski and her son Paul Ziolkowski for the wonderful teddy bear story; Lee Brown for being the best kitchen gossip in the world and all the other usual suspects.

Chapter One

Nobody understands the meaning of the word embarrassment unless they have travelled on a packed InterCity train with a small masturbating monkey, trust me on this. Although the monkey, Jicky, was packed into a wicker cat basket, he could be clearly seen indulging in his favourite, well, his *only*, hobby through the door of the basket.

At first, old women and children would peer in and coo sweetly at him, then they would turn away in disgust, or giggles, depending on their age and constitution, and I would get the hundred and fiftieth lecture of the day about how cruel it was to keep them as pets, and wasn't it illegal? I'd given up explaining that I was taking him to a monkey sanctuary, it was far too tedious, so I just nodded and agreed with them, whilst casting furious looks at Jicky, mentally imploring him to stop.

Last night as I cooked supper for myself, with Jicky draped round my neck as a sort of living fur stole that presumably only Anna Wintour would approve of, he stole an anchovy and spat it out in disgust, making little chattering noises. I laughed, and realised that although he'd only been with me a week, I was going to miss him. He was a ravishing-looking animal, mainly black with a fluffy ring-marked tail and white eye markings that made him look permanently surprised.

How I'd got him, and why it was me that was taking him to the sanctuary was all to do with my boss, *and* close friend, Davey.

It was the week before Christmas and Davey insisted that we go to his club for a drink and dinner; being Davey, it was never described as a Christmas works outing, or anything so vulgar, but that, in effect, was what it was.

Davey owned a small bookshop. Well, it had started out as a bookshop, with small inroads into very expensive hand-blocked stationery imported from Florence, and Mont Blanc pens. But Davey had begun to import some art from Thailand, China and Japan, as well as small figurative wooden carvings from Indonesia. The shop was a bit like the man, eccentric, eclectic but quite attractive. Everything in it seemed to be selling well enough, but we weren't exactly raking it in. Though as I tactlessly pointed out to him, the fact that we were busy at the moment could have more to do with the public's habit of impulse buying at this time of year than their sudden development of an aesthetic taste for foreign art.

'Thanks, Poppy darling, you do have the knack of cheering me up,' Davey said acidly.

I mumbled something about quite possibly being

wrong, and he suggested that we have dinner that evening at his club. So we set off towards Soho, and as always I was very intrigued indeed to see this private side of Davey.

I had worked for him for three years now, and we were very good friends, despite the obvious employer/ employee drawback to the relationship. He is a tall, fair, kindly man with a nice line in barbed wit. Gay, of course. Most men who manage to be all those things are, it seems. I used to cook dinner for him at least once a week, and we would always end up drinking far too much and getting severe face hurt because we made each other laugh so much.

When I had first applied for the job in his shop we had taken an immediate liking to one another, despite or maybe because of our vastly different backgrounds. He had gone to Eton ('Slough Comprehensive', said in a self-deprecatory drawl) and I had completely undistin- guished myself at a state-run, bog-normal concrete bunker in Suffolk.

Davey lived in the Chelsea flat belonging to his mad family who were based in Cornwall. He talked about them a lot and the more I heard about them, the more barking they all seemed. Still, I would beg him for more details, marvelling at the dotty things they did. The latest bit of gossip about them that had preoccupied our chats was his parents' decision to make a bizarre will. They had written it whilst gliding up the Nile on a felucca on one of their numerous buying trips to snap up Egyptian bits and bobs for their collection. I didn't

3

really know the fine details but it was worrying Davey rather a lot.

We walked to Soho, past glittering shop fronts that sparkled in the cold night air. Every window had fairy lights, and tons of tinsel. Davey sniffed disapprovingly. 'Decorations for the masses, my idea of hell.'

I laughed, because I knew that really, he was just reinforcing his personality. It was the sort of thing he was expected to say, so he obligingly did.

London was packed with Christmas shoppers, all looking exceedingly tense and agitated, hunched up against the cold and drooping under the weight of redundant presents chosen in a mad panic of nerves and paid for by credit cards that were soon going to be cut up in pieces by vicious shop assistants.

Surprisingly, I'd never actually been to his club before and I suddenly stopped in the middle of the pavement and clutched Davey's cashmere-coated arm, terrified by a stray thought that had popped unbidden into my head. 'Here, Davey, your club – it's not, well, it's not got boys *stripping* or anything, has it?' I asked rather nervously.

'Good God, woman! Where on earth do you think we are, Bangkok?' He peered down at me, laughing. 'No, no, nothing like that at all, it's just a club, you know, sells drink and food. Nothing to be scared of. Come along, you'll be fine.'

I doubted this. I didn't seem to be fine anywhere I went. I was out of kilter with the rest of the world, it seemed, too young for some things, or too old for others. Too fat, too thin, wrong sex, wrong class. I couldn't ever quite figure out where I had gone wrong. I felt I would have been quite all right if I had been born two hundred years ago to well-off parents who lived in Bath. I would have been a regular face taking the waters, and bowling madly along in a carriage. But somehow modern life had passed me by. Still unmarried at an age that made it seem impossible I ever would be, not even a risqué divorce under my belt, no circle of wildly wacky friends, not even an interesting family on the horizon. Just a very normal, slightly sporty, non-reading couple of parents in Ipswich. I was an adopted child – this had been made clear to me from an early age, and somehow I had never grown very close to them. Of course, when I was younger I had harboured secret thoughts that my real parents were romantic gypsies, or part of the Romanov dynasty, but I had grown out of that nonsense. Well, most of the time. I realised that my real mother had probably been a frightened young girl who gave me up for adoption because she was too young to cope by herself.

I'd had a series of low-paid, non-skilled jobs, a sort of one-up notch from Macjobs. The only good thing about them was that I certainly didn't suffer from ulcers worrying about redundancies in the middle of the night or how I was going to have to spout an acceptance speech for the Oscars. How very boring my life CV sounded, I thought. *Not* for the first time, I must admit.

Davey's voice interrupted my train of thought and I

heard him say, 'You know, Poppy, you just worry too much about everything, come on, do,' as he pulled me along in his wake.

I realised I had been dawdling. Something that as a child I was constantly told I did. Dawdling and day-dreaming had got me through the seemingly endless experience of the prison sentence that was school, so I was very grateful to them.

Davey pushed me through a revolving door and I was relieved to see that although his club was alarming, it wasn't frightening. You know, alarming in that it was filled with horribly confident, beautiful people. But not so far on the terror scale that it had me bolting out the door. Davey was obviously well known in there, and was greeted by several people. He pushed me towards an empty table and was soon pouring white wine into my glass and peering at a menu.

'Why is it a club?' I asked, not understanding that the rich of London like to pay membership fees, before they've had so much as a bite to eat. Oh, and of course famous people have to go where other famous people are. Even though, as I pointed out to Davey, the only famous person here was a model known for showing off her knickers in fashion magazines, now slumped at the bar, calling upwards to an unseen person.

I knew that she was called Babaganoush (obviously made up, and I thought it was something to do with aubergines, but I may well be wrong) and she was obviously drunk. Several people were gathered around her, helping her to try and coax something down from the ceiling. I heard her call out the name 'Jicky' and brandish a banana. The people grouped around her were becoming quite excited.

'Christ, it's a monkey!'

'Oh God, look what it's doing now . . .'

I craned my neck and saw that it was indeed a very small monkey, sitting on top of the highest shelf behind the bar. A barman had climbed on to a lower shelf and was slowly edging his way towards it, making little squeaking noises, presumably trying to fool the creature into believing he was a fellow monkey. The real one looked down at the barman with interest and then suddenly used his head as a stepping-stone from which to leap on to a light fitting, stopping only to whip the banana out of the model's hand. A chorus of voices joined in the general discussion about how to lure him down.

'My God, he moves like greased lightning, doesn't he?'

'Eow, look what he's doing now! Disgusting . . .'

'Oooh, he's so sweet.'

'Give him another banana.'

'Could turn nasty, you know. After all, it is a *wild* animal.'

'It's a cute little monkey, not a marauding tiger.'

'All I'm saying is that a wild animal is a wild animal, it's not a lap-dog, is it?'

'I left mine on the tube yesterday.'

'What, your lap-dog?'

'Oh, no, sorry. I thought you said lap*top*.'

7

'Where did you buy it?'

'Dixons.'

'Dixons are selling *monkeys*?'

A general madness had swept over the beautiful people as they tried to tempt the monkey downwards. Some very silly suggestions indeed were made, and I glanced at Davey to see if he was going to join in the fray. He looked as though he was enjoying himself, and I turned my attention back to the monkey. He seemed quite content perched on the light fitting, gazing at the mayhem he'd caused.

Davey leant forwards and said something to me. I had been expecting this, and had been trying to think of an acceptable way to decline. He invited me to spend Christmas with himself and his family in the West Country. Davey had asked me before, and I had always refused. Although I adored hearing about them, *meeting* his family would have my fear soaring off my own personal scareometer.

I was just making my customary, rather feeble, excuses when I heard the Greek chorus give a roar of approval and felt a small, hot, furry creature land on my shoulders. I leapt up, knocking my chair over in my confusion, but instead of being dislodged, the monkey merely tightened his grip and clung on to me.

'Ah, look, he's found a friend . . .'

'Oh, why didn't he come to me?'

'Not simian enough, darling.'

I glared at this remark, but realised that the effect was lost as one of my eyes was covered in monkey fur. I

8

tried to untangle his hands, which were scarily human, from my hair, and could feel his little heart beating through his ribs. He was making high-pitched whimpering noises, and I sensed that he was frightened.

The model, Babaganoush, was kneeling in front of me, reaching up to the monkey.

'Hees name is Jicky, he was geeve to me, by my good friend, and I promise to take heem to 'ow you say? Monkey home in ze country. But I am soo busy, eet ees impossible. Look, he love you! You take heem, yes?'

I gazed wildly at Davey for some help, but he just grinned broadly at me. The model tossed her hair around a lot and begged me to help her. She leant forward to reveal a lot of tanned cleavage to Davey, but immediately realised that it didn't cut any ice with him and so tried instead to become very girlie with me. I stumbled out a few objections but she dismissed them out of hand. She then promptly burst into tears, and pleaded with me. Scenes of any sort leave me feeling very flustered and so that, it seemed, was that. I was in sole charge of the monkey.

I won't go into the indignities of eating dinner in a very fashionable club with a live monkey doing really quite revolting things on my shoulder, or of Davey's very unhelpful suggestions and increasing hysteria at the situation.

'God, Poppy, it looks like you're wearing a very trendy hat, not madly you, I would say.'

I pleaded with him and demanded help till he went off and got a cat basket from the model and we forced

Jicky into it, with much squealing. After that things got a bit calmer, and Davey reiterated his invitation to spend Christmas in the country with his family.

'Now listen, sweetheart,' he said, kindly. 'I *know* what you're going to say. That you were planning to cook something special and watch the big movie on TV, weren't you? Well, it doesn't sound awfully exciting, does it? You've simply got to get out and live a bit, you know. Besides, the monkey sanctuary is about half an hour from the Abbey, so you see, it was meant to be!' He eyed me speculatively and added, almost to himself, 'Besides, who knows what might happen . . .'

'What?'

'Nothing. I just want you to come home with me, that's all.'

I squirmed in my chair and admitted that my Christmas didn't sound very thrilling, but it was what I wanted, and it was what I was used to, and why didn't Davey take Jicky with him?

'Because I am driving down tomorrow in my fabulous two-seater and leaving you and the Troll' – a very rude nickname that Davey had given to the temporary Christmas helper – 'in charge of my empire whilst I go and prepare green swags and polish glasses and help my poor parents with the usual hilarious snapdragon party.'

What?

'Oh, you know, it's one of those family things.' He waved his hands grandly around, implying that every family of any worth had odd traditions and I was simply being dim.

I was tempted, but very unsure of myself. Not only were his parents, as Davey said, 'rather eccentric' (I had inwardly snorted at this, coming as it was from a man who by no means could be described as normal), but there was also a batty-sounding sister, and a maverick brother and his American live-in girlfriend. Along with assorted friends, who no doubt were equally mad. It was intriguing to hear about them from a distance, but the thought of meeting them practically brought me out in hives.

'Davey, are you asking me because you feel sorry for me?' I suddenly demanded.

His pale blue eyes widened in surprise. 'God, no! Look, Poppy, the thing is, well, you really are good company, you know?' He fiddled with his cuffs, and then added, honestly, 'At least, you are when you're not worrying about whether you're in the wrong place, or saying the wrong thing. And it does worry me that you don't seem to go anywhere, or meet anyone.'

I was filled with gloom. He was quite right. I didn't know how my life had become like this. I had looked up one day and found myself here. Not such a bad place to be, but not great either. A tiny flat in South London, an untaxing job, hardly any friends, no partner and a wardrobe that had seen better days. Oh dear. I really must take myself in hand, I thought. I really must make more of an effort. The problem about making an effort was, it was just that. An effort. I was much happier dawdling. A good book, a good movie and Davey to talk to in the day. What else was there anyway? I sighed. This kind of thinking got you nowhere. And here I was with an invitation to spend Christmas with a large, mad, wealthy family where anything could happen. Take a chance and agree, I urged myself.

'Anyway,' Davey added, still fiddling with his cuffs, 'you're my special friend, you know? I'd really like my family to meet you.'

That stumped me for a while. It was unlike Davey to throw compliments around, and I was touched that he had described me in that way. I felt the same about him, and on dark nights had even wondered idly what it would be like between us if he wasn't gay.

'Besides, Jicky needs you to take him to his new home,' Davey said, taking out his fob watch and checking the time. (He always wore a fob watch, and always checked the time, even when he wasn't bored, though he probably was by now with my endless ability to procrastinate.)

I looked over at him and wondered for the thousandth time why he hadn't got a partner. We discussed it together endlessly at work over cups (bone china, of course) of tea and the matter was inconclusive. Davey was one of those old-fashioned young fogeys. Public school and a private income of sorts had enabled him to live the life of a gentleman of leisure, although he had confessed once to behaving very badly indeed on a buying trip in Thailand.

'But if you can abroad, why can't you here?' I'd asked, puzzled.

He'd rolled his eyes at me and said, 'That's the whole point, Poppy! Abroad simply doesn't count, surely you can see that?'

I'd pointed out that the only bit of abroad I'd seen was two package holidays on the Mediterranean which had been utter disasters. Sunburn on the first and shellfish poisoning on the second.

Davey rapped the table with his knuckles and taxed me again with the invitation. 'I'll even buy your train ticket,' he added magnanimously.

He'd have to, was my unworthy thought, with the wages he paid me. Like most wealthy people he was extraordinarily mean in some ways, and wildly generous in others. I'd once sent him out for tea bags for the shop, and he'd come back simply *horrified* at the price of them, but then thought nothing of spending fifty quid on a bunch of flowers.

'Poppy, come on. You'll have a great time, I promise. I'll make sure you don't get the haunted room and, well, look, I don't want to think of you alone. So go on, what do you say?'

He laughed when he saw the look of panic on my face and added, 'The haunted room bit was a joke; the Abbey is disappointingly free of ghosts, unless you count my sister, I suppose.'

I absent-mindedly stroked Jicky through the wicker door of his basket. His little black hand immediately grabbed my finger, and he rubbed his head against it.

What was I really worried about? Well, apart from meeting Davey's family, nothing. But that was enough for me to go into hyperventilation. I *hated* meeting new people. All that chit-chat and meaningless nonsense. It could be supposed that I was cripplingly shy, or that some awful disaster had happened to me at an impressionable age, but it hadn't.

There are more people like me than you suppose, I think. Centuries ago we would have been referred to as the parson's relict. The youngish spinster who made charity calls and dished out soup, or stayed at home and did the flowers.

Of course, nowadays there really isn't the room in our society for that strange and peculiar thing, the unmarried woman. Oh yes, I mean it's OK if you're brilliant at what you do, or you are obviously a dyke. But a normal, reasonably good-looking woman who, it seems, just wilfully refuses to have a partner, attracts sly whispers. What's wrong with her? Has she had her heart broken? Is she harbouring a secret married love? Is she, somehow, not *normal*? I think it is one of the reasons why Davey and I became such good friends; we formed a we-are-normal-but-single club, and rebelled against being seen as freaks of nature.

'Poppy . . .' Davey said patiently.

'Oh, God, sorry, I was miles away. Do you think people think I should be a nun or something?' I asked.

'What?'

'No, don't answer that, we'll be here all bloody night.'

'Look, I've been thinking. I'm not going to take no for

14

an answer. I'll set you up with a hunky Cornish fisherman or something. Don't look like that, you know I'm joking. Now, let's get the bill and I'll get you a taxi.'

I protested that I couldn't afford a taxi, and Davey insisted on paying for it, pointing out that Jicky would freeze to death waiting for the bus.

We stopped at our shop on the way home, where Davey pushed a very handsome copy of *South American Monkeys* by R. Angel into my hands, and then stopped again at a brightly lit greengrocer's, with hundreds of marked-down pine Christmas trees leaning on the pavement, where he bought grapes and bananas for Jicky. He even helped me up the steps into my flat, and kissed me on the cheek.

'Poppy, don't worry about it, you're going to have a lovely time. I'll see you tomorrow at the shop,' he called out to me, as he ran back down the steps to the waiting taxi.

I shouted my thanks for dinner, and bolted the front door shut. I bent down to release Jicky from his basket and he immediately wrapped himself around my neck, his little hands foraging in my hair. Probably searching for nits, I thought. I hoped to God he didn't find any.

That night I went to bed with a mug of hot chocolate, a bunch of grapes, a slab of lemon cake and a monkey that insisted on sharing my pillow. I had squirted him with some perfume, and he smelt a lot nicer than before. I realised that this probably wasn't the done thing, but if I had to share my bed with him, he needed to smell less like a, well, a monkey.

15

I leafed through the R. Angel book in an attempt to identify Jicky. It made very disturbing reading. Apparently, monkeys are classified under the dangerous wild animal laws, and can turn very nasty indeed. They can be vicious and aggressive. I glanced down nervously at Jicky. He was curled fast asleep on my tummy, his small hands were outside the bedclothes and he looked about as capable of attacking anyone as a bunny rabbit.

I looked through all the pictures of monkeys but couldn't find what species he was. None of them looked right. Maybe he was a cross-breed or something. Can you get cross-breeds in monkeys? I wondered. I'd always been very confused about nature, and had never really understood the mule, ass and donkey thing. You know, you breed one with one and get another one that is completely incapable of reproducing itself. Hmm, well, that made sense. We can all but assume that the Almighty really does have a sense of humour and gets a little bored now and again like the rest of us.

Jicky stirred in his sleep and made contented chuntering noises. I read on and found out that monkeys were very sociable animals, and needed to find the proper social hierarchy within a group. They foraged for plants and insects and led a very healthy life. I glanced down at him again. I had my doubts about the foraging thing, but I was willing to believe it.

The last few days of Christmas week flashed by, and

the Troll and I had very little time to pander to Jicky's whims. I hid him in his basket at the back of the shop, hoping that he would behave himself, which of course he didn't. At all.

Davey, true to his word, had left me not only a train ticket, but also a huge wodge of money with a scribbled note to buy a party dress (not from anywhere in Oxford Street) and have my hair done (ditto).

This filled me with panic. What *sort* of party dress? What *exactly* done to my hair? And why not Oxford Street? OK, OK, I sort of knew the answer to that, but it really didn't make it any easier.

In the end, I summoned up the courage to ask Jessy. Jessy owned the wildly expensive florist's which nestled next door to Davey's shop. She was a very tall, angular creature with conker-coloured poker-straight hair. I found her a bit intimidating really, but I could see that if you were going to ask fashion advice from anyone, it would have to be from someone stylish, and she certainly fitted the bill.

Her shop was a whirl of activity, and smelt, as always, divine. I put my problem to her whilst she was knocking up a very modern Christmas wreath which consisted of bleached twigs and bits of livid green moss. Her eyes lit up with pleasure, and she asked me how much money Davey had left me. I told her, and she whistled her approval.

'What a nice man he is, we'll have you looking like a babe in no time,' she said approvingly.

Babe, *babe*? I had no idea what that really meant, but

I didn't like the sound of it at all. I also rather hoped that we wouldn't have to spend all of Davey's money on this transformation.

Jessy darted forward to answer a phone, and said to me, 'Don't worry, I'll pick you up next door at five. Get the Troll to lock up and we'll hit the shops.'

I nodded glumly and caught sight of myself in one of the many mirrors in her shop. A small, brown-haired, slightly anxious woman looked back at me. I took a deep breath and tried to look confident and ready for the challenge of shopping. I looked again in the mirror, and gave up. Perhaps a cup of tea with the Troll and sharing a banana with Jicky would improve my morale.

Chapter Two

The train was making moving noises now, and still no one had sat at my table, despite it being Christmas Eve and very busy. I pushed Jicky's basket as far back against the window as I could and peered down to check that he was OK.

The woman that I'd spoken to last night at the monkey sanctuary had been very understanding, even when I'd told her that I had no confidence whatsoever in his foraging ability. He'd seen a moth once, fluttering around my bedside light, and had dived anxiously under the bedclothes, making frightened yelps. I'd had to comfort him with a cube of cream fudge that I had rather been looking forward to myself. The woman had laughed, and promised me that within days he would be nibbling at all available insect life.

I glanced up at the luggage rack above my head and hoped to God that Davey was going to be at the station to meet me. If he wasn't there, I wasn't sure I'd be able to carry the amount of luggage I had. That was mostly due to the bright idea of Jessy and the Troll.

On the day that we had arranged to go shopping, the

Troll had consented to lock up for me *and* look after Jicky, so I was waiting for Jessy at the door at five o'clock, clutching Davey's money.

Right on the dot of five Jessy swooped by and shoved me into a taxi. Before I had time to voice any doubts I was sitting in a hairdresser's in Soho, feeling acutely self-conscious. The stylist called Russell, a completely shaven-headed man, wearing black leather jeans and a string vest, was on kissing terms with Jessy and they screeched compliments to each other over my head. I had been divested of my coat and wrapped in a black shiny cape, and was sitting (very uncomfortably, I might add) in an old-fashioned barber's chair that was horribly reminiscent of those embarrassing encounters at gynaecologists'. I kept expecting it to tilt backwards and reveal my underwear to everyone.

'Now, Russell, what do you think?' Jessy demanded, when she had finally stopped hugging him and sending her love to all and sundry.

They both surveyed me via a mirror which gave me time to try and get a grip on myself and suggest a trim. I needn't have bothered, because it was as if I hadn't spoken at all.

'Bold. Definitely. Big change of colour, and bold, bold, *bold*,' Russell finally intoned, reaching for some scissors.

'How bold?' I'd squeaked.

Jessy laughed, and told me not to worry. 'Russell's a genius. Relax, enjoy.'

Ha, I thought to myself. I'd rather have root canal

20

than this. But I meekly let myself be led like a lamb to the colourist.

'We're so lucky it's late-night shopping,' enthused Jessy. 'Now, what I suggest is this. Generous Davey has left you oodles of lovely wonga, so I think we should go for a capsule wardrobe that *includes* a party dress, and not spend it all on one thing that you are probably only going to wear the once. What do you think?'

'Well, umm—'

'Great. So, what I'll do is leave you here and go on a find-and-buy mission. What size are you? And shoes? OK, now then, what sort of state is your underwear in? Oh, and are you wedded to the bookshop-assistant look? Because I really think we can do better.'

Most of the people in the hairdresser's were staring with great interest at me, and I could feel the beginning of a blush.

'Wanna say it any louder then, Jess?' I muttered, feeling the redness start to sweep over my cheeks.

To my surprise, nearly everyone in the shop began to make suggestions as to where Jessy should go shopping.

'Oooh, a makeover, how exciting . . .'

'God, I wish someone would do it for me.'

'There's a great sale on in Joseph at the moment.'

'If you need any boots, I saw a fantastic pair at Hobbs.'

'Mention my name at Browns, you'll get a ten-percent discount.'

Jessy laughingly thanked everyone and kissed my

cheek, promising to be back in a couple of hours and leaving the shop in a swirl of activity. She suddenly stopped at the doorway and called out, 'Poppy, tell me, is there any colour that you absolutely and positively *hate*?'

People started to call out their own pet hates, when Russell said, 'Don't forget, she's going to be a bronzed amber by the time you get back, so don't get anything yellow.'

Bronzed *amber*? Was I? Oh, well.

'Navy blue,' I piped up. 'Nothing navy blue, it reminds me far too much of my old school uniform.'

'Oh, me too,' said a woman next to me.

'It was maroon for me,' another woman said. 'I still can't stand it.'

It seemed that I had started off one of those Proust moments, and soon we were all chattering away about colour phobias based on terrible school memories.

'Oh, God, what about those bloody games lessons?'

'Don't remind me!'

'Divided skirts!'

There was a collective giggle at that, and we then moved on to school dinners. I was awfully surprised. Here I was, in a very trendy hairdresser's, actually *talking* to people. This state of affairs didn't last too long, though, as I was soon in Russell's hands.

'Known Jessy long, then?' he asked, sloshing a vile-smelling liquid on to my hair.

I explained about her shop being next door to where I worked, and that she was the most stylish person I knew, and about my upcoming adventure to the countryside with Davey's family.

'Radical change will sort you out. Always does with women. You can be anyone you want with a new hairstyle.'

Oh, yeah? I thought. What about if I want to be a brain surgeon? How's that gonna work, then? But of course, I agreed by nodding my head and looking grateful. I gave myself a talking-to – I must stop these interior dialogues. Perhaps it was because I wasn't used to talking to other people much. Practice makes perfect, I thought. Maybe that's why a cliché *is* a cliché. It's because they're true.

'So, your boss must really like you to do this?' Russell asked. 'Or does he fancy you rotten?'

I spluttered at the very thought. 'Oh, no, nothing like that. He's gay. And a bit non-sexual, if you know what I mean ...'

Russell continued to slap on the colour in silence, giving me time to reflect that I had described Davey to a complete stranger as non-sexual. Bloody hell, what did I know? The last time I'd had a date that had involved any sort of physical contact was so long ago that Wham were still together. Or was it Tears for Fears? Anyway, it was a *very* long time ago indeed. So long that I had really given it up, and no, if you were going to ask, no, I didn't miss it at all. Well, not the sex bit, anyway.

But Russell had planted a seed of doubt in my mind.

Maybe Davey was changing? I banished that as wishful thinking.

My scalp was starting to itch, and I asked Russell how long this had to stay on.

'Oh, until the burning becomes unbearable,' he grinned. He handed me a magazine and asked if I'd like a coffee, or a Baileys as it was so near Christmas. I declined both offers and leafed through the magazine, worrying that my hair was going to turn green and fall out.

The magazine had one of those pieces in it about buying the perfect Christmas presents for all your loved ones, and it hit me with a jolt that I'd have to provide gifts for all of Davey's family. Shit, what the hell was I going to buy? And with what? I started to make a mental list. Davey – well, obviously, but what? He was really impossible to buy for. He had everything anyway, and he was so damned fastidious about things. The one birthday present I had bought him that he had seemed delighted with was a box full of old mother-of-pearl buttons. Perfect, he had exclaimed. But what was I going to get him for Christmas?

Then there were his parents, Edward and Jocasta, his sister Tabitha and his brother Alex and the American girlfriend, whose name I'd forgotten. Oh, *God*. What was I going to do? I searched the magazine for tips. *Really* bloody useful. A cashmere hot-water-bottle cover for £200, or a silver antique perfume bottle, a mere snip at £1,000. Shit, shit, shit. Maybe I could pretend that I had left all the presents on the train? Maybe I could raid the shop and hope that Davey wouldn't recognise any of the stock? Fat chance. Then another thought hit me – supposing they were the sort of family that didn't give presents at all? Then I would look like a fool and they would feel awful. Or maybe they were like the Royals? I'd read somewhere that the Royals had all their presents, unwrapped, heaped on trestle tables in the great hall in Sandringham, with name cards in front of them. And they waltzed up and down, swigging G & Ts, hooting at the *faux pas* that minor members of the family had made. 'Ooooh, nooo, not another bloody jewel.' 'Very sweet of you, Charlie, but I have got several castles already, y'know.'

Russell was prodding at my scalp and announced that I was 'done'. A very young girl, dressed in what looked like surgical scrubs, washed my hair.

'Oooh, luvverly colour,' she said as she gave me a final rinse, swaddled my head in a towel and led me back to the uncomfortable gynaecologist's chair. There followed a very tortuous forty-five minutes. Russell had the look of an artist who must not be interrupted as he started to cut. And cut. And cut some more. It got to the point where I simply dared not look in the mirror. I was convinced that I was going to be as bald as he was by the end of it. I was already mourning my shoulder-length mousy locks when he finally stopped. He then lobbed on some wax, or gel, or something and gave my head an incredibly hard scrubbing. My view of the mirror was then blocked as he stood in front of me tweezing and fiddling. He finally stood back and announced in a very self-satisfied way that I was ready.

I tried very hard to look pleased, and all the others in the place oohed and aahed at me. I didn't look like me at all. A blonde with choppy short hair stared back at me. I put a hand to my head and brushed it against the back of my head; the hair there was so short that I could feel my scalp through it. Bits of hair stood up in all directions, and a spiky, uneven fringe fell across one eye. I couldn't judge if it was good or bad, it was so different. At least there wouldn't be any need for a hair-dryer, I thought, desperate to feel positive about something.

I squinted in the mirror, and saw Jessy come charging through the door carrying loads of carrier bags. She glanced around the room, and called out to Russell, 'What have you done with her? Where is she?'

I waved my hand at her and she did a double take. 'Oh, my God,' she said slowly. '*Poppy*, you look fabulous!'

I looked in the mirror again. Maybe it was OK. Maybe I'd just have to get used to it.

Jessy took me back to her flat and forced me to try on the huge numbers of clothes that she had bought for me. By the heap that was soon littering her floor I realised what an immense undertaking it had been, and stammered out my thanks.

'Not at all. I really enjoyed it. Don't tell Davey, or he'll have a fit, but most of them came from that knock-off design place,' Jessy said, sitting cross-legged on the floor and pulling out a scarlet (fake) suede skirt from a bag.

I looked around her living-room and felt a pang of envy. So this is what trendy young things lived in, was it? The room was different shades of white, with textured natural throws, rugs and cushions everywhere. Huge fleshy plants and trailing pots of ivy were the only coloured things there, and the contrast between this and my flat which was crammed with books and overstuffed furniture picked up at flea markets was too great a gulf to cross.

'Now do try on the pants, they were the only thing I was nervous of buying. Everything else would fit, I knew.' Jessy chucked me a pair of black trousers and I dutifully stepped into them.

'Aren't they a bit tight?' I said doubtfully.

'Not at all. Now try the party dress on, and before you say anything about it being over the top, it's *meant* to be a show-stopper.' She dragged a dark green glittering creation from a bag. It looked fantastic, with reptilian scales of a golden green shimmering all over it.

'My God, Jessy, it must have cost a *fortune*,' I gasped.

'Nah, it's a rip-off of last year's Lacroix. The only thing is, you have to wear it with a *lot* of confidence. That really is the only trick to looking good, you know. Now what about shoes? I couldn't find anything for that dress. Have you got anything remotely suitable at home?'

I nodded doubtfully. I did have a pair of high heels

27

that were lurking in the back of the wardrobe, they would have to do. Jessy zipped me into the dress, and turned me round to face the mirror.

'Wait a moment, I've got the very thing,' she said, disappearing from the room and returning with a huge metallic wrap that she floated over me. 'There. Perfection!'

It certainly was one hell of a dress, it draped and touched exactly where it should. I felt like a star. Maybe the new hairstyle was working after all.

Jessy went through the rest of the clothes with me, and padded them out with some very strange-looking Japanese black stuff from her wardrobe ('Looks like hell on the hanger, but fantastic on') as well as a liberal lending of scarves, belts, bags and jewellery. I was kitted out.

'Now, Poppy, here's a Christmas present from me,' Jessy said, handing me a bag.

'Oh, God, no! You shouldn't have. You've done too much already,' I stammered.

'Open it,' she commanded.

It was a bag chock full of make-up. It had things like glittering body powder, lip gloss and cheek bronze. I didn't know what half of it was, to be honest.

'Don't worry, it's really not as expensive as it looks. Try it all out at home, it needs practice, you know.'

I thanked her again.

'I've *loved* it! It's like the transformation scene in a panto ... Oh, God, I didn't mean that! Oh, you know what I mean . . .' Jessy sounded worried that she'd upset me.

I reassured her, thanked her again and made my way home. I knew what she meant, though. I was definitely a Marks-and-Spencer's-type dresser, you know? I would never, in a million years, have spent so much money on clothes, and certainly not in the shops that she had been into. Jessy had also lent me an old leather jacket ('funky *and* practical') and I wore that home, carrying what felt like a ton of clothes.

She waved me goodbye, shouting out, 'Remember, confidence! Not that you'll need it, because you look fabulous. Call me and let me know how it's all going.'

It was incredibly gratifying that a man stood up for me on the tube, offering me his seat. I thought that I really had been transformed into a new glittering creation, until I realised that he was drunk. Ho hum.

The Troll lived quite near me, so I picked up Jicky on the way home. Now that *was* gratifying – she didn't recognise me at all.

'Bleedin' hell, Poppy! You look like someone on the telly!'

I thanked her graciously and swept down the path. My exit was a little spoilt, it has to be said, by my tripping over a loose paving-stone and nearly dropping all the shopping and Jicky. But I recovered with aplomb, and was soon safe at home at last.

I let Jicky out of his basket and he flew to my shoulders. He was puzzled by the smell and the lack of hair to hold on to, and he chattered his disapproval.

But he soon forgave me. Well, I assume he did, because the quantity of honey-and-raisin flapjacks he put away was staggering. With Jicky clinging on to my neck, I laid out all my new clothes on the bed and gave myself a confidence-booster talk.

'Right. OK. You look great. Be confident. Have a good time. Smile. Don't dither. OK. Oh, shit, Jicky, you little sod, don't do that on my shoulder!'

He scampered away looking sly, but pleased with himself. Maybe I wasn't going to miss him that much after all.

The last day that the shop was open, before I closed it for Christmas, was manic. I even sold the R. Angel monkey book, that I had reluctantly returned to the shop, to a harassed-looking American woman who claimed that her nephew, who was studying zoology, would '*like, toadally adore it!*' The Troll and I toasted each other in sips of wine and mince pies in the back room whenever we got a chance.

'What yer got for Dave, then?' the Troll demanded, scornfully taking a fifty-pound note from a man who looked quite shocked only to get a fiver in change back for a copy of *Treasure Island*.

'It is an important edition,' I said apologetically to him, 'and it's got great illustrations.'

I then turned to the Troll and groaned. 'I haven't. I haven't got *any* of them *anything*. I've got a couple of hours after work today, and then I have to catch the train in the morning.'

'Did yer really make these?' The Troll gestured towards the mince pies.

'Yes. Of course, why? Are they awful?' I said anxiously.

'No. Bleedin' great. Make 'em all food or sumfing.' She turned away to contemptuously gift-wrap a three-hundred-pound pen. Well, when I say gift-wrap, I mean crush it into a bit of silver metallic paper and cover it with Sellotape.

I wondered whether she was a genius or whether she had come up with a plan to make me look really stupid. I settled for the genius bit, because I was broke, had no inspirations and the only thing that I was confident about, was that I could at least cook a mean mince pie.

At five thirty, before locking up, as instructed by Davey I handed the Troll her Christmas bonus. To my utter surprise she burst into tears, and hugged me. Had the world gone Christmas crazy? I waved her off, wishing her a happy time, and felt very Dickensian, as though she was Tiny Tim or someone, going home to provide her family with the festive goose.

I thought that the best thing I could do was head off to the late-night supermarket and buy the ingredients to make the presents for the Stanton family. It was too late to make a cake, well, a proper Christmas cake anyway, but I could make a dried fruit one, loaded with apricots and brandy, that would do as a sort of thank-you for having me. Davey could have some stuffed hot chillies in a jar of oil, he adored those and would pick them out of my fridge whenever I had made any.

31

Edward and Jocasta? Well, I thought I could make them a big box of handmade chocolate truffles, I'd tart them up with some fresh coffee beans, vanilla and nuts. Alex and his girlfriend? She was American and as far as I could tell they all loved cookies, didn't they? I'd make some shortbread and some florentines. That left the sister, Tabitha. Oh, God, what the hell was I going to make for her? Got it. Those Persian things that had buckets of rose-water and pistachios in them. They had a really cool name, something like in translation '*The Shah swooned with delight*' although that might well have been an allergic reaction to the nuts, rather than sheer delight with the sweets, of course.

I pinched oodles of wrapping paper, bows and gift boxes from the shop, locked Jicky firmly in his cat basket and headed home. The journey home was tough going. It was very cold and all forms of transport were jammed with people, most of them, it seemed to me, out on a mission to make me feel guilty about keeping a wild animal in a cat basket. I got home, dumped off the monkey and headed towards the joys of the supermarket.

By midnight, I was exhausted. Every bit of the kitchen was covered in melted chocolate, chopped nuts, dried fruit and flour. So was I, and what was worse, so was Jicky. He and I had had a bit of an altercation over some orange peel, and he was sitting on the top of the kitchen door, chattering his indignation at me and licking his fur, looking like an extremely naughty boy.

'You wait till you get to the sanctuary, mate. Then you'll have something to moan about,' I cautioned him, then relented as he leapt down from the door and nestled around my neck. I saw his small hand reach out to try and pinch some more pistachios, and gave up. I mean, he was a monkey after all, wasn't he? I gave him a handful and plonked him in his basket. I was so tired, I decided to clear up in the morning. I took the cake from the oven to let it cool on a wire rack, and indulged myself in breathing in the warm aromatic loveliness of it.

Tomorrow was Christmas Eve. All I had to do tomorrow was clear up, pack and be at Paddington station at eleven. I yawned and stretched and allowed myself to have one chocolate truffle. It tasted rather odd, then, as chilli flooded my mouth, I saw that the board I'd cut the chillies on was the board that the chocolates were resting on. Oh, shit.

It seemed a new flavour had been invented.

I went to the bathroom and scrubbed my teeth so hard they practically bled. It was a pretty horrible flavour, but they used chocolate in a hot sauce in Peru or somewhere, didn't they? I'd say it was from an old South American recipe, handed down directly from Montezuma.

I had a quick look in the make-up bag that Jessy had given me. I'd drop off some chocolates for her, too, in the morning. *Not* the chilli ones. What did you do exactly with cheek glimmer? I'd have to give that a go in the morning, as well. I studied my new hairstyle in the bathroom mirror, it was as if a stranger was looking back at me. Same blue eyes, same rather too wide and full mouth, but a stranger nevertheless. How odd. Maybe Russell had been right after all. New hairstyle, new person. I practised smiling in the mirror, and then tried to look sexy and confident. Hmm, that would take some work, I could see.

Chapter Three

You can but imagine the hell of Paddington station on Christmas Eve. I blessed Davey for the foresight (and deep generosity, having seen the price of it) of giving me a first-class ticket. But even so it really was hard going, especially as I was laden down with suitcases, the big box of food goodies, and a monkey in a cat basket. Not to mention sundry bits and pieces like handbag, coat, scarf, book, and newspapers. It really didn't help either, that people were careering wildly around searching for the number of their train platforms, staggering under the weight of badly wrapped Christmas presents, and dragging wailing, overexcited children behind them. Just to add to the chaos the tannoy system was relaying a very wobbly version of 'We wish you a merry Christmas' that could seriously drive you mad.

The ploy of spreading coats and books on the seats had seemed to work, but there were still a lot of people milling around, searching for their seats. I was amazed at the number of families, even in first class. Perhaps all the parents worked at something very high-powered in the City and earned a fortune. The train was definitely moving away now, and I had a fleeting moment of panic that I was heading in the wrong direction, and that I would be much happier curled up on my sofa at home, watching TV and coping with the familiar sensation that everyone was having more fun than me. Well, that was true, they usually were. I don't want you thinking I am some sort of recluse, or anything. I mean, I did go *out*. I'd even joined a few evening classes over the years – and believe me, that is something I wouldn't do lightly. I'd done upholstery, a dismal failure, involving a hasty visit to A & E when I stapled my hand to a chair frame. Then there was Chinese cookery. That was OK, I guess, but it was full of the most awful women who competed endlessly for the harassed teacher's attention. He, poor soul, was more interested in the only boy there, and they would confer in giggled whispers behind his wok. Then, to my shame, there were the I Ching interpretation classes. (I don't know why either, but it had seemed a good idea at the time.) I had met Gaia (real name Mary) there, though, a rather jolly single mum who I occasionally met up with for a pizza and a movie when her child-minding could be arranged.

It was not, I realise, the most exciting social life I could have, but I had fallen into it, and wasn't exactly struggling to get out of it. There was, of course, a network of old mates, but they had all paired off, bred, and were happy to discuss their baby's teething or their husband's snoring with me, but that was it.

I reminded myself that I was going to be ready for

any adventure that might come my way, and started to congratulate myself on the seemingly brave act (or so I thought) of setting out to Cornwall to spend Christmas with the Stantons. Wynn-Falcon-Stantons to give them their full name. I would be ready for fun, good times and socialising, I told myself firmly.

I was staring out of the train window, looking at my reflection in the glass, still amazed by how different I looked, and continuing my pep talk to myself, when I was aware of a tall, dark-haired man, looking very disreputable in a leather trench coat, three days' worth of stubble and sunglasses (which were completely redundant), who fell, panting, into the seat opposite me. He was carrying a can of Coke, which he gaspingly swigged from, muttering, 'Sugar and bubbles, it really is the only thing for a hangover . . .'

Somewhere from the depths of his coat his mobile phone rang and as he fumbled to find it he threw me a look of apology. Then he answered it.

It is impossible not to look interested in someone else's conversation and I buried myself in the review section of the newspaper and tried to compose an expression of neutral passivity. He was purring into the phone with an appeasing tone to his voice, obviously talking to a woman, I thought.

He ran his hand distractedly through his hair and said, '– and BA have lost my sodding luggage, it's probably on its way to Istanbul by now, all I've got with me is one change of sodding clothes. I missed the hire car and now I'm on the bloody train. This country seems to close down at this time of the year, so you're much better off where you are, I can assure you. As soon as this festive hell is over, I'll call you. Yes. Yes. Of course I will. Although we really have said just about everything there is to say, haven't we? Goodbye.'

He hung up and, to my utter surprise, stood up, slid the train window open and hurled his phone from it. I must have gasped my astonishment, because he caught my eye and said, 'A hangover and Claudia do not mix. I've been up all night and the sound of her voice could drive me to suicide. At least this way I can sleep all the way home.' He smiled at me and, unwillingly, I found myself smiling back.

Jicky was poking his hands out of the basket, in an attempt to untie the string of his door.

'My God – what the hell have you got in there? They look like the hands of a terribly small old man.'

'It's a monkey, name of Jicky.'

He bent forward and looked with interest into the basket. 'Nonsense,' he said.

'What?'

'Well, it's not a monkey, it's a marmoset. They were very popular pets in Roman times, quite a fashion amongst the wives of the senate. Filthy habits, I believe . . . The French court at one time was smitten with them too.'

He gave a huge yawn and settled back in his seat, wrapping his coat around him like a blanket. He removed his sunglasses and I saw that he had deep brown eyes that were red rimmed, but with a network of laughter lines around them.

'Would you be awfully kind and wake me when we get to Bodmin? I simply have to get some sleep . . .' He smiled at me again, then closed his eyes and was soon snoring gently.

I have to admit, I was intrigued. He was without doubt simply the most gorgeous man I had ever seen. *And* he was sitting opposite me on a very long train journey (how long, I hadn't yet realised). *And* he was getting off at my station. I wondered excitedly if Davey knew him. We were due in at Bodmin at four, surely he wouldn't sleep all the way? I surreptitiously got a mirror from my bag and checked my make-up. Then I called myself a fool and put it away again. Why on earth would this obviously attached, glamorous-looking man want to have anything to do with me? Or I with him, I added sternly to myself.

Still, I think that there is a romantic streak in us all, and what could be more romantic than a chance meeting with a beautiful stranger on a train? I'd always harboured a secret yearning for the golden days of the Orient Express, you know, the odd meeting with a Russian count, or a spy from Bucharest. Then of course there were the wonderful films; *Brief Encounter* usually had me in floods of tears. Then there was that fantastic one with Marlene Dietrich, where she leans back into the shadows of the train, with the sheer black veil from her hat falling over that peerless face, and says in a world-weary voice, '*It took more than one man to change my name to Shanghai Lily* . . .' Lovely stuff.

I took the opportunity whilst he was asleep to study him more closely.

Fascinating, definitely. He had a battered, husky, sexy charm about him, and I had to drag my eyes away.

A few minutes later, a stewardess with a left-of-centre parting came down the corridor pushing a trolley, asking people if they wanted 'refreshments'. The trolley made a hell of a racket and the man sitting opposite me awoke.

'Four large vodkas and tonic, please, sweetheart.'

The stewardess blushed with pleasure and faffed around with miniature bottles, lemon and ice. The trolley rattled its way onward and the stranger pushed a drink towards me, across the table.

'I try *very* hard never to drink alone, and it seems impossible to sleep.'

I smiled reluctantly at him. He was obviously one of those men who led a charmed life. I couldn't imagine that he had heard the word 'no' very much. He was endowed with the sort of charm that you think you are impervious to, until it is directly aimed at you. Then you realise that you are helpless before it. I took the drink and we silently toasted one another.

What the hell, I thought. It's only a drink, and it *is* Christmas. Perhaps this would be a good opportunity to try out my sexy look that I'd been practising to go along with my new hairstyle and clothes. I sucked in my

cheeks, pouted a bit and looked at him from under my
eyelashes.

'Are you all right?' he asked.

'Yes, why?'

'For a moment there you looked as if you were going
to be sick . . .'

I blushed and tried not to laugh. The sexy look still
needed some work then. I tried not to be flustered, and
in doing so, took a much larger gulp of my drink than I
would normally have done. Jicky was making little
squealing noises that I knew pre-empted his appalling
act of vice. I blushed *again* and looked away, desperately trying to think of a subject to talk about.

'My God, does he do that all the time?' the man said,
incredulously.

I nodded

'Typical male adolescent. I used to spend hours in
the bathroom at home locked in with a copy of *The
Lives and Loves of Frank Harris*, which was all that I
could find in our household that passed for erotic
literature. And that was pinched from my father's
library. What about you?'

I choked into my drink. What did he mean, what
about me? What about my *what*? Erotic reading? Or
bathroom habits? Both seemed to me to be equally
alarming subjects and not the sort of train conversation
I had been trying to think of. Oh, God, I could feel
another blush starting and I willed it to subside. I
glanced up and saw that he was grinning at me.

41

'I'm sorry, I always ask intimate questions. I find it's the best way of getting to know someone. Don't you?'

I fiddled with my plastic glass, and noticed with alarm that it was empty. I'd certainly knocked that back in a hurry. He tipped another miniature bottle of vodka in my glass and topped it up with a can of tonic. I vowed to sip at it this time, and not behave as if it was a glass of Tizer.

'I'm spending Christmas *en famille*, how about you?' he asked.

The vodka had certainly loosened my tongue and I found, to my utter surprise, that soon I was telling him about the lack of contact I had with my adoptive parents.

He looked sympathetically at me and said, 'I had a friend at school who was adopted, he made up all sorts of stories about his real mother, you know, that she was a duchess or something and he was the product of a wildly unsuitable liaison between her and the game-keeper. Made him feel displaced, he said, but he grew out of it. He's now a commodity broker, married with three kids of his own and shouts at them the whole time.'

I considered what he had just said. It was how I felt about myself, I really felt I didn't belong *anywhere*. It was the reason that I adored hearing about Davey's family. I longed to have that connection with a group of people. I smiled at him, and he smiled back.

The ticket collector was making his way down the train. He'd made his job a little more bearable by

42

sticking a bunch of mistletoe in his jacket lapel and draping tinsel around his neck. I wondered idly if he'd had to pay for them himself, or whether the train company had a budget for them. Probably the latter, as the marketing department would foolishly think that this was good PR. He stopped expectantly in front of our table, and I started to pull all the rubbish out of my handbag. Some of the junk from my bag fell on to the floor, and as I bent down to pick it up, I heard a cry of surprise from the ticket collector, followed by screams and shouts from the rest of the carriage.

Jicky, the little sod, had finally mastered the trick of undoing the cat basket. He was swinging with a look of triumphant glee from a luggage rack the other side of the train.

My glamorous stranger was snorting with laughter, and was no help whatsoever. I was reduced to climbing on to the table and reaching up to Jicky, tempting him with a banana, something I now never travelled without. I was horribly aware that the red fake-suede skirt that Jessy had bought for me was extremely short, and I tried to pull that down with one hand, whilst brandishing the fruit with the other. The carriage had joined in the fun and I was being advised by them on what to do.

'Grab hold of it.'

'Oh, he's so sweet . . .'

'Dad, Dad, can I have one for Christmas, can I? Can I?'

'It's not right, is it? Downright cruel, I call it . . .'

'Grab it, now.'

Jicky slapped quite hard the side of a man's head who was misguidedly trying to guide him towards me. 'Christ, the little bugger's attacked me!'

'It's like *Gremlins*, isn't it? Throw water over it . . .'

'No, God, don't do that, they multiply!'

I was pleading with Jicky to come down now, and to my relief he leapt on to my shoulder and buried his head in my neck. I think, to his credit, he was fearfully embarrassed by the fuss he'd caused. A crowd of children had gathered around me, jostling for a better look at him. But I didn't trust Jicky to behave himself at all.

I stammeringly apologised to everyone, and explained for the hundredth time that he wasn't a pet and I was just delivering him to a sanctuary. The whole carriage laughed then, because as I said the word 'sanctuary', Jicky clapped his hands over his ears and let out a high-pitched squeal. I took advantage of the lull in hostilities and bundled him back into his basket. I eventually found my ticket to show to the collector, who most definitely was *not* amused by the incident, and I apologised, yet again.

The man opposite me was still laughing weakly, and he said, 'I must say, this is a far more interesting journey than I had anticipated. I was going to introduce myself and ask you how on earth you ended up with the monkey, and your life's story, but . . .' he paused, leaning towards me, 'I've got a much better idea. Let's not do all that chit-chat that strangers do on trains.

Let's do something far more interesting . . . Let's play a game.'

Looking around nervously, I saw that the whole carriage was so busy that very few people were paying any attention to us. I did notice an attractive girl who was eyeing me with envy, and the stranger with lust. And, yes, that cheered me immensely.

'What?' I said, breaking my vow of not swigging my drink. I felt a delicious tingle of excitement start in my stomach. Then I told myself I simply had to calm down, for all I knew he was about to suggest playing Scrabble or something. His voice was wonderful, as dark and smooth as a really good plain chocolate, with a hint of money and privilege lurking somewhere in it. In my vodka-befuddled state I decided that he sounded a bit like Richard Burton. He glanced at me, and I got the idea that he was sizing me up, judging whether I was willing or able to play whatever game he'd got in mind.

'Is that your natural hair colour?' he asked abruptly.

It went through my mind that I could lie, but really what was the point? *No one* had this colour hair naturally. I shook my head.

'Oh, good. I find women who don't colour their hair have very little imagination.'

'Oh.'

We sat in silence, whilst his eyes travelled my face. Like an idiot I gulped the rest of my drink down, and he watched with amusement, smiling at me and staring into my eyes, making me feel wonderfully uncomfortable.

45

'Do you always drink so quickly?' he asked.

'Only when I'm nervous,' was my idiotic reply.

He laughed and stood up, stretched his arms above his head, and pulled down a beaten-up leather bag. He rummaged around, and drew out a bottle of brandy. He poured a large wallop into my plastic glass, and then into his own. I protested, and then resolved that I would *not* drink it. I really didn't want to turn up at Davey's home drunk. I could feel my stomach rumbling, though whether this was from nerves or hunger I didn't really know.

'Right. The game. It involves suspending disbelief for a few hours, do you think you can manage that?' he said in a teasing tone, though his eyes were very serious.

I nodded. I opened my mouth to tell him that my whole life consisted of suspending disbelief, but thought better of it and closed it again.

'Well, we're on the Trans-Siberian Express . . . Wolves are racing along the frozen steppes beside us. We know we are on the train for five days, icons are hanging in the carriage, and the Grand Duke is gambling his fortune away in the next car. We've just crossed the great Volga river, where every man on the train stands, with his hand over his heart, to salute the great waterway of Mother Russia—'

'Do they? Really?' I asked, entranced already.

'Yes. They do. I have the good fortune to be travelling with the favourite courtesan of the Tsar.' He nodded his head at me. 'A beautiful woman –'

He called me beautiful, my mind was screeching at me. Me. *Beautiful.*

'– she is travelling without an escort, she has only the company of her pet marmoset. The days are long and cold . . . I offer her my protection. And she accepts. We fall hopelessly in love –'

We do? *We do* . . .

'– but we know that it cannot be –'

Shit. Why not? Why bloody not?

'– for the Tsar will never allow it.'

Oh, damn. I can get round him, no probs.

'We are desperate, our mounting passion rises like endless tundra outside the frosted window . . .'

We glanced out of the window, and though I was quite prepared to see frozen wastes, we both saw the huge cooling towers of a nuclear reactor, and burst out laughing. I took a swig of the brandy, and realised that I felt glowingly alive, for the first time for a very, *very* long time. That could well be the booze, my sane mind warned me. My insane mind told the sane bit to mind her own business and shut up. I tussled for a while, and then gave in. This was far too thrilling to miss.

'Do try and ignore the delightful environs of Swindon,' I said. 'Please go on. I'm fascinated, what happens next?' I was trying desperately to appear sophisticated and insouciant, as if this sort of thing happened to me all the time. Yeah, right.

He leant towards me, running a finger up my arm. 'You beg me to leave you alone, you belong to the Tsar, you know that he will have me killed if I so much as touch your shoulder.' His finger moved up my arm, along my neck and caressed my face. Which was probably bug eyed, I realised. I tried to compose it into something more befitting the Tsar's favourite courtesan. 'But our love is too strong,' he continued. Pulsing electric currents ran through my arm and shoulder where his hand had been. 'We arrange to meet in the Grand Duke's private carriage, he has passed out with vodka in the dining-car. You run the length of the train, desperate to find me. You have a voluminous velvet cloak on, and you pull the heavy fur-trimmed hood over your head to protect you from curious eyes—'

'What colour?' I asked.

'What?'

'The cloak, what colour is it?'

'The darkest of greens, but it catches the light to make it the colour of your eyes, it's the green of the Volga by moonlight, it's the green of the darkest emerald you have ever seen, it's—'

'OK, it's green, then what?' I was practically hyperventilating by now and I had to control my breathing.

'You run down the endless dark, swaying corridor. You pass priests and monks who are lighting incense, the stars are burning as brightly in the night sky as your love for me. At last, at last you find the Grand Duke's carriage. I am standing outside, waiting, as you know I will always wait for you, my life will be dedicated to waiting . . .'

I dismissed my non-drinking resolve and gulped in a

48

fervour of excitement. Trust me here, this was unquestionably *the* most exciting thing that had ever happened to me in my whole life. With the possible exception of getting my photograph in *Judy* and winning a camera, of course, but I had only been eight at the time and that thrill had kind of worn off.

I was also hopelessly confused at this point. I mean, just how much of all of this did he mean? If he meant it at all, which I doubted. I was so drawn to him, and into the damn game, that I was prepared to believe practically *anything*.

'The train sways its way along the interminable track. The snow is shining under the cold moonlight outside, but inside the carriage we are warm. Too warm. We long for one another, and we take the only chance we know we will have. The one chance before the Tsar reclaims you and I have to report to my Captain at the front . . .'

He stood up, putting his drink down on the plastic table. He held his hand out to me and pulled me to my feet.

'Where are we going?' I asked.

He looked steadily into my eyes, and then said, 'To the Grand Duke's carriage, of course . . . Where else?'

Chapter Four

I stood rooted to the spot. I was aware of all the bustle and noise of the train, but they had receded into the distance. Whoa, there. Had I got this right? Was this man seriously proposing that we go and have a *quickie* on the train? Where on the train, for Chrissake – the *loo*? Maybe I'd got it all wrong, and this was some sort of hideous practical joke, maybe he was proposing that we go for a stroll to the buffet car or something. But one look at his glinting eyes told me otherwise. I felt a tremendous fool standing there, and wished desperately that I was more used to this sort of thing. I cleared my throat, and then said, with what I hoped sounded like mild amusement, and not appalled but delighted shock, 'Do you really mean to go and have sex in the loo of an InterCity 125, the Cornish Express? On Christmas *Eve*?'

(Why Christmas Eve was so sacred I do not know, and I seriously questioned my state of mind at this moment.)

'But of course! Sex with a beautiful stranger, I can't think of anything more exciting, can you?'

Well, no. Other than winning the lottery, I suppose. Or discovering that you had a long hidden talent for water divining. Who am I kidding? *Of course* it was exciting.

He ran his hand along the nape of my neck, and whispered something *very* rude, and *very* sexy into my ear. To my great surprise I felt my knees buckle. I really only thought that this happened in torrid romance books, but I am here to tell you that it does not. It happened to me. My legs actually turned to water. That in itself shocked me, the physical signs of longing were not something that I was awfully familiar with. I had to prop myself up on the corner of our table, as I was worried that I was going to keel over.

'What about Jicky?' I asked tremulously, trying to put off making a decision. Here I go again – dithering. And at a time like this. Honestly.

'*Il n'y a pas de problem*,' he grinned at me, rootling out a fiver from his pocket and asking the little boy sitting up the carriage to keep an eye on Jicky, and *not* to let him out of his basket.

As he did this, two thoughts flashed into my mind. One was, I have to tell you, – smooth bastard. I mean, really, who did he think he was? That thought didn't last too long, however. The second was – am I *really* going to go along with this? *Really*? I distractedly picked up my plastic glass of brandy and finished the not-inconsiderable amount in one gulp. I know, I know, there's no need to tell me, it really wasn't the most

51

sensible thing I could have done in these circumstances. Especially as I am *useless* when I drink spirits on an empty stomach. Oh, dear, I giggled to myself, I've turned into a drunken adventuress. Jessy *would* be proud of me.

The GS (glamorous stranger) waltzed back up the train to me, and took my arm.

'Well, madam, shall we go to the Grand Duke's carriage?' he said.

It was 'make your mind up' time.

He was standing so close to me that I could smell his cologne, and I picked up another disturbing scent as well. Musk, with a hint of acidity to it. Pheromones, probably. I felt giddy as I stared at the weave of his black jumper that was swimming slightly in front of my eyes; the cross grains of it were doubling into each other as I watched them. God, I must be more drunk than I thought!

'Well?'

I nodded, trying to look sophisticated, and he held my hand as I stumbled along beside him. I fell into his back on several occasions, earning myself quite a few disapproving glances from the families cluttering up the aisles with their luggage and presents.

He pushed me ahead of him, and swiftly opened the door of the charmingly named WC. As he locked the door behind him, he continued the make-believe story, only stopping to kiss me.

'The panting of the wolves is like your own breath now, we can see their yellow eyes glittering in the snowy moonlight . . . Your flesh is warm here and cold here, I press you to me . . .'

He was pulling off his jumper, and holding me in his arms. It really felt as if this was all happening to someone else, a curious lassitude and feeling of unreality had fallen on me. He kissed me again, much harder this time, almost as if knowing that I was feeling unconnected, and willing me back to him. Oh, well, I thought, responding. I might as well get into the spirit of the thing. He was pushing me against the door of the loo now, and we were both panting, our breaths coming in short hard rasps.

This really was turning into an adventure, I thought rapturously. I was kissing the GS back with a great deal of enthusiasm, whilst still trying to hold my stomach in, and worrying about the cleanliness of my teeth. We had very nearly got to the stage where I realised that sex really *was* like riding a bike – you didn't forget how to do it – when the train gave a tremendous lurch and the deafening screeching of brakes filled our ears. The train was fighting to stop, and I wondered if someone had pulled an emergency cord? Not Jicky, I hoped. Though I wouldn't put it past him. We clung to one another to try and keep our balance, but toppled over in a heap of tangled limbs on the very unlovely floor. I banged my elbow quite hard on the wall, and the GS cursed very loudly as his foot struck the sink. We scrambled to our feet, straightening our clothes. The brakes were still making the most terrible noise, and I realised that the train could well be in serious trouble and it was only alcohol and lust that were preventing me feeling more frightened.

I was lurching around, pulling on my boots, with the GS struggling with his head stuck in his sweater, when the train eventually came to a juddering stop. We looked wordlessly at each other and then both said at the same time, 'Are you all right?'

I nodded, and then he unlocked the door and we both burst out of it. The train was full of frightened people who were clamouring to know what had happened. All the lights had gone off in the train, and it was full of wintry half-light that came in from the outside. We made our way back to our seats, giving me time to notice, with great mortification, that my skirt had somehow swivelled around and was now on back to front. I tried to turn it around unobtrusively, but I had a hunch that the attractive woman sitting across from me, the one who had given the GS lustful looks, had a fair idea of what had been going on. She gave me a glance that managed to combine disdain and envy at the same time. Well, I rationalised, we hadn't actually *done* anything other than a great deal of what at my school used to be called snogging. But it was enough for me to know that I would willingly have done much more. I was elated to discover I didn't have even one pang of remorse.

I reclaimed Jicky, who was remarkably unconcerned and nibbling some sort of sweet that had been pushed through his basket by the little boy who'd been looking after him.

'He's been doing really, like, peculiar things! My dad said he'd been scratching himself,' the child told me importantly.

That was one way of describing it, I thought, as I thanked him, and hefted the basket back to my table. The ticket collector, who had shed the tinsel but kept the mistletoe, burst into the compartment and made an announcement. 'Ladies and gentlemen, Great Western apologises for any inconvenience, but the train had to make an emergency stop due to a failed signal. We will be resuming our journey as soon as possible. Thank you.'

A barrage of questions was hurled at him.

'How long are we going to be stuck here?'

'I've got to make a connection in Bristol, how long are we going to be?'

'Do we get our money back?'

'Is the buffet car open?'

'Do we get free drinks?'

The ticket collector answered these as best he could, and moved on to the next carriage to give out the good news.

The GS moved the brandy bottle back on the table and gave me a rueful grin. 'Thwarted on all counts. The Grand Duke's carriage will have to wait, more's the pity. Can I top you up?'

I shook my head. Brandy had got me into this trouble, I didn't want to compound it. Maybe I should bless the failed signal, perhaps it had saved me from making a complete fool of myself. On the other hand . . .

I wrestled with my feelings. I wasn't sure *what* I was feeling, to be honest. Relief? Or frustration?

Jicky was squealing in a high-pitched tone, and I bent down to have a look at him. He made piteous gestures towards me, and I knew that he wanted to get out of the basket and drape himself around my neck. I shushed him, and offered him a grape instead.

The carriage was full of indignant chatter about the incompetence of the railways, and the heartfelt wails of children who wanted to know how Father Christmas would find them on a *train*. I glanced at the GS, and saw that he seemed vastly amused by all this. He leant forward and stroked my hand. 'I *am* sorry. It seems the game has rattled to a halt, but don't worry, we're sure to be moving along soon. Do you think we should introduce ourselves after all, or should we keep the exciting anonymity?' He looked enquiringly at me.

I pondered this, for about a nanosecond. If we stuck to the game, how on earth would I ever be able to trace him? On the other hand, it was probably a safe bet that this sort of man would be pretty untraceable, anyway. Damn. And I was pretty sure that he wasn't going to be jumping around insisting on taking *my* phone number. Perhaps this was the real difference between men and women – sex with a stranger on a train was wildly exciting, but only if you thought it was going to lead to something else. (Woman.) Sex with a stranger on a train was wildly exciting. Period. (Man.)

He was still gazing at me with an amused smile on his face. 'Look, I'm sure you don't make a habit of doing this sort of thing, and as much as I'd like to continue our make-believe, perhaps if you told me your name, and where you're going, we might be able to meet up?'

I mentally cheered and punched the air like a football supporter.

'Yes, yes, that would be great.' Oh, shit, now I'm sounding like an overeager puppy or something. 'I'm Poppy, Poppy Hazleton.'

I held out my hand, and smilingly we exchanged a formal handshake.

'How do you do. My name is Alex Stanton, and I'm very, *very* glad to meet you.'

Davey's brother. Oh, my God! Davey's *brother*! I could feel my face flood with a deep red. I was horrified, I mean, I was going to spend Christmas with this man! That might or might not be a good thing, but how was he going to feel about it? How was I going to tell him? Oh, shit, how was I going to tell Davey? Perhaps I wouldn't have to, perhaps we'd be stuck in this train for days and we could all just go home and—

'What the hell's the matter? I've never seen such a reaction to a name. We don't know each other, do we? I'm sure I'd remember ...' he tailed off, looking with concern at my panic-stricken face.

'No, no. It's just that I'm a friend, well, I work for your, oh, *God*, I'm spending Christmas with you and your family. I work for your brother,' I mumbled, not looking at him. Then I added, 'Sorry.'

Now I'd *have* to stay on the train. Perhaps I could go straight back to London on it. To my horror I felt tears prick the corners of my eyes. It had all been so glorious, and I had felt so brave, and now it was all ruined. He was going to be horrified that he was stuck with a casual pick-up all over Christmas. Davey would be angry with me, and – I looked up, startled by a shout of laughter. Alex was hooting his head off.

'Good God Almighty, what a to-do! I shall annex you for myself, and insist that you go into the room next to mine. *What* a coincidence. Usually coincidences are very tedious and not all what one wants, but this is extraordinary . . .' He was actually wiping away tears of laughter.

He suddenly stopped laughing and said, 'Christ, wait a minute, what do you mean exactly? A *friend* of Davey's, what sort of friend?' he said suspiciously. His face had darkened, and it made me very nervous.

Davey would only have one sort of woman friend, and I didn't know what to say to him in reply.

'You know, friend friend. I mean, we work together and have dinner together and . . .'

'Nothing else?'

'No. What *do* you mean?'

Alex gazed speculatively at me. 'Davey hasn't *changed* at all, has he?'

'Umm, no. But I really haven't got a clue what you are talking about,' I said, mystified at this line of questioning.

He leant forwards and said confidingly, 'Between you and me, the lav scenario was going to be hard on the imagination, not to mention the flesh, wasn't it? Not

58

that I'm complaining, you understand. Though my foot still hurts like hell ... I wonder where we are?' He looked outside the window and I followed his glance. I could tell that we were no longer going to be talking about Davey, or what had just nearly happened in the loo. I felt disconcerted, and unsure of how to respond. I tried to tell myself that everything was OK, but there was an undeniable *frisson* of tension between us.

We were stuck somewhere in the countryside, and very unprepossessing flat fields stretched out either side of the train. The sky was an ominous dark grey, and it looked very cold. A solitary horse was standing head down against the wind, cloaked in a sort of equine raincoat. Poor thing, I mused. Not even in a stable on Christmas Eve. I saw Alex drain his brandy glass and refill it, and mine.

'No, no, really, I mustn't,' I said, pushing it away from me.

'Whyever not?' Alex asked.

'I really don't want to meet your family pissed, do I?'

'Best way, in my view,' he said, filling me with alarm.

I wanted to ask him about all of them and, of course, his American girlfriend, who I realised must have been who he was talking to on his mobile phone earlier. At least she wasn't here. The relationship sounded very rocky to me, so maybe a fling wasn't entirely out of the question?

I racked my brains to remember what Davey had said about him. All I could dredge up was that he was Davey's younger brother, and he lived in Paris. Davey had a very high opinion of his family. He admired them, loved them, even idolised them, but, I realised, he hadn't told me many practical details about them. I knew that his parents had inherited the Abbey from Davey's grandfather, who had the distinction of writing a book about the beast of Bodmin in 1930, *with* photographs (that were later to be proved fraudulent, and were actually enlarged pictures of the stable cat). That the Abbey had housed the last private court jester in England, whose specialities were sparrow mumbling (plucking a live bird, with his hands tied behind his back) and setting light to his farts for the amusement of after-dinner guests. Queen Victoria had slept there, but then so had Oscar Wilde, albeit at a different time.

I knew that his father was devoted to the farm and the deer, and would not allow hunting on his land. He was a passionate collector of antiquities, especially anything Egyptian, and was always dragging in shards of pottery with great enthusiasm. His mother wrote poetry, fished and dabbled in the arts. His sister was considered a bit of a 'problem' by the family, but Davey had never disclosed what the problem was. His brother – what *had* he told me about him? What did he *do* in Paris? I thought it was something to do with insurance but, looking at Alex, that seemed highly unlikely.

Jicky reclaimed my attention by trying to push a grape up his bottom, and making high-pitched whistling noises.

'Oh, Jicky, stop it, do,' I said, wishing that he was a

cute kitten instead of this embarrassing monkey, or marmoset, or whatever the hell he was.

Alex laughed again, and said, 'I assume that you're taking him to the monkey sanctuary near us?'

'Yes, on Thursday, the day after Boxing Day.' Davey had promised that he would drive me there.

'You know, I worked there as a teenager in my summer holidays. Put me off wild animals for life. They help stranded seals as well, all very worthy, I'm sure. But the people – smelly old hippies. Mind you, I thought they were very radical when I was fifteen. *God*, that was a long time ago . . .' He poured yet another brandy, and I hoped he was going to start talking about himself, so I could find out more about him. But no, he was off in another direction altogether. The charm had come back into his voice, however, and I no longer felt quite so anxious at his reaction when he had found out who I was. I thought I could still detect a slight hesitation in his voice, but the easy camaraderie there had been between us was beginning to return.

'I *always* try to come home for Christmas if I can. I find Christmas abroad too depressing, don't you? Or maybe with your family you prefer to be away from them?' he said reflectively.

I nodded, in what I hoped to be an agreeing sort of way, without actually lying. I had never, ever been anywhere more foreign than Suffolk for Christmas.

Alex eyed the family sitting next to us and gave me a huge wink. 'I was once in Phuket for Christmas and almost considered suicide,' he continued. 'The combination of the heat, the mosquitoes, and the bar girls was appalling. That and really, *really* bad acid was enough to nearly send me over the edge.'

Oh, God. The table opposite ours was filled with a family practically falling out of their seats trying to listen now.

'Yes,' Alex continued, warming to his theme and glancing with enjoyment at the family who were earwigging, 'the grass was great, of course, but then I got the runs for three days running. Probably dodgy tiger prawns. My friend told me that opium would cure it, but then, opium is very constipating, don't you find?'

The only opium I was familiar with was the perfume, and that gave me a headache. I tried to assume the air of a world traveller, and made another nodding motion with my head. It was very quiet in the train, without the sound of the engines, and it felt as if everyone in the carriage had fallen silent, eavesdropping on what they undoubtedly thought of as a drug fiend. I willed myself not to go red, and squirmed slightly in my seat.

'Of course, the only way to *get* the opium was to go back to Bangkok. Seven hours on a train having the shits is no fun, let me tell you . . . There's a very good reason why the Thais only eat with their right hand – no bog paper!'

The father of the family opposite was getting a little flushed in the face, and I was biting the inside of my mouth to prevent an attack of the giggles. I glanced at Alex, and he winked again at me, continuing his travelogue. 'Then there was the Christmas I was in Amsterdam. I'd been smoking in a coffee shop most of the day, and then decided to join in the skating along the frozen canals. You know how strong the dope can be out there, well, I was so stoned that I didn't feel the frostbite start – next thing I knew I was in hospital with a very pretty little nurse wrapping hot towels round the old chap! Seems he nearly fell off! *That* put an end to my skating, let me tell you . . . But to be fair, the red-light district nearly curtailed any other form of recreation as well. Once you've done Anne Frank's house, and shed tears, what's left? Only the drugs and the whores, so you do see—'

The train lurched forward. There was a small spontaneous burst of applause from the carriage, which then turned to groans when it stopped again. I tried to think of something that would change the conversation, as it looked as if the man opposite was about to have a stroke. I decided that Alex was doing it as a tease, but it had gone far enough. I glanced at my watch; we had been stuck here for an hour. If Alex hadn't hurled his phone from the window, we could have called Davey, and told him we were going to be late.

It was as if Alex had read my mind, because he suddenly stood up and said, 'Excuse me, but has anyone got a phone I could possibly use?'

The girl that had cast longing looks at Alex earlier, offered her mobile with the air of a magician producing a rabbit and handed it to him with a smirk, whilst smoothing her hair with her hand.

'Thanks, sweetheart,' Alex said casually, giving her the benefit of a slow smile, causing me to narrow my eyes at her.

He punched in a few numbers and had a very leisurely conversation with, I presumed, Davey.

' . . . And you'll never guess who I met up with on the train,' he said into the phone, turning to give me a huge grin. 'Yes! Too extraordinary, isn't it? Hmm, yes, I see. Well, I can't promise anything. Oh, and by the way, all my luggage is still with BA, I've only got the dregs of a bottle of brandy and one pair of socks with me. Dig out some of my old clothes, would you? Love to all, see you soon. Bye.'

He handed the phone back, and the girl gave him the benefit of a smouldering look which, I was pleased to see, he totally ignored. Well, I think he did, anyway.

'Davey says that I must be nice to you. I can't think why, I have been nice, haven't I?' he asked, with a slow lascivious smile.

There can't be any working blood vessels left in my face, I thought despairingly as I began to blush again.

The ticket collector made another appearance, and announced that the train would be leaving as soon as possible, but he was still waiting for the signal to be repaired. And the buffet was closed. Another chorus of groans met this announcement.

'Oh, dear. It seems as though we're stuck in the middle of nowhere with nothing to eat. Never mind, let's have a drink.' Alex poured the brandy into our glasses and magnanimously passed the bottle round the carriage. I got rather unsteadily to my feet and dragged down the box of food goodies. I plonked the box down on my seat and began to rummage around to see what we could nibble on.

'My God, it's like a hamper from Fortnum's, what's in this?' Alex held up a beribboned gold box, and shook it gently.

'Truffles, but I made those for your parents,' I said.

'Made them, *made* them? Good grief woman, is there no end to your talents?'

I laughed and dragged out some mince pies and a few bits of fruit, and watched Alex wrestle with the jar of stuffed chillies for Davey.

'Honestly, I'll just take a few, he'll never know,' he promised.

We had a small picnic on the train, and settled down with the rest of the carriage to wait for it to move.

Chapter Five

By the time we eventually arrived at Bodmin station it was pitch black outside and very, *very* cold. Alex was practically comatose, he had drunk so much brandy, and Jicky was shivering in his basket. I staggered off the train under the weight of all my luggage, and was aware that I didn't cut quite the figure I had intended. The traumas of the train journey, not to mention the loo incident, had left me dishevelled, and the amount of alcohol I'd consumed had given me a bleary-eyed, rumpled look. Although I had whipped out my make-up bag, and brushed my hair, it hadn't seemed to work the sort of transformation that I required.

The station forecourt was crowded with people, all meeting the delayed train, and the frosty night air was punctuated with cries of adoring relatives, clutching and hugging one another. They piled presents into the boots of cars and headed off towards a supper kept warm for them. One by one they disappeared and soon we were the only people left waiting. We made a forlorn little group, and I felt my spirits plummet.

'Shall we try and get a taxi?' I timidly enquired.

'Absolutely no point. It's Christmas sodding Eve, practically Christmas bloody morning now, and the one taxi available is probably ferrying people from the Hole in the Wall pub to the Westbury Hotel, which is the only place to get a drink past eleven in this sodding town. If a pregnant woman on a donkey arrived here tonight, they wouldn't find room in a sodding pasty shop – let alone a sodding stable.' I noticed that he'd changed his tune a bit about how great it was to be home for Christmas.

'Got any money? Change, I mean. I'll go to the end of the road and use the phone box. I've only got euros,' Alex said resignedly.

I searched around and pulled out my purse. I could feel my bottom lip begin to quiver, which was no surprise. I'm a real wimp when it comes to other people's emotions. Alex was working himself up into a bad mood, and I felt unable to cope with it, or him.

A pair of headlights appeared in the road, and I hoped that it was Davey. An estate car pulled up beside us, and an unfamiliar face peered out of the driver's window.

'Hello, my 'andsomes! Davey sent me. Climb in then. Good to see you, Alex. An' you must be Miz Hazleton. Bloody hell, what you'm got in that basket? Some sorta polecat?'

I explained about Jicky, who was looking very sorry for himself indeed, and started to pile the luggage in the car. Alex and the driver, who obviously knew each other well, started an incomprehensible conversation.

Incomprehensible because it mainly concerned people I didn't know and the man's accent was quite hard to understand.

A heavily pregnant woman was asleep in the passenger seat and she opened her eyes briefly and gave us a smile, then promptly closed them again, murmuring, 'Alex, how lovely . . . the children will be pleased you're home, they're in the back, asleep, well, I hope they are. You must be Poppy, 'tis lovely to meet you, do excuse me, I be so tired . . .'

I climbed into the back of the car and found myself sitting on several old copies of the *Cornish Guardian*, a horse's bridle and a sack of onions. I turned to see two ravishing-looking children who were curled up fast asleep in the back of the car on a pile of sacks and a bundle of hay.

'This gorgeous woman is Demelza, Thomas's wife . . . My God, Tom, she looks like she's going to give birth at any moment. You really do believe in keeping them barefoot and pregnant, don't you?'

Tom smiled fondly at Demelza's sleeping form. He had the expression of a contented man.

'Who are the children?' I asked, thinking that they looked like reclining angels.

'Toby and Eve, and I know what you're thinking, but trust me here, they are devils when awake,' Alex said, going on to quiz Tom about the whereabouts and health of the rest of the Stanton family.

'Oh, they'm all right. All over at Truro for drinks with the bishop and midnight mass after. Your ma's flitting

68

around goin' crazy about the snapper party. They'm right glad you've come this year. Full house, they'm sayin'.'

I peered out of the window and saw nothing but looming blackness. There was a signpost for Bodmin, but we turned away from it, and were soon speeding through twisting country lanes. Jicky was shivering in his basket, and I took pity on him and let him out, pushing him down the front of my jacket to warm up.

'Lucky monkey,' Alex murmured, sliding one hand on my knee.

I made an assenting sort of noise, whilst blessing the darkness of the car which spared my red face. I was glad to see that the arrival of Thomas had cheered Alex up. I guessed that he wasn't used to being stranded at a station, without a warm welcome.

''Ow's Paree then?' Thomas enquired. 'Still with that Yankee bird?'

'Maybe, maybe not,' Alex said, sliding his hand further up my leg, making me squirm. 'But Paris is still divine, thank you.' The two men obviously knew each other well, and they continued bantering and joking with each other, whilst the car bounced alarmingly along the dark road.

'Thomas is my father's tenant farmer,' explained Alex. 'Born here and never wants to leave. That's right, isn't it, Tom?'

'Don't know about that, things is pretty bad, you know, round 'ere. Terrible 'arvest this year. 'Melza's 'ad to get a job, only in the summer, mind, when all the

69

emmets swarm. Over at Padstow in that posh fish place,' Tom sniffed disapprovingly. 'And your dad, well, no disrespect mind, but he's more interested in 'is old bits of whatnots than he is in the farm. Still, I'm not complaining. Wouldn't catch me goin' up-country.'

'What's the emmets?' I whispered to Alex.

'Ants. That's what they call the tourists.'

I giggled slightly to myself, it was all becoming a bit *Cold Comfort Farm* for my liking. Jicky wriggled contentedly in the crook of my neck, and I stroked his head. All I knew about farming came courtesy of *The Archers*, and they seemed to lurch from one crisis to another.

'What are you in the panto this year, then?' Alex asked.

'I'm the demon king, right good part it is too, got a solo as well. You'm coming to see it, aren't yer?' Tom said anxiously.

'It's the cultural highlight of my year, of course we're coming. Where's it being performed?' Alex said, squeezing my leg.

'At the funny farm, same as ever.'

I glanced enquiringly at Alex. He pointed to a sticker in the car which read, 'Wake Up with a Young Farmer,' and then said, 'The young farmers put on a panto every year, Tom's their star turn. It's held in the theatre of the county asylum. It's usually quite a star-studded event, isn't it Tom?'

Tom gave a throaty chuckle. 'Better'n all that London fuss and bother. Proper good job, it is. We start rehearsin' in September, and your ma's done a right turn with makin' a load of costumes and paintin' the scenery. Mind you, I still don't know all me words, I sing me song to the sheep. They'm like it, anyway.'

'Who's playing the dame this year?' Alex asked, saying to me, 'That's a very hot ticket. Very sought after, probably because they all desperately want to put on female dress. I brought over a French friend, one year. He nearly peed his pants laughing. I had to explain that the lead boy was always played by a girl, and that the dame was always played by a man. He laughed and laughed, and said, "*But of course, my dear Alex, have you never heard of the Vice Anglais? It explains so much!*" The French take themselves far too seriously in my book . . . Anyway, who's the dame?'

'Arthur Yeo,' Tom said gloomily.

Alex burst out laughing, saying, 'How did he swing that one then?'

'Let's just say we suspect foul play, and leave it, shall us?' Tom replied.

I nudged Alex, and he said to me, 'Arthur's the local water bailiff, *and* the local salmon poacher, too. Very handy, as you can imagine. He's married to what I think is usually called our treasure, Odessa. She practically runs the Abbey, and us, single-handed.'

The car passed a farmhouse, and began to slow down. Tom stopped the car and carried the sleeping children into the house. Demelza groaned and clambered awkwardly out, waving goodbye to us, and followed Tom inside. Within seconds Tom was back

71

and we started upwards again. We passed two crumbling pillars with crouching dragons perched on top of them that held open a rusting ornate iron gate.

I could just make out the outlines of trees either side of us, but very little else.

'Are we here?' I asked.

Alex nodded. 'Nearly, it's a long driveway.'

The drive became quite steep, and at the brow of the hill, outlined by the starry night sky, loomed the Abbey. It was *huge*. I glanced at Alex nervously, and hoped that Davey had indeed been joking about the haunted room. It looked just the sort of place to have one.

Tom stopped the car in front of a massive oak nail-studded door that was lit by a lamp and we clambered out. I trailed behind Alex, holding firmly on to Jicky. We made our way to the door, which was flanked by a series of Victorian chimney-pots, resting on the ground. There were at least forty or so, and Alex began counting them.

'What *are* you doing?' I asked, shivering in the cold, helping Tom with the luggage.

'Old family custom. You have to add up the day and month that you were born, count the chimneys back from the right of the door and that's where the key will be. Twenty-three and three is twenty-six, so it should be –' he bent down, and lowered his arm into the depths of the chimney, '– in this one.' He triumphantly withdrew a large key, and walked towards the door.

'I had a nasty shock once, I put my hand down there and got hold of a frog. Very unpleasant.'

He unlocked the door and pushed it open. We were then standing in a hallway that left me gasping for breath. I had never seen *anything* like this. A riot of colour, and a simply heroic disregard for order hit me right between the eyes.

It was a massive vaulted room, with a minstrels' gallery at one end. It was crammed to the gills with objects, furniture, and well, just *stuff*.

The walls were dense with paintings from the classical – scimitared Turks assaulting captive nautch-girls, bloodied pheasants hanging upside down over bowls of grapes, amorous Nomads, Greek gods playing with the mortals – and the modern – enormous women with three eyes and one breast, dotted neon pop art, misty impressionists and a copy, I assumed, of a well-known Picasso. Dotted amongst these were icons, looking-glasses, stuffed animals in glass cases, antlers and horns of a lot of dead animals, religious parapher-nalia, plaster cornices, bits of columns, candle sconces, urns, stained-glass fragments and model aeroplanes. I could not, with any certainty, tell you the colour of the walls, as it was impossible to see so much as a gap between any of these disparate objects and adorn-ments. Vivid emerald-green silk curtains draped the windows.

The vast black-and-white tiled floor was covered, too. A huge wooden Gothic font stood in the centre of the room, with green rushes and branches soaring out of it. A harp with broken strings and a Victorian horse from a merry-go-round, with flaring nostrils and a barley-twist gilt pole coming up from its back, bearing the name '*Racer*', stood next to a grand piano that was swathed in mirrored shawls and smothered in framed photographs.

Persian rugs, sheepskins, and a very old tiger skin dotted the floor, along with about a thousand empty, old-fashioned soda siphons that were ranged along the walls, like thirsty skirting boards.

I clutched Jicky closer and moved forward, open-mouthed at such riotous abundance. It was like walking into Aladdin's cave, I quite expected to see an open treasure chest with jewels and doubloons pouring from it. Or maybe it was more like an overstocked junk shop, run by an owner who could obviously never bear to part with anything.

I heard Alex thank Tom for picking us up, and I turned to thank him too. They were both grinning at me.

'Always takes folk this way, the first time. You'm get used to it,' Tom said, waving goodbye.

I doubted it. This would take some getting used to. It was maximalist gone mad. God knows what the rest of the place was like. I gathered my wits about me and shouted 'Happy Christmas' to Tom's departing back.

'Tell Demelza I'll be down to see her and the kids soon,' Alex called out after him.

'My *God*, Alex. This place is—'

'I know, I know. I always forget how much I love it till I get back here. Now then, get by the fire, for God's sake, you probably haven't noticed it yet, but it's freezing in here.' Alex motioned me towards a wood fire that was smouldering at the end of the room.

I *had* noticed it, actually. The cold was quite extraordinary. It was, I swear, colder inside than outside, and when you spoke you could actually see your breath form in an icy mist in front of your face. I moved closer to the fire, but it was like trying to warm your hands by the flame of a match in the middle of an ice-rink. I took another look around the hall, there was a distinct lack of radiators. I wished that Jessy had bought me some thermal underwear, or at the very least a hot-water bottle.

An enormous Christmas tree was in one corner of the room, smothered in what looked like, and on closer inspection *were*, kitchen utensils. You know, graters, whisks, wooden spoons and so on, interspersed with coloured fairy lights. A heap of presents stood underneath, all wrapped in newspaper sheets. A sagging sofa that had an army of embroidered cushions, velvet throws and shawls stood in front of an enormous carved wooden sideboard that held a serried rank of cut-glass decanters.

Alex moved towards it, and said, 'I suggest you have a brandy to warm up. It's probably why I drink so much, you know, it's a natural reflex to keep out the interminable cold.'

He handed me a drink, and said, 'Knock this back and we'll go in the kitchen. It'll be warmer in there, and we'll have some food.'

As he led the way from the hall, I had time to notice

that there were signs of recent habitation there. A bowl of walnuts with the nutcrackers in it and a lot of empty shells was on the floor by a chair, next to a half-empty bottle of red wine. A heap of knitting, with the needles stuck into a ball of vivid purple mohair wool had been left on the arm of a red velvet, deeply buttoned chesterfield. A tray of tea things, including a vast silver teapot and a plate of butter that had been used in the toasting of crumpets (the butter hadn't even melted, which just goes to show you how very cold it was) was balanced precariously on the edge of the slate hearth. An overflowing ashtray, and a plate containing apple peel and orange rind, were incongruously placed on top of an empty plinth.

I trailed behind Alex as I had done on the train and fleetingly wondered if he was going to push me into a bathroom and continue our snogging from the train. I followed him down a stone-flagged corridor that had glass cases on the wall full of stuffed animals, mostly birds. We'd already passed several owls, a seagull, a heron and then, most disconcertingly, a huge case of stuffed cats, all sitting at a table, playing cards. One black cat had a pipe in its mouth, and another ginger one had a raised glass in its paw. It was *very* surreal. Alex called out what the various rooms were as we passed them.

'Flower room. It's called that but I don't imagine anyone has arranged any flowers in there for over fifty years. Study,' he said, pointing to another door, 'and strictly my father's. He goes in there to play records of

Billie Holiday very loudly and pore over catalogues from Sotheby's, but we all go along with the pretence that he's working. Cloakroom, *don't* go in there unless you're desperate, your bum will freeze to the seat. Painted Parlour, we eat in there. Sewing room. Butler's pantry, well, I suppose it was at one time, after it had been an office for the abbot, but now it's used for storing things, mainly wellington boots that all seem to be left-footed, and gardening tat. This door leads to the chapel, quite spectacular really, we'll go in there tomorrow. That door leads to the cellar, don't go down there unless you love spiders and really can't sleep without another bottle of port, it's where we keep the booze. This door leads to the gun room, don't worry, no guns, it's full of newspapers that my mother thinks she'll get round to reading one day, and her painting stuff, and this,' he said finally throwing open a door, 'is the kitchen.'

A delicious warmth washed over me, and I gratefully stepped inside. It was an incredibly large room, and had obviously been converted into a kitchen in the days of servants, who naturally didn't need windows with a view, which was just as well because the windows here started well above eye level. Tier above tier of chipped, mismatched china, mostly covered in a riot of flowers, rose upward to a hook-studded ceiling. Glass domes of wax fruit stood on one dresser, and a collection of Victorian scales with brass weights filled another. An enormous cooking range stretched out over one wall, and that, I saw, was the source of the warmth. The walls were painted a duck-egg blue, and had, in beautiful copperplate writing, dozens of maxims painted on to them in black ink.

'*Don't make it so awful good. Men, the pigs, will eat anything.*'

'*Nearly all soup will be improved by a slug of sherry. And so will the cook.*'

'*Never eat oysters with children around.*'

'*She was a good cook, as good cooks go, and as good cooks go she went.*'

A 1950s American fridge that had been painted a sunflower yellow purred in the corner of the room, next to a cardboard box that was overflowing with branches of holly and a sack of potatoes. Jars of pasta, tea and spices were dotted liberally around the room, along with strings of onions and garlic. The floor was slightly crunchy underfoot, with layers of dirt, and I saw massive spider's webs everywhere. Two trussed, uncooked geese sat in roasting dishes on the crowded kitchen table, jostling for space with jars of paintbrushes, piles of laundry, a plate of half-eaten toast, a box of cigars and an open dog-eared copy of a cookery book by Elizabeth David.

I thought of my mother's kitchen in Ipswich, with its gleaming white appliances, cling-filmed food and sterile clean floor, and grinned. This was *much* more exciting. Although I did make a mental note not to eat anything that had dropped to the floor.

I saw that Alex was grinning back at me, and he said, 'Bit different, I expect, from what you are used to?'

I nodded violently, wanting to tell him that I loved it all, but was feeling distinctly overwhelmed. I think he knew, though, because he gave me a reassuring smile and then moved over to stand in front of a spotted, ornate looking-glass that had a sheet of paper tucked into it.

'It's where we leave notes for one another. We've got one from Davey.'

I went to stand beside him, and read over his shoulder.

Dear Alex and Poppy,

How nice that you both met on the train. [Alex sniggered quite rudely at that, throwing his arm around my shoulders, till Jicky chattered a warning at him.] *It's a bore, but we've all had to go to Truro, and then home with the bishop for disgusting sherry, no doubt, and underdone sausage rolls.*

Please show Poppy to her room, Ma thought she'd like the Chinese room, but for God's sake make sure she's got a hot-water bottle. The traditional pie is in the bottom oven for you both. We'll probably be back quite late, so don't wait up.

Pa's driving, so wish us luck!

Davey X.

There was a scrawled message of love on the bottom from Jocasta, and a reminder to lock the door.

Alex decided that we should eat in the kitchen, and cleared a space on the table by simply brushing things to the ground. He rattled around the room, pulling out drawers and collecting cutlery, giving me more time to look around and get my bearings.

'It's quite a place your family has here, isn't it?' I offered, privately thinking that I was stumped for words to describe it. I bent down, holding Jicky safely, to retrieve the things that Alex had thrown to the floor, and put the books and laundry on the seat of one of the many chairs drawn up round the table. I saw something glittering on the floor, so bent down again to pick that up. It was a diamond ring.

'God,' Alex said, examining it, 'Jocasta's probably been looking for that for weeks. Well done, you *are* going to be popular!'

I held the ring in my hand and examined it. A largish diamond was held on to a band of white gold by two claws. There was some sort of engraving on the inside, and I held it to the light of a candle on the table to try and read it.

'*Draco custodiet aurum irreptum*,' I slowly read out, probably in an appalling Latin accent.

I glanced enquiringly at Alex, and he translated for me. 'The dragon guards the undiscovered gold,' he laughed. 'The family motto, don't you know! Please try not to worry, we really are all quite normal, I promise.'

I doubted that very much indeed, but I didn't say anything. If this lot proved to be normal, then I was the reincarnation of Marilyn Monroe.

He wrapped his hands in a tea towel, took a dish from one of the many ovens of the range, and plonked it on the table. He passed me a spoon, saying, 'You dish up, and I'll open the wine.'

I paused, with the spoon in my hands. It was the *most* peculiar pie I'd ever seen. Pinkish fish heads, eyes still intact, and scaly fish tails were peering upwards, surrounded by a sea of pastry.

'Alex, what *is* this?' I asked nervously.

'What?'

'The pie, what the hell is it? There appear to be whole fish leaping out of it,' I said in horror.

'Oh, it's stargazy pie. We all have it down here on Christmas Eve. The fish are gazing at the stars, hence the name. It's really not as bad as it looks.'

I gingerly poked around the pie with a spoon, giving myself as small a portion as I dared. I was relieved that once under the pie crust the fish were cut up, and I saw that the heads and tails were for decoration only.

I took a small mouthful, and was pleasantly surprised. Potato, swede, onion and fish were all combined with cream and parsley, but I avoided looking at the fish heads.

'It's a pie in honour of the starving children of Mousehole. An old fisherman, Tom Bawcock, braved the wildest storm you've ever seen to go fishing. This was on the twenty-third of December—'

'What year?' I interrupted, aware that I was being pedantic, but not caring.

'1868. I don't know actually, I just made that bit up to satisfy your craving for facts, although I could well be right, of course. I mean, starving children probably

81

didn't exist after that, and the kids in Mousehole now have all got hundred-pound trainers and Gameboys. Anyway. Old Tom caught seven sorts of fish and his wife cooked stargazy pie for all the village the following day. The fishermen all got pissed on cider and they and the fish were found gazing starwards, hence the name. I must say, I've got quite fond of it over the years, it wouldn't be Christmas now without it.'

I sipped my wine and looked around me. I took in the air of dilapidated grandeur, the mess, the dirt and the gleam of silver in the candlelight. The pie was like the Abbey, I decided. The whole place was a bit stargazy. It was more than just a building or a house, it seemed to have a personality all of its own. It was intimidating and grand, but it was also shabby and had a heartbeat. It felt alive, as if it were watching us. I put my wineglass down and smiled at Alex.

'I love this place,' I said emphatically, realising again that I was a bit drunk.

'I'm so glad. And I hate to change the mood, but did you know that Jicky was having a wank on your shoulder?'

Chapter Six

We polished off the bottle of wine in the kitchen, and I rather unsteadily got to my feet to follow Alex to my room.

'Shouldn't we do the dishes?' I asked.

'Are you mad? No, of course not, we've got stacks of plates,' Alex said airily.

That wasn't the *point* of washing up, I thought of saying to him, but decided against it as I saw a vast amount of dirty china leaning in a drunken tower next to the large stone sink. I quailed at the sight of it. A week's worth of dishes, at least.

'Don't your parents have any help in the Abbey?' I asked.

'Yes, of course, I told you, we have Odessa Yeo, Arthur's wife,' Alex said with surprise, then his eyes followed mine to the sink. 'Well, the thing is, Odessa is rather sporadic at the best of times and is easily distracted by my mother getting her to sit for her, or my father getting her to clean a bit of ancient pottery. But Davey will have assured you clean sheets, I promise.'

Alex picked my case up in the hall, and I pushed what was left of the box of goodies I'd made under the Christmas tree. We set off up a beautifully carved staircase that divided in two with a graceful curve. Although on every step there appeared yet another odd object to be stepped over, a 1920s Parisian hatbox, a tin can of beads from Biba, or a pile of pine cones.

'Follow me, we turn right, and go along past the gallery, your room's down there. *Very* near mine, I'm pleased to say. And you have the dubious pleasure of your own bathroom, although I can't vouch for the plumbing,' Alex said.

I duly followed directions, and found myself in a library that I realised looked over the hall. A carved wooden railing ran down one side, and the top of the Christmas tree poked up through the banisters. I saw that the top of the tree had been decorated with a bunch of silver pan scrubs, tied together to form a star. The other side of the room was floor-to-ceiling books, with a large roll-top desk in one corner. Statues dotted the room, and a daybed draped in tattered silk was pushed against the railings. I peeked over, and saw the jumbled array of the hall far beneath me.

A corridor ran out of the room, and Alex walked down it and pushed open a door quite close to the library, I was happy to see, as the long dimly lit corridor stretched out for a long way and looked decidedly creepy. The comforting warm presence of a benign spirit that I'd felt in the kitchen had long gone, and I shivered.

The door opened on the Chinese room, and I gasped with pleasure. It was *gorgeous*, with yellow silk on the walls with intricate peeling patterns of Chinese dragons and flowers. A four-poster bed, made of black lacquer and mother-of-pearl, matched the chest of drawers and wardrobe. A door led off the room, and I glimpsed a bathroom through the gap in the door. It was also *very* cold. But at least it wasn't scary.

Alex dumped my bag on the bed, which groaned rather alarmingly, and slid his hand inside the bed-clothes.

'Faithful Davey, he obviously didn't trust me with a hot-water bottle, and has put one in himself. But I can think of a much more interesting way to keep you warm.' He gave me a slow smile, and then said, 'Look, why don't you have a hot bath? Come and visit me afterwards, I'm three doors down from you. OK?'

I nodded, grateful for a moment to be left alone with my impressions of this amazing house. I also needed time to think about Alex. He had been all over me on the train, then it seemed had cooled a little, now he was back on again. I realised I was still more than a little drunk and gave up making any conclusions about any outcome. Live for the moment, I told myself firmly.

I walked round the room, touching the furniture and trying to peer out of the mullioned window. It was too dark outside to see anything, but I did notice the incredible silence. No traffic, no trains, nothing. I heard the hoot of an owl, and shivered. A hot bath was just what I needed. I was touched to see a bunch of green leaves and a few red berries in a pewter mug by the side of my bed, a copy of a book with the arresting title *Monkey Magic in Madagascar* and a bunch of grapes. I smiled. Davey had thought of everything.

Davey's hand could also be seen in the bathroom. Lovely new perfumed soap and big fluffy towels showed me that he had given some thought to my comfort. I glanced doubtfully at the bath though. It was gigantic, and made of copper with a mahogany surround. A large lever with brass plates was where the taps should be. It looked like a piece of heavy marine engineering rather than taps, and it took me several struggling moments to ease the stiff lever forward. As soon as I had, a torrent of boiling-hot water gushed into the bath, making Jicky scurry to safety. I cajoled him down from the curtains and enticed him into his cat basket with a grape.

I poured a handful of violet bath salts from a curved glass jar into the bath, and started to get undressed. After nearly giving myself a slipped disc by adjusting the temperature of the water, I stepped into the bath and sank back in the sweet-smelling steam. I felt myself relax in the water, it was the first time I'd been warm that day. I could already see that the wonderful party dress that Jessy had got me was going to be ruined by my wearing a lot of vests and T-shirts underneath it, to try and keep up some semblance of warmth.

I sighed with pleasure though, despite the cold of the Abbey. What a *fantastic* start to Christmas. The Abbey was fascinating enough by itself, but meeting Alex was the icing on the cake. I had to pinch myself. But yes, it was all true, and a very sexy man was waiting for me in his room down the corridor. So what if he was blowing hot and cold? I laughed to myself, Alex was my Christmas present! Perhaps I could exchange him if he didn't fit?

I tried to think what I could wear to swan down to his room. A fur coat would be handy. I wondered if I could possibly look sexy in three jumpers and a pair of long socks. Probably not.

I reluctantly dragged myself out of the warm water, and was horrified to see wrinkle marks all over me as I'd stayed in there so long. My face, I noted in the glass, was also lobster coloured. Oh damn. I massaged some moisturising cream all over my body, feeling like a film star (usually I only did my face). I hopped into the bedroom, swathed in a towel, and turned my case out, searching for something sexy but warm to put on.

The hot bath had given me an all-over glow, but the icy-cold bedroom soon started to make me shiver again. Whether from the cold or excitement I wasn't sure. All I knew was that this was the most thrilling assignation I'd had in years! Alex was waiting for me, for *me*, I kept repeating to myself, feeling like a child about to open a Christmas stocking. I had a moment's qualm about having a fling with what was probably a *very* unsuitable man, who may or may *not* have a girlfriend in tow, but the spirit of adventure that I had thought bypassed me completely, kicked in.

I stared at all the clothes littered on the bed and in

the end settled for my old thick cotton nightshirt. I know, I know, but it was *cold*. I tarted it up by wrapping a big soft scarlet shawl around me, and after chucking some perfume on my neck (I was worried that Jicky might have left an unpleasant smell there) I excitedly opened the door.

I closed it softly behind me, and the silence and the cold of the old Abbey pressed against me. I shivered delightedly and drew the shawl more tightly around me. Third door down, Alex had said. I turned to my right, and glanced down the corridor.

The next thing I knew, I was screaming my head off. A figure was standing at the end of the corridor, dressed in grey. I think it was a woman, as it had long dark hair falling over its shoulders. I closed my eyes and screamed again, and when I opened them, the figure was gone.

'Jesus Christ! What's going on? Poppy, are you OK?' Alex was running towards me.

I hurled myself at him, and said, between gasps, 'Oh Alex, I've just seen a ghost! I swear, I have! Oh, God, it was horrible, it was a woman, I think, all in grey with long dark hair—'

'Where did you see this?' Alex asked, holding me in his arms and stroking my back.

I shivered again, but this time it was because of his hands rhythmically stroking my back. Definitely.

I pointed with a trembling hand down the corridor. 'Down there, just sort of lurking at the end of the corridor. Oh, God, it was frightening. She looked all gaunt and thin, and all in a horrible grey sort of shroud—'

'Long dark hair and in grey? That, I am pretty sure, is not a ghost. I'm sorry to disappoint you, but it does sound remarkably like my sister.' He snorted with laughter. 'Come on, let's go and have a look.'

Oh, *great*. I hadn't even met her and I was accusing her of being a scary ghost. I cursed myself for adding the gaunt, thin and horrible bit. I hadn't really seen any of that, it was too quick, but I'd felt such a fool screeching in the corridor, I wanted to make it as scary as I could.

Alex was bellowing her name down the corridor, and I jumped as, sure enough, the figure reappeared.

'Tabitha, you frightened the hell out of Poppy! What are you doing here? Why aren't you at Truro with the others?' Alex said crossly.

I had a good look close up at the apparition, and could well be forgiven for thinking it was a ghost. She was deathly pale, and exceedingly thin; she looked most unwell to me, and I thought she should be back in bed. She looked a little bit like a very thin version of Kate Bush, when she was doing her 'Wuthering Heights' song.

'Oh, I'm sorry, did I scare you?' she said breathlessly. 'I heard noises so I came to see what it was.' She turned to Alex and put her hand on his arm. 'I'm so very glad you're here, you can help me feed the birds tomorrow. The ground's frozen, the poor little things must be starving. And who's this? Where's Claudia?'

I squirmed a bit and muttered that I was a friend of Davey's, and that he had invited me down here for Christmas.

'Oh yes, of course. He *did* say something about it, how nice to meet you. Do you like walking? There are some wonderful places to go to on the moors, I'll take you if you like.'

She looked anxiously at me, and I thanked her but privately thought that the only walking I was going to do involved some shops at the end of it, or a café at the very least.

She was wearing a thin pale grey nightdress, and I assumed she must be as freezing as I was, but she didn't look it. Perhaps she really was part wraith, and it was a well-known fact that they didn't feel the cold. We all stood around in the cold corridor making small talk, until my teeth began to chatter.

'Poppy, why don't you go back to bed? I'm going to have a long, cosy chat with my brother. See you in the morning. Good-night, I do hope you sleep well.' Tabitha gave a smile in my direction, and dragged Alex down the corridor behind her. He turned to me and mouthed the words 'I won't be long', and gave a rueful grin and a shrug of his shoulders.

I beetled back to my room, and hurled myself into bed. Then I got out again immediately to take Jicky out of his basket. I needed every bit of warmth that I could lay my hands on. I piled Jessy's leather jacket on top of the duvet, and swaddled myself in the shawl, trying to fight the icy sheets. The hot-water bottle that Davey had so kindly put in earlier was now lukewarm, a bit like Tabitha's blood, I decided. Now, she *was* strange. Admittedly it hadn't got us off to a flying start, me mistaking her for a ghost, but surely she could see the resemblance. Maybe she was mad? Maybe every abbey has its secrets and she was this one's? She certainly looked the part, with large staring eyes and wild tumbling hair. Although I thought she overdid the startled-faun act a bit. Jicky snuggled down, and I hoped that he would warm me up. My feet were like blocks of ice, and tired as I was, I was also in a hyped sense of alertness, waiting for Alex. Had he meant he would come to me? Or did he think that I was going to brave the corridor again, and go to him? I should cocoa. Nothing was going to get me wandering around this place late at night.

From downstairs I heard the chiming of a grandfather clock. Midnight.

'Happy Christmas, Jicky,' I whispered, giving him a squeeze.

I thought of all the Christmases past, and even with all of them put together, this *had* to be the strangest. I remembered when I had been about fifteen and had begged to be allowed to cook the Christmas lunch. My mother had reluctantly agreed, and the family had gathered expectantly around the dining table, clutching their sherry, waiting for the turkey and all the trimmings to come out. What we actually got was indeed the turkey, complete with a small plastic bag of giblets oozing out from above the parson's nose, which I hadn't realised was in there. The whole meal had been a bit of a disaster. Then there was the Christmas that the electricity had conked out, and we all realised that we had absolutely nothing to say to one another, and longed for the company of the telly so that we could revert to our customary silence. To my horror, my parents had made me go to the golf club with them, which was even worse, as I was forced to laugh at whiskery men's incomprehensible jokes, and admire the ladies' hideous new dresses. That was the Christmas I had finally given up any romantic yearnings about finding my real parents. I think I realised there and then that I would have to accept my adoptive parents as my own.

I glanced again at my watch, but it was only ten minutes later than when I had last looked at it. He probably wasn't coming. Or maybe he would, if I got out of bed and cleaned my teeth. Again. Oh, this was nonsense, how could cleaning teeth magic someone into a room? It was rubbish. I was *not* going to do it.

About thirty seconds later I was in the bathroom, fumbling for the toothpaste and reprimanding Jicky for having a wee on the bath mat. I gave the mat a quick scrub in the bath, after wrestling with the lever again, and made a mental note that I'd have to rig up a sort of litter box for him for the next couple of days. I spied a large bottle of what I took to be toilet water in the bathroom, and blessed Davey once again. I took the stopper out and liberally sprinkled it around to dispel any remaining monkey smells there might be. I was becoming immune to them, but I was aware that they existed. I sprinkled some more of the liquid on the floor. It smelt very nice, flowery, with a hint of green in it. I wiped my hands, and turned to leave the room and get back to bed. My feet disappeared from beneath me, and I went flying across the room, smashing the bottle, and landed very hard on my bottom.

The bloody liquid was bath oil, and I'd spread it all over the damn place! I groaned, and tried to stand up. It *hurt*. I managed to get to my feet, and pulled up my nightshirt to have a look in the mirror. Oh, God, there was blood! I saw a small sliver of glass embedded in my bum. I twisted to try and see it, and nearly put my back out. Oh, *great*.

I stood in an agony of indecision. What to do first? I managed to get Jicky out of the way, and pulled on my boots before I tackled the broken glass and oil in the bathroom. Every movement hurt, and I was hobbling like an old woman. I shut Jicky in his basket, and went to assess the mess in the bathroom. I needed hot water, a dustpan and brush, and a mop. (Not to mention a nurse to tackle my wound.) This was not the sort of house that had domestic stuff like that around, and I was *not* going to wander around downstairs dripping blood. Oh, God, think, *think*. OK, improvise. I found a newspaper, and gingerly picked up the shards of glass. That took ages. Then I ran some hot water and tried to mop up the oil with my flannel. It was useless, the oil just spread. What I needed was some sort of washing-up liquid to cut through the oil. I know, shampoo! I found my shampoo and dripped it on to the floor, I added some hot water and got on my hands and knees to mop. I watched in amazement as the whole of the bathroom floor became lather. It looked like one of those foam parties that they have in clubs in Ibiza. The more I rubbed, the more it foamed.

Shit. Well, maybe it would dry by the morning. Or not. I didn't really care by now, I was more concerned with what I was going to do about the bit of glass in my behind.

Right, think about this logically. What are the options? Well, OK, I could go and ask Alex if he's any good with a pair of tweezers, hitch up my nightie, and get him to have a go. No. Definitely *no*. Out of the question. Or Tabitha? Again, a most emphatic no. Right, I could sleep on my tummy, and tackle it in the morning. A favourite with me, even though I could well bleed to death and get tetanus or gangrene or something. Oh, God, imagine the horror of having to get blood off the sheets and explain why I chose to get bottom poisoning by leaving some broken glass in it all night. Shit, imagine having to explain *how* I got broken glass in it in the first place. OK, another option? I was rapidly running out of them, and I racked my brain. OK! Got it! Phone an ambulance. This was an emergency, wasn't it?

No.

Oh, OK. Right, there was only one thing left. I'd seen enough episodes of *ER* to know what to do.

I hobbled to the bathroom and washed my hands,

and the tweezers, in very hot water. My boots made a squelching noise and seemed to stick to the floor, and I had to prise my feet off the tiles to move. I persevered, took a towel from the bathroom and hobbled back to the bedroom.

I took the bedside lamp and put it on the floor in front of the old-fashioned long swivel looking-glass. Oh, why me? Why *now*?

I hitched and folded my nightshirt around my waist and made a belt out of the shawl to keep it in place. *Then* came the fun bit. I discovered that standing with my back to the mirror, I couldn't twist round far enough to see properly. Oh, God, now what?

I remembered a particularly gruelling power yoga class I'd done with Gaia months ago, and a horrible position that we were all meant to 'flow' into. I'd lasted about three minutes before pretending to have a coughing fit and fleeing the class on the pretext of getting some water, never to return. Maybe this was the time to 'flow' again.

Basically it involved standing with your legs as far apart as they could go, bending down and trying to push your head through your legs. It was worth a try. I took a deep breath, and stood with my back to the mirror. I stretched my legs, trying to keep a good balance in my boots, and turned upside down. Well, at least I could *see* it now (I could also see rather a lot of everything else as well). The blood was rushing to my face, and I struggled with the damn tweezers.

Ouch! It bloody hurt! I took another stab at the sliver

95

of glass, and saw, to my absolute horror, the bedroom door open.

'Poppy? What the hell are you doing?'

Alex stood in the doorway open-mouthed. As well he might. I knew, thanks to the mirror, exactly what he was seeing.

If I say that I prayed for death, does that sound too dramatic? If not death, then I'd settle for sudden oblivion.

Of course, sudden oblivion doesn't happen when you want it to, does it? My hands were scrabbling frantically to pull down my nightshirt, and I started to stutter some absurd explanation.

I'd tied the shawl round my waist very tightly, and it was impossible to untie. You know how when you're flustered everything simple seems to take for ever to do? Well, it was just like that, but worse.

My nightshirt was still hitched around my waist when I heard Alex say, 'Well, you were right about not being a natural blonde!'

It was the final straw. I did what I should have done five seconds ago, and burst into tears. Well, to be honest, I didn't need to force it.

It worked like a charm. Alex untied the shawl from my waist and held me in his arms, hearing through my muffled sobs how I'd got some glass in my bottom.

'Oh, you poor thing! Now then, lie flat on the bed and I'll get it out, I've always wanted to play doctors and nurses. Do you think it might need stitches? I must say, it was the most extraordinary sight, especially with your boots on – very disturbing. Now then, come on, that's right. Lie flat and try to relax.'

Yeah, that was really going to happen, wasn't it? The only good thing about lying down was that I could bury my head in the pillows and sob some more, mainly out of humiliation, but pain was starting to kick in as well now. I heard Alex go to the bathroom to wash his hands.

'Be careful, it's rather wet in there,' I warned him.

I heard him laugh, and then felt him sit on the edge of the bed.

'Now then, I'm going to be as gentle as I can. If it's any consolation at all, you've got a lovely backside.'

I pushed my head further into the pillow. I could feel him pick at the sliver of glass with the tweezers and gently pull.

'Oh, God, that hurts, is it out?' I cried.

There was a silence, and I felt Alex move the tweezers again.

'Oww! That *really* hurts, Alex! Just pull it out, will you?'

'Actually, Poppy, it seems to be, well, not exactly stuck, but well, quite hard to budge. At the moment, of course. I think it's in quite deep.'

In quite deep? How deep? Are there major blood vessels in your bum? Oh, *God*.

I heard Alex take a deep breath, then he said, 'OK, I'm going to give it one more go, and if it doesn't move then, well, I think I'll have to get Tom to run us to hospital—'

97

'No! Just pull as hard as you can!' I insisted.

'OK, maybe we should have a brandy?' Alex said hopefully.

'No! Just pull, damn you!'

'OK, one, two, three—'

'Yoo-hoo! Hello, Poppy, I can see the light's on, are you decent? I've got Ma and Pa with me, we've just got back from Truro and they're dying to meet you. How was your—'

I heard the door open.

'Christ almighty!' Davey's appalled voice echoed around the room.

I raised my head and saw a group of people in the doorway taking in my bare bottom and Alex bent over it. I prayed again for oblivion.

'Hello,' I said, forcing a bright smile, 'I'm Poppy Hazleton. Thanks for inviting me for Christmas.'

Chapter Seven

I thought wildly of self-suffocation in the pillow for a moment, but Edward and Jocasta Stanton were utterly divine about meeting a strange house guest having her bottom examined by their son. Davey was hysterical with laughter and had to sit on the side of my bed offering advice, between wiping away tears of laughter.

'Really, Poppy, I do think you might have waited for me to get back from church. Here I am filled with festive holiness, and I feel quite ready for another chat with the bishop. What good luck we didn't bring *him* back with us! I can see it in the parish magazine now . . .'

I buried my head further in the pillow and heard Jocasta say, 'Now then, Davey, that's quite enough! The poor girl is obviously suffering. I think you should pop downstairs with Edward and get us all a drink. Off you go.'

I heard retreating footsteps, and then Jocasta moving towards the bed as Alex made way for her. I squinted sideways to see her, and was delighted to find that she looked *exactly* how I'd imagined her, which I found immensely comforting. You know how sometimes you can imagine a person, and then on actually meeting them you become very disappointed? Well, not with Jocasta.

She was a tall, silver-haired woman, with deep blue eyes set far apart in a tanned and weather-beaten face, and with a *very* individual dress sense. She was wearing sheepskin garters, criss-cross-laced with leather thongs, another lot of sheepskin in a sort of jerkin affair and long, dangly, barbaric earrings. It was odd, yes, but she managed to look remarkably stylish.

'Now then, Poppy, I think I'll have a look. I used to be a nurse, so you're in quite safe hands—'

'Ma! You've *never* been a nurse!' Alex protested.

'No, darling, you're quite right, I haven't. But I thought it sounded soothing and now you've spoilt the illusion. Oh, dear, I wonder if we could ask Tom to pull it out? He's awfully good with the sheep when they're lambing,' Jocasta said thoughtfully. 'Although I do see it's not *quite* the same thing.'

'Oh, no, please,' I said. 'Please not. I really don't think I could stand any further humiliation. Have another go, Alex. Pull *harder*.'

'Wait, darling, for the brandy. We'll need to brace ourselves,' advised Jocasta. 'Anyway, Poppy, it's delightful to meet you. We hear such a lot about you from Davey, you know, I am glad you could come.'

I stifled a snigger, in between wincing with pain. I thought Jocasta was being great, lying so well.

'I really am so, so sorry,' I began to say, when I was

royally waved silent by an imperious hand studded with rings.

'Oh, look! Is that a monkey in the basket?' Jocasta said excitedly.

I explained about Jicky, and how Davey was going to take us to the sanctuary.

Jocasta was crouching in front of the basket making little crooning noises, and stroking him through the door.

'Ooh, lucky you! Edward and I were offered a squirrel monkey as a wedding present, but my mother made me refuse it. She said they do very rude things on top of shelves.' Jocasta sounded quite envious.

'Not just on top of shelves,' I said meaningfully.

She laughed, and then shouted down to her older son and husband to hurry up with the drinks. 'Poppy and I are practically dying of shock up here, not to mention loss of blood and monkey envy! So *do* hurry up!' She turned to Alex and said, 'What *can* they be doing?'

We heard footsteps and Edward and Davey reappeared with a tray of champagne flutes and an icy bottle.

Edward was the exact replica of Davey, but a good forty years older. Immaculately dressed, and with the same fair hair. He had a gruff voice and was obviously rather embarrassed by my predicament.

'Hold your horses,' he said, 'here comes the cavalry. We thought a bottle of the Widow might be called for, it *is* Christmas Day, after all.' Edward placed the tray on my bedside table, and studiously avoided looking at my bottom.

'Ooh, what a treasure you are. You always think of just the right thing,' Jocasta said adoringly to him.

There was a bit of fluffing around as the cork was popped and the champagne poured. Davey started to ask Alex about Paris, whilst Jocasta and Edward discussed the general beastliness of the bishop. ('But darling, I'm *sure* he's got false teeth.')

Now, call me a party pooper if you will, but I felt decidedly uncomfortable. Everyone seemed to have got used to my position of shame very quickly, and I had to make little whimpers of pain to bring this matter back to general consideration.

'Alex, please, *please* try again. It really is hurting now,' I said.

Everyone must have felt very guilty about standing around my bed drinking champagne, because now they all sprang into action.

It was decided that Alex would pull with all his might, and Jocasta would staunch the flow of blood. Alex was just readying himself with a gulp of champagne when Jocasta said, 'Now wait a moment, darling. Poppy, I think you should grit your teeth, and when that doesn't work, which it *won't*, swear very, *very* loudly. Forget all that nonsense about breathing. It never helped me at all during childbirth. A damn good swear, strong drugs and then lots of adoring relatives to look after you. Right, ready?'

I nodded and Alex heaved.

There was a burst of applause as Alex held the splinter of glass aloft, and Jocasta dabbed me with something that stung, and then put some lint and plaster on. I managed not to swear out loud, but it hurt very much indeed. The relief of pulling down my nightshirt was indescribable. I wrapped the shawl around me, and painfully tried to find a comfortable position to sit up.

'Jocasta, didn't you have one of those rubber cushion things, after Alex was born? We should find it for Poppy,' Edward said.

'Do you know, I did. I had the most *frightful* piles after you were born, Alex, I wonder where I put it?' Jocasta put her glass down, and looked ready to search the Abbey.

I caught Davey's eye, and implored him silently to make them stop talking about it.

'I think we should all retire and leave the patient what little dignity she has left,' Davey said dryly.

I smiled gratefully at him, and soon everyone was wishing one another Happy Christmas and good-night. Edward held up the empty bottle of champagne and said guiltily, 'We forgot Tabitha!'

'So we did, but you know she doesn't drink,' Jocasta said, bending down to kiss me good-night. 'Now, darling, I'm going to give you a sleeping tablet, otherwise you'll be in *agony* during the night. Do call if you need anything, won't you?'

I thanked her again and dutifully swallowed the offered pill.

103

Davey bent down and kissed me, saying, 'I *love* the hair, by the way. What a to-do! Are you sure you're OK?'

I assured him I was, and he waited at the door for Alex, who raised his eyebrows at me and smiled. 'Goodnight, Poppy. It was a pleasure meeting you, I can assure you! Sleep well.' He gave a shrug, and closed the door.

Thwarted again, I thought, as they disappeared. I heard Jocasta say something about a tetanus injection, or would I be all right if I drank a lot of red wine as that had iron in it? Their endearing and daft discussion drifted down the corridor, and after a few door bangs, and the gurgling of very old plumbing, the Abbey settled down for the night.

I shifted in the bed, and tried to find a comfortable position. I thought about taking Jicky out of his basket to warm me up, but I really couldn't be bothered. I thought for a moment that the sleeping pill was making me rather flushed and warm, but I stretched my hand out towards an ancient copper pipe in the room, and felt that heat was coming from it. Typical stargazy behaviour, I thought as I drifted off to sleep. They turn the heating on at one in the morning.

I woke up once in the night, and thought for a thrilling moment that Alex had stolen in to see me, as the bedroom door was just closing. Maybe it was creaking, or maybe Alex *had* come in, seen me snoring my head off, and thought better of it. Damn. Jicky was chattering away in his basket which made it seem a

104

possibility. I sleepily let him out and draped him over my neck. Just before sleep claimed me I heard a very strange noise outside, coming from the garden. A scraping, shovelling noise. It sounded remarkably like someone digging.

When I eventually woke next morning, sun showed through the incredibly threadbare curtains. I lay in bed for a few minutes, remembering where I was and the events of yesterday. So much had happened, and today was Christmas Day. Even though *no one* reaches the level of excitement about Christmas morning that you do when you are seven, there is, undeniably, still a little *frisson* of thrill there. I half-expected to see a knobbly stocking at the end of the bed, filled with toys and with an orange in the toe. I sat up and yawned. Good God, there *was* a stocking at the end of the bed! Davey, unquestionably. I snorted with delight, and grabbed it. It was full of the most wonderful girlie tat. Nail varnish, sugar mice, chocolate money, a pair of shocking pink fluffy gloves, some nuts, a pair of chopsticks, a set of fake nails and, of course, the ubiquitous tangerine.

'What a star that man is,' I said to Jicky, giving him the tangerine to play with. I got out of bed, and pulled the curtains back. My room was at the front of the Abbey, and I could see the long, steep drive falling away from the house. Bare-limbed trees crowded the drive, and if I turned my head I could see a lawn that was dotted with shrubs and quite a few large sculptures. I looked more closely at one of them, and saw that it was in fact an old granite headstone, complete

105

with a small crouching dragon surrounded by a low mossy wall. Good grief. I thought graves had to be on consecrated ground or something, but maybe Cornwall has its own laws about that sort of thing? It wouldn't surprise me if the Stantons buried their family wherever they happened to drop. I saw a small pile of earth to one side of a statue of a dragon, so perhaps I had been right, and someone had been digging in the middle of the night after all. But who and why was beyond me.

I cautiously touched the wound on my behind. It was very sore. I wondered if I should risk getting it wet by having a bath. I glanced at the clock. Was it a suitable time to go downstairs? I didn't want to look as though I was hanging around for breakfast, but on the other hand, I didn't want them thinking that I was never going to get up. They can be posers, those sorts of thing, when you are staying in other people's homes. What is quite normal and natural for you, may not be for them. They might well look at you askance if you asked for porridge and a kipper when they only nibbled on water biscuits and drank lemon juice for breakfast. Perhaps I could try and find Davey's room? Maybe not. My sense of direction was usually awful, and the Abbey was an unknown quantity.

I glanced outside again. The sky was a pale blue, but I could see the frost still on the grass. I had just washed, and was trying to find a suitable clothing combination, you know, warm, smart, Christmassy, and – dare I say it? – sexy, when there was a knock on my door.

'Come in, and a Happy Christmas!' I carolled out, wrapping my shawl tightly around me. I wasn't going to give a repeat performance of last night's bare-bottomed woman.

Davey came into the room wearing the most wonderful dressing-gown. He looked just like Sherlock Holmes in it, as I told him. He preened slightly, and said, 'Yes, it *is* rather wonderful, isn't it? I deserve to be coddled up in something gorgeous, I've been awake for hours, working, you know.'

I looked doubtfully at him. Working? At what?

He admired himself in the looking-glass and, glancing at the debris on my bed, said, 'Oh, good, you found the stocking then. I got a set of screwdrivers, very much the wrong present, I thought.'

'But didn't you bring mine in? I felt sure *you* were responsible for it. I was just about to thank you, and tell you it made me feel as if I was eight again. Sugar mice *and* a tangerine. Perfect.'

'No. no, it wasn't me. We have them every year, and every year we try to find out who delivers them. When we were children we tried to stay up all night and catch Edward, but we never did. He's very clever about it, because he gets a stocking, too, and he always acts as though it's a complete surprise and questions who's delivered it to him. But it must be him, because Jocasta has never been known to willingly get up before ten. She was even late for Tab's wedding because it was before eleven, and—'

'Your sister's *married*?' I asked, agog.

107

'Was, darling. Was. Now then, what are you going to wear? I intend staying in this very gorgeous dressing-gown. I'm going to drink port all day and play the piano in a Noel Coward sort of way.' Davey stroked the padded plum velvet of his dressing-gown, and started to pick out some clothes for me to wear.

I told him about Jessy choosing them all for me, and he approved greatly. But I was really more interested in the details of Tabitha's marriage, and tried to ask him questions about it. He was annoyingly vague.

'Oh, it was a long time ago now, I think it only lasted about three months, a distant cousin. Both as barmy as each other. Poor thing, really. She's never very happy, but being saddled with the surname that she's got, because he won't agree to a divorce – very strict Catholic, must be rather depressing, I suppose.' He tailed off, looking through the ever-growing mountain of clothes on my bed. He began to hang them in the wardrobe for me, and came across the slinky party dress.

'How fantastic, perfect for the snapper party. I might even be tempted myself, seeing you in that. Now then, hurry up, let's go and have some breakfast.'

'What cousin? What's the surname? What *is* the snapper party? And what do you mean, you might be tempted yourself? And what have you been working at?' I wailed to his retreating back.

'Oh, you know, the usual sort of thing . . . I'll see you in the kitchen. Tea or coffee? The name's O'Shag, so you do see . . . She swears that the "g" is silent, but . . .' He disappeared down the corridor.

I giggled to myself. O'Shag! No wonder the poor woman looked miserable. I dressed with care, paying a lot more attention to the state of my underwear than I normally would. Today had to be *the* day, didn't it? Or was I being far too presumptuous? Oh, God, maybe he'd gone off me? Or the horrid-sounding American girlfriend had hexed him somehow? Perhaps Alex and I could slope off somewhere and – oh, stop it, I told myself. Just stop it. I could sometimes give myself a headache whilst I dithered away, and I was determined not to do this today. Enjoy the day, and don't count your chickens, whatever *that* means, I thought happily as I picked Jicky up and put him in his basket.

I made my way to the kitchen, opening a few wrong doors en route, and found Davey staring in dismay at a note.

'It's the cooking instructions from Odessa, about the geese. Oh, dear. It looks very complicated, I'm sure it doesn't *really* say cover with sand, does it?'

I went to stand beside him and read the note. 'Salt, you twit! Although her writing's difficult, isn't it?'

'I think that's down to the wonderful benefit of never having gone to school,' Edward said, coming into the kitchen carrying a cardboard box. 'Happy Christmas to both of you! Now, I've got breakfast in the box, let's go to the Painted Parlour, shall we? Jocasta'll be down in a few moments, Alex has gone to dig the heather. Oh, I

109

suppose we should wake Tab – or maybe we should let her sleep? What d'you think, Davey?'

We trotted along, and I whispered to Davey, 'Why is Alex digging up heather?'

'Oh, you know, for luck. We all get a little sprig to wear today, well, we used to, but Jocasta thought we shouldn't go round picking it, so now we dig it up and plant it in pots. Same thing, really. Digging is jolly hard work, you know. Far harder than I expected,' Davey said, opening a door to his right.

I had no time to wonder why Davey had been digging, as I gasped with astonishment at my first sight of the Painted Parlour. It was a small room, well, small for the Abbey, and it was completely painted with scenes from the Bible. John the Baptist in the desert took up one wall, Samson and Delilah had another, whilst the parting of the Red Sea had two walls together. I looked up and saw Adam (who looked remarkably like Edward) and Eve on the ceiling. The colours were so bold as to be practically lurid, and the whole effect was quite extraordinary. A bit claustrophobic, certainly, but wonderful.

'Did Jocasta do this?' I said, staring at the tribe of Israel marching through the parted sea, complete with goats, donkeys, sheep and what looked suspiciously like a gorilla. Moses appeared to be carrying a bottle of beer, and I giggled. The whole thing was remarkably uplifting.

'Yes, I did, so don't say anything too awful,' Jocasta warned me, coming into the room behind us.

110

'But it's wonderful!' I stammered. 'I think it's brilliant, you're *so* clever.'

Jocasta kissed me on the top of my head, and wished everyone Happy Christmas. I felt extraordinarily happy. I *liked* feeling part of this strange family.

I saw that the large round dining table had been set with cutlery and glasses. Davey was lighting the candles, and Edward was pouring white wine into glasses.

They certainly drank a lot, I thought. I know it's Christmas and all that, but I didn't think I could face a glass of wine with my toast, perhaps I could ask for orange juice without appearing a wimp?

Alex came charging into the room, brandishing a small brass flowerpot with some heather in it, which he placed in the centre of the table. He was covered in mud, and was blowing on his hands to get them warm.

'Happy Christmas, everyone! It's positively brass-monkey weather out there! Whoops, sorry, Jicky. I think it could snow, you know . . .' He walked around the table and kissed everyone, including myself, which caused a blush on my face that did *not* go unnoticed by Davey.

'Mud must be brushed off when dry, do not attempt to use soap and water,' Davey said smugly, glancing down at his own immaculately manicured hands.

Alex ignored the advice and said, 'So, Poppy, did you sleep well? And how's the, er, wound?' A wicked grin spread across his face.

'Don't be impertinent, sir!' Edward boomed at him, casting a furious look in Alex's direction.

I felt my heart start thudding and I tried to answer as calmly as I could. 'Yes, fine thanks, and it, well, it's OK, but it's still quite painful,' I said primly.

Alex laughed, and ran from the room to get some cushions for my chair.

'He so thoughtful,' said Jocasta fondly. 'He takes after you, darling,' she said, blowing a kiss to Edward.

Edward was not displeased but made a harrumphing sort of noise which was meant to show general disapproval, I think.

'Nonsense, he's just trying to impress Poppy with his manners, which as we know can sometimes be lacking towards the opposite sex,' Davey said, picking up his wineglass and sniffing the contents. 'Umm, wonderful. The '67? Wonderful year, Pa, you do spoil us.'

Alex came back carrying two cushions that he placed on a chair next to his, and I gratefully sat down. It was still hard to sit, and I had to balance really on one cheek, which was as uncomfortable as it sounds.

Edward was untying the cardboard box at a side table, and said, 'Right, nearly ready. Davey, go and get the plate! Oh, and I'll need the leather glove, as well. I think I left it in the study. Run boy, run!'

I looked nervously at the cardboard box. What the hell was in there that required a leather glove? Something that bit?

Davey smiled and left the room to return with a massive platter that was chipped and cracked. It had the family motto inscribed around it and a picture of a sleeping dragon on the bottom. As he handed it to his father, everyone burst into applause.

'Happy Christmas, my darlings!'

'The Stanton plate lives to see another Christmas!'

'Oh, it really *does* feel like Christmas now, doesn't it?' Jocasta cried, clasping her hands in front of her.

I looked enquiringly at Davey as he passed the glove to his father.

'Oysters,' Davey explained.

Oh, *God.*

Edward was unpacking layer after layer of bumpy grey shells that had been packed in ice.

'Fresh as a daisy,' he declared. 'Now then, I think our guest should have the first one, a sort of welcome to the Abbey, my dear, and thank you for visiting us.' He put his leather glove on and shucked the first oyster.

Oh, *God!*

Now, I'm sure that oysters are deservedly expensive, and I'm sure that they are delicious. But my problem was, to my shame, that I had never tried one. And, here's the rub – they do not *look* delicious. They look *disgusting.* All eyes were upon me as Edward passed me the first one. I suppose I could have said that I was allergic to them, or something, but I felt I had caused so much fuss already, and they were all so delighted with themselves in giving me a treat that I steeled myself to swallow.

Right then, Poppy, just do it. Don't dither, just do it

113

without thinking about it. How hard can it be? I said to myself, trying to unclench my jaws.

I gingerly took the shell between my fingers and brought it to my lips. I tried not to look too closely at it, and I caught a smell of the sea, then without allowing myself any time to think about it, I tipped it in my mouth.

Immediately my tongue was flooded with a briny, salty tang. The texture was disconcerting, a bit thick and slimy, but the taste was, well, let's put it this way, it really was like having a mouthful of the sea. I swallowed it as quickly as I could and took a gulp of wine. That was better, maybe they weren't too bad after all! New experiences were coming thick and fast to me, and I felt almost giddy with it.

Everyone was getting stuck in to the oysters now. I tried another one with some shallot vinegar on it (*much* better, trust me) and happily listened to the chat about what everyone had got in their stockings.

'I had a beautiful new sable brush in mine, just what I wanted!' Jocasta enthused.

'Well, I had a toy Mercedes, damn it, which I think is a bit cruel, when everyone knows I want the real one,' protested Edward, pouring more wine.

'Oh, come on, Pa, we know it's you! You should get yourself something you *really* want,' Davey said, smiling fondly at his father.

'No, no. Really, it is most definitely not me,' Edward said, gazing round the table.

Everybody groaned.

'Edward, you always say that! But we know it is . . .' Alex said, slurping an oyster at the same time.

'It's *not*—' Edward began to say.

'*Really* it's not!' Jocasta, Alex and Davey said in unison, copying his tone of bewilderment.

We all burst out laughing, and the door opened, letting in a slight chill. It was, of course, Tabitha the wraith.

Jocasta and Edward jumped up to kiss her Happy Christmas and Davey poured her a glass of wine. Tabitha exchanged it for a glass of water, and shuddered at the sight of the oysters.

'Poor little things,' she said with compassion. 'I don't know how you can, it's so cruel, you know . . .'

The family smiled tolerantly, and I guessed that this was a much-discussed subject.

As she sat down she gave a little scream. 'Oh, God, what *is* that animal doing?' She pointed at Jicky in his basket.

I didn't need to turn round, I knew exactly what he would be doing.

Chapter Eight

When we'd got down to the very last oyster, Jocasta snatched it up and said, 'Come on, all of you, let's go and wish the Stantons a Happy Christmas, then we can sing Happy Birthday.' She started to gather herself together, knocking her napkin to the ground in her haste to stand up and taking her wineglass with her. I noticed everyone else did as well, so I stood up, clutching my glass.

I wondered where we were going, and envisaged a trip to an upstairs bedroom to wish an ageing relative a festive greeting, but no, we all trooped out the kitchen door and trailed over the lawn to the headstone that I'd seen outside my window. The sky had turned a pale grey, and the wind had dropped, but it was still *very* cold.

Jocasta placed the oyster on the stone, and Edward poured some wine over it. Then they all grouped together and I saw, with great surprise, that Edward had a tear rolling down his cheek. I was not used to a family that showed their emotions so easily. I searched my memory and couldn't remember seeing my father cry, ever. Not even when England lost at cricket.

Alex and Davey threw their arms round their father, and Jocasta held her hand out to him in what looked like a remarkably tender gesture, and I saw a glance of implicit understanding pass between them. It made me feel rather in the way, and I tentatively took a step backwards. Perhaps I should go back to the house, as this was obviously a family thing.

I felt Jocasta touch my arm, and she drew me towards her and said, looking down at the grave, 'Now, this is Poppy, a very good friend of Davey's, and I hope of us all, soon. She's come to stay with us for the first time, but not the last, we hope, so we thought you'd like to say hello.'

I looked nervously around me, but everyone was smiling fondly at the grave.

'Let me introduce my parents, Edith and Robert, *and* my grandparents, Grace and Harry,' Edward said gruffly. 'And a finer family no man could ever wish for.'

It sounds mawkish, but it wasn't. I cleared my throat, and said, 'Edith and Robert, Grace and Harry, it's Poppy here and, umm, well, I'd just like to wish you a Happy Christmas and say what a fantastic time I'm having in this beautiful place. Umm, and I think you're all lovely!'

Jocasta kissed me, Davey and Alex cheered and Edward looked so pleased that I didn't mind one bit feeling a fool. Tabitha even gave me her Peruvian hat to wear.

Usually my fear of meeting new people made me cripplingly shy, but with the Stantons I felt strangely at ease. Perhaps it was because being surrounded by such incredibly egocentric people left me no room to observe myself; I was too damn busy keeping track of what they were all up to. Also, I'd had a good training being close to Davey, we'd been friends for a long time, long enough for me to take this brand of eccentricity in my stride. That, and of course the fact that I fancied the pants off one of them. Even Edward, who I had thought of as being gruff and a bit intimidating, I now realised was just a growling teddy bear.

As we all turned back to the Abbey and some semblance of warmth, I pointed to the Latin inscription on the grave, which was the same as on Jocasta's ring that I had found under the table (for which she had thanked me profusely over breakfast and then promptly lost again) and asked, 'Is that what it means? The dragon guarding the hidden gold? Is that what the gold is, ancestors?'

'We like to think, so my dear,' said Edward. 'Although when I was young, and when these boys were eight or so, we used to believe that every time we saw a dragon, we had to dig like billy-o, and we'd uncover the real gold. But you know, the older I get, the more I believe that the gold's been here all along.' Edward held his back poker straight, and courteously offered me his arm. I squeezed it affectionately and earned myself looks of thanks and appreciation from the rest of the family.

I saw that Davey was looking quite smug, and was staring up at the roof. I followed his glance and saw that he was examining the dragon gargoyles on the roof.

'What is it?' Edward asked, as he too followed Davey's eyes.

'I still maintain that the family myth must have an element of truth to it, perhaps I should try the roof tomorrow?'

'Good God, no, I forbid it! Do you hear? Most dangerous,' Edward said, adding, 'If there really was any hidden gold, don't you think we would have found it by now?'

And then he whispered in a loud enough voice for all to hear, 'Boy's a fool! Bad enough that he's creeping around digging up the asparagus beds without having him clambering about on the roof!'

So Davey *had* been trying to dig around for some treasure.

Edward was still glaring at Davey, but the rest of the family sniggered, and I was beginning to get the feeling that Edward's bark was worse than his bite. I had guessed as much already, I mean any man who can weep openly the way he had done, couldn't be the bluff, tough man that he liked to portray.

'Well, I don't see what other chance I have!' Davey protested.

Jocasta gave him a 'not now' look, and he shut up.

I didn't know what Davey meant by 'other chance'. He didn't have money troubles as far as I knew, but then his finances were a complete mystery to me. As was his increasingly odd behaviour: *something* was going on, but I had no idea what. I couldn't quite put my finger on it, but Davey had been exceptionally nice to me. Not that he wasn't most of the time anyway, but ever since he'd invited me down here, he had been even *nicer.*

We all trooped back into the kitchen, stamping our feet to get them warm, and Tabitha began to chop up some slimy green stuff on a chopping board.

'Oh, good, darling, you're eating something!' declared Jocasta, looking pleased.

'I'm having some samphire. So good for one, anyone else?' Tabitha said with her back to us.

I saw Edward and Jocasta exchange agonised looks, and Davey sighed. Alex snorted with laughter, and muttered, 'God, no. Why don't you have some toast or something? Go on, treat yourself, it is Christmas Day, after all.'

Looking at her frail skinny back, I tended to agree with him. She really looked as though she could do with a decent meal. Was this the 'problem' that she had? Anorexia? I dredged up what I knew about eating disorders, very little as it turned out. I personally had no sympathy with it at all. It seemed utterly ridiculous, when half the world was starving, for the other half to make themselves throw up. Just think of Karen Carpenter, and I rest my case. I looked at her again, she *was* skinny, but she had a definite little bit of a tummy, maybe she was just dieting or something.

120

Jocasta clapped her hands and said, 'Right. Everyone to the chapel, and then I'm sure it's present-opening time, isn't it? Oh, and what time do we have to put the geese in? Does Odessa say?'

Edward scanned the illegible note.

'Shouldn't they be stuffed or something?'

We all stared at the birds. They looked massive to me, and I had no idea what to do with them.

'Where's the potatoes?'

'Oh, God, we haven't got to have sprouts, have we?'

'Oh, let's not worry about that now,' Jocasta said grandly, somehow implying that the geese would magically cook themselves. 'To the chapel, all of you. You too, Tab, if you've finished eating, that is, darling.'

'Well, I have. But if you're going to start cooking meat, you know I can't stay in the same room. How you can all poison your systems with—'

Edward and Jocasta had frozen smiles on their faces, but Alex interrupted her. 'Oh, Tab, do lay off for a bit. Come on, let's all go to the chapel.'

Tabitha smiled in a sort of pitying 'they-know-not-what-they-do' way at all of us reprehensible flesh eaters and managed to stop herself giving us all a lecture on the benefits of soya protein.

I clutched Davey's arm and whispered, 'Davey, who are we singing Happy Birthday to?'

Davey looked at me with amusement. 'Baby Jesus.'

'Oh.'

'Yes,' Alex said, walking behind us. 'It's the one Christmas thing that really is terribly embarrassing, but, well . . .' He shrugged his shoulders and gave an amused grin.

'We can hear you!' Edward and Jocasta cried, ushering us into the chapel. Alex blew them both a kiss and held the door open for me.

It was yet *another* room that floored me. It was dark and sombre and perfectly plain. Three rows of pews and the remains of an altar were the only structures. Tall wax candles flickered in front of a Madonna cradling a baby, and someone had placed a garland of green stuff around the base of her. It was old and still in here, and I could feel the past catch up with me very quickly. I had been to a church somewhere in Suffolk where I had felt the same emotions sweep over me. I had never been particularly religious, but sometimes it felt as though certain places held the memories of all the believers who had prayed in there years and years ago. It was definitely that sort of place.

'We sing Happy Birthday because we're all mostly tone deaf,' Alex whispered, running his hand up my back and giving me goose bumps.

Jocasta and Edward started the song off, and Alex and Davey fair walloped it out. I half-heartedly joined in, but Tab remained defiantly silent. She was the first one out of there, calling out as she headed towards the stairs, 'I'm going to do my meditation and then get changed, but I'll be quick, OK?'

Jocasta narrowed her eyes and opened her mouth, then obviously thought better of it and closed it.

122

Edward squeezed her arm, and said, 'Don't worry, darling, let's all have a drink.'

I accepted a glass of champagne and we all gathered in the hall.

'What do you think she meditates about?' Alex said truculently. 'I, for one, couldn't concentrate at all if there were presents to be opened ...'

'Nor me,' Davey said. 'Although having had some presents here, maybe we should all do a spot of meditation.'

There followed a discussion in which everyone competed to see who had received the worst present. Jocasta cited the example of the year she got a pair of slippers from Edward's cousin – 'I mean, *slippers*, I'm not a granny! More's the pity,' flashing a look at her two sons, 'And they were pink, *and* quilted ...'

Davey laughed and told them that he once got a ready-tied bow-tie, in black velvet.

Edward went suitably quiet at this terrible breach of taste. 'My dear boy, how frightful. What idiot gave you that?'

'Arthur and Odessa.'

'Oh, well, that's all right then, jolly kind of them,' Edward said with relief.

Alex was laughing at something his parents had said, and I cast a sneaky longing look at him. God, he was gorgeous. He saw me gazing at him and gave me a self-satisfied wink, which made me blush and quickly look away. I must be out of my mind if I thought that I stood a chance with him, but ... Well, he had made it abundantly clear that he was, at least, *interested*. And that was something to work on, I tipsily reminded myself. Even if he was the playboy of the western world, I just didn't care. So what if he had a girlfriend, she wasn't here, was she? I tussled with myself a bit about those last thoughts, it was probably the champagne talking, giving me confidence. Because I can assure you that, sober, I would care very much indeed about it. Oh, how I wished I'd read more of those magazine articles about how to attract men. I'd always turned to the recipe pages. Now I realised that there might have been something helpful in them after all.

Edward refilled our glasses and I hiccuped gently to myself. But Jocasta heard me and looked delighted.

'Now then, Poppy, I have the most wonderful cure for hiccups . . .'

The rest of the family groaned. 'No, don't, darling. Poppy, don't let her, you'll be here for ages, and then we'll never get to open our pressies,' Davey said.

'Rubbish. Now then, Poppy, I'm going to write something on your forehead and you just concentrate and tell me what it is I'm writing. OK?'

I nodded, hoping she wouldn't write anything too obscure that I'd never heard of. I decided that if she did I'd have to pretend I knew what it was and somehow bluff my way out of it.

Jocasta crouched in front of me and delicately traced the outline of a letter on my forehead.

'Umm, A? Or is it a T?' I said.

'You see? That's why it takes for ever! We could be here *hours*,' Davey wailed.

'Do be quiet, you monstrous child, and let Poppy concentrate,' Jocasta said, continuing her writing.

After much wrong guessing and many cries for help, I eventually spelt out aloud the letters that made up the word 'v-e-n-i-s-o-n-s-a-u-s-a-g-e-s'. I looked questioningly at Jocasta.

'Because that's what Edward and I had for our honeymoon breakfast, didn't we, darling? And do you know, he cooks them every Sunday morning and we feast in bed,' she said, beaming at me.

Edward looked fondly at his wife and I forgot that he'd seemed so abrupt at first. Any man that still has breakfast in bed with his wife every Sunday can't be that scary after all. I caught Alex's eye, and we both smiled.

'Poppy understands that we all have a great love for one another,' Jocasta announced grandly. 'You can tell, look at her brow bone, one can always tell by that!'

I gave a nervous feel to my brow with the back of my hand. Tell *what* by it? I couldn't help but wonder whether they had all mistaken me for someone else.

Chapter Nine

Jocasta insisted that we wait for Tabitha to finish her meditation before we opened any presents, much to the general disagreement of her husband and sons.

'Really, none of you boys are any help at all, and I am quite worried about her,' Jocasta said anxiously. 'She arrived here three days ago, she's hardly eaten anything at all, and she won't say where she's been, or what she's been up to. Anyone with half an eye – although why people say half an eye I simply don't know, as I've never seen anyone with half an eye, have you?' She paused reflectively. 'Although there was that blind piano tuner that we used to have, what was his name? Edward, what was that man's name, darling?'

'Mr Dresser, I believe, funny little man, although I don't think he was blind, Jocasta. He did have a limp, though . . .'

'Don't distract me. I was saying that anyone with half an eye can see she's not well. Poppy, perhaps you could have a chat with her?' Jocasta appealed to me.

I was horrified at the suggestion. I found it hard enough to chat to people I did know, let alone a

126

stranger who seemed distraught. I wanted to help out, but was eminently not qualified for the job of agony aunt to Tabitha.

I began to stammer, 'Oh, no, really, I don't think I'd be any use at all, I—'

'Good. Well, then I think if you want to have a talk with her, maybe this afternoon?' Jocasta said.

I threw a look of entreaty at Davey, who laughed and said, 'Jocasta, stop it. Darling, you're railroading Poppy, you know!'

Jocasta slumped in her chair at the kitchen table. Edward came to stand behind her and rubbed her shoulders.

'Am I? Oh, dear, I am sorry, Poppy. It's just that I am so concerned about her. I thought another young woman to talk to would help, you know.' She put her head in her hands, and gave a sob.

Alex poured us all some wine, and I watched with fascination as he and Davey and Edward all comforted her. I tried to imagine my own mother confessing to worrying about me. My father would have grunted behind the sports section of the paper, and that would have been it. This was a family that spoke its mind and cared for one another. It was quite a revelation to me. I nervously said, 'If you really think I'd be any help, I will *try* to talk to her, but I don't really know what's wrong.'

Jocasta smiled gratefully at me, and Edward gave me a slight wink.

'*Please* let's not spend Christmas Day talking about Tabitha and her endless troubles. Now, Ma, don't look

127

at me like that, darling. Those soulful eyes, pleading silently with me like a bad stage production of *The Miracle*, just won't work. We all grew up with it, remember?' Davey turned to me and added, 'My mother has a great capacity for endless worrying, but you must take it with a pinch of salt, and don't let her sweet-talk you into things, or the next thing you know is that you'll be posing nude with a bunch of flowers in your hand, freezing to death while she paints you!'

Jocasta threw her head back and laughed. 'He's quite right! No, we won't talk about family problems today. Now then, what shall we do about dinner?'

It seemed that Odessa usually cooked for them, but Arthur had demanded that she stay at home this Christmas and help him learn his lines for the panto.

We all looked dubiously at the geese.

'It can't be that hard, can it?' Alex said, poking them with his finger. 'Let's look up a recipe or something.'

We had a lovely couple of hours in the kitchen. Davey kept us entertained by playing the piano, and floods of music echoed down the corridor. We had snatches of Bach, ragtime, Noel Coward, Mozart and jazz. Edward peeled enough potatoes to feed an army, whilst Alex read directions from a cookery book. I washed up three times, noting that all the silverware had worn dragons embossed on the handles, whilst Jocasta kept up a running commentary on Davey's musical ability and the probable outcome of the meal.

'I can't *think* where we got this book from,' she said, brandishing a copy of *Middle European Jewish Cookery*.

'But it sounds delish. Apparently we stuff the geese with a mixture of mashed potato, apple, lemon peel and sage. Oh, and lots of salt. What does *render* the fat mean, exactly? How does one render anything? Edward, I think we need some more wine . . . Alex, why don't you go to the cellar and bring some up? Take Poppy with you, she's never been down there, has she?'

Oh, goody. I get to be in a dark room with Alex, I thought gleefully.

'Davey! Play that wonderful song from the show that I love, the lilac thing, you know . . .'

Alex glanced at me and gave me a smile which made my heart leap. I followed him down the corridor which was flooded with Davey's rendition of 'We'll gather lilacs in the spring again' which changed after a couple of bars to 'Mack the Knife'. We came to the cellar door and he paused, and held his hand out to me. I took it and we started down the steep dark stairs. Even though I was convinced that spider's webs were going to brush my face, probably *with* the spiders still attached, I found I didn't mind. We reached the bottom of the stairs, and Alex swung me round and kissed me.

'God, I've been waiting to do that for ages. Let's go back to the Trans-Siberian, shall we?'

He backed me gently against the dirty stone wall of the cellar, and started to whisper in my ear. I could still hear the faint sound of the piano tinkling out a Christmas song, and feel Alex's hands as they crept up my back.

'I think the Grand Duke will have left us his empty carriage, don't you? Shall we say tonight? About one?'

I nodded, breathless with excitement. I tried to work out how long it was, and then chided myself for such calculated thought.

Alex drew away from me and brushed some dust from my hair. I found myself behaving like a rabbit caught in the headlights, I seemed incapable of movement. We stared at one another until I thought my knees would actually give way.

'Are you all right?' Alex asked me.

I nodded again, seemingly unable to talk. Although I did have a fleeting thought that I'd better say something soon, or Alex would think that I was one of those nodding bulldogs you see in the backs of cars. I cleared my throat, trying to prepare myself to say something. Anything.

Alex was gently kissing my neck and shoulders, sending delicious shudders up and down my back.

'Oh, you do smell nice . . .' he said, in between kisses.

'Do I?' I said, stupefied with longing.

'Mmm, yes. A bit like a sun-kissed bowl of fresh apricots.'

I laughed, and Alex joined in.

'Poppy,' he said, 'I hope I'm not rushing you or anything? I know how overwhelming my family can be, and I don't want you to think that I'm jumping on you just because Claudia isn't here. Thanks be to the Lord,' he added hastily, drawing me closer to him. 'That particular nightmare has ended and—'

Davey's voice boomed down the stairs, 'What *are* you two doing? Come on, Tab's down, let's go and open presents!'

I jumped guiltily away from Alex, and he scrabbled around in the dusty wine racks, handing me bottles to take upstairs.

Davey was standing at the top of the stairs, peering down, and he gave Alex a scowl. Alex laughingly slapped him on the back and sauntered off. Tabitha was drifting around in a grey velvet Gothic number, and even though it was daylight, she still gave the impression of being from the other side. Her long dark hair was pulled away from her face, emphasising her huge, rather haunted eyes and prominent cheek-bones. She gave you an overwhelming feeling of wanting to fatten her up. A few weeks of force-feeding her alongside the poor geese from which the French make *pâté de fois gras* wouldn't have gone amiss.

The hall looked wonderful, and I could see Davey's hand in the huge swags of greenery everywhere. Even the fairground horse had trailing ivy around his neck and twisted up the gilt pole coming from his back, and all the antlers that sprouted from the walls wore haloes of green. Jocasta and Edward had lit all the candles, and the small flames glinted off the strange and fantastic objects in the room. It was very nearly warm, and the apple logs and pine cones on the fire gave off a heavenly smell.

Edward settled himself into a shabby deep leather armchair, and gave a grunt of satisfaction like a weary

131

badger returning to its set. Jocasta sat between her sons on a long plum-coloured chesterfield, diamonds glinting on her hands, a raspberry-coloured shawl draped around her. Tabitha perched on the arm of her father's chair, and as I looked at the group I guessed that these positions for the giving out of presents had been set, as it was, is now, and ever more shall be. I had a sudden stab of envy for them all, and thought treacherously of my own family who ripped open their presents to the background of the TV, and my mother's nervous flutterings in the kitchen. Here was the family I should have had, I thought, feeling slightly sorry for myself. I tried to put it down to drinking copious amounts of white wine in the morning – which I am *not* accustomed to – rather than feelings of jealousy.

I bent down to stroke Jicky through the door of his basket, and wiped a hot little tear of self-pity from my eye. Why hadn't I got an interesting, although admittedly slightly barmy, family? I might have been anything, become *anyone*, if I'd been born to all of *this*. God, what an awful thought, and how unworthy. Maybe we all got the family we deserved, I thought.

'Poppy . . .'

I looked up to find them all staring at me, and I realised that Davey had been saying my name for some time.

'Oh, sorry, I was miles away,' I said, feeling foolish.

Edward looked with concern at me, and said, 'Now then, feeling homesick? Perhaps you would like to call your family? I know I should if I had to be away from this lot at this time of the year. Takes you like that, y'know, Christmas. I remember the year that I had to be in Egypt trying to buy that sarcophagus. Good God, I spent the whole time blubbing on the phone. Awful, awful . . .'

'No, no, I'm fine, honestly,' I said, not feeling able to tell them all that I was not feeling homesick, just slightly jealous.

Davey pulled me down beside him, and squeezed my arm. Jocasta leant across him and said, 'Now, darling, is it your bottom? Because if it is, I can easily arrange a trip to the hospital—'

'No, no, not at all,' I said, feeling the hated blush start.

Alex sniggered and then, of course, they all had to explain to Tabitha the bloody (literally) incident of last night that she'd missed. Davey started to give an impression of me lying on the bed, doing *far* too much squealing to make it realistic, I thought.

'Oh, you poor thing,' Tabitha said, when we'd recovered. 'I think bathing it in witch hazel and tea tree would help, I could go and—'

'No, really, I'm fine,' I insisted, trying to ignore the snorts of laughter coming from the other end of the sofa.

I thought about what Alex had said to me in the cellar, and felt a glow of satisfaction. Although the look that Davey had given him filled me with alarm. Maybe Davey thoroughly disapproved of me as suitable girl-friend material for his brother?

The present giving got under way, and I was relieved to see that the presents were after all not so grand that mine would look out of place. Tabitha handed out her presents to us all and looked on anxiously as we opened them. A tangled mass of crochet spilt on to my lap. Caught up in the rather dirty beige string were bits of shell and feathers. I looked helplessly at it. What the *hell* was it? Some sort of hat? I glanced around and saw that everyone had one and they, too, looked bewildered.

'OK, Tab. I give up. Is it a hairnet?' Davey asked, holding his up and studying it.

'No, no, it's a sort of modern string bag, isn't it, darling?' Jocasta said, struggling to untangle her present from a diamond ring on her finger.

Tabitha smiled at us all, pityingly. 'They're dream catchers. I made them all myself. You hang them over your bed and they catch any nightmare you might be going to have. I put pieces of earth magic in them, so that the vibrations would all emanate to your own energy.'

Davey nudged me hard in the ribs, and I stifled a giggle.

'Jolly useful, darling, and well done,' Edward said loyally, hastily putting his down on the floor.

'We made them on the workshop that I went on this year, they are so vibey, aren't they?' Tabitha said, looking almost animated.

'Vibey?' Jocasta queried. 'Yes, I'm sure they are,' she

added warmly, giving Alex a swift kick to the ankle, I noticed.

'Ouch. Yes, just what I wanted,' Alex said.

My presents were accepted with rather more pleasure, and nobody seemed to notice that they had already been broken into on the train. Davey had to be stopped from scoffing not only his, but the chocolates as well.

Edward gave Jocasta a tiny box that she opened with cries of delight. It was, I was told, an uncut diamond, and traditionally she got one every third year. She gave Edward some second-century leaves of papyrus which he was equally delighted with. I marvelled at the oddity of the gifts. It certainly was a change from watching people open pairs of socks or saucy pants.

Alex excused himself, but promised bags of French goodies as soon as BA came up with his luggage. There was a chorus of unbelieving groans at this, it seemed that this was not the first time.

'Yes, but this time it's true!' Alex protested, fending off mock blows from his mother and brother.

Davey gave me a twisted triple rope of pearls. I stared at them, marvelling at such a wonderful present.

'Oh, Davey, they are fantastic, thank you so much. You really shouldn't—' I began to say, stroking them, before I was interrupted by Jocasta.

'Nonsense, of course he should. Nothing would suit you better, put them on now, and let's see.'

I fastened them around my neck, and held them in my hand. I had no idea if they were real or not, but I guessed that they couldn't possibly be, or they'd be worth a fortune. It didn't matter anyway, I loved them.

Davey stared at the pearls around my neck and said, 'Well, yes. How very lovely you look in them, Poppy.' His voice sounded a little stilted, and we all looked at him in surprise. This wasn't the sort of thing that Davey said at *all*. To break the rather uncomfortable silence I thanked him by kissing him, and Edward said, 'I've always thought women should be given jewellery, nothing prettier in my opinion. Remember that year I gave you an emerald, Jocasta? and you swallowed it by mistake . . .'

Swallowed it by *mistake*? How?

'What happened?' I asked, intrigued.

The whole family burst out laughing.

'Let's just say that for days the old nursery potty was in use and a bulletin board was posted in the kitchen to keep us all informed of the, er, movements!' Davey laughed.

I opened a small box from Jocasta and Edward and found inside a beautiful cup and saucer. It was obviously old, and had riotous poppies and gold swirls leaping over it.

'We thought, well, because of your name, you see. It's Rockingham, we do hope you like it?' Jocasta said, gazing earnestly at me.

I jumped up to kiss her and Edward thank you. 'It's beautiful! I've had the most perfect presents, I can't thank you all enough!' I said, hopping from foot to foot. I was really delighted.

Davey laughed and poured us all another glass of wine, and we sat in front of the fire admiring one another's gifts. Tabitha and I fixed fake nails on our hands from the Christmas stockings, whilst Davey played the piano again, picking out songs that he thought we might all know. Alex and Edward were playing a very acrimonious game of chess by the fire and Jocasta was knitting something with the vivid purple mohair wool that I'd seen earlier.

'I love your ring,' I said to Tabitha. It was a gorgeous silver and gold plait with small diamonds set in it. She'd been given it by her parents, who had beamed with pleasure when she'd slipped it on her finger. It was too big, so she was wearing it on her thumb.

She opened her mouth to say something, but obviously changed her mind.

I glanced at my watch and jumped to my feet. 'Oh, God, the geese! I'm pretty sure that they're done by now,' I said, running towards the kitchen.

'Oh, yes,' Edward agreed. 'Come on, all hands to the pump. Davey, have you laid the table? Alex, you open the wine.'

We crashed around in the kitchen, getting in each other's way, and I watched Tabitha make herself her Christmas dinner. It seemed mainly to consist of various seeds and nuts, with a dollop of yoghurt. I saw Jocasta glance at her, but she was restrained by Edward from saying anything. Edward carved whilst I made a watercress and orange salad, and Jocasta made a redcurrant and red wine sauce.

137

The meal was lovely, and we all made pigs of ourselves, with the exception of Tabitha who picked at her health-food concoction. We all sat round the table, feeling like pythons that had swallowed whole chickens, idly cracking walnuts and drinking port. The whole meal had been a cracking example of the Stanton family at its most stargazy, I rather drunkenly thought. They had laughed and argued, made up and bickered good-naturedly again. Alex had spent a lot of the meal with his hand on my knee, and I suspected that Davey had seen this, but hadn't said anything, although he had favoured Alex with another glare. Tabitha had kept to water throughout, and was looking tired. She stood up to excuse herself, and said that she was going to bed.

'But darling, we haven't had the telling yet!' protested Jocasta, trailing her shawl in a plate of empty walnut shells and orange peel. 'And it's so early, do stay for a while longer.'

I didn't like the sound of the telling, whatever that was. I imagined Jocasta hypnotising us all so that we told our secrets to all and sundry. Well, other than harbouring a passion for Alex I had no secrets, but I didn't want that broadcast. I glanced at Davey, who was happily chattering away to his father. I tried to forecast how he would take the news that I was expecting a clandestine nocturnal visit from Alex. He'd been acting strangely since I'd been at the Abbey. Maybe he would be pleased? Maybe not. It was very hard to tell with Davey. I knew he wanted me to have an adventure, and get out more, but that probably didn't involve having a fling with his brother.

'No, really, Ma, I am *so* tired. I don't think I'll be doing Brown Willie tomorrow, either,' Tabitha said, edging towards the door.

Brown Willie? The telling? It was like living in the movie *Highlander*. They'd be talking about the quickening next. I gave a tipsy giggle to myself.

'Let the girl go to bed if she wants to,' Edward said, pulling Tabitha towards him and planting a kiss on the top of her head. 'Sleep well, sweetie. You look as if you need it. You are all right, aren't you?'

'Yes, I'm fine, Pa. Really, I'm just so tired.' Tabitha was swinging on the doorknob, blowing kisses at the rest of us.

'A good meal would help,' Jocasta said, hating herself for saying it, I could tell.

Tabitha just smiled at her, and drifted away upstairs.

Jicky distracted us by making squawking noises and Jocasta begged me to let him out of his basket. He immediately wrapped himself around my neck, much to the envy of Jocasta.

'Oh, do you think he'd come to me?' she cried.

'He'd come over anything!' Alex said, earning himself schoolboy sniggers from Davey and Edward.

I unwrapped Jicky and handed him over to Jocasta. He immediately started to groom her head, and she gave a little sigh of pleasure, scratching him behind his ears.

I put my elbows on the table, and watched in alarm

139

as one of them slid right off the edge. Oh, God, no more port for me.

'Please tell me, what is the telling? And who is Brown Willie?' I said owlishly, careful not to slur my words.

'Oh, well, the telling is just my parents' way of worming things out of us,' Davey smiled. 'You know, what we've been doing over the past year. I think she secretly expects us all to be on trial for major fraud, or married into the royal family, or—'

'It's nothing of the sort!' Jocasta retorted. 'We just never know what you're all up to, and we hardly see you any more.' She turned to me. 'I'm sure your parents are the same, they must want to know what you are doing?'

Well, no, not really. But I just nodded.

'And Brown Willie, it's a hill, or tor, rather, on the moors,' Alex added. 'We climb it every Boxing Day. Bloody exhausting it is, too.'

'But we Stantons are a hardy breed,' Edward said proudly. 'And every year, we climb the tor. We used to be able to say that we could see only our land from the top, but not any more, I'm afraid. Still, the deer will be visible.'

I hoped I had footwear up to the job. Jessy had shopped with parties in mind, not an enforced yomp through heather and gorse.

Jicky had settled contentedly on Jocasta's shoulder, and she was feeding him grapes. I warned her not to let him scoff the chocolates that I'd made, as they had a disastrous effect on his digestive system. But there was a chorus of 'Spoilsport' and 'It is Christmas!', so I gave up.

'Now then, which of you boys is going to start?' Jocasta said, looking at Alex and Davey from over the top of her glasses, with Jicky's fluffy tail wrapped around her neck.

Davey groaned dramatically. 'Honestly, Ma! I have nothing to tell, the shop's OK, Poppy is a star there and keeps me on the straight and narrow. That's it.'

'Well, what about a, umm, well, a prospective *partner* for you?' She said the word delicately, as though she had wanted to say girlfriend but had thought better of it. She gave Edward an encouraging look, and he jumped and made his obviously rehearsed speech.

'Yes, you know old boy, we're very open-minded. Umm, anyone special on the horizon?'

Davey said with fake pomposity, 'You both know I have friends, rather than relationships, but if there ever is that special someone you shall be the first to meet them.' And then he glanced towards me in a way that made me feel distinctly uncomfortable. What *was* Davey up to?

'I *knew* we shouldn't have sent you to Eton,' Jocasta said absent-mindedly, feeding Jicky titbits from her plate. 'All that fagging, it must have been subconscious, mustn't it? Boys together are so unhealthy . . .'

Snorts of mirth came from Alex and Davey.

'. . . But it never changed you, Alex, did it? Now then, what about you? How's Clara? How's Paris?'

'*Claudia* is fine, Ma.'

My heart shrank a little. But I was cheered no end to discover that Jocasta couldn't remember her name, either.

'So is Paris. The art insurance business can't do without me. I'm flying to Tokyo next month to see if a Renoir is fake or not,' Alex said.

'Are you? Oh, how interesting! You do have such a fascinating job, darling. Did you hear that, Edward? *Tokyo*,' Jocasta exclaimed, gazing proudly at her son.

'And you know, Ma, Claudia, well, she's probably going back to the States soon, so . . .' Alex said, looking at his plate.

Is she? Oh, goody.

'She's a very beautiful girl,' Jocasta said to me. 'She came here the once, didn't she? But she was called away very quickly on some assignment for suntan oil. Very peculiar. But Alex, you're not too heartbroken, are you?'

Beautiful is as beautiful does, I thought, hiccuping slightly.

'No, Ma. I'm not.' Alex then added under his breath, 'I'm most definitely not.'

Chapter Ten

'Dear God, I hope you've stocked up on ship's biscuits and grog,' Davey said rather gloomily, pointing out of the window.

'What on earth are you talking about, Davey?' I asked.

'Look for yourself. Snow,' he said, gesturing outside.

It was true, I looked out of the window. Small white flakes were flurrying around.

'Do you think it'll settle?'

'Well, it's cold enough,' Edward said grumpily.

'Come on, let's go and look,' Jocasta suggested, tipping Jicky into his basket with a handful of nuts to keep him company.

We charged drunkenly down the corridor, pausing briefly to pile on coats and scarves. Jocasta plonked a trilby hat on my head and I wrapped a scarf around Davey's neck. We were all giggling as we fell outside the back door. It was beautiful out, very dark and silent with the snow falling sparsely around us. A small amount had settled on the roof and gables of the Abbey, and the ground had a light dusting on it. Jocasta grabbed Edward and hummed a waltz under her breath as they swirled around.

'Dotty, aren't they?' Alex said, smiling fondly at them.

I agreed. We all stood watching Edward and Jocasta dance around the lawn. Bare skeletons of winter trees stood over us, and I saw an owl glide amongst the flakes of snow. A frosty moon shone low in the sky, and I couldn't remember ever feeling quite so happy. I hugged myself and moved closer to Davey. I reached up and plonked a kiss on his cheek.

'What's that for?' he asked.

'For all my lovely clothes and wonderful pearls, and giving me the best Christmas I think I've ever had,' I said.

'I'm so glad, Poppy. You deserve it. If I may, I'd like to talk to you later, in private.'

I wondered what on earth he had to tell me. Perhaps it was going to be a warning to lay off his brother, and I glanced anxiously up at him. Davey smiled reassuringly back and squeezed my arm.

'Can't you tell me now?' I whispered, feeling that if it was bad news I'd rather have it immediately than wait for it.

Davey shook his head, so I pointed out the owl to them both. We watched it silently swoop down over the lawn and across towards the moors. Some poor little field mouse was going to end up as a snack.

I turned back to look at the Abbey. A golden stream of light was flooding out of the open kitchen door, and I could see some light coming from an upstairs window.

'Is that Tabitha's room?' I asked.

They nodded and I went to stand underneath it. I called up to her that it was snowing, and wouldn't she come down and look at it with us. It was quite forward of me, and I wondered if it was at all feasible to have a glass of port every day if this was the effect it had on me.

She eventually came to the window, but declined to come out and play. Edward and Jocasta started to serenade her with Christmas carols, and we all joined in. Tabitha clapped her thanks and disappeared back inside. We trooped back to the house singing 'We Three Kings', and stamped around in the kitchen, getting our feet warm.

Davey made hot chocolate and tea, and we went into the hall. As I sat down to drink my tea from my beautiful poppy cup and saucer, I remembered Jicky and ran back to the Painted Parlour to collect him.

A scene of devastation hit me as I opened the door. Broken china, spilt wine, ripped napkins, and the total absence of all the chocolates, even the chilli ones. The prime suspect was swinging unrepentantly from the chandelier fitting on the high ceiling.

'Jicky! You little bastard, get down here at once,' I called to him. He chattered his reply and started doing the vile thing whilst continuing to swing on the light fitting. Oh, *God*. Could anything else go wrong? I wearily began to clear up, keeping an eye on the monkey. Two plates and a glass were the only casualty, but he had thrown scraps of food all around the room, as well as fruit peel and nut shells. Tiny handprints of chocolate were trailed all over the biblical murals, adding a touch of Daliesque surrealism to them. I hoped I could clear everything up before anyone came in, and I was scurrying madly around, trying to hide broken bits of china, when the door opened and Davey arrived, demanding to know what I was doing.

'Oh, Davey, I am so sorry, I seem to do nothing but wreck this place. Could you get me some rubbish bags?'

Davey laughed and went to fetch some cleaning stuff. Jicky was full of energy after his sugar-laden meal and swung round the room like a hyperactive – well, like a hyperactive monkey.

When Davey returned we cleared the room up, and I had even managed to wipe off Jicky's handprints from the lower reaches of the wall.

'My God, it looks like a dirty protest at the Maze prison, doesn't it? Well, I suppose if all the inmates were midgets, that is,' Davey said, staring at the last tiny handprint.

Jicky was swinging from chandelier to curtain pole with monotonous regularity now, and nothing I did, including bribery with grapes and pleading, did any good.

'The little bugger's drunk!' Davey exclaimed.

'What?'

'Well, I think he's had all the dregs in the glasses, look at him, he's positively pissed!'

I thought that Davey was right. I could only hope that Jicky would soon fall asleep and I could get hold of him.

Davey and I closed the door firmly behind us and carried all the plates and glasses to the kitchen. It was in an unbelievable state of squalor: the picked-over carcasses of the geese were sitting on one end of the dresser, flanked by dirty bowls, plates and dishes. The floor had onion skins in amongst the other debris, and every surface, already covered in decorative rubbish, was also sprinkled liberally with dirty cutlery and glasses.

'I bet your mother's kitchen isn't like this,' Davey said, looking with distaste at the remains of Tabitha's meal.

'God, no. It's very boring. Boring but clean,' I laughed, rescuing a gravy boat from behind a huge glass dome of wax fruit.

We washed and cleaned and chattered till we'd broken the back of it. I was drying the last of the plates when Davey said, 'Poppy, I think you should know that my brother is – well, let's just say that he's a little free and easy with his affections, shall we?'

'I knew it! I knew that this was what you wanted to talk to me about!' I said, bending down and retrieving a fork, so that he couldn't see my face. But was he warning me off him, or preparing me for when Alex got bored with me? But then, supposing he didn't? Get bored, I mean. Perhaps Davey just didn't want me involved with his family?

'Poppy, are you listening or are you dithering mentally?'

'Oh, dithering, I expect. But yes, I am listening. Go on.'

'Look, I'm not blind. And I do see that he's devilishly

attractive but, well, he's not going to be able to shake Claudia off that easily. If you think you can handle an affair with my brother, and I use the word affair loosely – some less charitable people might say a one-night stand – if you think it might be fun for you, then go ahead . . . I'll be here for you to cry on my shoulder, but don't say I haven't warned you. OK?'

'OK,' I said, abruptly banging some plates down on the table. I felt a bit of a fool. So Davey had seen all the hand-holding that had been going on. At least he didn't know about the train journey, I comforted myself with thinking. A further comfort was that not anybody, maybe especially a brother, really knew another person *that* well.

'Anyway, that is *not* what I wanted to talk to you about. But I think the object of my discussion may well be redundant by now.'

I really wished sometimes that Davey didn't speak like a page from a civil service manual.

'What is it, then? Spit it out, or for ever hold your peace,' I said flippantly.

'Later on, I'll tell you later on. But be careful with Alex, that's all. Things are a bit more complicated than you think . . .'

You can imagine what that little statement did to my overworked imagination. *How* were things complicated? What was it? Money problems? Family problems? Maybe Alex was the local Romeo and had a habit of seducing all of Davey's friends? Oh, God.

'Come on, let's go and put Jicky back in his basket, shall we?' Davey said kindly, sensing my awkwardness.

I nodded, and we went to the Painted Parlour. Jicky was fast asleep in the bowl of fruit, and he made no complaint when I put him in his basket. The door of the room opened and Edward put his head around the door and said, '*There* you both are! We thought we'd play shops. Oh, I say, you've cleared up! Good show. Come along, or Jocasta will have bagged the best shop.'

A circular rosewood table had been drawn up to the fire and cleared of all its tat, apart from an elaborate Venetian glass candelabra. Jocasta and Alex were sitting expectantly, waiting for us. Jocasta had two packs of cards in front of her that she was shuffling.

'Oh, good, we've been waiting for you. Now then, Poppy, as you're the guest, you can choose first. What shop do you want to be?'

What *shop* do I want to be? Oh, God, this was going to be another family thing that I knew nothing about and was going to fail dismally at. I sat down, as far away from Alex as I could, and said, 'I don't know, what is it? I mean, why do I have to be a shop? I should warn you, I am absolutely *hopeless* at cards. I expect you all to get very cross with me, as I seem to have a blank where it comes to adding up, or remembering what people are holding and—'

'No, no. It's absolutely nothing like that at all, I promise. It's snap. But instead of shouting "snap" you have to ask for something from the person's shop, do you see?' Jocasta said earnestly. 'For instance, if I'm a butcher and you're a baker, and we both turn up a three, I'll ask you for some fruit buns and you ask me for some sausages, and whoever says it first gets the cards, OK?'

I nodded doubtfully.

There was then a ten-minute argument as to what shop everyone was going to be. After some wrangling, as it seemed that a haberdasher's was favourite, Edward settled on being a fish shop, Jocasta got the haberdasher's, Davey an antique shop, Alex an off-licence, and I was a florist. Jocasta dealt all the cards out, her diamonds flashing in the fire and candlelight.

'Oh, stop sulking, Edward, I'm far more suited to be a haberdasher than you! I've always wanted a job, you know, in a material shop, I *love* the sound when they cut you a length of satin . . . And do remember, all of you, once someone has asked for something, that's it. You can't ask for it again. Now keep your wits about you. Poppy, don't worry, this game tends to get very loud . . . Right, are we all ready?'

One by one we turned the cards over: a ten, two, ace, jack, five, then another five. Edward sprang to his feet and shouted, 'A walnut Victorian tallboy!' At the same time, Davey pushed back his chair and roared at his father, 'Two pounds of haddock!'

Edward conceded that he'd been a little slow and the cards went to Davey.

A two, three, queen, nine, king, six, nine, jack, then another jack.

'A zip, and some shirt buttons!'

'A bottle of Tio Pepe!'

Jocasta and Alex were shouting at the tops of their voices at one another.

'Sherry, I said sherry! You know I said it first!

'Zip and buttons! Zip *and* buttons!'

Jocasta gave in with many muttered complaints.

An ace, three, three.

Oh, God, it was me. What the hell was Edward? Oh, yes, fish.

'Sardines!'

'Roses!'

The cards were flying round the table now, and there was a long run, where no two cards turned up together. Five, three, ace, king, two, four, then another four.

'A sodding carriage clock!'

'A poxy bottle of cider!' Edward snarled, grabbing the cards.

We were all hysterical with laughter. 'Edward, really! Poxy, *poxy*! Where on earth did that word come from?' Jocasta laughed.

The game continued with the insults and orders becoming louder and louder. The air of the hall was shattered with wild cries of impossible-sounding orders and shrieks of laughter.

'Herrings!'

'A packet of crisps! Cheese and onion, if you have them . . .'

'A bunch of daffs!'

'Sorry, sir, they're out of season, could I interest you in some poinsettias?'

'Yes, all right, damn you!'

I had to remove my shawl, I was getting so hot, and Jocasta's hair was becoming dishevelled. Edward had loosened his collar, giving him more room to shout with, and Davey was in danger of toppling off the back of his chair. Alex had a concentrated scowl on his face and was muttering under his breath the shopping list that he'd composed in his mind for every eventuality. One by one people went out, and soon the only two left in the game were Alex and myself.

Two, seven, queen, three, five, ace, nine, jack, and another jack.

'A bottle of gin!' I screamed.

'Carnations! White ones!' Alex shouted, making a grab for the pile of cards.

I grabbed back and soon we were tussling for the cards.

'Poppy was definitely first with the gin, she's won!' Davey said.

'Absolutely,' said Jocasta, slapping Alex's hands away from the cards. 'Let go, you little beast!'

I sat, panting, at the table, feeling as triumphant at my win as if it had been an Olympic medal. We were all flushed and laughing, and as I caught Alex's eye, I remembered what Davey had said to me in the kitchen. I just didn't care. I was happy and contented, and if it didn't work out with Alex, so what? I'd have one night to look back on. One perfect night.

Chapter Eleven

The one perfect night didn't happen. Instead, Christmas night at the Abbey turned into a particularly gruelling episode of *Animal Hospital*.

Alex had a nightcap with his parents and Davey, whilst I kissed everyone good-night and carried Jicky upstairs.

I let myself into the Chinese room. I had plenty of time for a long soak. Perhaps I should reapply my make-up? Oh God, it was dark anyway, what the hell. I forced the heavy lever in the bathroom for the hot water and poured in a lavish amount of smelly stuff. I ran around the room, hurling clothes into the bottom of the wardrobe, and hiding my shoes under the bed. I even went so far as to light a few candles.

Should I shave my armpits? I ran a finger under my arm, there was a slight bristle, but really, who would know? I was too excited to trust myself with a razor, anyway. I lay in the hot water, thinking of the delights to come. I hoped. Oh, my God. I sat up abruptly in the bath, hot water sloshing over the side of it. Contraception. Oh, *shit*. Why hadn't I thought of this before? I suppose that modern young things carried around condoms as a matter of course. Well, I'd just have to assume that Alex had something. He looked like the sort of man who would, if you know what I mean.

I thanked whoever it was who had built the Abbey that the walls were so thick you couldn't possibly hear what was going on in the next room. I would have *hated* to be overheard – but maybe I was jumping the gun a bit. Perhaps there wouldn't be any sort of moaning or laughing, although I was rather hoping that there would be.

I hopped out of the bath and rubbed moisturising cream all over. I gingerly took the dressing off my wound and gave it a quick once over with some antiseptic cream; that smelt vile, so I dabbed it with some perfume, which stung.

'Ouch,' I said to Jicky, who opened one bleary eye at me. Davey had been right, Jicky looked as if he was suffering from a bit of a hangover. 'Serves you right,' I said to him, turning his basket so that he was looking at the wall. I didn't want him spying on me.

I fluffed up my hair, had a quick squirt of perfume and jumped into bed. It was freezing, so I rubbed my feet together to try and warm the sheets up a bit. How long was Alex going to be? I wasn't sure if I should feign sleep or be nonchalantly reading a book. I decided on the book thing as, quite frankly, sleeping, even *pretending* to, was out of the question.

Delayed gratification has its points, I suppose. But really, anticipation is not my thing. I was practically gnashing my teeth with anxiety when, with great delight, I heard a faint knock on my door and the handle slowly turn.

'Do come in,' I said, in what I hoped was a husky, sexy voice, and I draped myself over the pillows in a sort of come-hither mode.

Tabitha put her head round the door and said, 'Oh, hi. I just wondered if you wanted any of that tea tree cream for your cut?'

Duh! No. No, I don't.

'Umm, no thanks. That's very kind of you, but I'm fine, thanks!' I said brightly, then faked a huge yawn to drive the message home.

'Oh. OK, then. Sleep well. Shall I put your dream catcher up for you? Just in case—'

'Honestly, Tabitha, that's such a kind thought, but I've, umm, I've packed it, ready to take home. Thanks, anyway.'

She backed away reluctantly, and I instantly felt mean, perhaps she just wanted a chat. But really, this was *not* the time for it.

'I'll see you tomorrow,' I called after her.

She put her head around the door again, and said hesitantly, 'Yes, maybe I could take you to my own special place on the moors, if you'd like?'

'Great. See you tomorrow then.'

Wouldn't you just know she'd have her own special place on the moors? Oh, hello sky, hello wind, hello heather.

I settled back down, and saw Jicky cleverly stick his

155

tiny hands out the side of the cat basket and open the door.

'So *that's* how you do it! Little sod . . .' I got out of bed in search of some string or something that I could tie the basket back up with. Jicky sat in the middle of the floor watching my search with puzzled eyes. I had my back turned to him and was scrabbling in my suitcase for some ribbon that I thought would do, when I heard the most awful noise. Then immediately my nose was assaulted by the vilest smell imaginable.

I spun around to see that Jicky was crouched on the floor having a violent attack of monkey diarrhoea. The smell was making me gag, and I backed away from him, horrified.

'Oh, Jicky! No, no . . .'

I ran around the room, throwing open the window and scooping him up to put him on some newspaper. Too late. He got me. I tore my nightdress off and threw it in the bath, then wrapped a towel around me and tried to think of what to do. Oh, God, oh, *God*. I'd gone from a sex siren (well, I thought so, anyway) to a monkey-poo-stained lunatic in the space of two minutes.

Jicky was hopping around the room, depositing evil-smelling pools wherever he stopped. I caught up with him, and holding him at arm's length, put him in the bath. Dear God, the smell was awful! I grabbed a loo roll from the bathroom and was mopping up as best I could, when, yes, *of course*, Alex knocked on the door.

'Please wait a moment,' I called frantically.

156

I won't describe to you what I was holding in my hand at this moment. Let's just say that I really needed rubber gloves and a mask.

'I've been waiting all day, I simply won't wait any longer,' he said, opening the door.

'Stay out!' I hissed, mopping up yet another puddle.

'Christ almighty!' Alex clapped his hands to his nose and looked wild-eyed around the room.

'I know, I know, it's awful!' I wailed. 'It's Jicky, I—'

'Well, I didn't think it was you! Where is he?' Alex said, looking a bit green around the gills.

'I put him in the bathroom, but I wouldn't go in there if I were you. It's not a pretty sight,' I said, clamping my arms to my side to keep my towel round my body.

Alex ignored me and went into the bathroom. He came out pretty soon. 'Poppy, I think he's really ill. What should we do?'

'I don't know!'

We stared at each other, and Alex started to laugh. In the end I joined in as well. It was either that or I'd burst into tears.

We decided that Alex would go and get some cleaning stuff, I'd wash myself and put something warm on, and then we'd try and do what we could for Jicky. I swabbed and washed my hands, and climbed into some clothes. Poor Jicky was shivering in the corner of the bath, making terrible whimpering noises. I threw my nightdress into a plastic bag, ready to throw away. When Alex came back with hot soapy water, scrubbing brushes and, best of all, some rubber gloves, we

157

quickly cleaned the room as best we could. The smell was still terrible and the open window made the air icy, so we scurried around.

Alex and I sat on the edge of the bath, looking at Jicky. He was a pitiful sight, and my heart went out to him. I felt him, and he was very hot.

'Oh, Alex, what shall we do?'

Alex bit his bottom lip. 'Perhaps we could call the sanctuary that you're taking him to? Oh, God, watch out, he's erupting again!'

I rushed to my bag to find the phone number, and after spilling the entire contents of it on to the floor – why did I have such *crap* in my bag? – I feverishly found the scrap of paper and headed out the door. Then stopped. I had no idea where the phone was, and even if I did, would anyone really answer a phone at a monkey sanctuary at this time of night, at Christmas? I doubted it somehow.

There was another knock at my bedroom door and Jocasta put her head around. 'I heard some noise . . . Oh, my God! Jicky, the poor little thing. Alex, you must phone Patrick immediately.'

Alex had a look of truculent mutiny on his face. 'If you think I'm going to phone that man—' he began.

'Don't be silly. He's a wonderful vet. The number is in the study, and hurry up!'

I had my doubts that any vet, wonderful or not, would be willing to come out on a cold Christmas night for a sick monkey, but I did hope so. Alex crashed out of the room and Jocasta and I settled down to wait.

Chapter Twelve

The vet, Patrick, did eventually turn up and was remarkably efficient. Alex sloped off, leaving Jocasta and me and the vet forming a trio of monkey nurse-maids to Jicky.

Patrick gave Jicky an injection and asked me about his history of which I was remarkably ignorant. I explained how I had come by Jicky, and Patrick said, 'Yes, I can see that you are the sort of person who hangs around in swish London clubs!'

How wrong can you be? I thought to myself as Jicky was spectacularly ill again.

Jocasta swept out of the room, telling us she was going to make us all a hot drink, and would be back soon. Patrick grinned at me, and I noticed, now that the initial panic with Jicky had worn off, that he was a very good-looking man. He had curly hair which was rather too long and kind smiling blue eyes. He was wearing what was obviously his pyjamas underneath a pair of jeans and I apologised for getting him out of bed.

'Oh, not a problem,' he replied cheerfully enough. 'Makes a change from sheep and cows, and I was on call anyway. Besides, it's always a pleasure to come to the Abbey. I'm going to the snapper party, of course, but I do like to get up here. It's an interesting place, isn't it?'

I nodded. That was one way of describing it. The more I looked at Patrick and talked to him, the more I simply couldn't understand Alex's reaction when Jocasta had asked him to call him. What was wrong with Patrick? He seemed perfectly agreeable to me.

'He's dehydrated,' Patrick said. 'We must try and get him to drink some water.'

We fussed over Jicky who was pathetically grateful for our attention.

I know that it is wrong to anthropomorphise animals, but honestly, he looked so human it was heartbreaking to see him ill.

'Oh, God, I hope he's going to be OK,' I said anxiously.

'He'll be fine,' Patrick assured me.

I couldn't tell if that was his professional voice or if he really meant it.

We gave Jicky some water, and wrapped him in another towel. He held on to my finger with his tiny black paw and trustingly took all the medicine we gave him. He felt very hot, and his tummy was swollen and tight.

Jocasata came back holding a bottle of brandy and some glasses, this time with Davey and Alex, and we all congregated on my bed.

Jocasta was swathed in scarves and shawls over the

top of a scarlet flannel nightie, she was still dripping with jewellery and her silver hair was in a long plait hanging down her back. Davey was still in his wonderful dressing-gown and Alex had wrapped himself in his long leather coat. Patrick had taken off his woollen coat to reveal a sloppy red sweater. They would have made a fantastic-looking cast to a very strange play.

'Poor little mite, poor little Jicky,' crooned Jocasta.

Jicky flickered his all-too-human eyes at the mention of his name and I could swear that he almost gave me a wink.

'This reminds me of when the children were young,' Jocasta said dreamily.

'What does, darling? Sitting on a bed getting pissed on brandy? No wonder we all grew up to be so very odd,' Davey said.

Patrick sniggered, earning himself a scornful glance from Alex.

'No, don't be tiresome, you dreadful child – no, the nights I spent simply *hovering* over your sick beds, it was awful. You,' she said, turning to Alex who was stretched out fully on the bed, hogging most of the space. He was now totally ignoring Patrick who, luckily, seemed to be unaware of it. 'You were the worst, although you'd never think so by the look of you now. Do you remember when you had scarlet fever? You were *terribly* ill . . .'

'Yes, as a matter of fact, I do. It was bliss, I got sent home from school and we made up names for the twelve months of the year, do *you* remember that?' Alex said, taking a hefty swig from his glass.

Jocasta laughed and then they both chanted together, 'Snowy, Flowy, Blowy, Showery, Flowery, Bowery, Hoppy, Croppy, Droppy, Breezy, Sneezy, Freezy!'

'Oh, it seems like yesterday,' Jocasta sighed. 'You boys were *so* sweet, especially when you both got that wobble in your voice when you were growing up, it was that half-boy half-man voice, it used to make me cry . . . I don't know why, really, it just did . . .'

Davey and Alex exchanged amused glances. I kept very quiet, hoping to hear more childhood stories.

'*Then* there was that time that Davey broke his ankle by falling under a car because he was reading a book in the street,' Jocasta continued. 'And I had to paint over the *very* rude words that Alex scribbled on his cast—'

'Yes, Ma, but *you* painted a very rude picture, if I remember rightly,' added Davey dryly.

'There is absolutely nothing rude about the naked human form,' retorted Jocasta.

'There is when you're twelve,' Davey said.

We all giggled. Apart from the fact that poor Jicky was ill, it was quite jolly. A bit like a dorm party at boarding school, I fondly imagined, having gleaned all my history of those institutions from Enid Blyton.

Jicky gave a cry of distress and emitted yet another foul smell. We all groaned.

'I really think that should be the last of it,' Patrick said.

'Let's hope so, for Chrissake,' Alex said. 'We could all do with some sleep,' he added pointedly.

'I blame you, Poppy,' Davey said sternly. 'If you hadn't made those choccies so delicious we wouldn't be in this trouble now.'

I poked my tongue out at him and reminded him that I had begged them all not to give them to him.

'Now, then, this is silly,' Jocasta said, '*all* of us staying up. You boys are hopeless anyway, so get yourselves to bed. I'll stay here with Poppy and Patrick and we can take it in turns to monkey-sit.'

'No, not at all, I shall stay with Poppy *and* Jicky,' Patrick said, seemingly unaware of the furious looks that Alex was giving him and, to my surprise, that Davey seemed to be doing too. 'I shall pinch a blanket and curl up on the sofa—'

'Daybed,' Alex corrected him coldly.

'Whatever. Off you all go, and don't worry about him. He'll be fine.' Patrick waved them all away.

Alex and Davey left the room, Davey looking relieved that he wasn't being called on to nurse Jicky any longer, and Alex looking distinctly unhappy. Jocasta was crooning a lullaby to Jicky, and rocking him in her arms. It seemed she was enjoying having a surrogate baby in her clutches again, and I didn't think that she was going to be dissuaded from her Florence Nightingale devotions.

Patrick managed to persuade her that all would be well, and she left, trailing hairpins behind her after

163

making us promise that we would call her if she was needed.

Patrick swaddled Jicky up in another towel and held him, whilst I clambered into bed. I'd lost all trace of embarrassment with Patrick by now, and it seemed the most normal thing in the world to share a room with him for the night. I wondered if I should offer to take turns on the daybed, or whether I should offer him the proper bed?

Patrick soon absolved me of any decision and with a practical neatness made up a bed for himself.

'Don't worry, quite used to it. Usually in a barn somewhere or other. I shall wait for a couple of hours to make sure that he's over the worst of it and then creep out and go home.' He snapped out the lights and the room was plunged in darkness.

I felt amazed at my own acceptance of this situation. Perhaps being around the Stantons had changed me. I no longer even felt remotely nervous of being alone with Patrick, though to be honest, if he had been a creepy sort of man I would have felt very differently.

'How do you know the family?' Patrick asked me.

I explained about being friends with and working for Davey and how he had often invited me down.

'I'd always refused up till now. They all sounded far too intimidating to cope with . . .'

There was silence for a moment.

'But you don't feel like that now?' Patrick asked, his voice seeming very distant in the cold dark room.

164

'Well . . .' I wasn't too sure how I really felt collectively about them. I was still rather in awe of Edward, and Tabitha was not the cosiest person in the world, but Jocasta was lovely, and knowing Davey as well as I did made our friendship no problem. As for Alex – well. I tried to formulate an answer for Patrick when I heard the gentle sound of snoring coming from his direction. I stifled a giggle and tried to get some sleep myself.

I managed to sleep surprisingly well, and was relieved to find that Jicky seemed to be well in the morning. The only sign left of Patrick was a neatly folded blanket on the daybed. I peeked out of the bathroom window and saw that the small patches of snow were still on the ground, and the sky was a pale, sullen grey. It looked, and was, freezing. I piled on as many clothes as I could and headed downstairs.

Davey was in the kitchen, pottering around making toast. That in itself seemed to be a bit of palaver. It involved putting slices of bread in a sort of large wire contraption, and opening one of the lids on the range, then keeping an eagle eye on it, before flipping the whole thing over to toast the other side.

He was spreading butter and honey on a vast plateful of brown toast, and piling it on to a tray that had a squat brown teapot on it.

'Come on, let's take it up to my room, at least it's warm in there. I'm glad to see you're well wrapped up, did Jessy buy that sweater?'

I nodded, it was a particular favourite of mine. It was quite tight, and very long in a textured, knobbly linen

165

and wool mix, and a fantastic colour. A sort of mishmash of squashed prune and blueberry.

I helped Davey carry the breakfast tray upstairs, and we were soon in his room, which was glowing with warmth (thanks to a portable heater). The room itself was very like Davey, a replica of a gentleman's club in St James', *circa* 1930. I sat in a dark green leather buttoned chair and munched some toast, looking around me.

Books seemed to make up the bulk of the decor, and they had flowed over the shelves and made themselves into piles on the floor. I looked down and read the first title that I could see, *How to Grow Flowers by Candlelight in Hotel Bedrooms*.

How very, very useful.

Then I saw a magazine that made me choke on my toast. What the hell was Davey doing with a copy of *Playboy*? I stared at it, to make sure that I had read the title correctly. A pneumatic raven-haired beauty dressed in a scanty pixie outfit was spread unbecomingly over the knees of a bogus Santa Claus on the front cover. I glanced over at Davey, but he was looking out of the window.

'Christ, it looks cold out there. We're going to *freeze* climbing Brown Willie, have you got any suitable footwear? And I warn you now, there's no point in lying and saying no, because you won't get out of it. My mother will probably fashion you some out of sheepskin or something,' he said, sipping his tea. His eye

166

caught sight of the *Playboy* magazine, and he blushed and put his foot over it, sliding it under his bed.

'I can explain—' he said, when there was a knock on his door and it was thrown open by Edward, wearing a tweed suit and carrying a flask.

'Good morning all!' he boomed at us. 'Now, how's that poor little monkey? Better? Good, now Alex is ready, I've woken Jocasta and Tabitha, so we'll all be set to go in about half an hour. Right?'

Davey and I nodded with a poor imitation of enthusiasm.

It seemed that Edward was one of those hearty morning people, and I guessed that much as Davey loved his father he would have been a great deal happier pootling around at home than going striding over the moors.

Alex was the next person in Davey's room, looking hungover, and clutching an enormous mug of coffee.

'I hope you all slept better than I did,' he growled. Then, shooting me a dark look, 'Did bloody Patrick try to jump on you or anything?'

'God, no, of course not,' I said indignantly.

Alex sneered slightly at this and turned away.

Oh, God, what was it between the vet and Alex? Something must have happened, or was Alex always this moody? I did hope not. My heart sank slightly and I forced a smile on my face.

'Well, I think the walk up Brown Willie is going to be the equivalent of a cold shower, so we'd all better get ready to freeze,' Davey said.

Alex groaned. 'I know, I know, and Pa is already stomping around the hall filling his flask with apricot brandy. It's going to be hell ... How's Jicky, by the way? If he was still ill, we could stay behind and monkey-sit him,' he added hopefully. I could see that he was trying to placate me, and I glanced gratefully at him.

'Wipe that unworthy thought from your mind, we're going on the moors, and what's more, we're going to bloody well enjoy it,' Davey said despairingly.

I went to my bedroom to pile on even more jumpers and to make sure that Jicky was OK, and secure in his basket. I was determined to find out why Davey had got a soft-porn magazine in his room, it was just *so* unlikely. But a lot of things had been unlikely with Davey recently. All those strange looks he'd been giving me, and his devoted attention. I still hadn't recovered properly from the pearls he had given me. It was very odd. Perhaps he always behaved this way at home?

I wandered down the corridor, and heard Jocasta call me from her bedroom. On putting my head round the door I was confronted by a glorious, royal disregard for order. An easel was set up in the centre of the room, a table with a roll of silk ready to have patterns painted on it stood in front of a window, and the bed was covered in half-completed chalk and charcoal sketches. Hats and necklaces were dripping in profusion from all the light fittings, and a huge portrait of the family took up nearly a whole wall. A log fire burned in the grate, and Jocasta was still in her scarlet nightdress.

'I am glad that Jicky's so much better!' she called from her bathroom, over the sound of running water. 'I think that we can happily leave him while we go up Brown Willie, but we can come back and check on him, if you like, before we go into Padstow.'

I'd heard from Davey that after the terrible moor climb, they all traditionally went into Padstow to stare at the harbour, get rather plastered in the pubs and watch the locals do something odd singing dreadful songs with shoe polish on their faces. Really, nothing was surprising with this lot.

I stared at the portrait on the wall, in which Jocasta was sitting in a low chair with two babies on her lap. Edward stood behind her, a hand on her shoulder. Davey, aged four or five, stood next to his father, looking up at him, and a very young Alex was standing, leaning against the chair that his mother was sitting on.

I looked again at the picture, why two babies? Who was the other one?

Jocasta came from the bathroom, and saw me staring at the picture. She sighed.

'Yes, I can tell what you are wondering. Tabitha had a twin, Pandora – she died when they were ten months old. Poor thing, I do wonder you know, if—'

Edward put his head around the door and shouted, 'My God, Jocasta, we're all waiting for you, you know! Even Tab's up, she's going to come after all, she wants to show Poppy something . . . I've got the flask, and some slabs of cake, so do hurry, woman!'

I scuttled out of Edward's way and went to wait in the

hall with the others. So, Tabitha was a twin? What was Jocasta about to say to me, I wondered. Something to do with Tab being lonely, and missing her dead twin? Maybe. We heard Jocasta calling from the library a few moments later, and we all went to see her. She was holding a variety of coats, jackets, capes and scarves, all made from what seemed like nineteenth-century sacking. I opted for a fetching little number in dark green, trimmed with velveteen ribbon. It made me look like something from Robin Hood, possibly Friar Tuck, but then everyone looked pretty dreadful in them, so I didn't mind too much. Tabitha had her own version of outdoor gear, which consisted of ethnic stripy jumpers and coats. We piled out of the back door, and were instantly hit in the face by a bitingly cold wind. My eyes started to stream with the cold immediately, and I heard Davey positively whimper.

I could see as we progressed up the garden that the Abbey was placed in a fold in the moors. A secluded garden, peppered with trees, rhododendrons and velvet-like grass that had had generations of monks tending it, had kept the moors from invading it, but all we had to do was step over a low wall and we were on the moor proper.

Heather, gorse and dead bracken, with outbreaks of granite slabs spotted with lichen, and dotted with sparse patches of snow, stretched as far as the eye could see. The sky was pressing low to the horizon, looking ominously like more snow, and the wind was howling. We all walked as quickly as we could, clothes flapping in the wind, with Jocasta belting out a hymn at the top of her voice. I kept my hands clamped over my ears to stop them singing in the cold, till Alex tied a woollen scarf over my head, securing my beret. I *dreaded* to think what I looked like.

Tabitha materialised beside me and said, 'I love it out here! Don't you? I'm glad I wasn't too tired to come out. I makes me feel so free . . .'

I wiped my streaming eyes (and nose) and didn't have the heart to tell her that she could be free as a bird any time she liked if only I didn't have to walk in this icy wind a moment longer.

She pulled my arm and pointed to a dip in the moor that had a small pool in it. 'There! Isn't it wonderful? A magical place really, I do my meditations there, the earth energy is so strong . . .'

Meditating in this weather was unthinkable, so I nodded and smiled brightly but continued yomping up the hill.

Alex was pushing Jocasta from behind, and Davey was pulling her from the front. I looked on enviously. I could have done with some help myself. I was panting like crazy, and my legs were killing me. Standing in a shop all day was obviously not the equivalent of a thrice-weekly workout at a gym. I wondered, for the hundredth time, if I should take up some form of exercise. Something not too taxing that would give you the body of a supermodel and that you could do in a warm room, obviously.

I was scrambling up a large slab of stone when I felt a

pair of hands creep round my shoulders. I turned to face Alex, who kissed me on the mouth, and then quickly pulled away from me as Edward and Tabitha came into view. He laughed and pulled me up the rock behind him.

'If it wasn't so bloody cold . . .' he said meaningfully. 'Still, I could always bring a few sheepskins out here, it would be very like the Russian steppes, don't you think? We could pretend we'd sneaked off the Trans-Siberian.'

'I think you're barking mad. We could get frostbite!' I laughed.

'Are you sure bloody Patrick didn't try anything?' he demanded.

'No, of course not!' I said indignantly, wondering why Alex seemed to be so obsessed by Patrick.

'Hmm, well, you tell me if he does . . . Sorry, by the way, about Patrick, it's old history between us. I think he's a bit of a prat . . .'

I looked at him, puzzled, but he didn't say any more. Until now Alex had been much cooler with me today than at any time before, and I'd been hoping that the innocent night I'd spent with Patrick hadn't changed anything. But the way he was looking at me now made my spirits soar. Perhaps I could summon up some courage and sneak into his room tonight?

After half an hour we were near the top of the tor. We stopped and had a swig of apricot brandy and Edward handed round the slices of the cake that I'd made. We all fell on it and gobbled it down.

172

'Delish, darling, you are clever,' Jocasta said admiringly to me.

'Look, that's Bodmin beacon . . . and over there is the Iron Age settlement,' Edward said, pointing out the landmarks for me.

'I've never understood why anyone would want to settle here, Iron Age or not. I mean, no shops, no bars, no restaurants,' Davey said, wiping crumbs from his chin.

The Abbey looked like a toy doll's house from up here, with threads of smoke coming from its numerous chimneys. The farmhouse beyond it looked tiny. Moving white cotton-wool blobs revealed themselves as sheep; even with all that shaggy wool on their backs, they must be frozen. It was desolate at the top of the tor, and although the view was awe-inspiring it was so cold that we scuttled down, back to the comparative warmth of the Abbey, as quickly as we could.

I had enough time to check on Jicky and slap on some lipstick, and then I was bundled into a really old, I mean vintage old, car that Edward drove us to Padstow in. It was a bit like riding with Toad, I felt like shouting out 'Poop, poop' whenever we turned a corner. The countryside whizzed by in a blur, we sped down a steep hill and soon we were parking in a harbour car park.

Padstow was beautiful, a horseshoe-shaped, pocket-sized harbour, with bobbing fishing boats in the port. All the boats were decorated with Christmas lights, and it looked very jolly till you saw the large illuminated cross and all the names of the fishermen that had been lost at sea. Very posh restaurants were side by side with pubs and chip shops. Pirate-like seagulls swooped down on anything that looked like food, even taking chips from the unwary hand. A small brass band was playing in the icy air by the customs house, and a lot of people, dressed very strangely with boot polish smeared on their faces, were singing.

'Right,' said Alex. 'The Shipwrights Arms first, then the London Inn, then the Golden Lion, then the—'

'First things first, old boy,' Edward said, looking conspiringly at Davey. 'We'll meet you there, just got to pop in to see Sonya . . .'

Edward and Davey practically ran off and disappeared into the village, while the rest of us walked around the harbour to the pub at the far end.

'Who's Sonya?' I asked.

'Edward's second wife,' joked Jocasta. 'She's lovely, she runs an antique shop here, Jacob and his Fiery Angel. I think she stays open today because of Edward. He'll come back with something or other, he always does.'

We stopped at every pub in Padstow, and were joined by Edward and Davey in the last one. They were carrying a small cardboard box, and they looked very pleased with themselves.

'Sonya sends her love, and is looking forward to the snapper party,' Davey said, edging his way through the crowded bar.

'Yes,' boomed Edward, struggling to make himself

174

heard over the raucous noise of the black-faced singers as they burst through the pub. 'She wants to know if she can bring anything? I said no, but I wouldn't mind having a look at that picture of a woman with the parrot on her wrist in situ. Now, who's for a drink?'

The pub had a huge log fire and we were all crowded around it. Our small table was full of glasses that seemed to be continually topped up by people wishing Jocasta and Edward a Happy Christmas. I gathered that these two were not, as you might first have assumed, considered to be too grand or posh for this place, but were a well-accepted part of the community. Although there were a few raised eyebrows at the dress sense of Jocasta and Tabitha, the whole family seemed to be held in affection and respect.

The singers were kissing all and sundry now, making sure that we all got smeared with the boot polish, causing great gusts of laughter. The accents here were so strong that I had great trouble comprehending what people were saying, although when I did catch some of the lyrics of the songs, I was quite glad *not* to understand everything. A plate of hot pasties appeared, and was demolished by the hungry crowd in the pub.

A very old man, who sat in the corner nursing a pint, was encouraged to sing. As he struggled to his feet, silence was called for. His thin reedy voice, cracking with age, sang a timeless Cornish sea song. We all joined in with the chorus. I sniffed away a sentimental tear, and had to keep pinching myself to see if my happiness was real. Feeling such a part of this crazy family was a special feeling, and one that I wanted to savour.

Chapter Thirteen

I sat on Alex's lap on the way home, in a happy, slightly tipsy haze. Even Tabitha, who'd only drunk apple juice, seemed jolly, and she was squashed up against Davey, who complained that her hip-bones were cutting into him. Jocasta was in the front of the car next to Edward, who took the bends in the road as a personal challenge to his driving ability.

As we went past the farmhouse, we saw Tom walking out of the door, muffled in jacket, scarf and wellington boots. Edward stopped the car to talk to him.

'Happy Christmas, Tom, all set for tomorrow?'

'Course, Mr Stanton. I'm just off to get 'em sheep down to the lower field. Don't like the look of the sky. Him going to snow again, I reckon.'

We all peered anxiously upwards although, to be honest, I didn't really look *that* anxiously, I mean, what was a bit of snow here or there?

'Need any help, Tom? And how's Demelza?' Jocasta asked, leaning out of the car window, and dropping a scarf.

Tom handed it back to her with a smile. 'No, we'm be

all right. Melza's looking right forward to the party, she wants to know if you need anything?'

Jocasta said no, and we continued upwards to the Abbey. As we struggled out of the car, Edward stood outside the front door, and sniffed the air.

'Do you know, darling, I don't really believe that you *can* smell snow,' Jocasta said, laughing.

'Of *course* I can . . .' Edward said indignantly, sniffing in every direction.

'What does it smell of?' I asked, intrigued.

'Oh, this and that, trees, bit of grass, iron, you know . . .' Edward said with authority.

Tabitha said that she would ask the runes, if he liked, and he thanked her absent-mindedly.

'The last time we had a heavy snow, we lost so many sheep,' Davey said, opening the front door. 'That's why we worry. That, and we ran out of brandy. It was awful!'

A small, perfectly round woman wearing a flowery crossover apron, the likes of which I had only ever seen on characters portraying cleaners in soap operas, was welcoming us in, wiping her floury hands.

'Mind you all wipe 'em feet,' she cautioned. 'I made some soup, an' that be hot, 'tis waiting for you in the kitchen. I'm making bread, and I ordered from the store. Arthur sent you a salmon. You can have that for your dinner. He'm be going to snow, and we don't want to be caught out, do we? Not with your party coming up, like.'

Alex and Davey made a beeline for her and lifted her off her feet in a double bear-hug, much to her delight.

'Odessa! As gorgeous as ever!'

'Happy Christmas, my lovely. Have you been teaching Arthur his lines?'

She was as pleased as punch with all the attention, and her face glowed.

'Wher'm your manners?' she demanded. 'Put me down, you great big loafers, I 'aven't seen your sister yet. And who's this young lady?'

I was introduced, and we shook hands. She gave me an astute looking-over with sharp blue eyes, and then graced me with a big smile. She turned to Tabitha, and took her in her arms.

'Well, my lovely, you look right nesh, and that's a fact. I'm right glad you'm back here, you need some proper food, I reckon.'

Tabitha smiled at her and assured her that she was all right. We drifted into the kitchen and had some of Odessa's wonderful soup. It was delicious, and had a good pint of cream in it, I thought. I smeared butter on some warm bread, and thought that I'd soon be letting out buttons on all my clothes if I carried on like this. Tabitha had a mouthful, and then pushed her plate away, turning rather green. I saw Jocasta look worried, and bite her lip. Davey and Alex were too busy arguing with Edward over some esoteric point about taxidermy not being art, to notice. I was just convincing myself that I could really manage another hunk of bread when Odessa handed me some. I looked up in surprise and thanked her. She answered me with a wink.

'Tabitha, have you had some of this bread?' I asked.

'It really is good, I wish I could bake, do *you* know how to?'

'No, I mean, I used to, but I can't eat wheat now . . . or dairy,' she said, smiling wanly at me.

'Why's that? Are you allergic or something?' Nearly everyone was on some sort of faddy diet. I knew people in London who'd paid a fortune to have their *hair* analysed, for God's sake. The results turned out to be that they were all allergic to beetroot, tonic water, radishes and chocolate. They all claimed it to have worked wonders for them, but I have to say, I wasn't convinced.

'No, no. It's just that when I was at the sacred sister workshop –'

The *what*? Oh well . . .

'– and I did the testing for my earth energy, I discovered that I could only eat green and goat.'

'What?'

'Oh, you know, green food – vegetables, obviously – and goat products. Not goat *meat*, naturally. Oh, and nuts and seeds of course.'

Of *course*. Silly me.

'Well, it doesn't sound great, don't you miss other food? I mean, do you think you're getting enough vitamins and things?' I tried to sound knowledgeable, but my nutritional advice was not sound. I know we are all meant to eat five portions of fruit and vegetables a day. I had once tallied my daily intake and just scraped by if you count potatoes in the shape of crisps, and the raisins in a bar of Fruit and Nut.

''Tis nothing wrong with a bit o' chocolate now and again, like,' Odessa muttered in the background.

What? Was she reading my thoughts?

'Oh, yes, I mean the ultimate goal, of course, is to live on air,' Tabitha continued.

Air? Air!

I remembered a woman in the news a couple of years ago who'd taken a tent and a copy of a terrible book that had sold millions, and had gone to try out the air diet. She'd died.

I gazed in horror at Tabitha. Oh, God, was she really that mad? I'd seen a TV programme about people who fasted for weeks at a time, to try and work up to the point where they could live on air in some American crank spiritual place. They were keeling over like flies by the end of a couple of days. I'd watched the programme whilst eating a huge plate of spag bol. With cheese. *And* garlic bread.

I glanced around the table, seeking help. All the others were involved in a noisy discussion that had evolved somehow on to the merits of Gilbert and Sullivan. I tried to think of what to say to her, that either wouldn't put her off talking to me, or make her even more firm in her ideas.

'You know, Tabitha, that it can be very dangerous, fasting and things?'

She smiled at me. 'Everyone says that. But you don't really know much about it, do you?'

No, I didn't. But it doesn't take a doctor of science to tell you that if you don't eat you will eventually die.

I sighed, and shook my head.

Jicky was making squeaking noises, and was begging to be let out of his basket. I bent down to retrieve him and he chattered his pleasure at me, whilst curling round my neck. I reminded myself that he was going to the sanctuary tomorrow, and stroked his head. I was really going to miss him.

'He'm won't be leaving you, you know.'

Odessa was standing behind me, and I turned to face her.

'What did you say?' I asked.

'Same as my cat, Shadow. Some is born that way. He is, with you. Get him by accident, did you?'

If you call a monkey falling on you from the ceiling in a club, an accident, then yes. I nodded. I stared at Odessa. She had a cat called Shadow, and she was insinuating that Jicky was some sort of familiar. Oh, God, what the hell was she, a witch or something?

She laughed at me, showing a mouthful of gold fillings. 'Don't you be daft, my 'andsome,' she said, moving around the other side of the table. She put a mouth-watering apple pie down, with a jug of cream next to it. She deftly sliced the pie up, and pouring cream over a small portion, she put it in front of Tabitha.

'I put a right good spell on that one,' she said, winking at us all, 'so you make sure you'm try it. All that workshop nonsense, you'm might learn something from me. What do all them women from London know? Nothing. I ask you, London!'

Tabitha smiled and dutifully had a small mouthful. When I tasted mine, I had to restrain myself from licking the bowl and begging for more. Maybe Odessa really had put a spell on it?

Odessa was buttoning herself into a voluminous black and tan coat, and clamping a red felt hat on her head.

'Right. I'm be off now. Don't forget, the salmon's cooked, all you got to do is some potatoes and a salad. I'll be seeing you all tomorrow for the party.'

'Odessa, do let me drive you home, it won't take me five minutes and it's very cold out,' Edward said, rising from his chair.

'No, thanks, Mr S. I never do, as well you know. I go through the field and up the lane, besides I want to look in on Melza, on me way. She'm near her time again.'

My God, was she the midwife as well? I could see the comfort in that, much more safety in the presence of Odessa than all the sterile nurses in a hospital, offering futile pain relief.

Odessa waved us all goodbye, and was gone. I glanced round and saw that Tabitha had eaten all her apple pie. Jocasta caught my eye and we smiled together. That clinched it, as far as I was concerned. I had just met my first witch!

Davey made hot drinks and I cleared the kitchen, balancing Jicky on my shoulder. We all settled round the table with various cups of tea, coffee and, in Tabitha's case, hot water. The conversation turned to the snapper party, being held tomorrow night.

'What was the word last year, darling?' Jocasta asked Edward, scooping up the crumbs of the apple pie with her finger.

'Flesh-eating. And remarkably difficult it was too,' Edward said.

I thought I'd keep quiet and concentrate, maybe that way I would understand the rules to this damn snapper party. I was hoping that I'd pick it up, then I wouldn't have to ask plaintive questions about it, as I usually did.

'What about espalier?' Davey mused.

'What the hell is that?' Alex asked.

'Oh, you know, it's when you train trees to grow flat against a wall . . .'

'Don't be daft, no one's going to know that.'

'Crystals!' Tabitha called out.

There was a groan of dissent.

I felt as if I was going mad, I'd *have* to ask. It made no sense at all to me.

'Please, someone tell me, what *is* the snapper party, and why are you all choosing words?' I appealed to them.

There was a very jumbled explanation given to me by them all. After listening to everyone, I gathered that the object of the party was to choose a word, fairly obscure, but not so obscure that nobody actually said it. And then when talking to people you could try to sneakily edge the conversation around to a related subject, hoping that one of the guests would say the word. When one of them *did*, you shouted 'Snapdragon!' at the top of your voice, and the whole of the Stanton clan came to snap, a mixture of kissing and slapping, I discovered, and claim the person as the snapper of the evening. Prizes were involved, and also some sort of arcane wearing of heraldic buttons, but by then, I'd completely lost the thread.

We all sat around, trying to think of a word.

'What words have you had in the past?' I asked.

Everyone looked to Davey who, it seemed, they believed had the best memory. He was also, apparently, the keeper of the book. He produced a large leather-covered notebook and started to read out the words.

'Flesh-eating, as we've said. Teasel, Anvil, Sweetmeat,' Davey said, frowning in concentration.

'Well, I do remember one year getting the bishop to say Gusset,' Jocasta interrupted proudly.

Everybody sniggered.

'Carbuncle, Gregorian, oh, yes, and do you remember Doxographer?' Davey said, snapping the book shut.

'What the hell is that?' I asked.

'It's a cove who writes down a list of philosophers' opinions,' Edward said. 'That year was hell, we were all still up at five in the morning, and in the end I think a bit of cheating went on, because Odessa won, of all people!'

I thought of my own parents, who if they ever *had* a party, prepared by buying a couple of bottles of sherry and splurging out on a packet of cheese biscuits. The

185

conversation would be strictly limited to the weather and subtle boastings of new cars and foreign holidays. I tried to imagine my parents here at the Abbey, joining in with the snapdragon party. I giggled to myself, the image it conjured up was impossible.

Jicky jumped off my shoulder and began to exercise by running up and down the shelves of the dresser. The Stantons were squabbling over the chosen word. Voices were raised, and even Tabitha was getting hot under the collar.

'Jeroboam!'

'Balthazar!'

'Crescendo!'

'Gondolier!'

'Don't be so damned silly, you might as well go for Matador!'

'Oh, don't be so cruel, how anybody can torture those poor bulls the way those bloody Spaniards do—'

'Do shut up, Tab. We're not saying the bullfighting is a good idea, it's just a word, you know.'

'I know. But I still don't like it, those poor bulls are—'

'Minotaur!'

'Who, in the name of *arse*, is going to get that?'

Jicky was squeaking and jumping around the shelves. I tried to coax him down with a grape, worried in case he broke anything. He jumped back on to my shoulder and I stroked his head. He made little chattering noises, and started to groom me. I had sort of got used to it, but I dreaded the day he actually *found* anything.

'Got it!' Davey shouted, pointing at Jicky. 'Simian. What do you all think? You know, monkey-like.'

'We do know what it means, darling,' Jocasta said, rather put out, I guessed, because she hadn't thought of it herself.

'Perfect,' Edward said.

'What happens if no one gets it?' I asked.

Everybody stared at me.

'What do you mean?' Alex said.

'Well, you know, supposing nobody actually says Simian. What happens then?' I said, gazing at them all.

They all stared glassily at me.

Edward cleared his throat. 'No one, in the entire history of the snapdragon party, and I assure you of this, *no one* has ever *not* said the chosen word. The party will continue. For *days* if necessary until the word is said. The doors will be locked, and the guests counted. No one will be allowed to leave.'

We started giggling helplessly.

'The very idea,' continued Edward, warming to his theme, thumping the table. 'The very idea of not guessing the word. Incredible! *Impossible*. And what's more, it has not, and will not happen! There, I have spoken!'

'Oh, Edward, you would have made a wonderful politician, all that tub-thumping you could have done!' Jocasta said admiringly.

We went to the hall and gathered around the fire. Jocasta picked up her knitting and instructed Davey to show me the family photographs. He dragged out a huge book from a drawer of a carved chest. Photographs and, to my surprise, X-rays, spilt out of it. Alex pounced on an X-ray, and said, 'This is mine, my ribs, I think. God, that hurt.'

Jocasta looked fondly at him, and said to me, 'I find bones rather beautiful, don't you? Clothed in the right flesh, I mean.' I nodded helplessly. As if I'd given it some serious thought in the past, and found that I agreed with her. 'I have kept *all* the children's X-rays. And do you know, I think my children, collectively, have broken nearly every bone in their bodies. But then, they did do such *very* dangerous things. They regularly had the roof race, they could all have been killed!' She fumbled with her knitting, pulling at the purple wool. 'But I do see that the Abbey roof is a *perfect* place to play if you are a child. It's positively perilous. I begged them not to, but every summer, at midnight, they would hold the silly race. Edward and I used to hear them scrabbling and scrambling amongst the chimneys. Nothing we could do, of course. Still . . .'

'The roof race,' Alex said, his eyes sparkling. '*God*, that was fun, wasn't it? I used to be so scared!'

'Not as scared as our cousin Adam, he wet himself,' Davey remembered, grinning.

'I used to think that if I won it, I'd be able to fly right off the edge and land on the moor,' Tabitha said wistfully.

I bet it was tough growing up with Alex and Davey, I thought. Neither of them would ever have let you win the roof race.

'Did you, darling? Oh, how sweet,' Edward said fondly, looking at his daughter. 'But still, your mother is right, you know. It really is very dangerous, and I don't think you should have done it.'

There was an explosion of protests.

'But Pa, *you* were the one who told us all about it! You did it when *you* were a boy!'

'Nevertheless,' Edward continued calmly, 'I forbid you all to do it again.'

I thought of the Abbey roof and shuddered. It was immensely high, and had steeply angled ledges and gullies all over it. Not to mention crumbling dragon gargoyles. I could see that it would have been fun, but I would never have been brave enough to try it. I looked at Tabitha with admiration. She was obviously not the wimp I'd thought.

Jocasta went to have a bath and change before dinner, and Alex and Davey started to play a duet on the piano, with much wrestling for the keys. Edward sloped off to his study, and soon the strains of Billie Holiday were competing with the piano.

Tabitha asked me if I'd like my runes read, and I declined as politely as possible. I'd rather planned to have a quiet word with Davey. I wanted to worm out of him the past history between the vet and Alex, and also I was desperate to know what he was doing with a copy of *Playboy* hiding in his room. I was sure that if I could spend some time with him I could get it out of him. But Tabitha's face fell, so I said hastily that yes, of course I would really, as long as it wasn't too much trouble for her.

'No, no, I'd love to. Let's go to my room, though. It's so much more sympathetic,' she said, glancing at Davey and Alex who were trying to push each other off the piano stool.

I followed her upstairs, cuddling Jicky for warmth. It was dark outside, and away from the fire in the hall, the Abbey was very cold. Although I felt quite comfortable downstairs, as soon as I climbed to the first floor, I always felt slightly ill at ease. Maybe it was because the place was so damn huge. I was used to a two-bed-roomed house in Suffolk, or my own tiny flat in London. All this space just for one family.

Her room was at the far end of the corridor and was painted a blinding white. Crystals dangled from every window, and diagrams of astral chakras were pinned on the wall, along with posters for the sacred *sistah* workshop, showing a group of women smiling ecstatically at the camera. 'Celebrating Sistahs' unique womb-an-ness' the headline on the poster shouted. I cringed, and turned my back on it.

I saw a copy of the air-diet book by the side of Tabitha's bed, and glanced through it while she found the runes. The book seemed to imply that we could all live on air if we were spiritual enough, and if you couldn't – well, you didn't really deserve to live, did you? I slid the book under a pile of pamphlets from

Sistah Baluuu on the importance of earth balancing, and hoped that Tabitha would think she'd lost it.

She made me sit on the floor, and ceremoniously shook out a crumpled bit of rather grubby white velvet. She spread this in front of me and handed me a small pouch that I was instructed to shake while formulating a question in my mind. Then I was to throw the runes on to the square of velvet.

Oh, well, I thought, shaking like mad. I'll give it a go. Perhaps I could ask about my future, if any, with Alex.

I chucked the small wooden cubes on to the velvet. The various squiggles painted on them stared up at me.

Tabitha caught her breath, clasping one hand to her head and one to her heart.

Oh, no. She's going to go into that shaman-like thing, and pretend that it's really stunning news.

'Oh, look, that's great, really good alignment,' she said encouragingly. 'A big change in your life, umm, that's good. Oh, yes, I like that . . . How odd, a pair of something features very strongly indeed. A pair of something that gets separated, but comes together in the end . . .'

Shoes? I thought, that's the only thing I've got a pair of.

'Oh, Poppy, this is excellent, really great. Yes, I know I'm right. A simply massive change, all for the good, is going to happen to you very soon indeed.'

Whoopee, I thought, now losing my cynicism at good news. Maybe Alex and I *do* get married . . . or at the very least have a wonderful affair.

'Yes, really good. I think it's a complete new direction for you, very different from what you have been doing. *Very* different indeed.'

Well, let's be honest. Anything would be very different from what I had been doing, which mainly consisted of going to work, chatting with Davey and then going home.

'Oh, but what's this? Umm, I don't know about this. It looks like someone is going to stop you. I don't like this at all, you must be very careful indeed. There will be a person who doesn't want you to be happy.'

Here we go. The danger bit, it happens all the time. Even if you have a laugh on the end of the pier with a palmist there's always a danger bit. It probably makes them think that you're getting your money's worth.

'I am sorry, Poppy. It all looked so great, and then this had to come along. You must take care. You will, won't you?' Tabitha looked at me with worried eyes.

I laughed. 'Of course I will! But don't be worried, I don't really believe in it, you see, so—'

'Take care, anyway. OK?' She stared at the runes again. 'Now this is interesting, there's something here for all of us, I think. It's connected with the sky, or clouds, or something high, like a mountain or something. I wonder what that could be?'

She looked so thin and puzzled, hunched over the runes, that I impulsively hugged her and told her not to be daft. I decided to go and have a bath, and said that I would meet her downstairs in half an hour. Tabitha gave me a pamphlet from the *sistahs*, that I said I would read (I did have my fingers crossed when I said it) and I hurtled through the cold corridor to my room and tried to choose what to wear tonight.

I thought about the runes, and as much as I wanted to believe in them, I just couldn't. I only ever read the horoscope page as a bit of light relief from all the terrible news. I was pretty sure there were forces out there that we all knew nothing about, but I didn't think they were to be found in Tabitha's room, interpreted by an underweight stand-in for Kate Bush. Still . . . you never knew. Now, what to wear? Nothing that would leave strap marks on my body, I decided, astounding myself. Tonight, after all, was *the* night that I was going to be creeping around the Abbey in search of Alex – if I was brave enough.

Chapter Fourteen

I thought it might be time to try on some of Jessy's rather peculiar Japanese clothes for dinner. I struggled with a few garments. One of them I wasn't quite sure what it was, the sleeves seemed to be legs, if you know what I mean. But when I looked in the mirror, she was right. They did look awful on the hanger, but great on the body. I added Davey's pearls and admired the effect.

With my new hairstyle, which I was still thinking of as the new hairstyle, and would do for ages, I looked, well, I honestly thought I looked great. Sophisticated, grown up even. Ha, how appearances can deceive. I drifted around the room slapping perfume on. I was in a whirlwind of excitement; the more I saw of Alex, the more I liked him. OK, OK, fancied him rotten, but I did like him as well. He was such fun to be around, with his unflagging enthusiasm for life, and his ability to laugh at everything. And then he'd shown me an understanding of myself that I'd never had before. So yes, I *really* did like him. Now that, in my rather limited experience, I admit, was unusual. But then, I liked the whole family.

Davey was even nicer amongst them than he was in London, and I was even getting fond of the loopy Tab. I checked myself in the mirror again, delighted to see that I looked as good as I felt, and allowed myself a bit of a preen before I went down to the hall.

As I passed through the library, I peeked over the railings and saw Edward in the hall, with a bottle in his hands. It was strange looking down on people, it gave you a different perspective on them. From here, I could see that Edward had a thinning spot in his fair hair, and that his shoulders were bowed. You would never see that if you were facing him. He gave every impression of a well-groomed, upright and healthy man. But from here, you could see his age. It made him look vulnerable, and I felt compelled to hurry down the stairs to join him. A day or so ago, I might have hesitated about being with Edward by myself, but something had touched me, and I rushed downstairs so that he wouldn't be alone.

'Poppy, m'dear! You look very lovely, and just in time to help me open the champagne. Davey is far too busy doing something or other in the Painted Parlour, he and Jocasta are the arty ones in this family, you know. They always make everywhere look wonderful, don't you think?' he said gruffly.

I agreed warmly with him, and went to fetch some glasses. I managed to find enough space on the crowded table to put them down, and Edward moved around the huge hall, drawing the vivid emerald green curtains. He stopped at one window, and peered outside. 'It's going to snow again. I'll eat my hat if it doesn't, you see. I hope it stays off till after tomorrow, though. Very difficult for the snapper party if we're snowed up.'

He poured two glasses of champagne and handed me one. 'Lovely to have you here,' he toasted.

I thanked him and asked how many people were coming to the party tomorrow.

'Well, it's usually about a hundred and fifty, give or take.'

A hundred and fifty! My God, this was going to be one hell of a party.

'Yes,' Edward continued, his eyes sparkling with pleasure, 'it's counted as one of the best gatherings in the county. We have the clergy, although the bishop isn't exactly a party man – though his archdeacon, well, that's another matter all together – and the fishermen, now they really do know how to enjoy themselves. The artists over from St Ives, all my farmers, of course, neighbours, relatives, friends. Oh, yes, I really think you'll enjoy it. We were worried that it might have been a bit too quiet and boring here for you . . .'

Yeah, right.

'God, Edward, not at all! It's been perfect, the party sounds wonderful. I just hope I can get someone to say the word Simian,' I said, sipping my drink.

'That's the spirit! I remember one snapper party that went on for a couple of days, people sleeping all over the place, great fun. It was the year that Tabitha and Pan—, that Tabitha was born. Jocasta looked so wonderful, people were standing on chairs to get a good look at her, just like Lily Langtry! Proudest man in Cornwall, I was. Still am, of course. But those days, oh, what fun. I wish you'd seen her then, she was a stunner . . .'

'I think she still is,' I said stoutly, earning myself a top-up from Edward. I meant it, too – stylish, eccentric, striking and quite, quite mad, Jocasta was a woman that people still looked at, no matter what age she was. Having seen the portrait in the bedroom, what wasn't quite so obvious now, was that she had indeed been stunningly beautiful. But eyes lose the lustre, hair the gleam and skin the bloom. How very unfair. Especially, I would think, for a beautiful woman.

We were still chatting about the party when Alex came running down the stairs.

'There you are, Poppy, I've been looking for you,' he said meaningfully.

'Have you? I've been here talking to Edward about the snapper party, trying to get a strategy together to win it,' I said sweetly.

Alex laughed. 'Well, I warn you now, there will be some stiff competition—'

'What's all this talk about stiff? I do hope you're not corrupting my friend Poppy?' Davey said, walking into the hall, holding out his hand for a glass of champagne.

'Typical, I can tell you boys are home!' Jocasta called out from the library, making a regal entrance down the staircase. 'Why you persist in awful bottom jokes is beyond me! Now, Davey dear, do come and do me up at

197

the back, I simply cannot reach it, all those tiny little buttons! Ridiculous. Made, I suppose, when we all had maids, or madly jealous lovers that ripped the clothes off your back and to hell with the consequences . . .'

She turned her back to Davey and he obligingly did up the small buttons on the back of her dress. It was a violet silk, full-skirted, long, fluid, yet figure-hugging number. She was right, it certainly had been made in the days of ladies' maids. The dress shrieked of some long-ago grand couture house. Balenciaga? Worth? One of those, anyway. She looked gorgeous in it. She had a huge jet choker and enormous swagged necklaces of jet covering her bosom, and she looked as if she'd stepped straight out from the pages of *Vogue*, anywhere from the year 1950 to 2050. Incredible. She even had a wonderful jet tiara in her abundant silver hair. I eyed it enviously.

Edward handed her a drink, and silently applauded her with his eyes.

'Jocasta, you look fantastic,' I said. 'What fabulous jet!'

'Thank you, Poppy. I was going to save it all for tomorrow, but I like to wear something I can leap around in more easily at big parties, so what better than a family Boxing Day dinner, I thought. Now, where is Tabitha? I want to give out the buttons.'

She held a small silver box in her hand. Davey and Alex called upstairs to their sister, who trailed downwards dressed in the obligatory grey. I had a sudden stab of pity for Tab, it can't have been easy growing up with Jocasta as a mother. She looked fabulous, had done everything, and was so overpowering that it must have been hard for Tab to carve out her own corner. But I noticed that Tab gave a small special smile to her father, before anyone else. Maybe she and Edward were close.

Jocasta opened the silver box and handed out small brass buttons, each of which had a worn carved dragon on it. The little badges were surprisingly heavy, and had a sturdy pin on the back.

'Ooh, the snapper badges!' Davey said, immediately pinning his on to his lapel.

Alex fastened mine on to my shoulder, allowing me ample time to gaze at him close up.

'Now, then, all the family, and I count you as an honorary member, Poppy,' Jocasta said to me, pleasing me greatly, 'must wear these tomorrow, otherwise it's not fair on all the poor guests.'

'They're lovely, where do they come from?' I asked, twisting mine upside down so that I could read it properly. Latin script of the family crest twisted around the edges, and a small sleeping dragon curled in the middle.

'They were all from Edward's grandfather's wedding waistcoat, I had them made into pins when we first had a snapper party. Edward wore the waistcoat itself at our wedding, didn't you, darling?' Jocasta said.

I glanced enviously at Edward and Jocasta. What must it be like to be so in love with one another after all these years of marriage? I simply couldn't imagine it.

Was I ever going to find my own place in a family? I did hope so.

Alex came to stand next to me and squeezed my arm. 'Are you thinking about love and family?' he asked in a teasing tone.

I nodded and he laughed.

'I thought so. It must be difficult, sometimes, but you can willingly borrow our family, you know, any time you like.'

I thanked him. But it wasn't the same. I so desperately wanted to belong somewhere, I hadn't realised just how much till I had been amongst the Stantons.

I glanced around and saw that the rest of the family were all chatting to one another. I moved closer to Alex and said, 'You know, I think I *would* like to borrow all of you, if I may . . .'

Alex smiled at me and said, 'Feeling a little lonely?' He spoke without a shadow of innuendo and seemed genuinely concerned.

I found myself telling him how much I longed to belong somewhere, to feel connected to a group of people that I could call my own.

Alex gazed down at me, his eyes full of understanding and sympathy.

Edward ushered us into the Painted Parlour and I saw that Davey had been very busy indeed. The room was studded with tiny night-lights, and a magnificent cold salmon had been decorated with cucumber scales. A tiny silver salt cellar was in front of everyone's place, as well as home-made crackers and an impressive array of mismatched glasses.

Jocasta said proudly, 'I even made mayonnaise!'

Alex and Davey laughed, and Edward smiled proudly at her. I guessed that Jocasta didn't find her way into the kitchen very often. Tabitha had some salad, and even one tiny potato, but steadfastly refused any wine. The amount of candles in the room made it acceptably warm, and cast a soft glowing light on us all. Alex had made sure that he was sitting next to me, and I felt his hand brush against my leg now and then, which was very nice, but disconcerting as it made me jump.

Edward was explaining to me how the salmon, courtesy of Arthur, had been caught. 'Honestly, really stinky cheese on a bamboo rod. He swears by it . . .'

We all stopped in our tracks as the sound of a car hooting outside could be clearly heard. A minute later there was a pounding on the front door of the hall.

'Quick! Down on the floor!' hissed Edward.

Huh?

'Stop it darling, it might be Tom, or Demelza, or—' Jocasta said, reasonably.

'Don't be so bloody silly,' Edward said, quite rudely for him. 'They'd come round the back as they always do. No, I bet it's some damn fool turning up on the wrong night for the party. Or the bloody bishop asking for a donation. No, I will not have it!'

I looked around and saw that Davey and Alex were stifling laughter.

'Edward hates unannounced visitors,' Alex whispered to me. 'We usually have to pretend we're out.'

Tabitha was soothing her father who was bristling at the idea of an interrupted dinner.

This family was getting odder and odder, I decided. One minute Edward was telling me how much he loved inviting a couple of hundred people for a party, the next minute he was crouching on the floor, hiding from a knock on the door.

The car hooted again, and the banging continued. Edward eyed us all furiously. 'Well, one of you must answer and say we are not at home,' he insisted.

'Darling, we can't,' protested Jocasta. 'Besides, it's perfectly obvious we are! It might well be your cousin Carlotta, she said she might come for the party, and she could well turn up a day early.'

The banging was a regular thumping noise now.

'Oh, bugger bugger bugger,' Edward said, glaring at us all. He suddenly looked at me, and his eyes lit up. 'Poppy, you go! Say that we've all gone out and tell whoever it is, cousin or not, that they'll just have to bugger off and come back at the proper time.'

I glanced doubtfully around the table, but was met with encouragement by them all. Only because none of them wanted to go, I thought. I unwillingly pushed back my chair. They were all, even Tabitha, convulsed with laughter. All apart from Edward, of course.

'I can't really tell them to bugger off, can I?' I asked nervously.

'No,' whispered Alex, wiping away tears of laughter.

'Just say you're the new cook, and that we've all gone to bingo or something!'

As I moved to the door, I said to them, 'I think you're all an absolute shower!' making them laugh again, as I prepared to cross the hall and struggle with the huge bolts and chains on the front door.

Whoever it was who was knocking heard me drag the bolts back, and stopped, waiting expectantly for the door to open. I glanced behind me and saw that all the Stantons, with the exception of Edward, were hiding behind bits of furniture in the hall.

'I can see you!' I whispered frantically to Davey who was crouched behind the piano. He moved marginally backwards, stuffing part of the fringed shawl that covered the piano in his mouth to stop himself giggling.

I finally dragged the door open, letting in a blast of icy air. The most beautiful blonde, long-haired, long-legged woman was standing there, surrounded by luggage, wearing a dark squashy fur coat and hat.

'Hi!' she said, flashing a smile and showing blindingly white teeth. 'I thought nobody was home!' she drawled in a parody, almost, of an American accent.

I gaped at her. I couldn't possibly imagine telling her that she had to come back tomorrow, or to bugger off.

'If you could grab my bags, I'll just pay off this sweet man who's driven me all the way here from some itsy-bitsy airport.' She peeled off what looked like a small fortune from a pigskin wallet and handed it to a bemused-looking taxi driver.

'Now then, where are the old folks? Oh, gee, you

don't know who I am, I must be forgetting my manners!' She laughed again, and held out her hand to me. 'I'm Claudia, Alex's fiancée, and you are –?'

Oh, fuck.

Oh, fuck.

And I am? Who? I went blank for a moment. Oh, yes, I'm the woman who your boyfriend picked up on a train, who's had her bare bottom inspected by him for a bit of broken glass, who's held hands with him under the table, snogged him in the cellar and has even moisturised her elbows for him in readiness for the big night of passion which was meant to be tonight. The woman who has confessed that she feels apart and lonely and wishes she had a family just like his.

I fought the urge to push her back in the taxi and beg the driver on bended knee to take her back to whence she had come.

'I'm Poppy, um, a friend of, well, I work for Davey,' I said, hating her already. I glanced around and saw that Alex had stepped out from behind the harp. I was glad to see that he did not look pleasantly surprised.

'Honey!' Claudia cried, dropping her bag on my foot in her rush to get to him, 'I've tried you on your mobile? Then the number here is just impossible, so here I am!'

'Yes, here you are,' he said evenly.

Davey and Jocasta were gradually stepping out from their hiding places, looking a bit shamefaced.

'Clara, how lovely to see you,' Jocasta said, stepping forward to welcome her. 'How are you? This is a surprise, I must say. Naughty Alex didn't tell us you were coming, I rather thought that you'd gone back to Ameri—'

'Yes, well. Hello, Claudia, and Happy Christmas to you,' Davey said, giving his mother a warning glance, which I was happy to see Jocasta completely ignored.

Claudia kissed Davey, who flinched slightly, probably from her power grip, I thought, looking at her toned and lithe body. She crushed her jaw against Jocasta and looked around the hall. Tabitha was sitting on top of the fairground horse, and Claudia waved at her and said, 'Hi there, Tabby, you're looking so well. Nice to see you again. And where is Mr S?'

I found myself unable to meet anybody's eye as we all drifted back into the Painted Parlour, where Edward was tucking into his dinner. His innate good manners triumphed over his inclinations, however, and he stood up to shake hands with her.

We all sat down again, and Davey poured Claudia a glass of wine.

'Oh, no thanks, really, I have to be sooo careful, you know. My skin reacts real bad to alcohol. Do you have any Volvic?' Claudia said, flashing her gnashers at us all.

'Any what?' Edward said, looking alarmed.

'Volvic, water,' Claudia said, smiling for Texas.

'Good God, no,' Edward said, tipping back his glass of wine and swallowing it rapidly, as if in fear that the need for water might be contagious.

I sat gaping like an idiot at her. I have to say, she was astonishingly beautiful. She had gorgeous, peachy,

205

lightly tanned skin and a mane of blonde hair. Her very pale blue eyes were set almond wise into her face, echoing her fantastic cheek-bones. Her jaw was razor sharp, and I tried to look for tell-tale signs of the surgeon's knife. What did I know? This creature was probably born like this. I glanced at Davey, who gave me a quick look of implicit sympathy, and was faintly cheered. Alex, the swine, wasn't looking at anyone, but was fiddling with his cutlery. Tabitha was pushing a bit of salad around her plate, giving her father anxious glances. Jocasta was royally unaware, or so I thought, of any tensions around the table, and continued to call her Clara, much to my joy.

'So, Clara, how are you, my dear? How was that suntan-oil promotion that you had to do last time you were here?' Jocasta asked, smiling brightly at her.

Claudia threw her head back and gave a melodious tinkle of a laugh. 'Oh, you guys! I always forget your great British sense of humour! You *musta* seen me, I was the face and body for Labella suntan last year. It was a great contract, it got me the front cover of *Vogue*, now, you musta seen that!'

Her voice had the very annoying habit of rising at the end of every sentence. It made each statement into a question. I could also foresee that it would be catching. Soon, if we weren't all careful, we'd sound like the cast of an Australian soap opera.

'My dear girl, if you weren't in the *Cornish Guardian*, *Antiques Weekly* or *Garden News*, we certainly wouldn't have seen you,' Jocasta said firmly, adding afterwards, 'but don't worry, we won't tell anyone. It must be shameful for you to be splashed all over the place. Face and body, you say? I can't think why, I certainly wouldn't want to paint you ... Models are far too thin nowadays to be interesting, although I have always thought that must be an oxymoron, don't you? You know, models and interesting, I mean, it's a bit like sports personality, they simply don't have one. Anyway, the human skeleton must be clothed in some sumptuous flesh to be remotely fascinating, don't you think, Alex?'

This was a side of Jocasta I had never imagined. She was looking triumphantly sly, with a gleam of determination in her eyes. I didn't know why she had taken against Claudia, but I was immensely glad she had. If I hadn't been so winded by Claudia's arrival, I would have enjoyed, in a vicarious way, Jocasta's rather snide comments. I looked around at Davey, who was watching his mother with the sort of fascination a needle phobic has being given an injection. You don't want to watch, you know you shouldn't watch, but somehow you are incapable of not watching. Claudia seemed impervious to anything that Jocasta said, and was smiling at Alex, whilst toying with a tiny portion of salad.

'Oh, gee, no, no thanks, no fish for me. I've had my protein allowance for today. Is there oil in this salad dressing? Oh, right, I thought so. Maybe someone could wash it for me?'

Wash a salad? No protein? Oh, God, maybe she too

was on the air diet. Tabitha jumped to her feet and volunteered to go and rinse the one lettuce leaf that Claudia had on her plate.

Claudia smiled her thanks, and turned to Alex. 'You know, I had such trouble getting hold of you, honey. What happened to your cell phone?'

I sniggered rudely to myself, remembering Alex hurling it from the train window.

'And then I rang and rang here, and just decided to come right on over anyway!' she drawled at Alex, looking at him from under her eyebrows. A look I recognised as the one that I had practised as being sexy. No wonder Alex had asked me if I was going to be sick.

'We never answer the phone if we can help it,' Edward said, glowering at her. 'It's usually just damn fool people asking damn silly questions. Answered it once and a chap asked me if I had considered double glazing! Bloody fool.'

Tabitha came back to the room with Claudia's washed leaf, and reverently placed it in front of her. I looked at my own plate and saw that in my nervousness I had consumed everything on it. I reached out for some more bread, slathered it with butter and started to nibble at it.

'You know,' Claudia began, looking at me, 'dairy is real bad for you.'

'Oh, it is, isn't it?' Tabitha said enthusiastically.

'Nonsense,' Jocasta said, putting a huge dollop of mayonnaise on Claudia's plate, making sure that it trailed over the washed salad. 'Absolute stuff and nonsense. I and my entire family have always had butter, absolutely nothing wrong with any of us! Now, let's all have some brandy, for God's sake, and stop this boring conversation.'

The evening went downhill from there. We sat around the table, listening to Claudia bang on about the importance of drinking a litre of water a day, till Davey and Jocasta dragged us all into the hall for a rousing game of shops. Claudia had to be a health-food shop, of course, which meant that she won because nobody, apart from Tabitha, could with any certainty name anything that was on sale in one.

I spent the whole game avoiding looking at Alex or Claudia. I was very glad when Jocasta called for an early night, so that we could all be ready for the party tomorrow. Jocasta made a great fuss of Jicky, as it was his last night here, giving him grapes from her plate, but no chocolate, I was relieved to see. Davey was angelic, guessing, I thought, how I was feeling, and spent a lot of time chattering to me. But I was out of kilter and couldn't concentrate. As soon as Jocasta said good-night to everyone, I did the same and followed her up the stairs, clutching Jicky to me for comfort.

Jocasta kissed me good-night at the top of the stairs, and I clung to her for a moment. I had just opened my bedroom door, when I heard my name being softly called. I turned round and saw Alex leaning against the wall.

'Poppy, I didn't know she was coming here, really I

didn't. Look, let me deal with her tonight, OK? I'll talk to you tomorrow. I'm so sorry.'

I looked blankly at him.

Me too. I thought. Very sorry indeed.

Chapter Fifteen

My eyes were still piggy and red-rimmed in the morning, and I spent ages splashing cold water on them. I felt empty and sad, but had to keep reminding myself how much worse I would have felt if Claudia of the shining gnashers had turned up today, instead. Or would I? At least I would have had a great night of passion; as it was now, I felt cheated. I told myself that I was behaving like a spoilt brat, as though someone had taken my toys away. Stop it, I said to myself firmly, just stop it.

I looked at Jicky in his basket, and started to cry again. This was the morning that Davey and I were taking him to the monkey sanctuary. As much as his revolting habits grated, I was really going to miss him. I was still sniffing when Davey came bounding into the room.

'Well, last night was beastly, wasn't it?' he said, taking note of my blotchy face and runny nose. 'Still, I must say, I'd forgotten what Ma is like when she doesn't like someone. Positively dangerous! Now, come on, Claudia's ghastly, so don't worry. I'm sure Alex can give her the slip for a night, if that's what you're fretting about.'

Men. Honestly.

I felt too tired and miserable to point out to Davey that yes, Claudia might well be ghastly, but she was *gorgeous*, and I didn't want Alex to give her the slip for a night, for God's sake. And how could he possibly think that I would even contemplate a night with Alex with his girlfriend next door? I wanted much more than that now, I realised. A fling might have been on my mind when I first met him, but now I was thinking of a time-scale that went into *decades*, and involved anniversary presents.

I listlessly picked up Jicky's basket and headed out the bedroom door, praying that I wasn't going to bump into Claudia, who'd probably look exhausted but happy from the reunion sex that she'd had with Alex. Or so I imagined. If I'm honest, I'd done nothing *but* imagine that all night long. I'd tortured myself with visions of them together, doing exotic things and laughing together about the poor besotted woman (me) a few doors down the corridor.

We walked downstairs and had tea in the kitchen. I'd had a quick glimpse outside, and it looked freezing. I hoped Jicky was going to be warm enough in his new home. But then, I thought, if he'd withstood the intense cold of the Abbey, he'd be OK anywhere. They probably had special monkey central heating or some-thing.

'Where is everyone?' I asked.

'Still in bed, I suppose. Come on, let's get this over with,' Davey said in a brisk no-nonsense voice. The sort of voice parents use to their children when visiting a dentist.

We finished our tea and went out. I wanted to get Jicky settled as soon as possible. We set off in Davey's very low, fast car, bumping down the steep driveway. We waved at Tom, who was getting out of his Land Rover, and nipped along the country lanes. The surrounding countryside looked bleak and bare, and I shivered. Perhaps it was just my mood, maybe the countryside was magnificent, but I just couldn't see it. I gave a dramatic sniff, and resolved not to be so gloomy.

'Don't distract the driver's attention,' Davey cautioned. 'It can be very dangerous, and I assure you, another sniff of that dimension and we'll have an accident. Now, cheer up, do. Jicky's going to a lovely new home, and will find a pretty monkey wife and stop having to play with himself all day long. Jocasta will probably have killed Claudia by the time we get back, and then there's the snapper party tonight to look forward to. Lots of lovely times ahead, darling. OK?'

'OK.'

We sang along to a tape of (naturally) Judy Garland doing her 'Over the Rainbow', very, very badly, and that did in fact cheer me no end. By the time we got to the sanctuary I felt much better.

Davey pulled up, and we stared at the huge red-brick building.

'My God, it looks like a very minor public school,'

said Davey. 'I do hope he won't get ragged by the other boys and have his head put down the bog. Still, knowing his luck, he'll probably get a very good-looking fag who fetches his grapes for him. Amongst other things.'

'He'd probably like that,' I said, taking in the huge grounds, sections of which were covered in wire netting. Presumably to stop the monkeys from escaping. Or humans getting in. Though it did make it look like a prison.

'I do hope you've got his games kit, and sewn his name tags on in the right place. Other children can be so cruel, you know.'

'Shut up, Davey, I'm feeling quite nervous,' I said, walking to the front door and ringing the bell.

We were met by a man with a beard, who took charge of us. He gave us a bit of a pep talk about the monkeys that lived there, and how he would gradually introduce Jicky to them. He asked me questions about Jicky that I was incapable of answering. How old was he? What was his history? And so on.

'Look, honestly, I was having dinner one night, and he simply fell on my head. I offered to bring him here, that's all. I really don't know anything about him at all,' I said.

Beardie lifted the basket on to a table and peered at Jicky. He then asked me to take him out, which I did, and immediately Jicky curled himself in to my neck. The man gave Jicky a quick once-over, and started to shake his head.

'What's the matter?' I asked.

'Well, I'm afraid he's just too old for us. You see his teeth? You can always tell by them ... He'd be too difficult to readjust into a normal social group. I'm sorry.'

'What am I going to do with him, then?' I asked.

Beardie smiled, rather patronisingly, I thought, and shrugged his shoulders. I looked at Davey, who shrugged as well. Maybe Odessa was right, it looked as though Jicky was staying with me after all.

'How old is he then?' I said, stroking Jicky absent-mindedly, wondering what I was going to do with him and whether Davey would mind if I took him into the shop every day.

'Difficult to say, but he's probably about eight or nine.'

'And how long do they live for?' Davey asked.

'Ten, maybe eleven.'

'Oh. I see.'

Davey and I walked back to the car with Jicky in his basket. A few snowflakes started to fall as we drove away from the sanctuary.

'How are you feeling?' Davey asked. 'Do you mind being saddled with a small, elderly, masturbating monkey?'

I wasn't sure. I had been crying earlier at the thought of him going, but now the practicalities of actually having him all the time began to dawn on me. It seemed terribly unfair that he had been rejected, it was like turning up to a retirement home and being told you

215

couldn't come in because you were past it. The cost of grapes alone was going to bankrupt me. Perhaps I could wean him on to something cheap, like carrots?

'Poppy?'

'Oh, sorry, I was just thinking about carrots.'

'Of course you were, and why not? A very underrated vegetable, I've always thought. Puréed with sherry, butter and parsley they are absolutely delicious.' We laughed, and headed back to the Abbey. As the car was bowling along the country lanes I thought it was time to tackle Davey on the subject of *Playboy*. He blushed and laughed and stammered and I knew that he was not going to give me a satisfactory answer. I let the matter drop – for now.

The sky was a pearl grey and the snow had stopped by the time we got back. We found Odessa in the kitchen, sleeves rolled up above her elbows, rolling out huge quantities of pastry.

'Mornin', you two. Where you'm been then?' she asked, elbows moving like pistons across the heavily floured table.

I explained about the sanctuary, and she snorted with laughter. She didn't actually say 'I told you so', but it was heavily implied.

'Odessa, where is everyone?' Davey asked.

'Mr and Mrs Stanton are having their breakfast in bed, Tabitha is out walkin' the moors, Alex is helpin' Tom with some sheep, and that *woman*, that American, is fiddlin' about with the lavs!' Odessa said in tones of great indignation.

'Doing what?' Davey asked, laughing.

We were still laughing when Claudia came into the kitchen. She looked rather tight-lipped and was clutching a bottle of bleach. She was wearing a very thin cashmere twin set and a knee-length floaty chiffon skirt, and I knew that she must be as cold as the rest of us because her nipples were sticking out under her jumper.

'Hi, you guys,' she flashed at us. You almost needed sunglasses to combat the shine of her teeth in daylight. 'Have fun? I've been cleaning, this place is like, *real* dirty, we could all come down with something if we're not careful.' She turned to Odessa and said, 'OK, I've done the johns, where do you keep the furniture spray?'

'We'm don't,' Odessa said firmly, fixing her with a basilisk stare. 'All the furniture here is polished every three months with beeswax and that's that. If you want to do somethin' useful, why don't you unpack the glasses for the snapper party in the hall?'

Claudia knew when she was beaten and headed back for the hall armed with a tea towel and a pair of rubber gloves. Odessa thumped the pastry with great violence and glared at her retreating back.

Davey and I glanced at one another, and I timidly asked Odessa what I could do to help.

She beamed at me and soon I was enfolded in an apron, chopping up vast quantities of potatoes, carrots and onions for the pasties she was making.

'Load of rubbish,' Odessa grumbled. 'The lavs here

217

are perfectly clean. Where does she think she is, some sort of hospital? Come down with something! Cheeky hussy. I could give 'er something proper nasty to come down with if I chose to.'

I stifled a giggle and wondered if I could bribe Odessa to vex Claudia with something. Nothing too awful, you understand, but something lightly disfiguring. Like warts. On her face. Or turn her teeth yellow. You know, something mild like that.

Odessa glanced sharply at me, and said, 'Don't you tempt me, missy!'

I gasped at her.

'Don't you be daft. 'Twas perfectly obvious what you was thinkin'! Soft on Alex, are you? Well, you'm not the first and I doubt you'll be the last – though I don't know about that. What will be will be, and that's the truth. Now then, you finish that veg and we'll have a nice cup of tea and a mince pie.'

I nodded meekly, and carried on chopping. I didn't care what she said, I knew a witch when I met one.

I found that I was quite content pottering in the kitchen with Odessa, and I tried my hardest not to think about Alex too much, or give any credence to what Odessa had said.

Davey was floating around adding touches of glamour to the Abbey with huge displays of foliage and setting candles up everywhere. He was also, I noted, removing any valuables to the gun room for safety. He was staggering under the weight of an enormous crystal candelabra, and panted, 'Oh, do give me a drink, I could well die of thirst soon.'

'Tea, or d'you mean a drink drink?' I called out, as he shuffled backwards into the gun room.

'Oh. Yeah, tea would be real nice,' Claudia said, walking up the corridor. 'Do you have camomile? I find that real soothing. Hey, Odessa, I need a new cloth? This one's kinda had it.' She waved her tea towel around to show that it was grimy.

Odessa silently handed her a new one, and we all watched as Claudia inspected it. It seemed to pass muster, and I breathed a sigh of relief. A showdown between Odessa and Claudia was not what we wanted. Although I knew which one I'd put my money on. I heard Davey snigger, and I hurriedly said, 'Tea, then?' and rushed to put the kettle on.

I gave Jicky a piece of celery to toy with, and Odessa advised me to take him out of his basket.

'He'll have to spend enough time in there tonight, when the snapper party is goin' on. You'm better off lettin' him out now.'

I agreed with her, and made the tea with a living stole around my throat. I was sure I'd seen herbal teas somewhere in this huge kitchen but I couldn't find them now, so I poured Claudia a weak cup of China tea, and called along the corridor that it was ready.

She gave a little scream when she entered the kitchen. 'Oh, my God! Have you been cooking with that animal loose? Are you crazy? That is real unhygienic! You put him away now, you hear?'

219

I opened my mouth to say something, when I felt Odessa's hand on my back.

'Now then, you stop being a daft bugger! That animal. Him be cleaner than you. Besides, he's a cold little mite, and is doin' no harm. Leave him be. Do *you* hear me? Leave him be,' Odessa said in a steady voice, fixing Claudia with a stony stare.

Claudia spluttered a bit, but subsided into a chair at the kitchen table, keeping a belligerent eye on Jicky. There might have been an awkward silence around the table, but Claudia was too thick-skinned, Davey was too socially adroit, and Odessa was impervious. It was only me, it seemed, who was awkward. Claudia was horrified at the amount of meat, fat and flour that went into making a Cornish pasty, and suggested that we'd all be better off with sushi and raw veggies for party food tonight. Davey shuddered and Odessa merely snorted with laughter.

'You'm no idea! We'm feedin' all the county tonight, they'm be expectin' my pasties, and that's what they'm getting. Raw vegetables indeed. An' sooshee, what's that then when it's at home?'

When it was discovered that it was raw fish, Odessa rocked with laughter, and said scornfully, 'Oh, I'd like to see the bishop's face if we'm gave him that! Or the boys from the farm. I reckon the fisher boys would have a right laugh, think we'd gone mad, they would!'

I thought that if it only took a plateful of raw fish to make the Stantons mad – well . . .

I offered to take some tea up to Jocasta and Edward,

but Odessa told me that they would come down when they wanted anything. Claudia sniffed and drawled that she thought she'd make herself some lunch, if that was all right, looking with distaste at the mince pies that we were all shovelling into our mouths.

'These really are good, Poppy,' loyal Davey said, wiping crumbs from his chin.

'Yes, I reckon you'm got the touch,' Odessa said, looking at Jicky and me.

Claudia scraped her chair across the flagstoned floor and marched to the fridge, yanking the door open. I was pretty certain that she wouldn't find anything suitable in there, unless Tabitha had restocked her seeds and samphire.

Odessa and Davey started to talk about the snapper party and I cleared the table in preparation for the assembly line Odessa was planning for the pasties. Odessa was in charge of the filling, Davey was on crimping, and I was on brushing the finished product with beaten egg. Claudia was mainly in charge of complaining about the fat levels. We soon had trays and trays of the pasties ready for the oven, and before long the delicious smell of baking filled the kitchen. Odessa promoted me to chopping parsley, and sprinkling it into a large jug of cream.

'What's it for?' I asked, mixing the vivid green specks into the yellow liquid, and admiring the effect.

'That's the secret of the snapper pasty,' Odessa said proudly. 'You make a little nick in the top of a cooked pasty, and pour in the cream and parsley. They'm be so good, I reckon even Tab'll eat one.'

'Talking of Tab, I hope she's all right on the moor,' Davey said, standing on tiptoe to look out of the impossibly high kitchen windows. 'It's going to snow again, and this time it might settle.'

'Don't you fret your fat,' Odessa said. 'She'm know this place better'n you. Look lively, that tray needs takin' out the Aga, and that one puttin' in.'

We all jumped to obey Odessa's orders. It was like being summonsed by the head acolyte of some medieval coven. The kitchen, under Odessa's care, came into its own, too. Dark shadows filled with herbs, antique oddities and tattered cookery books gave it the air of an apothecary shop. Pestles and mortars, copper utensils and ancient kitchen artefacts glinted in the pools of light. The huge dresser groaned under the weight of surviving bits and pieces of glorious Victorian dinner services, the pinks as pink as roses, the gold leaf solid and intact. Jars of bottled fruit, dusty copper moulds, strings of garlic and bunches of dried herbs all added to the calming chaos of the room. Spoons for every occasion hung down from a rack, wooden spoons worn smooth with age and use, spoons shaped for skimming cream, flowered china ladles and a silver jam-making spoon with a handle over eighteen inches long and a worn bowl eroded away after generations of summer stirrings.

I watched Odessa's expert hands dance over the waiting trays of pasties, and was almost hypnotised.

Claudia had taken herself off to her room, muttering about doing some stretch work, whatever the hell *that* was, and Davey was polishing a massive silver punch-bowl, ready for tonight. I think we all jumped when the kitchen door opened and Tabitha came in. She looked frozen.

Davey leapt up and made her sit down, while Odessa pushed towards her a steaming cup of something milky, that I realised she'd made just moments before Tabitha came in.

'Oh, thank you,' Tabitha said, smiling at Odessa. 'It's so beautiful out there, the snow has just started again, and I—'

'Never you mind about that. Drink up and go and get yourself a proper hot bath, my lover, then I want you to lie down for a tidy bit,' Odessa commanded.

Tabitha meekly went from the kitchen, clutching her hot drink.

I smiled. I could see where the power lay in this household. I hoped Tab would take more notice of Odessa that she seemed to of her parents. I could see that her parents loved her, but they were such strong characters themselves that unless you were a shining beacon of eccentricity or endowed with a great deal of charm and ego, as Davey and Alex were, you could well sink in this family.

I heard a phone ringing and ringing in some distant part of the Abbey, but it was completely ignored.

I glanced at Davey. 'Aren't you going to answer it?'
'God, no.'

I could never do that, I decided. Then I had a sudden thought – supposing it was Alex calling from the farm? He might be ringing to say that he was going back to Paris and then I'd never see him again, or he might be calling from a pub in Bodmin, too drunk to get back for the party tonight, or—

'Have some more tea and relax,' Odessa advised, smiling at me.

She reached out for another mug and poured some tea into it, stirring in three large teaspoons of sugar. The kitchen door opened again and Alex breezed in, blowing on his hands and stamping his feet to get them warm.

'Christ, it's cold out there!' he said, giving Odessa a great big smackeroo on the cheek. She pushed him away and handed him the mug of tea and a hot pasty.

'Oh, delicious,' he said between hot mouthfuls. 'The sheep are all in. I'd forgotten what stupid sodding animals they are, all they're good for is mint sauce, in my opinion. We fed the deer, too.'

He suddenly caught sight of Jicky who was perched on a shelf between a stuffed cockerel and an ancient straw hat that was studded with crumbling paper roses.

'What's he doing back here? I was just about to commiserate with you for being recently bereft, but I see I was wrong.'

I steeled myself to talk naturally to him, and tried my best, but it was hard to meet his eyes. When I finally did, my heart melted. He was looking at me with great compassion, sorrow, gentleness and, it must be said, a hint of amusement.

'Jicky was too old, they wouldn't take him—'

Jocasta swung through the kitchen door. 'Too old, who's too old?'

I explained about Jicky and she clapped her hands and positively cooed with delight. I could see that if I wanted to keep him, I was going to have a custody battle on my hands if I wasn't careful.

'Now then, Mrs Stanton, that animal he be young Poppy's. We'm find you somethin' else. All right?' Odessa said sternly.

I saw that I'd been right, Jocasta would have wanted to keep him.

Jocasta agreed and regretfully sighed as she looked at Jicky who, of course, being the centre of attention, immediately started doing the unmentionable. Everyone burst out laughing, and I could feel the dreaded blush heat my face as I avoided looking at Alex. He laughed even more, and squeezed my shoulder as he walked past me.

'I'm off for a hot bath. Davey, have you got any clothes I could borrow for tonight?' Alex called to his brother.

Davey looked mutinous. 'I am *not* going to lend you anything. The last time you took my best silk shirt that I had only just bought, and I've *never* got it back. You're like some bloody great cuckoo, or whatever bird it is that steals things –'

'Magpie.'

'Crows . . .' Jocasta said dreamily, 'a *murder* of crows, what a lovely name . . .'

Odessa was watching the family with the same amused, indulgent grin that I was, I realised.

'Anyway,' Davey said, firmly guiding the conversation back to the impossibility of lending any of his clothes to Alex, 'I think you've put on a little weight since I last saw you, and you wouldn't fit into anything of mine, so—'

'Weight! *Put on weight?* How dare you, sir!' Alex lunged towards Davey, holding out an imaginary sword.

'I have you now, Sir Percy!' cried Davey, stabbing him back with another imaginary rapier.

'Never, never shall I concede!' shouted Alex, running past him and colliding with Edward coming in to the kitchen.

'Steady, boys, steady,' Edward said, in a furious voice. He was carrying a small tattered bit of tapestry in his hand, and he looked very anxious.

'What is it, darling?' asked Jocasta, shushing Alex and Davey who were still indulging in what my old head-master would have called horseplay.

'Look, look! I found this in the downstairs cloaks,' Edward said, his voice filled with incredulity and anger. 'Some fool has been using the family banner to clean the lav with! It stinks of bleach! Who would *do* such a thing?'

I slid my eyes towards Odessa, and we met in guilty but delighted conspiracy.

226

Chapter Sixteen

Claudia was going to be in *so* much trouble, I thought gleefully, but I was damned if I was going to be the one who dropped her in it. I think Alex knew who the bleach culprit was, but he didn't say anything, either.

'What time is everybody arriving tonight?' I asked Edward, to take his mind off the desecrated family banner.

'Nine thirty-one,' he said.

Davey laughed, and explained that they didn't open the front door till then; usually people gathered in the courtyard and queued up the drive, swigging from hip flasks till Edward threw open the door.

'What, you mean you keep them all herded in the cold?' I asked incredulously, marvelling at such royal bad manners.

'Oh, yes,' Edward said, not mollified at all by the talk of the party, and still waving the offending bit of cloth around. 'We never let anyone in till the correct time, damn bad manners if you ask me, turning up early.'

'Oh.'

Odessa made Edward a cup of tea, and he stomped

off to his study with it, muttering under his breath about the stupidity of anyone who could use bleach. I really hoped that he didn't think it was me.

'Oh, God, it was Claudia, wasn't it?' Alex said.

Odessa and Davey nodded.

'It really is too bad of her, Alex,' Jocasta said quite crossly. 'Now Edward will be in a bad mood, and we all know what that can be like, don't we?'

They nodded gloomily.

'Don't worry, Ma, I'll go and talk to him in the study,' Alex said, leaving the room.

'Silly woman!' Jocasta said, looking at her son's departing back view. 'And *very* unsuitable. What is she doing here? I thought she was going back to America. Why my son has to attract such a ghastly specimen of feminine charms is quite beyond me, I must say.' She banged around the kitchen, till Davey made soothing noises to her as one might to a child having a tantrum.

It was bad luck, really, that Claudia chose that moment to appear in the kitchen.

'Hi!' (*Big* smile.) 'Is Alex back yet? I kinda want to see him, I have such a knot in my neck, I figure he could massage me. It must be from sleeping on those real lumpy pillows last night.'

I glanced at Jocasta, but she merely drew her lips back in a snarl, rather than a smile. Davey, the coward, slunk out of the room and Odessa busied herself with the pasties. I persuaded Jicky to get in his basket, and started to make my way upstairs.

'Stop!' called Jocasta, and I froze. 'I think, Poppy, that

228

we should give Claudia a tour of the Abbey gardens,' our hostess said sweetly.

Claudia gave her a horrified look and said, 'Oh, that's real kind of you, but I want to find Alex and—'

And it was bitingly, bloodishly cold I thought to myself.

'Nonsense. Besides, he's locked in the study with Edward, calming him down, and must not be disturbed. Follow me.'

Jocasta swooped out of the room and handed me a rainbow-coloured long scarf and a tweedy jacket. She pulled open the back door and commanded us outside. It was only mid-afternoon, but the sky was dark and the snow was falling in little flurries. Claudia shivered rather dramatically and tried to go indoors to fetch her fur coat.

'Oh, I'm sorry, my dear, I had to ask Alex to hide it,' Jocasta said. 'Seeing fur on human form *so* upsets Edward, and Tabitha, of course, and we wouldn't want that, would we? Now then, this is the family grave, but I don't think I'll introduce you just yet, let's look at the gardens, shall we?'

I smothered a giggle. Jocasta was being *awful*. Funny, but awful. It was a good job, really, that Claudia was impervious to any slight. Jocasta dragged us through the herb garden, the greenhouses and the old stables. We admired the pet cemetery. The church spire was pointed out, the holly tree that was meant to be cursed, the place where she hoped to grow asparagus next year, the rainwater tank, the row of wooden hives where there would have been bees if there hadn't been a terrible bee disease last year, the bamboo thicket, the beginnings of a maze, the molehills, and the remains of a well said to date from Norman times. Jocasta, of course, had a story to tell about all of these places. I kept my hands in my pockets and my mouth tucked into the folds of my scarf, and tried to avoid Jocasta's eye.

Claudia kept trying to slope off, but with a firm hand that brooked no resistance Jocasta kept her firmly by her side. It was well over an hour later that I saw that Claudia's lips were actually starting to turn blue. She had made many attempts to escape, but Jocasta was having none of it. But by now we had circled the Abbey and were in welcome sight of the kitchen door. With a wild cry, Claudia made a final break for freedom, and her long legs covered the distance remarkably quickly.

'It was real interesting, but it's so goddam cold . . .' she called out, waving to us as she slammed the door behind her.

'No stamina, that woman, none at all,' Jocasta said with grim satisfaction. 'Now, Poppy darling,' she added, her voice changing to her customary tone, '*you're* not too cold, are you? There's something I'd like to show you.'

I followed her meekly to the old stables where in a far corner, under a pile of straw, was a litter of kittens. The mother cat, who was obviously feral, viewed our approach with arrogant indifference in her topaz eyes.

'Edward simply hates the wild cats, so I have to feed

230

her in secret, but I am rather hoping that I can befriend one of her kittens. What d'you think?' Jocasta said, eyeing the litter enviously.

I thought it doubtful, wild cats were always wild, but I didn't have the heart to tell Jocasta that. She changed the subject abruptly, and said to me, 'Poppy, have I behaved *very* badly to Claudia?'

'Well,' I said slowly, playing for time, 'I think you might be a little—'

'No need, no need to say any more. But the thing is, you see, I really can't bear the thought of that woman turning this place into a health farm, or installing proper central heating, much as that would be nice, of course, but you do see that she is so unsuitable, and if she and Alex are the first, well . . .' Her voice tailed off and she gave me a somewhat sly sideways glance. 'I *was* rather hoping that you and Alex . . .'

'Me too, Jocasta. But . . . What do you mean, if they are the first? First what?' I wasn't quite sure what to tell her, and was aware that I'd probably said too much anyway. I didn't think that confiding in the mother of the object of one's affections and fantasies would be a good idea. I hesitated to tell her that really I was probably way out of Alex's league, and that only a makeover and new clothes from Jessy, and the fact that he had been sitting next to me on the train, had kindled his interest. That and, of course, that I had seemed perfectly willing to go and have sex with him in the loo of the train.

Jocasta seemed preoccupied and as I sighed, she

231

merely squeezed my arm affectionately. We headed back for the Abbey, only stopping to flap our arms at some crows that were threatening a robin.

Odessa was engaged in the perilous task of finding enough flat surfaces to balance the trays of pasties on. Jocasta advised me to grab a hot bath, and to start getting ready for the party.

'Won't I be rather early?' I asked, glancing at my watch.

'Oh, no, not at all. We'll all meet downstairs and have a drink and things,' Jocasta said vaguely, waving me out of the kitchen. She was looking intently at Odessa and I knew she wanted me out of the way. God knows what those two were going to be talking about, but Odessa was blessed with a great deal more common sense than Jocasta, so I didn't worry about it. I picked Jicky up and made my way upstairs.

I had a cosy chat with Davey in his book-strewn room (absolutely no evidence of the offending magazine) till he, too, advised me to go and get ready. So Jicky and I made our way to the Chinese room. The bath water was decidedly cool and I had a hasty wash. I then laid out on the bed the glittering dress that Jessy had got me, and eyed it doubtfully. It seemed frightfully grand, and I wasn't sure I was up to it. I decided to go and ask Jocasta what she thought, and to see what she was wearing as well. I gathered the dress to me, and started off down the corridor.

As soon as I stepped outside my door, I could hear voices rowing in Alex's room. Claudia was screeching at him and, although I was delighted that they were having an argument, I didn't want to be caught eavesdropping. I was just scuttling along the corridor towards Jocasta's room, when Claudia shouted something that made me stop in my tracks.

'. . . And as you're going to be a father, and be the goddamn first in this crazy family of yours, I think it's time you stopped flirting with that real Plain Jane, you know, that Poppy woman . . .'

Father? *Father!* Oh, great. First? First what? Then the Plain Jane bit sunk in. I glanced down at the dress in my hand and stood rooted to the spot. What *was* I doing? Who was I trying to kid? A new hairstyle and a few new clothes hadn't changed me at all, I was still the woman who was more comfortable wearing Marks and Sparks. And even if I did pull myself together and put this fabulous dress on, what was the point? Claudia was pregnant. It didn't matter what Alex had said to me, he obviously hadn't known, and now he did, he would never leave her. Not that I'd want him to, I added hastily to myself. I felt all my happiness ooze away from me. I walked back to my own room and closed the door. I sat on the bed, and stared out of the window.

I'd seen a TV programme once about the life of some sort of prehistoric mud worm, or fish. Apparently, when there's a drought they close down. They slow their heart rate and breathing, and simply *exist*, waiting for the next lot of rain. Well, that was going to be me. I'd wall myself up in my mud, and concentrate on just being, not living or being happy, but just *being*. I'd leave the Abbey as soon as I could, and get myself home. I'd watch TV, cook dinners for one and forget all about Alex and the rest of the wonderful, loopy, stargazy Stantons. I'd have to find myself another job as well. Working with Davey would be far too much heartache.

I felt great big fat tears of self-pity start rolling down my face. I sniffed, threw myself down on the pillow and gave way to a full ten-minute sobbing session.

It didn't make me feel any better at all.

I was still sniffing and splashing cold water on my face when there was a knock on my bedroom door. It was Tabitha.

'Oh, Poppy, I just wanted to show you what I was wearing tonight, and to see if you thought I . . .' She tailed off, looking with concern at me. 'Are you OK?' she said.

'Yes,' I sniffed. 'I'm sorry, I just had a moment of the blues,' I replied, not knowing what else to say. 'What was it you wanted?'

'Well,' she continued doubtfully, looking worriedly at my red eyes and blotchy face, 'if you're sure you're OK. I just wanted to ask if you thought I looked fat in this, only I bought it some time ago and, well, I'll try it on, and you tell me, OK?'

'OK.'

The thought of Tabitha looking fat in anything would normally have made me roar with laughter. She struggled out of her clothes and slipped into a pale grey (of course) long dress. Surprisingly enough, it did make her look rather fat. OK, well, not exactly fat, that would have been impossible, but there was something about the dress that gave her a definite bulge in the tummy area.

Oh, my God.

A bulge in the tummy area! No, no, it wasn't possible, surely? Not bloody Tabitha as well? Shit! I stared at her.

'Tabitha,' I said slowly, 'forgive me, but, well, you're not . . .' I left the word hanging in the air.

Then I saw her face, and I knew.

Of course! All that feeling sick, and not eating. Well, I hoped that Jocasta was going to be pleased anyway. Not one but two grandchildren were on the way to grace the Abbey and continue the mad inheritance of the Stantons. And I was firmly put out of the picture.

The relief of someone knowing was too much for Tabitha. Words streamed out of her mouth, and I put the story together as best I could.

It seems that she had met a man at the sacred sister workshop – yes, men were allowed, welcomed even, as long as they were sisters in their hearts. (I snorted a bit at this, but let it go.) And he and she, well, the rest was obvious. 'He is so wonderfully free, Poppy, you know? And of course, I couldn't tell him . . .'

'Why?'

'Oh, because he hasn't given me a number or anything so, so earthly, you know? I mean, he's just on another plane altogether. He has travelled far beyond anywhere I could go, I mean, he's on his way in this astral plane, and I, well, I couldn't possibly tie him to me, or keep him from his own karma. He said he would see me again, so, well, I'm just waiting. I did write to him, giving him my address, but, well . . . I don't even know where he lives . . .'

'So how did you know where to send the letter?'

'I didn't. But I sent it to Amya, she runs the workshops. It's funny, you know, because I thought at first that he and she were involved, but she said not. So she said that she'd send the letter on to him, but couldn't possibly tell me where he lived as it would be betraying a confidence, but that she saw him often and would make sure he got it, that was some time ago, but, well, I'm just waiting, you see . . .'

I saw only too well. What a mess.

She twisted her new ring on her thumb and looked down at it. 'I hope Ma and Pa won't be too upset when I sell this. The workshop takes up so much of my money and Amya is so right about the more I give, the more free I become.'

Oh, so that's what she said, did she?

Tabitha was becoming agitated now, and her normally pale cheeks were flushed pink. She paced the room excitedly.

'But, Tab, why haven't you told anyone? I mean, I know that I hardly know your parents, but they don't seem to me the sort of people who would mind, I mean, they'd be delighted, wouldn't they?' I said.

She shot me a look of surprise. 'Oh, no. No. They'd mind. They'd mind dreadfully, Daddy would, anyway. I'm not even divorced yet, and they minded that awfully. This would be the last straw. And what with

236

the will and everything, it's going to cause the most awful fuss . . .'

This stumped me. But I still wasn't convinced. I thought Jocasta would be delighted, and very understanding, and if she was, then Edward would be too. I didn't know the details of this damn will, but it was sounding more and more ominous. I knew that it had been worrying Davey dreadfully and now Tabitha too.

There was another knock on my door, and we both jumped. Before I could call out, Tabitha grabbed my arm and whispered intently to me, 'Promise you won't tell anyone? Promise?'

I nodded.

Odessa walked into the room, carrying a tray with two cups of steaming, fragrant liquid in them. She put the tray on the bed and handed Tabitha one cup, and then me the other, saying, 'Hot blackcurrant for you, and that raspberry one be for you, Tab. Now then, what you two be mithering about?'

I didn't dare look at her, as I was convinced that she really did possess supernatural powers and was quite capable of reading thoughts. She stared intensely at Tabitha and smiled. 'Well, well . . . a proper pair of tykes they'll be, I reckon.'

Tabitha and I stared at one another. Pair? *Pair!* Oh, my God, she was going to have twins! Maybe Tab's rune readings had been nearer to the truth than she knew herself. I started to say something, but Tabitha laid her hand on my arm, so I stopped.

Odessa picked up my dress and held it against

herself. 'Now that be a right proper job, I reckon. Don't you let Jocasta see it before you put it on, or she'll have it off you for the panto costumes, or 'erself!'

I laughed weakly, and glanced at Tabitha. She was sipping her hot drink and gazing at Odessa. I desperately wanted her to tell Odessa her news, to get it all out in the open, but she didn't look as if she was going to. She didn't need to, I realised. Odessa knew.

Odessa bustled away, leaving us to get dressed.

'Tabitha, don't worry, I'm sure everything will be OK,' I said despairingly.

Tab smiled at me. 'Oh, I'm sure it will too, the baby, or maybe *babies*, are going to be special, you see. Once *he's* seen me, he will want to be with us, so all I have to do is wait.'

I sighed, this was beyond me. As much as I'd promised not to tell anyone, I knew that I'd have to; but then, it was going to be pretty obvious soon, and everyone would know without me telling a soul. The sooner she got away from this awful-sounding workshop that was swallowing her money, the better.

Then there was bloody Claudia.

I sighed again.

Tabitha got up to get dressed in her own room, and rather touchingly, I thought, gave me a kiss before she left.

I dispiritedly began to dress. Maybe Jessy *was* right, after all. It was a matter of confidence with clothes. I slapped on as much make-up as I dared and hooked myself into the dress. After just a couple of days of clotted cream and butter it was very tight, and my cleavage impressed even me. I made sure that Jicky was safe in his basket, and taking a deep breath, and fixing a smile on my face, I ventured downstairs. I practically collided with Davey, who was tearing out of his room, frantically trying to fix his cuff-links.

'Christ, Poppy! You look amazing!'

I was immensely gratified, and thanked him. You know how it is, when you are feeling unsure of yourself and wearing something that is most definitely not in your usual spectrum of rather dull, conservative clothes, you need approval, and Davey had just given it to me. I could tell that it was genuine, as well, by the sheer admiration on his face. I fiddled with his cuff-links for him, and we proceeded down the stairs. Davey crept an arm around my waist, and I stared in surprise at him. He was never a very touchy-feely sort of person, and it seemed out of character.

Edward was fussing over the punch-bowl that Davey had burnished earlier in the day. He was pouring the contents of a bewildering array of bottles into it, followed by some lemon rind pared with a very old silver knife. He too expressed great approval for my dress, and I could see exactly where Davey and Alex got their wonderful manners from. It must be intensely gratifying, I thought, to be married to such men, they actually *notice* how you are dressed and what you have on, instead of the usual bland remarks or grunts that most males seem to think are compliments.

Edward handed us both a small glass of the punch,

and we sipped it judiciously. It was *incredibly* strong. I choked, and Davey thumped me on the back. I put the glass down immediately. If I swigged that, I'd be comatose before the party even started. I decided that I would put firmly from my mind any thoughts of Alex and the horribly fecund Claudia, or even Tabitha, and just try to have a nice time at the party, however hard it was going to be.

Jocasta was next down, wearing tight, black *leather* jeans, a long-sleeved Vivienne Westwood bustier, and what looked like, and probably was, a million-pound diamond necklace wrapped round her throat. Her long silver hair was piled on top of her head, and was already coming down, in fact she was shedding hair-pins as she walked. She looked quite incredible.

Odessa had been right about my dress, because Jocasta made a beeline for me, and started to stroke the fabric, eyeing it jealously.

'Poppy, you look fantastic,' she said.

'Thank you, so do you, I love your jeans, and that necklace!' I said.

She touched her neck, and glanced at her husband. 'Don't tell Edward, but it's a copy,' she whispered. 'I sold the real one years ago to pay for the new roof!'

She made sure that we all had our snapper badges prominently pinned to ourselves. She declined a glass of punch.

'No, Edward, I will *not* have one, look what happened to the bishop last year, poor man, no wonder, when I think of what you pour into it. It's probably illegal the amount of alcohol that's in there, like those artists who used to drink absinthe in Paris, they went blind or mad or something, it's the wormwood in it, I think. What *is* wormwood exactly? I must ask Odessa, she'll know.'

'She's probably brewing up a batch of wormwood as we speak,' Davey said, coming to his mother's rescue and pushing her hairpins back in.

Edward went off to open some champagne for Jocasta, and we all stood chattering in the hall. I kept glancing upstairs, trying to anticipate when Alex and Claudia were going to come down, and rearranging my expression into what I hoped was a neutral sort of look, rather than the self-pitying sorry-for-myself grimace that was on my face right now. I wondered if they were going to make an announcement about the baby, and I tried to plan ahead so that I could join in the congratulations without actually bursting into tears. I took a coughingly large swig from my punch glass to give me some Dutch courage.

Davey was fiddling with his fob watch, and Edward was glancing at one of the many grandfather clocks that were dotted around the Abbey. The clocks were a problem, because none of them showed the right time, and they had a disconcerting habit of chiming in the middle of the night, the noise reverberating around the place, making us all think it was far later than it really was. We could hear a few cars outside, and some slamming doors. Davey went to peer out of the window. 'Snowing again!' he said, in tones of great satisfaction. 'And people are arriving.'

'Damn fools,' growled Edward. 'They know what time the door opens, more fool them if they want to freeze to death!'

'Now, Edward, you know they all like gathering outside, they get to chat and things,' Jocasta said vaguely, absent-mindedly pushing a hairpin into the back of her head. 'Now where are the others? Oh, Tab, darling, there you are!'

Tabitha glided down the stairs, her tiny, slightly swollen tummy, to my eyes very prominent indeed.

Edward smiled at her and she came to rest beside him. Her snapper badge was pinned to the front of her dress, and she was playing nervously with it. She glanced towards me, and I smiled encouragingly.

'Poppy, you look wonderful,' she said.

'So do you, don't you think so, Edward?' I said.

'Indeed, yes, though I really think, darling, you're not eating enough . . .'

Jocasta gave him a warning glance and interrupted him. 'Tabitha, you do look very nice indeed, but do you know, darling, believe it or not, I think that dress is a little bit too tight!'

Davey looked at his sister and laughed. 'My God, Tab! Have you been sneaking some pasties in? I could almost believe I see the outline of a stomach, or are you going for the medieval look, you know, they all wore those high-waisted things that you like, apparently they all wanted to look pregnant—'

The word was like a talisman, it seemed to float in the air. I saw Jocasta glance sharply at Davey and then back at Tabitha. Her face sagged, and she suddenly looked every year of her age. She knows, I thought, she has just found out.

It was a test of Jocasta's strength, and she passed it with great style. I guessed that for all her possible secret longings for grandchildren, the idea of Tabitha, patently not her favourite child, having a baby out of wedlock, was not the great delight that I thought it would be. But you would never, ever have guessed it. She squared her shoulders back, plastered a great big smile on her face and went to stand beside Tabitha, putting a protective arm across her shoulders.

'Ignore Davey, you do look really lovely, my darling. Now then, why don't you have some orange juice or something . . .' She guided Tabitha to a seat and threw her husband a private 'I'll talk to you later' look.

Alex and Claudia came down the stairs. Claudia was beaming and dragging Alex by the hand behind her. He looked haggard. I averted my eyes, as I thought I knew what was coming.

They reached the hall at the same time that Odessa arrived from the kitchen carrying an enormous platter of food.

'Oh, great! You're all here,' drawled Claudia, looking absolutely bloody perfect in a pale pinky-beige layered chiffon dress. 'We've something kinda exciting to tell you all, haven't we, honey?'

243

Chapter Seventeen

I kept my eyes firmly on the ground, as I had absolutely no wish to witness the grand announcement that I knew was going to take place. I felt dread in the pit of my stomach, and started to panic.

'Well, whatever it is,' Edward said, consulting at least three different time pieces, 'you'll need to make it damn quick, I have to open the doors in two minutes. What time do you make it, Davey?'

'Nine thirty exactly,' Davey said, fob watch in the palm of his hand.

Odessa placed the platter of hot food down on a table and stood squarely in the centre of the hall with her arms crossed over her ample bosom. I saw that she'd changed into what was obviously her party outfit, a strongly upholstered number in a dusty black velvet. She stared at Claudia and said in a slow, firm voice, 'Well, I reckon that whatever you'm be planning of saying, you'm want to think on first. It be time to let those good folk in, we'm never late here at the Abbey, not for the snapper party, we'm not.'

Claudia threw Alex a glance of appeal, but Alex too, I

noticed, had his eyes firmly on the ground. Claudia let out an exasperated sigh and flounced back upstairs. Alex followed her.

'Well, let's open the doors, Davey!' called Edward happily. 'And I'd like to wish you all a very happy snapper party, and may the best man win!'

Odessa smiled grimly to herself, and then winked at me. I didn't quite know what to make of this, but felt I had at least gained a reprieve. It hadn't made my anxiety disappear, but I had time now to get used to the idea of Alex being unavailable.

Davey and Edward ran forward and dragged the heavy front door open. It seemed that only moments later the Abbey hall was full of people. They streamed in from the cold outside, laughing and stamping their feet to get warm. With dizzying speed I was introduced to the fishermen and antique dealers from Padstow, the clergy from Truro, the farmers from the moors, the art contingent from St Ives and Penzance, the local doctor and Odessa's husband Arthur; I was also reintroduced to Patrick the vet, and Tom and his ravishing and very pregnant wife Demelza. The faces all blurred into one, and my punch glass was kept constantly topped up by Davey. Patrick made a beeline for me, and kissed me hello. I responded a little more warmly than I should have, but hell, it was Christmas and I was starting to feel reckless. Alex and Claudia still hadn't re-emerged from upstairs, and it was getting to me. I kept imagining them coiled round each other, talking baby talk or something equally nauseating.

It was an extraordinary mix of people. Somehow I didn't think it would work in London, but I suppose that being in the country made everyone comfortable with one another. Weather-beaten fishermen were nose to nose over the punch-bowl with a man who was the editor of *Cathedral Monthly*, apparently arguing over the merits of the best way to cook crabs, whilst Patrick was trying to persuade Odessa to tell him some country remedies for curing colic in cows. Arthur was regaling everyone with tales of the upcoming panto-mime, and complaining that the best song had not gone to him, but to the local traffic policeman who was playing Baron Hardup, the baddie of the piece.

'He'll make a proper cock-up of it, I reckons. I ask you, a copper! What do they know about singin'?'

'More than a poacher, Arthur?' one of the fishermen called out.

'Water bailiff, if you don't mind!' Arthur called back with a huge wink.

Jocasta was darting about everywhere, trailing hair-pins in her wake. Edward and Davey were busy dispensing largesse in the form of punch and pasties. Tabitha was in deep conversation with Demelza on a sofa, I wondered if they were having baby talk. The Abbey seemed to be turning into a superannuated nursery. I looked for Claudia and Alex but still couldn't see either of them.

Even more people were arriving now, and the noise of the party had become one huge background roar. Everyone, according to their means, had made a tremendous effort to dress up, I could see. Most of the women were in spanking new dresses, or vintage cocktail gear, all apart from the art lot who featured heavily with home-made creations that had a lot of vegetable dye splattered over everything. Even the men, the majority of whom, I guessed, would have been far happier in jeans, were stuffed into suits or dinner jackets, some of which had definitely seen better days. There were odd incongruous touches, like Patrick who was wearing an ancient dinner jacket, white shirt and silk bow tie, but had his trousers tucked into wellington boots. Jocasta was singing the praises of Jicky to him, and guiding the conversation, quite unfairly I thought, round to him saying the snapper word. He, to my joy, however, seemed completely unaware of it, and avoided it skilfully, albeit unknowingly.

'You know, Patrick, that monkey is nearly human, despite him being, oh, what's the word?' Jocasta said hopefully.

'Monkey-like?' Patrick said.

Jocasta narrowed her eyes at him, and I snorted into my drink. Davey glided up behind me and said to his mother, 'Shameless, that's what you are, darling, shameless.'

A woman arrived wearing a gilded wreath of ivy leaves on her head, and the party cheered and crowded around her. She ceremoniously lifted the crown from her head and held it aloft. 'I give you last year's snapper's crown! And good luck to this year's winner!' Everyone whooped with approval and the

247

family got down in earnest to making someone say the word. The crown was placed rakishly on a large bronze bust of Balzac.

'Quite barmy, aren't they?' Patrick said to me.

'Oh, yes, absolutely. But such great fun,' I said.

He leant forward and whispered to me, 'Tell me, is this year's word Simian, by any chance?'

I nodded violently.

He laughed. 'I thought it must be! Do you want me to drop it casually into the conversation? Then you can win, and I get to wear that rather natty crown for a year.'

I admired his planning, and was quite tempted, but then a group of people parted and I saw Tabitha's pale face. If anyone needed cheering up, it was her.

I explained to Patrick that Tabitha deserved to win, and he seemed quite amenable.

'Do you want me to have a quick check-up of Jicky?'

'Oh yes, please, that would be great. But you are at a party, you probably don't want to do any work, do you?'

'I'm used to it. Besides, it really is quite a novelty treating a monkey. My colleagues over at Looe get to do the monkey sanctuary. I just get the farm animals.'

We made our way through the crowds. Patrick seemed to be quite popular, and was stopped every three paces by farmers greeting him. He was in no hurry, and I learnt more about lambing, colic, lameness and mastitis than I ever really wanted to know.

People were sitting all the way up the stairs, glasses

248

in hand or munching on pasties, and we had to step over them. As we passed through the library, I glanced downwards and saw the tops of everybody's heads. I scanned the craniums for Alex or Claudia, but they were nowhere to be seen.

I pushed open the door to the Chinese bedroom and Patrick closed it firmly behind him.

'He moves like greased lightning, doesn't he? We don't want to let him loose on the punch; it's lethal to humans and I dread to think what it would do to a monkey!'

He bent down in front of Jicky's basket. Jicky was, of course, doing something quite disgusting.

'Don't worry, animals are always being embarrassing, aren't they?' Patrick said.

I realised that this was a man who spent most of his life with a hand up various animals' bottoms, so Jicky's antics probably left him unabashed. I wished that I could say the same for me.

Patrick examined Jicky, feeling his tummy and looking at his teeth.

'Yes, the man at the sanctuary was right. He's an old fellow now, in monkey terms. He wouldn't have settled in there, you know. How are you going to cope with him?' Patrick said, stroking Jicky.

'I just don't know, but I'll find a way.'

'You beautiful determined women always do, don't you?' Patrick said.

Beautiful? Determined? *Me?* I made a promise to myself that I would cook Jessy dinner when I got back.

'Do you really work with Davey in his shop?' he asked.

'Oh, yes, it's great fun. Why, did you think I was a traffic warden or something?' I said stupidly.

'No, not at all. It's just that in that dress you could pass for a model,' Patrick said, smiling at me.

I felt a bit flustered, and true to form, started to blush. Patrick laughed again, and put Jicky back in his basket. I sipped at my drink, thinking it would be a good moment to join the rest of the party. But as I stood up, Patrick very slowly put his arm around me, drew me towards him and kissed me on the mouth. He did everything very slowly, as if to give me every chance to move away from him, but I didn't.

He eventually pulled away from me and said, 'I've been wanting to do that from the first moment I saw you.'

Well, this was the high life, I decided. Being kissed by Patrick was very nice. I mean, not *disturbingly* nice, like Alex had been, but nice, nevertheless. And sod it, I kept reminding myself, it was Christmas after all, and bloody Alex had now got a pregnant girlfriend, which put me firmly out of the picture. If I wanted to have a snog with the vet, why shouldn't I?

Patrick still had his arms around me when the bedroom door was flung open.

'Poppy, I've been looking—' Alex stopped, and stared at us.

It felt as though I'd had a bucketful of ice cold water thrown over me. Alex just stared at us, for what seemed

250

a very long time. His eyes were contemptuous, which I thought was a bit rich, considering *his* behaviour, but it did make me feel awful, all the same.

'Alex, I was just, well, we were looking at Jicky and, umm, well you know, it's Christmas,' I said sheepishly.

'Don't be so bloody silly, of course it's Christmas,' Alex snapped.

Patrick smoothed his hair and held out his hand to Alex. 'Hi, Alex, nice to see you again, how are you?'

Alex completely ignored him. 'I think it's time we *all* went downstairs don't you? Or is there a further medical examination that needs to take place?' he said in a very flat, cold voice.

I felt my face turn scarlet, and tears spring to my eyes.

Bloody, bloody men. How Alex had managed to make me feel an absolute slut, I don't know. But he had. It was so unfair! He had got a gorgeous, *pregnant* girl-friend, and I was just having a nice time with Patrick, and he had to burst in and spoil everything! Bloody, bloody men.

I pushed past Alex and practically ran down the stairs. I heard Patrick calling my name, but I made a beeline for the punch-bowl. I felt marginally better after I had swigged a few glasses of the punch. Well, to be honest, I didn't exactly feel better, I felt drunk.

Davey was playing old foxtrots on the piano, and I danced with Arthur, who was quite as drunk as I was rapidly becoming, and then with a few of the fishermen. Jocasta whirled past me in the arms of Edward, and

251

called out that she hoped I was having a marvellous time.

Oh, yes. Yes, I am. My heart might be breaking, but I was having an absolutely bloody marvellous time.

I stopped to catch my breath and Patrick claimed me. Davey started to play another song, and Patrick held me in his arms as we moved to the music. I'd love to be able to tell you that we floated around the hall, but to be honest, I was too drunk, and it was far too crowded. It was a good job I was being held up in Patrick's arms, or otherwise I'd have fallen over.

'Are you OK?' he asked.

I nodded. Then I blew a kiss at the bishop.

'Don't let Alex upset you. I don't know what's going on, but I can guess. He's a bit like athlete's foot, I've always thought. One's wife or girlfriend catches it at one time or another, but it doesn't usually last long.'

I suddenly felt a bit sick.

'Poppy, are you sure you're OK?'

No, of *course* I'm not. I'm just an ordinary woman who's been dropped in amongst these people, and I really, really believed, just for a moment, that Alex was going to be the one. The one who would take away my loneliness, the one who would tie me to these crazy people. And now? Well, now I've found out that his bloody girlfriend is pregnant, and that he flirts and makes people fall in love with him all the time. So, no, now that you ask, I'm not all right. I feel sick and I want to go home.

I abruptly sat down on a seat. Oh, God, I really did

feel sick now. I glanced around to see where the nearest door was. I rather unsteadily got up again and pushed my way through the crowd till I found the cloakroom. I locked the door, turned the cold water on and splashed my face. The room smelt very strongly of bleach, and I knew that bloody Claudia of the impossible ivories had been in here. I heard Patrick knocking on the door and calling my name.

'Please go away. I'm fine, I'll be out soon,' I said, sliding down the door and sitting on the cold stone floor.

My advice is as follows: if you should ever find yourself in the unfortunate position of feeling unwell due to a massive intake of unaccustomed alcohol – count. Get cold, and count. It doesn't really matter what you count – floor tiles, wall bricks, number of towels folded up on a table, books on a shelf, anything will do.

I'd reached two hundred and nine bricks in a wall, and had a freezingly cold bottom, before I felt even remotely better. I stood swaying slightly in front of an old spotted mirror that had seen better days, and looked at my reflection. *Not* good. Shiny nosed, piggy eyed and no trace of make-up left. My hair was sticking out at very odd angles, and I was still a bit green around the gills. I splashed more cold water over myself, cupped my hands and gulped some down. Then some more. I straightened up, and then set to with the lipstick and powder. I wished desperately that Russell the hairdresser was here, but I did the best I could.

There was a knock on the door, and I heard Patrick again, saying, 'Poppy, if you don't come out now, I'll have to break the door down! I'm worried about you.'

'I'm coming, hang on a minute.'

I had one final look in the mirror, took a deep breath and left the sanctuary of the cloakroom. I decided that I had nothing to be ashamed of, and if I wanted to kiss Patrick again, I would.

It was a scene of Bacchanalian debauchery in the hall. The punch had really kicked in now, and people had let their hair down. The bishop was dancing with Sonya, the woman from the antique shop, whilst the bishop's wife was leaning on the piano belting out an old showbiz tune. Two fishermen were riding the fairground horse, and Tom, Edward and Arthur were dancing around the harp, in a sort of free-form expressionism that Isadora Duncan would have approved of.

I assured Patrick that I was OK, and he very kindly went to get me a glass of water. Tabitha was leaning against the wall, talking to Odessa, and I made my way towards them.

'You'm all right?' Odessa enquired, looking at me with her piercingly knowing eyes.

'I'm fine,' I assured her, thanking Patrick for the water.

He was sweet, I decided. For he immediately launched into a spirited conversation with Tabitha, and skilfully guided her into letting him say the snapper word.

As soon as it left his mouth, Odessa and Tabitha gave

a mighty cry of 'Snapper!', and soon the whole party was crowded around us, taking up the chant.

'Sna-pper! Sna-pper! Sna-pper!'

Patrick had the gilded crown plonked on his head, and Tabitha was being kissed and snapped by the whole family and guests alike. She was so pleased with herself that a rosy glow was on her cheeks, and she was beaming with pride. Edward had his chest puffed out, and was hugging her with delight. Even Jocasta, who I knew had really wanted to win, was looking proudly at her daughter. Davey produced the vast leather book, and the word, winner and date were inscribed.

I pulled at Tabitha's arm, and whispered, 'Tab, why don't you tell Edward now . . . Go on, do.'

She looked doubtfully at me, and I cursed myself for being interfering. I think it was the effects of the punch that I was still suffering from, but it just occurred to me that Edward was in such a good mood that it would be a great time to tell him. Perhaps she would also tell him about selling her lovely new ring.

The crowd were still chanting, and then all the men started to sing. It sounded a bit like a hymn, the chorus being something about a man called Trelawny.

'And shall Trelawny live? Or shall Trelawny die? And thirty thousand Cornish men will know the reason why!' was being belted out by all the guests. It was quite a rousing song, but I had no idea who Trelawny was, or if he died or not.

255

I saw Tabitha take her father into his study, and close the door. Oh, dear. I hoped all would be well.

I caught a glimpse of Alex from the other side of the room, and my heart contracted. He had a bottle of whisky in one hand, and a glass in the other. He raised his glass to me in a sort of toast, with a smile on his face.

Bastard.

I turned away from him and talked to Patrick, determined not to show how heartbroken I was.

'Thank you for letting Tabitha win,' I said.

'My pleasure,' he replied. 'I have to be going soon, I'm on call in about two hours. Are you going to the pantomime tomorrow?'

I nodded.

'Oh, good, I shall see you there.'

He kissed me, quite chastely on the cheek, and started to say his goodbyes. I went to the door to see him off, and was entranced to see that the snow was about two inches deep. The moon was shining on it, and it looked spectacularly beautiful.

'Oh, shit!' Patrick groaned.

'What?'

'Well, I know it looks lovely, but you have no idea of the chaos that this is going to cause, it's going to be hell,' he said gloomily, kicking some snow off one of the many chimney-pots stacked against the Abbey wall.

I had harboured a romantic idea that he would kiss me again under the moonlight, but no such luck. He

256

was much more concerned with clearing the snow off his car.

I waved him off as he drove very slowly down the steep snowy drive. I turned back to look at the Abbey. It looked wonderful with a coating of snow, and the voices from inside echoed around the grounds. A shaft of golden light spilt out from the half-open front door and made spooky shadows against the wall. I heard someone, the bishop, I think, but I can't swear to it, say, 'Bugger me! Look at the snow!' and soon the guests had piled out of the Abbey to stare at it.

The fishermen started a snowball fight versus the farmers, whilst the arty lot made a non-gender-specific snowperson. I wandered back indoors and, glancing at the time, was surprised to find that it was three in the morning. Bedtime, I thought. I was very tired.

Davey caught up with me and swung me around to face him. To my utter surprise and shock he kissed me, on the mouth.

Chapter Eighteen

Jicky woke me early in the morning, by doing something very unattractive on the pillow. I groaned, and pushed him away. I felt dreadful. I mean, really, *really* dreadful. My head was pounding and I felt sick. My mouth was very dry, and it drove me to the bathroom to gulp down torrents of icy water. I peered out of the window and saw the snowy landscape. I shivered and crawled back to bed.

I remembered with a shudder all of last night's events. The final corker had been as I was going to bed, and Claudia had popped her head around the door of Alex's room.

'Oh, thank God someone's here, I've been calling that strange housekeeper woman for ages, but I guess you'll do. I mean you're practically staff, right?'

I had stared wordlessly at her.

Well, Plain Jane and now staff, was I? I gathered she thought that if I worked for Davey I was quite capable of running around after her.

'Odessa is very busy, what do you want?' I had in fact seen Odessa staggering around the hall under vast trays of kedgeree. I knew that I had tried to speak evenly but had rather spoilt the effect by hiccuping.

'Well, I really need some food, yeah? So maybe you could get me something? You know, like, some fruit, or maybe a small salad, but no protein or fat though. Oh, yeah, and I really need some mineral water? OK?'

I had hiccuped again.

'Looks like you're pretty pooped,' Claudia said, flashing a (caring) smile at me.

'Pooped or not, I recognise a manipulative bitch when I see one,' I said.

As I had fallen asleep last night the only thing that made me smile was remembering, with intense satisfaction, the sight of Claudia with her jaw wide open with surprise at the Plain Jane who had bitten back.

Depression draped itself over me and I hugged my misery and my hangover to me for a while, and then decided that I was just dithering, and had to do something, *anything* about it. But what?

I had screwed everything up. Patrick, Alex *and* Davey, it seemed. Last night had been awful. Alex was with his pregnant girlfriend, Patrick was probably horrified at my behaviour, and Davey, well, Davey had kissed me, for God's sake. I felt so confused and miserable that I huddled under the bedclothes wondering what I should do.

I had to go home.

That was it, I would leave.

I had to get away from here and sort myself out.

I knew I couldn't stay a moment longer. Once I'd

259

made the decision, I felt much better. I knew that I could never be comfortable in Alex's company, and to tell the truth, I felt pretty awful about being around Claudia, too. And as much as I loved Davey, I was still angry with him for his inexplicable behaviour last night. I longed to see Alex again, just to say goodbye, but I knew I couldn't. Home, home, home, the words drummed in my ears. Nothing very exciting might happen there but at least I would be safe.

I washed, dressed and packed as quickly as I could, moving in a frenzy in my desire to leave. I left my snapper badge on my stripped bed. I gazed around the Chinese room, mentally saying goodbye to it, goodbye to everything, really. The Abbey, Odessa, the snapper game, the Stantons and, of course, Alex.

I scribbled a note for them all and bundled Jicky into his basket, after wrapping him in my flannel nightdress for some extra warmth, and crept downstairs. I felt like a thief in the night.

The hall was littered with empty glasses, bottles and overflowing ashtrays. At least fifty empty plates, with residues of rice and fish, were the only remains of Odessa's kedgeree. Even the Christmas tree was leaning at what looked like a rather dangerous angle, as if it, too, was suffering from a hangover.

I knew I was running away from what might have been a wonderful experience, but I was like a child crying on the first day of school. I felt an urgent need to be in my very own flat.

I gingerly pushed open the door to Edward's study,

and finally ran to earth the phone, which was hiding under a pile of auction catalogues. I dialled Talking Pages and asked for a taxi company. I scribbled down the number on the back of my hand, and eventually spoke to a man who seemed vastly amused at my request for a taxi to the Abbey.

'You'm looked out the window, my lover?' the man's rich Cornish accent enquired. 'I'll not get a car up to there, I did me last run about five this mornin', to the Abbey, an' that was hard goin'. It's been snowin' again since then.'

'You have to,' I whispered into the phone. 'This is an emergency!'

I pleaded with him, and in the end he relented, but we had to reach a compromise. He would pick me up at the farm, and I would have to make my own way down the long, steep drive.

'But I'll need skis!' I said, horrified at the idea.

He laughed, and said he'd be at the farm in half an hour. More or less. I let myself out of the kitchen door, and was enchanted by the snow. It was at least six inches deep, and every surface had a fat white eider-down topping. The grave in the garden looked like a film prop, it was so improbable. The sleepy dragon was smothered in white, but you could just make out the outlines of its tail. I trudged through the snow, dragging my suitcase round the side of the Abbey, and glanced nervously up at the windows. I certainly didn't want to be seen making my undignified exit, but I needn't have worried, all the windows had drawn curtains, and there was no sign of life.

The steep driveway might well have been the black run in Gstaad. I had absolutely no idea how I was going to get down it, but get down it I must. I couldn't endure the humiliation of seeing Alex or Davey. I felt as though I was fleeing from the scene of a crime, my haste was so great.

I tentatively put one foot forward and immediately slipped over, dropping the basket that Jicky was in. He chattered his fury at me, and I shushed him, fearful that in the snowy silence he would wake someone up.

I sat on my suitcase, cuddling the basket to me, and contemplated the task in front of me. Got it! I would slide down on my case. I'd like to point out here that if you knew how famously unsporty I am, the mere idea of doing this would probably earn me a medal.

I was full of dread and anxiety when I turned the case over – as well I might be – and clutching Jicky, pushed off. At first it seemed quite pleasant, but then the suitcase, with the inevitability of a grand piano being hurled over a cliff, seemed to take on a momentum of its own. I was soon being hurtled downwards, spinning wildly out of control; blurred icy whiteness was all I could see. So I did the sensible thing and closed my eyes. I also, I'm ashamed to admit, made very girlie yelping noises of distress.

The mad toboggan ride ended, as was probably inevitable, with me being hurled into a bush at the end of the drive. I very narrowly missed a crumbling pillar, with a snow-covered dragon on the top, that was guarding the permanently open gate. The suitcase crashed into it, though, and at the last minute I let go of Jicky's basket and watched it somersault out of the gateway.

I jumped up, wincing at the sharp twinge in my shoulder, and slipped and stumbled over to collect Jicky. He was absolutely furious with me, and I tried to comfort him as best I could, without actually taking him out of his basket. That would be all I needed, a runaway monkey in the snowbound Cornish countryside. I could see the headlines now, it would be a retake on the beast of Bodmin, with Jicky being stalked by police marksmen.

I brushed myself down, and went to inspect my case. It was remarkably unscathed, perhaps I should write an unsolicited testimonial to the manufacturers? You know, along the lines of . . . *and I would just like to say that whilst making my escape from the madhouse of a man who toyed with my heart, in the early hours of a snowy morning, your suitcase played no little part in my safe exit* . . . Perhaps they'd be so impressed with my letter, I'd get free baggage for life.

I managed to get as far as the farm, and stood beneath a snow-smothered oak tree, waiting for the minicab. There was no sign of life at the farm, either. Perhaps Tom was doing whatever it is farmers do in the snow. Digging sheep out of drifts, or something equally rural that I knew nothing whatsoever about. I peered anxiously at Jicky, he was very quiet. Perhaps the cold had got to him; after all, he was used to tropical climes, not a Cornish winter.

I heard the cab before I could see it. The sound of a lone laboured engine was echoing around the silent countryside. I ran into the road, well, slipped and slid into the middle of the road, flailing my arms around. After we had packed my case, the cat basket and myself into the cab, and I had agreed with the driver that the snow was beautiful but treacherous, and that yes, I did love Cornwall and the Abbey, and *yes*, I was aware of what Jicky was doing, he asked me where it was I wanted to go.

'Bodmin station, please,' I said, peering out of the window and wishing that the driver could move a little faster. I had a horror of suddenly seeing any of the Stantons, or Tom.

The driver laughed. 'You'm out of luck there, my lover. Tryin' to get to London, are you? Well, you'm not be goin' today, an' that's a fact. Proper snowed in, we are. So where to now?'

Oh, *shit*. Where to now indeed? I stared out of the window. The cab was crawling along a country lane. All I could see either side of me was banks of snow, and hilly fields under a white blanket. Where the hell could I go? A hotel?

I asked the driver, who roared with laughter again. It seemed that he knew for a 'proper fact' that it was full. And all the B and Bs were closed.

'You'm in a right pickle,' he chortled.

Ha bloody ha. I was determined *not* to go back to the

Abbey, under any circumstances. I racked my brains, trying to think of somewhere suitable to go. The monkey sanctuary? Perhaps they'd take Jicky if I was included. Hardly likely, I agree. Odessa? No, I couldn't. What about that nice woman from the antique shop in Padstow, what was her name? Sonya, that was it. No again, I didn't even know her, or where she actually lived. What about the bishop? He had to take in waifs and strays, didn't he? I stroked Jicky through his wicker basket, and he pathetically took my hand into his small black paw. He felt *cold*.

'Do you know the vet? Patrick?' I asked.

'Course I do. Everyone knows Patrick.'

'Then take me there, please,' I said, relieved I'd finally thought of somewhere to go. I'd throw myself on to Patrick's mercy.

The car edged its slow way into Bodmin. There was no traffic at all, and the roads were still thick with snow, even in the high street. We took a road leading towards Wadebridge and eventually pulled up in front of a flat-fronted stone cottage, set well back from the road. The sound of dogs barking could be heard for miles around, which was probably why Patrick lived here, I thought. No neighbours, and endless woods to walk the dogs. I couldn't honestly think of any other reason why anyone would choose this location.

The driver pounded on the door, and told the dogs to shut up. I stood pathetically like an orphan in the snow waiting for the door to be flung open and words of welcome poured into my ears.

Five minutes later, when I had joined in the pounding of the door with the cab driver, I gave up. He wasn't in. The driver shrugged, and suggested we go to the back door, which was bound to be open, and that I wait inside for him. I expressed grave doubts at this, the dogs alone would probably rip me to shreds, let alone Jicky. Plus, I felt I couldn't just waltz into his house, uninvited. The driver, it seemed, had no such compunctions, and opened the back door, yelling at the surge of dogs to shut up, and it was only him, George, and a friend. The dogs, a greyhound, a boxer and a labrador, to my surprise heeded the order and retired to a series of dog baskets. George lugged my suitcase in, and left, assuring me that Patrick would probably be back soon, and was more than likely on call at a farm.

I sat myself down at the kitchen table to wait.

I stared around the kitchen. After the chaos and muddle, but sheer beauty of the Abbey, it was odd to be in a normal house again. Patrick's kitchen was small, orderly, neatly scrubbed and completely devoid of daft eccentricities. It was also (and this was a *good* thing) warm. It actually had central heating.

The dogs regarded me with friendly, or so I hoped, eyes, and I made sure that Jicky was safe in his basket on a worktop. I decided to make myself some tea, and as I put the kettle on, and searched for mug and tea bags, the dogs suddenly rushed to the front door. They had obviously heard their master's car, I thought, and anxiously prepared a speech for Patrick. I felt very nervous, and quite shy. I mean, it's not every day you

266

come home to find a comparative stranger, with a monkey and luggage, plonked in your kitchen. Oh, God! Supposing he thought I was trying to move in with him? I kicked my suitcase behind the kitchen door.

As soon as I heard the front door open and Patrick greeting the dogs, I called out to him.

He forestalled my speech by saying, 'Hello, Poppy, how nice to see you. I saw George up the road and he told me that you were here. Got the kettle on? Good.'

Well, so much for being nervous. George the gossip had deprived me of a *frisson* of fear and I felt distinctly put out.

Patrick laughed. 'I know what you're thinking! Yes, George is a great gossip. But you know, living in the country is like that. Everybody knows everyone's business. So come on, what's up? Why the escape from the Abbey? But before you tell me, let's have some tea and something to eat. I've got a raging hangover from last night, haven't you? And we've still got the hell of the pantomime and New Year's Eve to look forward to. My liver is going to be ruined! If I was a dog I'd probably put myself down . . . Now then, bacon and eggs?'

'Oh, yes, that would be lovely. But let me do them, you must be shattered. Have you been out all morning?' I said, opening the fridge and busying myself at the electric cooker.

Patrick gave a jaw-breaking yawn and sat at the table, stretching his long legs out in front of him. The greyhound came to sit with her long elegant nose in Patrick's lap, and he absent-mindedly stroked her ears.

'Thanks, I must say I am completely knackered. I've been on a moor farm most of the morning, a lot of trouble with the sheep, they've got—'

The phone rang, and Patrick stretched out an arm to reach it. The conversation that I could hear consisted of him grunting into the phone, and promising to be somewhere within the hour. He stood up and stretched. 'How long for the bacon and eggs?'

'Five minutes. Do eat something before you go out again, won't you?' I said, turning the heat up under the frying-pan and slapping some butter on the toast.

Patrick wolfed his breakfast down, and drank his tea standing up.

'I'll be back in a couple of hours, make yourself at home. Ignore the phone, I'll redirect it to my mobile. If you want a sleep, the spare room is quite acceptable, although not up to the Abbey standards.'

He headed towards the door, pushing the dogs back inside after him. He reappeared a second later, and put his head through the door. 'Oh, I forgot to say, it's a very pleasant surprise having you here. Tell me all about it later. Bye.'

He slammed out again, and I heard the sound of his car chugging away through the snow. I slowly washed up, and then sat down again, cradling a mug of tea in my hands. It was terribly quiet. The snow deadened any noise from outside, not that there would be any noise, I realised. This, after all, was the *country*. I wondered how people stood it, the lack of noise, I mean. I could quite see that it was beautiful, but it would drive me to very odd behaviour if I had to live here. I'd end up trying to talk to the squirrels or something, or take up making unsuitable friends on the internet.

I tortured myself by wondering if they were all awake at the Abbey yet. Odessa was probably making them breakfast, and they were all pitching in to help clear up the Abbey after last night's party. I felt very guilty about creeping off without saying goodbye, what a way to thank them all for their hospitality. Perhaps Alex and Claudia were making sleepy love together right now. Maybe Davey was feeling terrible about kissing me last night and wanted to explain why?

I sighed, and clutched my now empty mug to me.

The greyhound clicked her ivory spindles across the kitchen floor, and delicately pushed her muzzle under my hand for a stroke. Her amber eyes gazed into mine, and I immediately felt less sorry for myself. Perhaps that was the answer? I could surround myself with animals. That way, I'd never have to deal with men ever again, it was just too heartbreaking. I could be self-sufficient in the affection game, I mean, animals loved you no matter what, didn't they?

I jumped when the phone rang, but remembering Patrick's instructions, I ignored it.

I opened the fridge and stared straight at the bum end of a chicken. I decided to make a casserole for Patrick. It was the least I could do, he'd probably be starving when he came back. I found the radio, and switched it on to keep me company whilst I rootled

269

round a stranger's kitchen to find vegetables. I soon turned it off, though, as it was too damn Christmassy, and full of requests for close family and loved ones in this 'special festive season'. Oh, shut up, I said aloud, to the puzzlement of the three dogs who looked up at me, hoping for scraps.

I couldn't find anything to glam up the casserole with. It was a typical man's kitchen, if you know what I mean. No touches of extras, just the basics. I thought longingly of the Abbey kitchen, bursting with cream and saffron, garlic and peppers. I sighed again, and chopped some very wrinkled mushrooms that I'd found in the back of the fridge. I gave the casserole a final grinding of black pepper and put it in the oven on a very low heat. I gave the dogs a biscuit each and learnt from the tags round their necks that the greyhound (already the favourite) was called Dotsie, the boxer Buster, and the labrador, rather unimaginatively, was Labby.

I explored the rest of the cottage. The living-room held no surprises, other than a wincingly patterned green carpet and loop after loop of Christmas cards all signed from grateful patients.

I took Jicky, still in his basket, upstairs, and quickly deduced that the spare room was the one *with* the single bed, but *without* the vast quantity of dirty socks trailing out of a hamper. Maybe Patrick was right, perhaps I should try and get some sleep. My hangover had subsided, but I was very tired. I let Jicky out of his basket, and lay down, fully dressed, on the bed.

The next thing I knew, I was being awoken by the barks of the dogs. It took me a good few moments to remember where I was, and there was that disorienting moment of looking wildly round the room, searching for clues that would jog my memory.

I heard Patrick call up the stairs, 'Poppy, don't worry, it's not a mad axe murderer, it's me! What's that absolutely delicious smell coming from the kitchen?'

'Casserole,' I sleepily called downstairs.

'Fantastic! You wouldn't like to move in, would you?'

Well. It was the best offer I'd had for days, and it cheered me up no end. I called back that I'd be down in ten minutes. I got out of bed and found the bathroom where I splashed cold water on my face and dragged a brush through my hair. I tried hard not to look at the tidemark in the bath, or the toothpaste-spattered mirror. Why was it, I wondered, that although the Abbey was considerably dirtier than Patrick's, I minded less? Perhaps I was a snob at heart. The Abbey was so grand, the filth and squalor of certain aspects of it appeared to be like the tarnish on antique silver. Whereas the dirt in Patrick's bathroom was merely sordid. Oh, God, I hoped I wasn't going to turn into Claudia and demand bleach. I looked again at the bath, and knew with certainty that I couldn't possibly get into that till I had cleaned it. But then, I had happily climbed into an antique copper tub that had definitely seen better days. Maybe I was in love with all of the Stantons, and didn't mind their dirt? And although I'd snogged Patrick, I couldn't bear his personal dirt. I

271

pulled myself together and tried not to read too much into my unwillingness to have a wash.

'Poppy, where are you?'

Dithering about dirt. Deciding really, I suppose, that although you are very fanciable, I could no more sleep with you than I could fly in the air. Oh, *God*, what had I got myself into now?

'Coming! Put the heat on under the potatoes, will you?' I called down, going into the bedroom to collect Jicky. I glanced out of the window, and saw that the light was starting to fade. I looked hopefully for signs of a thaw, *surely* the trains would be running by now?

I made my way downstairs and hoped that Patrick did not misunderstand my motives for coming here. I walked into the kitchen and glanced nervously at him. He was feeding the dogs, and greeted me cheerfully.

'Did you manage to sleep, then? I *am* pleased. Jicky OK? What do you want me to do to the potatoes?'

I was glad to see that he was bright and breezy, with no hint of flirtatiousness, which I didn't think I could stand at the moment.

'Oh, I was going to mash them. How was your day? I still feel pretty awful, and I've slept all day, you must feel shattered!' I said, getting out plates and finding a colander.

Through mouthfuls of chicken casserole I heard all about the state of sheep on the moors, how the snow was really hard work for the farmers, how the native ponies coped with it, and how very, very stupid chickens were, on the whole. I glanced down at my plate, and saw the bones of the stupid chicken. Oh, dear. I was pretty sure that if I was a vet I'd be a vegetarian.

'Right, enough about my day. It's your turn. Why are you here? Not that I'm complaining,' Patrick said, smiling at me.

I started to tell him about the train journey down here, and my encounter with Alex. As I spoke, I was well aware that he could totally get the wrong impression of me, but he just nodded and listened. I then told him about Claudia's arrival (but not her pregnancy) and was very indiscreet and told him about Tabitha.

He whistled. 'Well, that is a turn-up for the books, could well be the making of her. On the other hand she might just dump it, or them, if what you say about Odessa is true, on Jocasta and Edward, and run off with the workshop thing, whatever it's called. Still, about Alex. I know you probably don't want to hear this, but he really has got quite a reputation, you know.'

'So I've gathered,' I said gloomily.

'Look, cheer up do, you never have to see any of the Stantons again, although I suppose unless you want to get a new job, you'll have to see Davey.'

That was the whole point, I felt like screaming at him. I *do* want to see them again, *all* of them. Desperately. Otherwise I could well be stuck in a place like this, with someone like *you.*

Oh, God, that was unfair. Patrick was nice. You know, *nice*. Like a cup of tea is *nice*. It's probably the most

273

damning word in the whole of the English language, isn't it?

'Look, Patrick,' I said, 'do you think I could phone the station? I really have to get home, you know.'

'Be my guest, but there's absolutely no point. There won't be any trains, the whole of Cornwall and Devon is blocked off.'

I sighed.

'Look, I have to go out tonight to the pantomime, I assume you don't want to go?'

I shook my head. I couldn't possibly face them all.

'I thought not,' Patrick said. 'Then may I suggest you make yourself comfortable in front of the TV, and have an early night? I'll be very quiet coming in. Then tomorrow we'll tackle the problem of how to get you home. Oh, and mum's the word. I won't tell anyone you're here – though, mind you, George has probably broadcast it to the entire village by now!'

I thought of all the fun I was going to miss. Arthur belting his song out, Jocasta's set designs and costumes, Odessa's mince pies, Edward and Davey's enjoyment of the whole proceedings, even the policeman playing Baron Hardup. And, of course, Alex.

Well, it was all of my own doing, I reflected, curling up in an armchair half an hour later with the dogs at my feet and Jicky around my neck. I opened the box of chocolates that Patrick had given me, and started to work my way down the layers.

Chapter Nineteen

I slept like a log. Probably due to the disgustingly large amount of chocolate that I'd gorged on. I don't care what anyone says, if in trouble, eat. That's my motto. I wondered how that would translate into Latin. *Troublus Gorgeum*, or something. Perhaps I could have it inscribed on a coffee mug. The first thing I did when I woke was to kick off the bedspread (very horrible, acrylic and a fetching shade of mauve) and look out of the window. The damn snow was still there. The sky was a shadowy dark grey, and I could detect small flurries of snowflakes tumbling from it. I felt unbelievably homesick – homesick for the Abbey, or homesick for my own poky little flat in London, I couldn't tell. I could hear the dogs barking somewhere outside, and I heard Patrick in the kitchen. I called out good morning to him, and went downstairs to quiz him on last night's events. I had meant to stay up and catch him when he came home, but I'd fallen asleep in front of the TV, and later dragged myself to bed.

The kitchen was buzzing with the washing machine

going, the radio on, and slices of bread popping out of the toaster.

'Morning, Patrick. How was the panto?' I asked, trying very hard to be cheerful. 'Did Arthur's song go down well? And what about Baron Hardup? Could everyone get there because of the snow? How was Jocasta? Did she say anything about me? And Alex? Did you see him? . . .' I tailed off when I saw the expression on his face.

'What's the matter?' I asked.

He looked at me, and said slowly, 'Poppy, I don't know. I think there's something very wrong. None of the Stantons turned up. None of them. They're not answering the phone, which isn't strange at all, but for none of them to come to the panto, well, that *is* unusual. Everyone was talking about it.'

'Maybe they're snowed in?' I said.

'No. I mean, it's very difficult to get up and down to the Abbey, but Jocasta and Edward would have walked there if necessary. They never, ever miss it.'

Oh, God. Maybe they were all ill? Maybe Alex had killed Claudia? Maybe Edward had killed Tabitha? Maybe Davey had gone berserk with a carving knife? Or maybe they just hadn't felt like it, I told myself firmly. I voiced this possibility to Patrick.

'I don't think you quite understand. Last night was the final dress rehearsal, which, traditionally, all the friends and family, in fact *anyone* who has had *anything* to do with it, goes to. Then the first night is January the first. I mean, Jocasta is *always* there, you know, making last-minute alterations to things, and Edward and

276

Davey are behind her carrying her notebook and picking up after her. Even Alex, if he's at home, goes. *Always*. None of them would miss it.' Patrick sounded worried.

I went to make myself a cup of tea, as I can't even think straight in the mornings without one. As I put my hand on the kettle, there was an abrupt cessation of noise. The radio stopped, the washing machine was no longer whirring and the lights went out.

'Oh, shit!' Patrick said.

'What? What is it?' I asked, my hand still on the kettle, wondering if it was something I'd done.

'Power cut,' Patrick said gloomily. 'It happens sometimes in the snow. Damn nuisance it is, too. Everything's electric here, no gas. Damn!'

The room was very quiet and gloomy. I had a leap of imagination to the Abbey where at least they had the Aga, open fires, and an abundant supply of candles. Here was all central heating, an electric oven and microwave.

'Have you had a bath yet?' Patrick asked.

'No. Why? Do I pong? It's probably Jicky, he does tend to live round my neck and—'

'No,' Patrick laughed. 'All I meant was, go and have one now, there'll be absolutely no hot water later. I'm going to go and see if I can get any wood for the fire in the living-room. I usually just switch on the electric fire, but the chimney *does* work.'

I went upstairs and had a lukewarm bath, cursing the weather and the circumstances. I tried very hard not to

277

touch the sides of the bath, which of course is impossible when you are actually in it, but I had scoured it as best I could beforehand. Why, oh why, had I left the Abbey? I turned over in my mind what could have kept them all from going to the pantomime. I could only come up with Cassandra-like configurations. Maybe Edward had ordered Tabitha out from the Abbey, and Claudia reigned supreme, ordering them all to stay at home and bleach everything in sight. Ridiculous thought.

I dressed as quickly as I could. It was surprisingly cold already upstairs without the central heating. I went down and helped Patrick to carry in a pile of snowy logs.

'They're damp now, God knows how long they'll take to dry out. Still, let's try for a fire, shall we?' he said.

We crouched in front of a very sulky fire, and pondered what to do.

'Poppy, I don't want to disappoint you too much, but there really is very little chance of you getting back to London. Tomorrow is Sunday, and the trains are erratic, to say the least, at this time of the year. We're sandwiched between Christmas and New Year. You are very welcome to stay here as long as you need to, you know.'

'Thank you, Patrick, that's very kind of you.'

Patrick smiled at me, and held my eye a fraction too long. Oh, God, here it comes, I thought. I'd been expecting it for some time really, but was still not sure what to do about it. The last thing I wanted was a tussle with Patrick in front of the fire. He moved slowly towards me along the couch. Oh, God, oh, *God*. I was like a rabbit frozen by indecision, caught by headlights. Had I really snogged him the night before? The punch must have been as strong as I thought it was. Your Honour. How could I? I mean, he was good-looking and all that, but I didn't want *him*. I wanted Alex. Oh, *pooh*. I felt the accursed blush start on my face. Supposing I pushed him away and in a fit of pique he threw me out in the snow? Then what? That was just plain silly, I realised. He wasn't like that. Was he?

I wriggled away from him, and said, 'Patrick, the thing is—'

'I know, I know,' he groaned. 'Just my luck, really. I get a gorgeous woman in my house, we're practically snowed in and she's hankering after the local bounder!'

'The local *bounder*? Really? That's a bit Edwardian, isn't it?' I said, secretly horrified, but trying to cover it up with a show of what I thought was sophistication. Don't think that the gorgeous bit had left me unmoved either.

'Well, you know what I mean. I just don't get it with women and Alex, you know? I mean, he's a looker, I suppose, and he's funny and charming. But he's always got a trail of broken-hearted women following him around . . .'

I suspected as much.

'. . . and then there's Claudia. Well, I mean, she's a *knockout*, isn't she?'

'And knocked up,' I said.

279

'What?'

'Oh, yes, I overheard them. So, you do see, I *know* he's out of the question but, well, I'm sorry, Patrick. I rather think I'm in love with all of the Stantons, not just Alex. Sorry,' I said lamely.

'Well, maybe you'll get over it,' he said cheerfully, patting my shoulder.

I doubted that, but I tried to smile in an encouraging sort of way.

'What about you?' I asked, trying to change the subject, but genuinely curious as well. 'Don't you have a girlfriend or anything?'

'I was married. She, rather, Moira, left me about two years ago.'

'Oh, I'm sorry.'

'That's OK. She hated my job, hated living in the country and didn't like animals much. So, you see—'

I burst out laughing. '*Not* the best qualifications for the wife of a vet,' I said.

'No.'

We stared at the flames of the fire for a while.

'Alex gave her a lift to London. I haven't heard from her since,' he said distantly.

I see. No wonder Alex wasn't his favourite person around here.

We had a fairly miserable sort of day. Most of our time was taken up with finding dry firewood (I did see a particularly horrible reproduction Georgian set of coffee tables, that I thought would be better off as firewood) and searching for candles.

'Well, the dogs won't starve, but I don't hold out much hope for us,' Patrick said, his head in a kitchen cupboard. 'Have you ever tried Kennomeat?'

'Yuck. Don't even joke about it, what am I going to do about Jicky?'

I knew from experience that only hothouse grapes, supplemented by a banana, would do him.

'Well, let's worry about that after he's polished off the fruit bowl, shall we? I'm more worried about us. I'm bloody starving, aren't you?'

We dragged out the contents of the fridge and settled in front of the fire. We had a picnic of Stilton, some limpish celery and water biscuits.

'Oh, well, we can always get stuck into the chocolates,' Patrick said.

''Fraid not, I think I overdosed on them last night,' I said guiltily.

Patrick's mobile went off, and he answered it immediately. After he had finished his conversation, he said, 'That was Tom, he—'

'Did you ask him about the Abbey? Are they OK?' I interrupted.

'No, he wants me to go over there, he's got a horse in foal. Would you like to come too? It's going to be a hell of a drive, but at least we'll get a warm meal over there.'

Patrick found me an old sheepskin coat of his, and tried to persuade me to wear his boots, stuffed with socks, but I had to decline the offer. We decided to take Jicky with us, and pushed a blanket in his basket for warmth. The dogs piled into the back. As I clambered in his car, I said, 'I thought all you country types had Land Rovers?'

'Hmm, well, my partner's got it, and he's in Plymouth, so we'll have to make do with this.'

This was a very old station-wagon that had stacks of vet equipment scattered all round it, and I was very pleased to see had a large bar of chocolate in the glove compartment. Although, judging by the weather outside, we should by rights have Kendal mint cake. That's what all the mountain climbers had, wasn't it?

The car toiled through the country lanes. I was willing it to go faster, as I was dying to know what was wrong with them all at the Abbey. I'd even prepared myself for the embarrassment of seeing Alex again. *And* Davey. Although I had racked my brains, I still couldn't come up with a plausible reason why he had suddenly kissed me.

It was very gloomy out, with small flakes of snow falling softly from the grey sky. The fields all looked frozen, and I pitied any animals left out in this. It took us ages to reach the farm, and when we finally pulled up outside, I jumped out of the car, taking Jicky with me. I slid along in the icy courtyard, and Tom opened the door to greet us.

'Patrick, I'm proper glad to see you! Let's go straight to the stables. Oh, hello, Poppy, you'll find Melza and the kids in the kitchen, go and get yourself warm.'

I watched Patrick and Tom disappear round the side

of the courtyard, and headed off to the warmth of the kitchen.

Demelza was standing stirring something at the Aga, in the classic pregnant woman's stance. One hand holding a wooden spoon, the other pressed palm flat in the small of her back. Her tummy was huge, and it looked as though she *must* give birth any second. The two children were at the kitchen table, industriously colouring in something by candlelight.

'Hello,' Demelza said, smiling at me. 'So, that's where you got to! They'm all worried 'bout you up at the Abbey, seeing as there's no trains an' that. You must be cold, would a cup of tea suit?'

'That would be lovely,' I said, glancing around the kitchen. I'd never actually been inside a farm before, and was a bit disappointed to see that it didn't look anything like my idea of one. Granted, my ideas were about sixty years old and were a cross between the *Archers* and *Cold Comfort Farm*, but there was no sukebind draped over the fireplace, nor were there horse brasses, or bits of tractors *á la* Pop Larkin, littered over the surfaces. There was, however, an Aga, and that would have to satisfy any rural urges I seemed to have.

The two children were introduced to me, Eve and Toby, who I had only seen fast asleep in the back of the car on Christmas Eve. They were ravishingly beautiful, with grave dark eyes and curly black hair. They were, of course, entranced with Jicky, and I reluctantly agreed to let him out of his basket. He immediately clung to my neck, and the children stroked him. They were incredibly gentle and quiet.

'They'm a bit shy, so make the most of it, the noise level will soon go up. They were overexcited this mornin' at the prospect of being snowed in with no electricity, but that seems to have worn off,' Demelza said, smiling at them. She gave me a mug of tea, and went back to stirring at the Aga.

'So, how's everyone up at the Abbey?' I asked.

She glanced at me, and then bent down to take a tray of something out of an oven. Eve and Toby stopped being little angels, and turned into normal clamouring children, pleading for a hot biscuit.

'Guests first,' Demelza warned, giving me two golden nutty biscuits. 'Now, why don't you two go into another room and play?'

They went off resentfully, clutching sticky hot handfuls of biscuits, with a resigned look about them. I remembered that look well, it was an 'oh God, grownup stuff' look. Banishment back to being a child.

Things *must* be bad, I decided, if Demelza had to send the children away to talk to me.

She came to sit at the kitchen table, slowly lowering herself gently on to a chair.

'It's right bad, I can tell you. They've took on somethin' awful,' she said with a certain amount of relish.

'What, though? I mean, what exactly is the problem, why didn't they go to the pantomime?' I asked, relieved that I was just about to find out.

'Well,' Demelza said, blowing gently on her tea, drawing out the story for all it was worth. 'Well, we've not seen the likes of it. The Stantons not talkin' to one another! And them all had a fight. Alex an' Davey, then Jocasta and Edward. Took on somethin' awful, they did. Even Tabitha, who don't normally say boo to a goose, she's proper upset with her brothers. And as for lady muck, you know, that Claudia, well, she's had 'em all runnin' around after 'er. Upset Odessa, she'm left the Abbey! Said that if that madam was goin' to be there, she'd have to leave! Can you believe it? Odessa gone? Somethin' awful, it is. Awful.' She rubbed her huge swollen tummy contentedly.

'Yes, but Demelza, what was it all *about*?' I said, resisting the urge to shake her.

Eve and Toby came tumbling into the kitchen, demanding more biscuits. Demelza gave me a definite 'not in front of the children' look.

'Mum, can I take the sledge out?'

'Mum, can I go to the stable to see the horse being borned?'

'Mum, can I have a monkey?'

'Mum, can I have three biscuits? Then I won't have to have any soup!'

'Mum, can I, can I? Please, Mum, can I?'

Demelza said they could *not* go on the sledge without their father, and even *with* their father they could only go on the drive up to the Abbey, and *not* on the road; yes, they could go in the stable, but had to be very quiet ('We *know* that, we're not stupid!'); and no, they

285

couldn't have a monkey; and three biscuits was not for small children, it was for pigs.

They oinked their way from the kitchen, pulling on hats and getting tangled up in coats and scarves.

'It must be lovely, growing up here,' I said. Thinking of the vast fields, with hidden treasures to play in, the animals, the wonderful food and the peerless Demelza as the sort of mother that all children deserve.

'If you count the highest unemployment figures in Britain, poor education and non-existent public transport. Oh, yes, and then there's rich Londoners buying up cottages so that the kids'll never be able to afford to live in the place they were born in, an' their poor parents workin' every hour there is – Oh, I'm right sorry! Ignore me, I'm very nitzy, I'm due any day now, and I get like that.'

I could well imagine. If I had been as pregnant as Demelza, and was practically snowed in, I'd put good money on me being more than 'nitzy'. I'd be near hysteria.

I jumped up and went to fetch the teapot to pour Demelza another cup.

'Thanks, but I'll be peeing all day if I have another one!' she said. 'Why don't you try and get up the driveway to the Abbey? I reckon they'd be right glad to see you.'

I longed to go up there, but didn't feel brave enough. Brave enough to face the icy treacherous slope, or brave enough to see them all again.

I shook my head.

Demelza rubbed the small of her back and winced.

'Is there anything I can do?' I asked anxiously.

She gave me a weary smile and said, 'Oh, I'll be all right in a minute. All that fuss up the Abbey, though, has made me realise that making a will is important. Think of all the trouble Edward and Jocasta have caused with it!'

'What about the will?' I asked eagerly, hoping that Demelza would shed some light on it.

But she just shrugged. 'Why don't you go over to the stable, and bring the kids back in half an hour for some lunch. Patrick an' you, too, of course. Could you tell Tom—'

She stopped talking and hunched her shoulders.

'Ow. Oh, shit! Poppy, go and get Tom! Now! Tell him the baby's coming!'

I stared at her. Oh, my God. She was having the baby! Now. Oh, *God*. Oh, shit shit shit. I found that I was breathing very quickly as I fumbled for the door handle. Snow hit me in the face as I stood outside the door, the sky was raining white down feathers on me. I went back inside and said, 'Demelza, where's the stable? Which building is it?'

'End building, other side of the courtyard . . . Ouch.'

'OK, I'm going. Please don't worry . . .'

I ran outside, hearing her shout after me, 'Poppy, don't run! Walk slowly, you'll fall over!'

I had a nightmare five minutes while I pulled open every farm door I could find; tractors, tools and a puzzled-looking cow stared at me. I started to call out

287

for Patrick and Tom, and guided by the voices I tracked them down.

'Tom, Tom, it's Demelza, she's having the baby! Quick, do hurry!' I was jumping up and down in front of him, trying to impart the urgency of the situation to him. 'She's saying ouch a lot, oh, please hurry! What shall I do? What *can* I do?'

The children were delighted with the news. Tom told me to calm down, and it would probably be hours before anything happened.

I stared at him in disbelief, and called on Patrick for support. Patrick, who was kneeling on some straw, doing something I didn't really want to see to the nether regions of a horse, agreed with him.

'Bugger about the snow, though, Tom, I don't know we'll get her into the hospital. Here, take my mobile and call an ambulance.'

I felt a fool, why hadn't I thought of that? I snatched the phone from Patrick, and began punching in the deeply thrilling triple nine. I pressed the phone to my ear, and heard nothing. I looked at it, and saw that there was no signal. I'd try outside.

'Right, you kids stay with Patrick. Come on, Poppy, let's go and help Melza,' Tom said, striding outside. 'You might as well pack that in,' he said, nodding at the mobile. 'You won't get a signal down here in this weather, and the main line is down, we'll have to manage on our own.' He took my arm as we fought our way through the snow to the kitchen door. I could understand people getting lost in blizzards. The whiteness seemed to be blowing horizontally, making everything shift in distance and location. The snow had picked up, and was swirling dangerously around us.

Tom shoved the door open, and called out to his wife. Demelza was still sitting at the table, head in hands.

'Tom, thank God you're here. There's something wrong! It don't feel right! Get Odessa, now!'

Something wrong? Something *wrong*! Of *course* there was. It was the ideal situation for something to go wrong.

I stood in the kitchen wringing my hands, looking on uselessly as Tom comforted Demelza. Tom glanced at me, and I could see the confidence that he'd shown in the stables was gone. He looked worried. Which, in turn, scared the shit out of me.

'Poppy, stay here with Demelza, I'm going to get Odessa.'

'No! Stay with me Tom, please.' Demelza's voice was urgent.

'Yes, stay with her.' My voice was equally urgent. 'Do, *please*. I'll go and get Odessa, where is she?'

Please don't leave me with Demelza, I can't even accurately describe the facts of life, let alone assist in a home delivery. Please. Don't. Leave. Me. With *your* pregnant wife.

Tom looked doubtfully at me, then Demelza gave a terrible groan and clutched his arm. I could see blood seeping through her skirt.

'Where *is* she?' I shouted at him.

'Turn right out of the farm, down the lane, over the first stile on your left, stick to the right-hand edge of the field, over the stile at the other side and you'll see her cottage. Take my torch, and put Melza's boots on. Hurry!'

Trust me, here, I hurried.

'Don't bother telling Patrick, he can't leave the horse now anyway,' Tom shouted hopelessly after me.

I had absolutely no intention of telling Patrick. I was on a *mission*. OK, don't panic, don't run, walk quickly. Breathe. *Right* out of the farm, along the lane to a stile on the *left*. How long down the lane? A couple of yards? A couple of *miles?* Jesus. I was stumbling in the lane, the snow hitting me in the face, making it hard to breathe, let alone *see*.

The going was hard. That's what they say on Channel Four about the racing, don't they? Hard going at Goodwood today. Well, this was fucking hard. I could feel my chest tighten in panic. Where was the sodding stile? I switched the torch on, and was immediately hypnotised by the vortex-like pattern of the snowflakes seeming to rush into the beam. I switched it off again and, bent nearly double against the wind and snow, staggered on down the lane. I saw what I took to be a gap in the fence, and kicked some snow around. Yes, it was a stile. Thank God. I climbed over it, taking care not to slip. OK, stick to the *right*-hand side of the field. This was even harder than the lane. I was practically knee deep in snow, and it was getting dark. I switched

290

the torch on again, and thought I saw something move on my left. Shit, what was it? Surely, no animals would be out in this? I couldn't let myself stop, so I hurried on, trying not to be frightened.

All the old stories of the beast of Bodmin came rushing into my mind, and I clenched the torch very hard, almost crushing my numb fingers. Christ, supposing I got lost out here? Supposing I got frostbite? I brushed some snow out of my eyes, and hurried on. The field seemed enormous, and the ground was rising.

I was panting now, and sweating under the layers of clothes that had been forced on me. Patrick's sheepskin coat was very heavy, and was rubbing the back of my neck. I pulled my scarf away from me, and stumbled on. Where was the other stile? Where was the end of this interminable bloody field? I thought of the blood that I had seen coming from Demelza, and quickened my steps.

I was starting to wonder if I was even in the right bloody field, it seemed *endless*. I could hardly see where I was going, and the torch was about as helpful as a lit match in a high wind. I kept thinking that I could see something ahead of me, and told myself over and over again that I was being fanciful. Right, breathe, walk, check for fence, stop thinking about wild beasts, spooks and ice witches. I put my hand in front of my face to try and shield my eyes from the blinding snow – there *was* something in front of me.

A small, spherical, silver shape. It had light coming from it. Christ! What the hell was it? It didn't look like anything I had ever seen before, and I'm quite sure you will question my sanity here, but I honestly thought it was some sort of alien life form. Oh, *great. Really* sensible idea, beam down in the middle of a field in a sodding blizzard! What should I do? What in the name of *arse, what* should I do? I stumbled forwards, falling over and dropping my torch. Oh, God, I was practically on top of it now.

'Welcome, we mean you no harm,' I croaked out, feeling utterly ridiculous, and quite terrified.

'You'm be a right daft bugger,' came a well-known voice.

Chapter Twenty

'Odessa!'

She helped me up and I fell upon her, laughing hysterically. She was wearing the most extraordinary jacket and trousers, made from what looked like tin foil.

'It's the latest outdoor techno cloth,' she proudly bellowed in my ear. 'My Arthur gave it me, what d'you think of it? Keeps you right warm, it does.'

'What are you doing here? I was just coming to get you,' I stuttered.

She grabbed my arm and turned me round, marching me back towards the farm.

'Demelza's in trouble—' I said.

'I know, I know, that's where I was goin'. Didn't expect to see you, though. Right proper fool you looked! What did you think I was?'

I was glad that the darkness and the snow prevented her from seeing my blushes.

We hurried down the field. It seemed a much more benign place with Odessa by my side.

'But how did you know?' I persisted.

'I saw her yesterday, right nitzy she was, I reckoned I

should come down. I tried to phone, but all the lines is down.'

I'd like to say that I helped Odessa over the stile, but it was, in fact, the other way round. We trudged up the lane, and saw that someone had put a lit candle in the window of the farm. That small flickering light was such a welcome sight, I nearly cried with pleasure. Odessa ran through the courtyard and pushed open the kitchen door. I followed behind, struggling out of my boots and taking the heavy sheepskin coat off with relief.

A flood of warmth coming from the Aga washed over me, and I gazed round the kitchen. Tom was bending over Demelza, who was clinging on to the kitchen table; her hair was wet with sweat and was sticking to her face.

Odessa wasted no time at all, and bent over her, murmuring in her ear. Then she straightened up and started issuing orders.

'Poppy, heat some water and make an infusion from this.' She handed me a packet of what looked like leaves and twigs. 'Tom, get that table clear and scrubbed. Now come on, my lover, let's get you comfy, shall we? I'll want pillows and cushions, blankets and towels.'

Tom and I leapt to her bidding. I poured hot water over the strong-smelling bits of vegetation. It smelt quite disgusting, and I nervously prodded it around in the mug.

'Put a drop of honey in it,' Odessa commanded. She

had divested herself of her space-age clothes, and was rolling her sleeves up. She washed her hands at the sink, and glanced at my white face. She followed my eyes to the puddle of blood on the kitchen floor.

'Clear that up, there's a good girl,' she said in a neutral voice, and gave me an encouraging smile. I found a bucket and mop, and did the best I could. Tom came bounding back in the room with piles of cushions and blankets.

'Right, I'll need some more candles in here. Now, Poppy, you help me get Melza up on the table.'

Oh, God. Oh, *God*. As I came closer to Demelza and helped her up, I could feel her trembling. I stroked her back, and tried to be as gentle as I could in touching her. There was a certain smell coming from her as well, I realised. A warm, animal smell. Odessa and I lifted her to the table, and she groaned in pain. I very nearly groaned in sympathy, but was too frightened of Odessa's scorn to do so.

Odessa made a high nest of the pillows and cushions, and gave Demelza the mug of herbs to drink. I gazed at Demelza with a mixture of horror and admiration. It seemed impossible to me that anyone would put themselves through all of this willingly. I mean, she'd even done this more than once! Impossible! Demelza gave a shout of pain, and drew her knees up to her chest.

I think I decided right there that I was very happy to be everybody's and anybody's universal aunt, as long as I never, *ever* had to go through this myself.

Odessa was talking to Demelza, and urging her to finish her drink, and rest for a while.

'Where are the children?' Demelza whispered.

'Still in the stable with Patrick, it seems you both are giving birth tonight,' Tom said, smiling at his wife. But Odessa soon put a stop to that.

'Tom, I want you out of here now, go and do something useful, there's a good boy. Birthin' be women's business, so you make a move, you hear? What a load of nonsense, having *men* around at a time like this. Go and see Patrick. Tell him I might need his bag later on, off you go.'

Need Patrick's *bag*? This was more than I could *begin* to cope with. Awful visions of brutal veterinary instruments came into my mind. I glanced nervously at Demelza, but I suppose she had other things on her mind at the moment. Tom kissed his wife and reluctantly left the room. Odessa took control again, clearly not believing in any modern nonsense like the husband having anything to do with this process at all.

It was like being in the cave of an Arthurian witch, and the candlelight lent itself beautifully to this primordial scene. Odessa was the head of the coven, without a doubt, or maybe some medieval apothecary, dishing out potions. Demelza was the beautiful girl, going through the ordeal of fire, and me? Well, not even a bit player in this grand drama. Just helping out. Yes, that was me, just helping out.

I made another foul-smelling brew under Odessa's

direction, and spoonfed it to Demelza. Whatever it was, it seemed to have the right effect.

Demelza clung to me, crying and groaning.

'Right, my handsome, push. Come along with you, push!' Odessa called.

This went on for longer than I really thought was humanly possible. Then amongst the blood, tears, sweat and just sheer gore, it happened. The only day-to-day miracle that goes on around the globe. A new baby came into the world.

I was crying, Demelza was crying and only Odessa remained in charge of her emotions.

'It's a girl, a right handsome, beautiful baby girl,' she said, in tones of deep satisfaction. I helped Odessa to wash her, then Demelza, and then I was dispatched to fetch Tom, Patrick and the children.

'Make them wait for ten minutes whilst I get Melza lookin' human again,' Odessa said.

I nodded happily and, grabbing at torch and coat, stepped outside. I gasped at the beauty of the snowy landscape. The wind had dropped, the snow had stopped and the moon was out. It shone down on a magical night, a new baby was ready to welcome it. I crunched through the crisp snow to the stable and pushed my way in. There, too, the everyday miracle had happened; a stumble-legged, long-eyelashed foal was nuzzling its mother. It looked ridiculously like a Disney cartoon.

'Congratulations, you've got a beautiful baby daughter,' I said to Tom.

He shouted with delight and picked Eve and Toby up and whirled them round.

'Come on, let's go and see her!' he shouted.

Patrick grinned and we all started to congratulate one another. I joined the children in dancing round and round in the hay-strewn stable. They, I have to say, were far more interested in the new foal than their new sister.

'What are you calling it, or him, or is it a her?' I asked them.

'It's a boy, silly!'

'Oh.'

'We don't know yet, I want to call him Racer, like the fairground horse in the Abbey, but Eve wants to call him Snowflake, which is so soppy, besides being a *girl's* name, so we have to wait till we can agree,' Toby said seriously.

We all made tracks in the deep white snow back to the farm, where we saw Odessa holding a heavily wrapped baby up to the moon. She handed the bundle to Tom, and he stared delightedly at his new daughter.

Patrick and I hung back in the kitchen, which was now clear, for a few moments to give Tom time to greet Demelza, then we followed into the living-room. Demelza was on the couch, cuddling her children and being fussed over by Tom.

'Do you think we should go?' I whispered to Patrick.

'Don't be so daft,' Odessa said. 'We'm got to wet the babe's head. 'Sides, you'll never shift that car in this.'

'She's got a point,' Patrick said, looking out of the

window. 'It must be ten inches out there at least. Looks like we're here for the night.'

That pleased me immensely. I didn't feel in the way, or at all unwelcome. I had been being polite when I thought we should scarper, and it was lovely to feel part of this family. Nearly as good as being at the Abbey. Nearly.

Odessa piled bowls and spoons on the table, and all of us, apart from Demelza who had been carried to bed by Tom, greedily spooned delicious soup and hot bread into our hungry mouths.

I spied a banana in the fruit bowl, and asked if I could have it for Jicky. I went to his basket, and then froze. The door was open.

'Where is he?' I asked.

No one answered.

'Where is he? Has anyone seen him?'

The children looked guiltily at each other.

I ran around the farmhouse, calling his name, but heard no answering chatter anywhere. I tried to keep calm and remember when I had last seen him. It was impossible, so much had happened that day and we were all confused. The children searched the upstairs and I looked downstairs. Odessa was putting her coat on in the kitchen, as was Patrick.

'Where are you going?' I asked.

'We'm having a look outside,' Odessa said.

Oh, shit. Outside? He wouldn't last a moment.

I grabbed my coat and joined them.

'Which way you'm go, when you went to fetch me?' Odessa asked.

'Why?'

'I reckons he tried to follow you.'

Oh, no. Poor little Jicky.

We trudged around the back of the courtyard and went down to the lane. Patrick and Odessa played the beams of light streaming from their torches over the ground. I called and called to him till I was hoarse. Then, to my delight, I spotted him. He was a small dark shape huddled against the base of a tree in the lane. I rushed over to him, and gathered him to me. He was so cold.

'Patrick, he's very cold, can we do something?'

Patrick took him from me, and I felt Odessa put her hand on my shoulder.

'Poppy, I'm so sorry. He's dead,' Patrick said.

'No, no, he's not, honestly. He's just very, very cold. It's all my own stupid fault. Here, give him to me, I'll warm him up,' I said, reaching for him.

'No. Poppy, leave him with me. I'm sorry. He's gone. There's nothing we can do.'

'But you're a vet!' I screamed. 'You must be able to do something!'

Odessa's hand tightened on my shoulder and then I knew it was true. I stood and cried in the snow.

Patrick strode away carrying Jicky, and Odessa stood beside me.

I couldn't believe it. He was the reason that I'd come down to this mad place, after all. And although I know

300

that I'd moaned about his bad habits, he had been such a comfort. Never again would I feel his tiny paws delicately stroking my hair, or feel his warm little body cuddled into my neck. Or hear his answering chatter when I called his name. I stood sobbing in the cold night air, oblivious to the snow and my icy feet.

After a while Odessa said, 'You have a good cry, my lover, you've lost a friend. That's right. Another one will find you, because that's what he did, he found you. So will the next.'

I thought about what she had said, maybe she was right. Jicky had found me, and led me into this Cornish adventure. If Odessa believed another friend would find me, I believed her. I snuffled and sniffed and found that Odessa with her usual second guessing was holding out a tissue for me.

'That's right, my handsome. No more tears now. We'm a new life waiting in there for us. Let's go indoors.'

I nodded, and wiped my eyes. I looked longingly up at the moon, wishing that I had the power to turn back time and make sure Jicky was safe in his basket.

Odessa laughed and handed me another tissue. 'No man, or woman, come to that, can change time. 'Tis impossible. An' it weren't your fault either; if his time was ready, he were ready. Same as all of us has to be, man nor beast it makes no difference.'

She reached for my arm and we slowly walked towards the farm.

'What was it you said again? When you saw me in the

301

field? We mean you no 'arm – what did you think I was? Some little green man?'

I nodded again and she laughed delightedly.

I gave a weak smile and followed her back to the farm.

The children greeted me with hugs, and Eve clung to me.

'It's OK, really,' I said, squeezing them both.

'We've decided what we're going to call the foal,' Toby said importantly. 'We're going to call him Jicky.'

I felt the tears spring to my eyes again, and said unsteadily, 'I think that would be lovely!'

Patrick smiled anxiously at me, and I smiled back. Tom came into the room carrying a bottle of champagne, and we cracked it open and drank to the baby, and to Demelza. The children clamoured for a glass, and Tom let them have a tiny amount each. They pretended to be instantly drunk, and staggered around the room, clutching each other, till Tom decided it was their bedtime.

To my horror I saw that Odessa seemed to be getting ready to go outside. She was clambering into her tin-foil trews, and I said, 'Odessa, you can't possibly go home in this! Tom, Patrick, tell her!'

They all laughed, and Odessa said, 'I've been walkin' these fields for over fifty years, it's a lovely night, now. A full moon, and deep snow. I'll be home in a jiffy, 'sides Arthur'll be waiting for me. He don't like me to be out late, so don't you fret, you daft bugger.'

I was very disappointed. I had been hoping to get

Odessa to myself to hear the truth about what had been going on at the Abbey. I pleaded with her not to go, but she was insistent. I guessed by Tom and Patrick's behaviour that there was nothing to be done to dissuade her, although I was very pleased to see that Patrick was donning his outdoor gear, and said he was going to walk her across the field, and then check on the horse and foal in the stable. She seemed happy with this suggestion, and didn't complain too much.

'You'm only trying to get hold of my cures, I knows that. Well, don't think you'll be lucky, 'cause you'm won't.' She turned to Tom and said, 'Now, first thing, you get Melza to that nasty hospital, they'll need to check her, mind. Not that they know anything!'

Tom smiled. 'I will. And Odessa, thank you.'

She made a dismissive sound and headed towards the door. She stopped and looked me in the eyes. 'And as for you, yer daft bugger, get yourself up to the Abbey. I reckons Davey needs to see you, and as for Alex, well, I said before, what will be, will be. But the sooner that lying, scheming trollop leaves, the better it'll be for all of us. You'm the person to do it, you hear?'

I gaped at her. What the hell did she mean? Me? How on earth was I going to get rid of Claudia?

'Odessa, what do you mean? Lying? What's Claudia lying about?'

'If she's pregnant, then I'm one of them supermodels!' Odessa swept out of the door, Patrick trailing in her wake.

303

My mind was whirring. Claudia was lying? Was she? How could Odessa be so sure? Maybe if you were a witch of the Cornish woods, you just knew those sorts of things. But supposing she was wrong? Then what? Then I'd be even more broken-hearted, having been given some sort of false hope. Perhaps it was better to do nothing at all. Not that I'd got any grand plan anyway.

Tom interrupted my day-dreaming by asking if I'd go and say good-night to the children, and did I want to see the new baby?

I nodded, and we climbed the stairs.

'You know, I'd do just what Odessa says, she'm always right, much as we sometimes wish she weren't,' Tom said, pushing open the door to the bedroom.

Maybe, maybe.

Demelza was fast asleep, with a soft smile on her face. A candle was by the side of her bed, and I could see the baby, nestled against her. It really was a beautiful sight, and I felt a tear start again.

'What are you going to call her?' I whispered, brushing the tears away with the back of my hand. I couldn't remember ever having cried quite so much as I had here. Whether it was bawling out of frustration because Claudia had turned up, or weeping over Jicky. And now the tears were tears of pure emotion at such a wonderful sight.

'Bianca, because of all the snow an' that,' Tom whispered back. 'Bianca Poppy.'

Oh, God. That was it. The tears started in earnest now.

'Oh, Tom, how lovely!'

Tom ushered me out of the room, muttering something about women crying all the time. I hit him good-naturedly, and he smiled at me. The kids were sitting up in their bunks, a night-light flickering in a saucer.

'Why are you crying?' soft-hearted Eve asked, stroking my arm.

''Cause she's just seen the baby, women do that,' Toby said scornfully.

I laughed and kissed them good-night. They smelt deliciously of childhood: pencil shavings, a hint of boiled sweets and apples. I hugged them tightly till Toby complained that he couldn't breathe. I promised them that I would go with them to look at the foal, Jicky, first thing in the morning.

Tom was propped up in the doorway, yawning his head off.

'Go to bed,' I whispered, 'I'll let Patrick in.'

'Thanks. I will, fair done in, with all the excitement today. I put some pillows and that downstairs, the sofa opens up, and the other couch's a bit lumpy, make Patrick have that one.'

'I will. Good-night, Tom, and congratulations again.'

He kissed me on the cheek and gave another jaw-breaking yawn. I wandered downstairs again, stopping off at the bathroom where I very nearly broke my toe on the edge of the bath, it was so dark. The only light in there came from the moon that was shining through the window. The cold silver light flooded the room, and I washed my hands and face, seeing a pale ghostly reflection of myself in the mirror. Even in that light, I could tell I looked knackered. My hair had been flattened by a succession of hats, my eyes were puffy through all the high emotion, and my lips were chapped. I felt along a shelf for some sort of moisturising cream, and slapped some on. That would have to do.

I tiptoed downstairs, going very slowly as it would just be my luck to fall over and wake the whole farm up. I'd probably break my leg, and Patrick would have to set it with the aid of some sort of horse anaesthetic. I groped my way into the living-room, and threw the duvets over the sofas. I tested the couch and smiled. Tom was right, it was bloody lumpy. Patrick could definitely have that one.

I picked up a candle, and shielding the flame made my way into the kitchen. It was lovely and warm in there, and I decided to do the washing-up whilst I waited for Patrick. I also pinched another biscuit from the tray that was still on top of the Aga. As I wiped the table, I found it hard to believe that this had been Demelza's delivery room. As scary as it had been, I thought that it was probably a far nicer place to give birth, than the, as Odessa would say, *nasty* hospital.

At least this was familiar, comforting. It smelt of baking bread, coffee and soup, not some horrible disinfectant. Although I was well aware that when I saw that pool of blood, this was the last place that I wanted

Demelza to be. I had then wanted phalanxes of white-coated professionals with stethoscopes flung around their necks. Not to mention a full complement of modern drugs. And that was just for me.

Thank God for Odessa.

The candlelight picked up some of the children's drawings that had been pinned to the kitchen wall. I could recognise the hand of Jocasta in some of them. She probably had them up at the Abbey for art lessons.

My face felt a bit sticky and itchy, and I absent-mindedly scratched myself. I hadn't rubbed the moisturising cream in properly. I massaged my face with one hand, whilst heaving the kettle on to the Aga with the other. Patrick would be back soon, and would probably welcome a cup of tea.

I looked out of the window at the snowy moonlit landscape. I wondered if the owls still hunted in this weather. I also had a horrid jolt as it occurred to me to ask Patrick what he had done with Jicky. Where was his cold little body going to rest this night? In the distance were the moors, I tried to imagine what they looked like. Tabitha would probably have gone out there today, it was the sort of elemental weather that she adored. I bet Jocasta didn't, though, she and Davey would make themselves a snug corner and argue with Edward over the merits of certain artists. They'd make themselves toast in front of a fire, or maybe crumpets smothered in butter, and Davey would play the piano. Maybe Alex would join them, and they'd all start

307

singing. I threw a few bottles of wine into the equation as well.

I made the tea and poured myself a cup. I took heart in what Odessa had told me. Even if it wasn't true, tomorrow I'd go up to the Abbey. I heard footsteps coming up to the kitchen door and then a soft knock. Patrick was back at last. I went to open the door for him. I gasped.

Even though he was muffled up to the eyes I could see that it wasn't Patrick. The hat alone, a rakish purple trilby, would tell me that it was Alex.

'Poppy!'

'Oh, God, Alex! What are you doing here?'

He was unravelling a long multi-coloured Dr Who scarf from around his neck, and he stepped into the kitchen, closing the door behind him.

My heart was pounding in my chest, and my hands had become very damp. These physical manifestations alone told me that I was, as I had suspected all along, hopelessly in love.

'Oh, Alex, Demelza's had her baby, here! And I had to go and fetch Odessa, and then poor little Jicky died and then—'

'Poppy, why is your face purple?'

I put my hand to my face and felt the cold cream on it. I took my hand away and looked closely at it by the light of a candle. Bloody hell, he was right, it was purple!

Chapter Twenty-one

'Why are you putting gentian violet cream on your face, has something happened to you?' Alex said, staring at me.

No, no, of course not. I *like* looking like a baboon. Or is that just the colour of their bottoms when they are in heat, or whatever the hell it's called?

'How do you know what it is?' I said, hoping that the mauve cream at least covered up the redness.

'Because as a child it was slapped on both my knees with monotonous regularity whenever I fell over. Toby and Eve normally have bloody great mauve stains all over them, like some weird mark of the blood royal. Don't tell me, let me guess, you put it on in a dark bathroom, thinking it was something else?'

I nodded.

'Bloody hell, well, don't just stand there, wash it off as quickly as you can. It's hell to shift, you'll probably have to scrub half your face off!' Alex was laughing as I rushed to the kitchen sink and started to scrub. He handed me some soap, and I rubbed and rubbed. Alex brought over a candle to see better.

'Christ, you look like my Aunt Eudoxia, she was famed throughout Montenegro for her pale violet complexion, not to mention her heavily hennaed hair—'

'Alex, you don't have an Aunt Eudoxia, do you?'

'No, I don't. But I thought it might make you feel better.'

'Oh, I have missed you!' I said involuntarily.

'Me you too.'

We looked at one another in the candlelight. There was complete silence in the kitchen, and outside. Not even the hum of a boiler or a distant rumble of traffic could be heard. Only my own rather laboured breathing. I was drawn to his eyes, and was staring at him. I knew that I shouldn't be, but it was impossible not to.

Alex looked away, and said, 'I suppose you've heard about the stuff going on at the Abbey?'

'Well, sort of.'

We were whispering for some reason and it made our conversation sound conspiratorial. Alex moved towards me, and I found that I was holding my breath. He put both of his hands on my shoulders, and looked down at me. Just as he opened his mouth to talk, the kitchen door was pushed open and Patrick came in, stamping the snow from his boots.

'Odessa is a marvel, isn't she? How she walks so quickly I— Oh, Alex, what are *you* doing here?' Patrick said, looking with surprise and faint hostility towards him.

Alex dropped his hands from my shoulders and said, 'I might ask you the same thing.'

Oh, God, bloody men.

They were both eyeing each other with distaste. Patrick sat down to take his boots off, and Alex leant against the kitchen wall and folded his arms across his chest.

'Tea, anyone?' I asked, taking some mugs down from a shelf.

My question was met with stony silence.

There was a very uncomfortable quietness to the kitchen, and I bustled around making tea, just for something to do, really. I glanced up and saw that Alex was following my movements, and Patrick was just staring at the floor. I gave a tentative smile to Alex, who grinned back.

Well, that was an improvement anyway.

I pushed a mug of tea towards Patrick, then handed one to Alex. Still in silence.

I cleared my throat, and said, 'Well, what a day we've all had! But Demelza has a lovely baby girl, they are going to call her Bianca *Poppy*, isn't that nice of them? Oh, and poor Jicky—'

Patrick cleared his throat and said, 'Don't worry, Poppy, I have him in the car. I'll take him to the surgery in the morning and I'll, well, umm, dispose of him for you—'

'You'll do no such thing!' Alex said. 'Give him to me, and I'll bury him in our pet cemetery. We'll have a proper funeral for him, Jocasta's great at that. She'll make a coffin, and we'll have hymns and then a funeral supper. We always do when any animal dies at the

311

Abbey.' Alex sounded confident, and was glaring at Patrick indignantly.

Alex then looked anxiously at me, and added diffidently, 'If that's what you would like, of course?'

I couldn't think of anything better, so I just nodded.

'Anyway, I haven't established yet, where the hell did you get to? Davey just found a note saying that you had to go home. Where have you been?' Alex continued.

'She came to me,' Patrick said softly.

'What?' Alex hissed. 'Why? What the bloody hell did you go to *his* for?' He jerked his head towards Patrick. 'Everyone knows that he bored his wife into leaving him—'

'Stop it!' I whispered as loudly as I could.

We were all trying to keep our voices down, aware of the children and new baby upstairs. The dogs were picking up on our anxieties, and Dotsie, bless her, came and laid her long nose in my lap.

'Traitor,' murmured Patrick, looking at her.

'Look, Alex,' I said as quietly and with as much authority as I could summon, 'I tried to get a train back to London, but the snow made everything so difficult, and then I didn't know where to go, and I thought of Patrick and he very kindly put me up for a night—'

'I bet he did,' Alex hissed rudely.

I gave Alex what I thought was a disapproving look, but he completely wrong-footed me by winking at me.

'OK, OK, I am sorry, Patrick. Please accept my apologies. Things have been a little strained around here and I think it best if I take Poppy back to the

Abbey. We've all been very worried about her.' Alex stood up, and held his hand out to Patrick.

They solemnly shook hands, and I marvelled, not for the first time, on the unpredictability of the public-school-educated Englishman. Oh, well. I guess it was a boy thing.

'I'll bring your luggage tomorrow,' Patrick said. 'Tell Edward that the new foal is called Jicky.' He smiled at me, and then mouthed 'Good luck'.

I thought I'd need it.

I stroked Dotsie goodbye, and bundled my coat back on, as well as pulling on a pair of boots. I was so thrilled to be going back to the Abbey, and at being near Alex, that the cold and the snow didn't seem to bother me.

It was a different matter when we left the relative safety of the farm courtyard. The moon had sailed behind a cloud, and the darkness seemed to come from the sixteenth century. I had never encountered such blackness in the modern world before. There were small reflective patches of snow, and that was it. Alex gripped my hand and we stumbled along together, concentrating on where we were walking.

'Alex, how the hell are we going to get up the drive?' I asked, panting to keep up with him. 'I had to slide down on my suitcase, you know.'

'Did you? How very enterprising of you!'

He pulled me towards him, and kissed me hard on the mouth.

All my thoughts of Claudia disappeared. I kissed him

back with a great deal of passion. He dragged me onwards, and I stumbled behind him.

'Where the hell are we going?' I whispered, convinced that we were heading in the wrong direction.

'To the barn, of course. You don't honestly think that we could get up the drive in the pitch black, do you?'

I giggled, and allowed myself to be pulled into the barn. The mare and her foal barely blinked at us, and in the light of the lantern that Patrick had slung up, they made a wonderful sight.

I watched as Alex bustled around, piling up bales of hay. (Well, I *assumed* it was hay. I wouldn't put any money on me being able to distinguish between hay and straw.)

'What are you doing?' I asked.

'Making a bed. Idiot. Otherwise we'll freeze.'

'Oh.'

I felt that this was not the time to start the Trans-Siberian game again, and was just about to voice my doubts, when Alex kissed me a second time.

The hay (I discovered that it really *was* hay) was very, very scratchy, and I was terrified that there would be mice, or worse, in it. But those thoughts did not last long.

It was bliss.

At one point, I found myself laughing and Alex drew me back towards him, asking me if I always laughed when I was making love.

'Probably. I'm a simple girl at heart,' I said.

'Thank God,' Alex said, pulling hay from my hair, and

smiling at me. 'You've no idea of the relief of being with you. I have missed you. I am so sorry about Claudia—'

'Oh, please don't say anything,' I begged, terrified the moment would be spoilt. Knowing that I would have to bring this memory out in the future to remember.

'No, Poppy, I don't think you understand. Let me finish. Claudia is lying. She's not pregnant.'

'What?'

He repeated it.

I was so elated, I felt like bursting into song.

'But Alex, how do you know?'

'I know. And what's more, so does Odessa. I'd trust her on anything, but the problem is that Claudia won't back down. I wanted to get her back to Paris as soon as I could, but what with the snow and everything it was impossible. I feel sorry for her now, I'm really not that much of a bastard that I want to publicly dump her. Also, Jocasta and Edward are going through hell at the moment with Tabitha—'

'Oh, so they know about her, do they?'

'What? How do you know?' Alex sounded surprised.

I told him about Tabitha telling me she was pregnant.

He laughed and said, 'Well, what you don't know is that she and Davey had a terrible row about it. Davey is convinced that she is going to dump the baby – or rather *babies*, if what Odessa thinks is true – on Jocasta and Edward, and that she is going to traipse around after this dreadful man. It's all frightful up there at the moment. They've all been worried about you, too. Especially Davey.'

315

I felt a bit guilty and also remembered that I still didn't know why Davey had kissed me. But lying in Alex's arms in the scratchy hay was so delightful, it took the edge off any really bad guilt I might have.

I gave a huge yawn, and Alex chuckled.

'I suppose it'll sort itself out. Things usually do. Now, before we try and sleep, come here again.'

All I can tell you is that making love in a snowed-in barn, in the company of a mare and her foal, is very thrilling indeed. Perhaps not the warmest or most comfortable of places to be, but I wouldn't have changed it for all the tea in China.

After some time, I wriggled out of Alex's arms and dressed myself.

'What are you doing?' he asked sleepily.

'I'm sorry to be so desperately unromantic, but I really need to go to the loo,' I said apologetically.

Alex snorted with laughter. 'Well, make sure your bottom doesn't freeze, though if it does I do have ways of warming it up!'

I edged my way to the door and walked across the courtyard to find a bush to go behind. The wind had dropped, and the moon was out again. It all looked so enchantingly beautiful, I wished I was doing something a little less prosaic than having a wee behind a bush. I gazed around me and decided that perhaps it wasn't such a bad place for Jicky to have died. Certainly it was a long way from the hot country that he had presumably been born to, but it was beautiful. When I entered

316

the barn again, Alex held his arms out to me and I willingly scampered into them.

After much very silly conversation we eventually drifted off into a fitful sleep. Most of the night I spent pressed against Alex, breathing in the smell of him, and the hay. I had to keep pinching myself to make sure that this was happening. I kept looking over at the horse and her foal, Jicky, to check on them too. They seemed supremely unconcerned that I had just consummated the grand passion of my life. Unfeeling beasts.

In the grey, cold dawn, we stretched and groaned and, I have to say, I did think longingly of a hot bath and a cup of tea. I refused to kiss Alex as I was terrified that my breath would smell, but he insisted anyway.

We pushed our way out of the barn, and saw that the thaw had set in. The snow was distinctly patchy now, and we thought we could trek up to the Abbey. I was a bit nervous as to how I was going to be received, but Alex assured me that everyone would be glad to see me.

'Well, nearly everyone,' he added truthfully.

I gathered up enough courage to ask him what was going to happen to Claudia.

He smiled grimly and said, 'Well, I shall borrow Davey's car and take her to the airport. Then I'm coming straight back to sleep with you properly in a feather bed.'

Goodness.

'You know, Alex, that it's Sunday today, and the day

317

before New Year's Eve. I bet there won't be a flight out anywhere and—' I started to say.

'If I have to *buy* a sodding plane, she's going. Now stop worrying and start climbing,' he said, pushing me from behind.

Although the melt was definitely starting, the drive was still treacherous. We slipped and tripped our way to the top. At my first sight of the Abbey I felt like bursting into tears, I was so happy. We crept round the back and let ourselves into the kitchen.

The usual regal decay greeted us. Piles of plates and glasses jostled for space amongst the antique kitchen equipment. Alex put the kettle on, and tried the light switch. The light immediately snapped on.

'Thank God for electricity, that means hot water. Go and run yourself a bath and I'll bring you a cup of tea upstairs,' Alex said.

It sounded like a wonderful idea to me. I ran up the stairs, pausing to look at the hallway. Signs of the snapper party had long gone, but there was an ominous quantity of empty wine bottles. I hesitated outside Davey's door, but decided that a bath should come first. Also, I knew I would have more chance of a warm welcome if I left it till a more civilised hour.

I pushed open the door of the Chinese room, and hugged it to me. It really did feel like coming home. I breathed in the familiar scent, and went to run a bath. As the hot water tumbled from the brass fittings, I looked in the mirror. My face was a delicate shade of violet, hay was stuck in my now not very chic hair, and

318

I had smudges of mascara splodged under my eyes. But I looked ecstatic. I was humming as I threw my clothes off and jumped in the hot water.

I heard Alex softly calling my name, and I answered him.

'Don't worry, I shan't compromise your dignity. Though God knows, I've seen you in some highly undignified situations. I shall leave your tea outside. Back in a minute ... '

I heard the bedroom door close, and I sank under the water. Well, this *was* the life, and no mistake. Alex was packing off Claudia, and coming back to me! Hoo-bloody-rah. The warm water felt great, and once again I sank under the surface.

The next moment I was coughing water and screaming my head off. I opened my eyes as I resurfaced to find Claudia standing in front of me. It was just like that scene in *Fatal Attraction*, and I rapidly scanned her hands for any knife that she might be holding.

'Bloody hell, Claudia! You frightened me half to death, what are you doing?' I said very angrily, leaping out of the bath and wrapping myself in a towel. I had no wish for Miss Bloody Perfect to see *my* cellulite.

'Oh, so *you're* back, are you?' Claudia sneered.

'Umm, yes. What are you doing?' I insisted.

'Well, I thought I'd give you a bit of advice. Alex is mine. OK? You get that? He is kinda having problems about acceptance at the moment. But he'll come round. As soon as I get him home, away from this crazy

319

goddam family of his, everything'll be fine. You hear me?'

I stared at her. She looked completely barking mad. Her hair was a bird's nest and her skin was blotchy. I guessed that a lot of midnight crying had been going on.

I know, I know. I *should* have felt horribly guilty. But I didn't. What can I say? The bedroom door swung open and Alex walked in.

'I thought I heard screaming, what's going on? Are you all right?' Alex asked me.

Claudia turned on him in fury. 'Where the hell have you been? You said you were going to the farm to check up on Demelza. That takes all night, does it? I might have guessed you'd found this little tramp. I cannot believe that you are even looking at this, this *pathetic* excuse for a woman. You're gonna be a father, you know, and—'

'No, I'm not. You know I'm not. Let's not get into this again, shall we? And don't talk to Poppy like that. Let's go downstairs. Come on.' Alex looked grim-faced, and I felt very awkward indeed.

Claudia stood in front of him, shrieking at the top of her voice, 'You are going to be a father, you are, you are—'

I wondered if it would be permissible to slap her. Apart from giving me a great deal of satisfaction, that's what you did to hysterics, wasn't it? My right hand positively itched to do so.

To his credit, Alex dealt with her very gently, taking

320

her arm and leading her outside. I heard him murmuring to her that they had been all through this again and again. He was *not* going to be a father because she was *not* pregnant.

I scrambled into my clothes and stood uncertainly in the passage. I thought I could safely wake Davey now, but knew I would be more welcome if I took him up some coffee.

I managed to find a clean cup and saucer in the chaos of the kitchen and hunted down the coffee. I eventually found it in a chipped Victorian container marked 'Rice'. I carried it with care up the stairs, as Davey loathed slopped drinks and I didn't want to antagonise him any further than my flight of absence probably already had. I tapped at his door and pushed it open. He was fast asleep, wearing, of all things, a nightcap. I stifled a giggle, he looked like a drawing from something by Charles Dickens.

'Davey?' I said, putting the coffee down and repeating his name.

His eyes snapped open.

We stared awkwardly at one another for a few seconds, then, to my relief, Davey smiled.

'Poppy Hazleton, as I live and breathe! Where the bloody hell did you get to? No, no, don't tell me till I am properly awake. Good God, woman, what has happened to you? You look different!'

I could tell he was pleased to see me, as he was beaming from ear to ear.

'Do I?'

'Yes ... Oh no, let me guess. You have finally, after years of abstinence, succumbed. *Not* with the vet, I hope?'

I shook my head.

'Thank God. I mean, he's very nice, but so boring. That can only mean one thing ... Alex?'

I nodded, and as he sipped his coffee I told him all about it. It was heavenly talking to Davey, just like being back in the shop. And the best thing was that he knew exactly what you meant, and asked all the right questions. I told him about my slide down the drive, Demelza, my walk to get Odessa (he spluttered with laughter when I told him about mistaking her for an alien), the birth, Jicky, and, of course, the night of rapture in the barn with his brother.

'Well, dear, what an adventure you've had. Now, let me tell you what's been going on here,' he said, propped up in bed amongst loads of pillows.

'Oh, please do. You've no idea how much I've missed all of you!' I said, curling up on his bed and tucking my feet underneath the quilt for warmth.

'Well, let me start by saying it has been bloody. Claudia is bonkers, quite, quite mad in my opinion. She insulted Odessa, who walked out. She is *not* pregnant, but insists that she is. Tabitha, on the other hand, *is* pregnant and is driving Ma and Pa mad with worry. It's quite obvious to me that she intends leaving the baby – yes, yes, I know about the twin theory – leaving them here and going off on this damn fool workshop that intends touring in America next year. We've all been

322

rowing and shouting at each other and now I can't quite remember who's talking to who.'

'Goodness.'

'Yes, quite.'

We sat in a very companionable silence for a while. Then I asked if Jocasta and Edward were cross with me.

'No, not at all. I think they just thought that you'd had enough of the Stantons, but they have been worried about you. Well, so have I, of course.'

'I know. Oh, Davey, I *am* sorry, I just had to get away, and then with the weather and the trains I was stuck, and—'

'It's OK. I *do* understand. But what about Alex? Don't tell me he's going to make an honest woman out of you?' Davey said in an amused tone of voice.

Personally, I didn't think it warranted such amusement, so I stuck my tongue out at him.

'Very sophisticated, dear. Still, you could marry in the chapel and I could do the flowers, or I could always give you away if your father doesn't want to—'

'Oh, don't tease, Davey. I am so happy!' I said.

'I can tell. But, well, you know, don't count—'

'– Your chickens. I know, I know.'

He cleared his throat and said, 'Well, I feel I owe you an apology as well, lunging at you as I did. I see now that it was quite stupid of me, but I was desperate—'

'Yes, you bloody do owe me an apology. What *was* that all about?' I asked.

'Well, you see, I simply *had* to try ... But it was absolutely no good at all. You are my best friend, so

323

you do see I thought that might help, but I think it made it worse. You looked so attractive that night—'

I stared aghast at him. 'Do you mean to say I was some sort of experiment?' I said incredulously.

'I really am sorry, Poppy. I thought it was worth a go, what with the will and everything. But I've known I was gay since I was about twelve and used to have lovely but very disturbing dreams about Roman centurians . . .'

'Oh, Davey, please explain about this damn will business. I don't understand,' I wailed.

He groaned. 'You know how I hate explanations . . . but if you insist. The will which my bonkers parents have made leaves the fate of the Abbey, amongst other things, to the first one of us that has a child. So you see, I am quite out of the equation! I thought I could try—'

'Try and get me pregnant?!' I collapsed in laughter at the idea. Even the thought of Davey getting physical with me was too much. I mean, it wasn't even offensive, it was just absurd. It was like trying to imagine Julian Clary and Julia Roberts having a wild night of passion. Simply not going to happen.

'I just wasn't thinking clearly,' Davey said. 'I then tried the old family myth thing, you know, digging under all the dragons I could find in the hope of unearthing something—'

I knew then what the scraping sound was that I'd heard in the early hours of Christmas morning. It had been Davey, digging up the garden. I stifled another laugh. He smiled at me and squeezed my hand, then hopped out of bed and went to the bathroom. I allowed myself the luxury of a day-dream that involved a summer wedding at the Abbey, with my parents hitting it off with Jocasta and Edward, and Tabitha heavily pregnant and looking well and vowing to buy a cottage in Bodmin. I had just got to the honeymoon destination (*not* Paris, where I felt I would be too likely to bump into Claudia, but somewhere romantic like Venice) when Davey reappeared, slapping cologne over his face.

'Come along, Poppy. Wool gathering, as usual, I see. Let's go and face the hell of the family conference, shall we?'

'What?' I said, looking alarmed.

'Oh, yes. Didn't Alex tell you? There is to be a meeting, and let me stress, this is *not* going to be fun. The last one we had was when Edward and Jocasta discussed their will with us all. It was frightful, shouts and slaps all round as I remember.'

This sounded like something I should avoid at all costs.

'Oh, well, it really has nothing to do with me. I mean, I'm definitely not family and—'

Davey gave a very unsympathetic laugh. 'Hmm, well, you soon might be,' he said, to my secret delight. 'Anyway, you're here now, so come along, do. And don't dither, there's a dear.'

Chapter Twenty-two

I didn't care what Davey said. The family conference was not going to be for me. We made our way downstairs, and saw that Jocasta was ahead of us. She was wearing a trailing garment, a sort of dressing-gown, I suppose, in a bluey-green material, the folds of which were billowing behind her. Her hair was piled up on the top of her head and skewered in place with a pair of ivory chopsticks. Davey called out to her, and she turned to face us. I was shocked by her expression. I'd only seen her two days ago, when she was in full snapper party gear, and full of life and vitality. She now looked drained and tired, every year of her age showing on her face.

'Poppy, dear! I'd heard you were back! Oh, I *am* pleased to see you . . .' She embraced me and I felt like sobbing on her shoulder, as well as trying somehow to comfort her. I settled for hugging her back with a great deal of enthusiasm.

Davey, I saw, was smiling fondly at his mother. That was a bit of a relief, at least they were on speaking terms.

'Poor darling Jicky! And I hear that you were there when Demelza had her baby? How lovely, but of course, gruesome at the same time, I bet. Birth always is. Oh, God, here we go again, talking about birth, it's the only subject we seem to be talking about round here at the moment. I suppose you know all the news here?' she said to me.

I nodded.

She tucked her arm into mine and we continued down the stairs. Jocasta gave a heavy sigh, and sweeping Davey and me into the kitchen, said, 'It really is too bad, you know. Tabitha is a very, very silly girl. I mean, who on earth is going to look after it? It's only too obvious that *she* can't, or won't. I'm too old for all that shenanigans. I want to be a doting grandmother, not some sort of unpaid nurse! Then there's that simply *dreadful* woman Clara, or Claudia as she insists she's called . . .'

I cleared my throat, convinced that Jocasta was about to launch into a rant about Claudia and that the woman in question would leap out from behind a column, brandishing a knife.

'And *what* she said to Odessa! It doesn't bear thinking about! Odessa is part of this family, I will *not* have her insulted so – besides, who will cook? I can't possibly, I'm far too upset . . .'

I stifled a giggle and caught Davey's eye. He gave me the ghost of a wink but for all of Jocasta's theatricals I could see that she was genuinely upset. This was a

327

woman who really did love her family, but on completely her terms. I think I had the same look of approving indulgence on my face that I had seen on her children's and husband's faces when they looked at her.

She threw her hands in the air, and wailed, 'Just *look* at this mess, I am meant to be making Edward some tea. What *shall* I do?'

Davey wrung his hands ineffectually, and made an attempt to find a clean cup and saucer for her. Really, they were both as useless as each other. Jocasta unearthed a large yellow soup bowl and clasped it to her bosom. 'Do you think Edward would mind his tea in this?'

'I should think he'd hate it, Jocasta. Sit down, and talk to Davey. I'm going to wash up, then I'll make some breakfast for us all. OK?' I said, rolling my sleeves up.

'Oh, darling, you're *so* practical,' Jocasta said admiringly.

To my complete surprise I discovered a dishwasher, that in the past I had mistaken for a washing machine. I loaded it up, and switched it on, laughing at the comments from Davey. (He swore that it had been a present to Odessa last year. She refused to use it, vowing that it would break the china, but Edward suspected it was because she couldn't read, and the instructions were beyond any of the Stantons to interpret for her.) The machine hummed into life, and I tackled the endless quantities of glasses by hand.

Jocasta and Davey sat at the table, and I made tea

and toast whilst trying to keep an ear open to their conversation.

'How is Pa?' Davey asked.

'Oh, don't even ask. Awful. That's how he is. He wanted to go and shoot thistles, till I pointed out to him that he wouldn't even see them because of the snow . . .' Jocasta said gloomily.

Shoot thistles? Probably another stargazy Stanton family custom that I knew nothing about, I reasoned.

'He's really terribly upset by all of this, you know. I do so wish you'd change your mind Davey . . .' Jocasta said pleadingly.

I glanced at Davey. Change his mind about *what*? His face looked set and stormy. I knew only too well what that meant. He had his stubborn face on. Whatever it was Jocasta wanted him to rethink, I knew what the answer would be.

'No, Jocasta, I simply can't. Or won't. It's out of the question. The shop is doing very well at the moment –'

He had the grace to glance at me as he spoke, and I averted my eyes. The shop might well be doing a variety of things at the moment, but to my certain knowledge, doing very well was not exactly one of them.

He continued: '– So for you to expect me to sell up and return the money to the trust is quite impossible! Besides, if you and Pa insist on this ridiculous will, what do you expect? All your children will simply squabble endlessly. Anyway, darling, I really can't see me living here, can you? No theatres, no restaurants to speak of, no galleries, and no, I do *not* count the Tate at St Ives as a feasible alternative to Cork Street before you say anything, and—'

'– and no opportunities to go bungalowing!' Jocasta finished knowingly.

Davey exploded with laughter. 'Bungalowing? *Bungalowing!* What in the name of God are you talking about, woman? Do you know, Poppy?' he appealed to me.

I thought I did, but kept well out of it, and just shrugged.

Jocasta said, 'Of course she knows what I mean! And so do you, you wicked child! It's where men of a certain age go and importune other men in public lavatories. Highly unsavoury, I've always thought . . .'

'Cottaging, you mean! Really Jocasta, where do you read such things? Of *course* I don't do that!'

Jocasta sniffed unbelievingly, and I turned my back on them to giggle in private. I tried to imagine my mother accusing anyone of 'bungalowing'. It was an impossible image to conjure up.

I made some toast and put the dangerously delicious Cornish butter, home-made marmalade and honey on the table. I had just poured the boiling water into the teapot when the kitchen door opened and Alex came in. He gave me a reassuring glance, and then asked Davey if he could borrow his car.

'No, you may not. The last time you borrowed it, it took two days to clean the interior alone!' Davey said indignantly.

'Oh, stop being such an old woman. I need to get

Claudia to an airport and the snow is clearing, the roads are passable, and I don't want to waste any more time. She has just admitted to me that she knows she's not pregnant. I *think* she feels terribly bad about her behaviour and wants to bolt. Or do you want another evening like the night before last?'

Davey and Jocasta shuddered at the memory, and I made a mental note to worm out of Davey all the sordid details.

'I bitterly resent the old woman insult, but if it means you are delivering us from the evil that is Claudia, then yes, you may borrow my car. But for Chrissake be careful, the roads will be like ice, and I gather that you didn't get much sleep last night,' Davey said, grinning wickedly at me.

I, of *course*, blushed.

Jocasta sprang to her feet. 'You mean that Clara is going? Oh, thank God. I am sorry, Alex, but really, the woman is deranged! I really think it's too bad of you— Wait, wait a moment, what do you mean, Davey, that Alex didn't get any sleep last night? Where were you? You went to the farm to check on Demelza and then . . .' She stopped and swivelled her eyes to mine. She took in my red face, and then smiled sweetly at her sons. 'Oh, I see. Well, all I can say again is thank God. And about time, too. Now do hurry, darling, she might change her mind.'

'Who might? Claudia or Poppy?' Alex said with a grin on his face.

331

'Both,' replied Jocasta tartly. 'You're not *that* much of a catch, you know.'

Davey sniggered, and Alex dropped a kiss on the top of his mother's head, then mine, and then his brother's. He waved his goodbyes to us and quite soon we heard the car start outside.

Jocasta and Davey heaved a collective sigh of relief. I felt extremely uncomfortable. Delighted as well, of course, but I am really not used to such an open discussion about my love life (not that I normally had one, you understand). It also felt so abrupt to be carting off Claudia so publicly.

Davey patted my hand, and whispered, 'Don't worry about Claudia, she'll be fine. She really is terrible, you know. Mad as well. Good riddance to bad rubbish, is what I say.'

Jocasta beamed at me, and said, 'Oh, Poppy, I am so glad I can't tell you. I must go and tell Edward, it will cheer him no end—'

'Oh, please don't,' I cried. 'I mean, nothing really has happened yet, and Claudia hasn't even gone properly—'

'Christ, you don't think she'll come back, do you?' Davey asked anxiously, practically looking over his shoulder.

I gave up. The manners of the Stantons were simply appalling.

The back door to the kitchen opened and Davey and Jocasta clutched one another in anticipated horror.

'You'm proper daft buggers,' a very familiar voice said.

Jocasta rushed to hug Odessa, much to her embarrassment. Even Davey gave her a smacking great kiss on the cheek.

'Oh, I really think things can't be that bad,' Jocasta said, 'if Clara has gone, and Odessa has returned. How lovely! But what's that?' She motioned to a smallish bundle that Odessa was carrying.

'I met Patrick comin' 'ere. This be poor little Jicky. Patrick's dropped your luggage off, Poppy, he didn't want to come in, for some reason.'

Davey pursed his mouth at me, and I wriggled uncomfortably.

Jocasta was in full flight of fancy for the funeral. 'Oh, the dear! It's so sad, but don't you worry, Poppy, we'll give him a wonderful send-off. Tomorrow, I think, don't you? New Year's Eve – *how* appropriate. It's a very lugubrious day, I always think. I shall have to make and decorate a coffin, and Davey and Alex can dig him a little grave in the cemetery—'

'Digging in *this* weather!' groaned Alex.

I shot a glance at Davey, who looked rather pleased with himself, as he alone could vouch for the difficulties of digging frozen ground.

Jocasta frowned at him, and made some tea to take up for Edward, promising that as soon as Alex returned she would have the family conference. Just before she made her exit from the room, she turned to Odessa. 'Now, Odessa, I can only apologise for my son's guest. I

333

know that Clara was very trying indeed, but you are back for good, aren't you?'

'That I am,' Odessa said with grim satisfaction.

'Oh, the *relief* . . . In that case I think your wonderful kedgeree for lunch, don't you? Then we could have roast lamb for dinner. Edward *will* be pleased. Now, I must go and make a coffin.' She bustled out of the room, and Odessa smiled at her departing back view indulgently.

'Now then, you take up a cup of this to Tabitha. I reckons she needs cheerin' up, no mistake.'

Odessa handed Davey a cup of steaming liquid, and he did as he was told.

She fixed me with a stare, and then, to my surprise, started to chuckle. 'Well, well. You'm got your wish then?' she said.

I knew very well what she was referring to, but I chose to try and remain aloof. It didn't cut any ice with Odessa. She gave me a great nudge in the ribs and said, 'Alex be a right little sod where women are concerned, you'm make sure he comes home every night, d'you hear?'

The thought of making Alex come home every night to me not only seemed highly improbable, it also made me faint with lust. I merely smiled and nodded.

She laughed again. 'Well, as I've said before, what will be, will be. You'll both be right happy here at the Abbey, I reckon. Make a proper job of it, too.'

Both of us happy *here*?

'Oh, no, Odessa, I don't think so, I mean Alex and I

334

are not even, you know, seeing each other or anything like that. It's probably just a Christmas fling, you know, and he's only just said goodbye to Claudia and . . .'

She was hooting with laughter now, wiping tears away with the back of her hand. 'They can never see it, quite remarkable, fair mazy you are! You'm set to stay, so's he. You just don't know it yet, that's all.'

I stared at her. Stay at the Abbey? How, for God's sake? I'd had a lovely time here and with Alex, but to count on anything else was madness. I decided to ignore her forecasts and asked what I could do to help her.

Still shaking with laughter, she asked me to hardboil some eggs and chop parsley. I meekly did as I was told, watching Odessa move about her kingdom.

She was stirring some uncooked rice into an enormous amount of melted butter when the kitchen door opened and Edward came into the room.

'Odessa! And Poppy! Well, how lovely. Jocasta told me that you were both back, and it was the best bit of news I could possibly have.'

He smiled at both of us, and I was almost tempted to hug him, but knew that it would not be appreciated, so I grinned back instead.

'Sorry to hear about Jicky. Jocasta's making the coffin now. Funeral tomorrow, so I understand.' He took a pencil from an overflowing Japanese vase that was balanced on a kitchen shelf, and ripped a bit of paper from a notepad that was lying on the table. 'Now then, any requests?'

'What?' I said stupidly.

'You know, favourite hymns or songs or suchlike. Anything that reminds you of the little chap?' he said gently.

I gazed at him, wondering, not for the first time, how anyone ever got used to the Stantons. I mean, here was a man whose beloved daughter was expecting a baby out of wedlock, and whose sons were arguing about a will or trust, and here he was arranging the funeral of a monkey with utter seriousness and dedication.

I promised him that I'd try to think of something.

Edward and Odessa embarked on an incomprehensible conversation about unknown farmers, and the health of the various animals surrounding the Abbey, whilst I burnt my fingers on shelling hot eggs.

Tabitha was the next one into the kitchen, and I jumped up to greet her. She returned my hug tentatively. She looked alarmingly thin apart, of course, from the tiny bump in her middle. She smiled at Odessa, and pointedly refused to look at her father.

Edward tried to engage her in conversation, but she turned away from him, burying her head in the enormous fridge, and eventually bringing out some fat-free yoghurt.

Odessa shook her head warningly at Edward, who had begun to say something. He subsided, and Odessa stroked Tabitha's hair as she walked past her.

Oh, dear. I had thought that Edward would forgive Tabitha and support her because he so clearly loved her. I could quite see that she was not the daughter

Jocasta and Edward might have wished for themselves, but they were such larger than life people, I couldn't believe they wouldn't find it in their hearts to help her.

Tabitha mooned around the kitchen for a while, studiously ignoring her father, but giving a word or two to Odessa. She was spooning yoghurt listlessly into a bowl and transferring minute teaspoons of it to her mouth. Odessa narrowed her eyes at her, and motioned for Edward to leave. I got up too, but Odessa pushed me back in my chair. Edward took the hint, though, and left the room abruptly.

Odessa started to tell Tabitha of the birth at the farm, leaving out the gorier details, I was relieved to hear.

Tabitha interrupted her. 'Odessa, I know what you're trying to do, but you see Ma and Pa have made it very clear that they don't want the baby here, and they've also made it clear that they think I shouldn't look after it myself, although there are quite a few babies in the travelling workshop. I mean, everyone gets to help out with them, so it's just like being in a family, really. Besides, I have to go, it's like having a calling, you know?'

'All I know, missy, is that you are havin' two babes, and it's no place to bring up Stantons, in some sort of travellin' circus. The very idea! We'll all find a way, so don't fret. Soon as Alex gets back, we'll sort everything out. Things have a way of happenin', if you want them to.'

I was intrigued. I could tell that Odessa had some-thing in mind, but God knows what. I spent the rest of the morning helping to assemble a huge kedgeree for lunch, and chatting to Davey. It was quite my favourite sort of thing to do, fiddling in a kitchen and talking. It's why I loved working in his shop, the work itself was hardly arduous, but the joy of having Davey to chat to every day, not to mention some of the customers, was bliss.

Davey and I had wandered over to the piano where he was picking out tunes with one finger, and I was racking my brains for a suitable funeral dirge for Jicky.

The conversation turned to the subject of Tabitha, and Davey sighed.

'It really is very difficult, you see Ma and Pa set up a trust fund, and we've all had some. Well, most of it, really. Then there's the Abbey to consider. After the last big family row, it was decided that the Abbey mustn't be sold, and it has been left to all of us. Well, all of us in theory, but in practice it goes to the one who has the first child. Then we all get to stay here but the one who has the child decides what we actually do with the place. Jocasta has this mad idea that Alex and I should give the trust money back so that Tab can buy herself a little place somewhere. Ridiculous.'

He banged a discordant chord on the piano and I winced. Trust funds and wills were something that I knew absolutely nothing whatsoever about. I felt fairly certain that I would inherit my parents' golf clubs, and that was it. I couldn't see me having sleepless nights

338

deciding what to do with a very dismal bungalow in Ipswich.

'But Davey, even if Tab had some money, I still don't see how that would solve everything,' I said.

He looked at me speculatively. 'Have you ever known *anything* that doesn't seem so bad when you have enough cash?'

Hmm, I suppose he'd got a point.

'The thing is,' he continued, 'that Tabitha won't give up her share of the Abbey. She says that she might well want to live here some day. Edward is convinced that Alex and I don't care enough about the place, and we'll stand by and let Tab turn it into some sort of commune or something. You know, running workshops on living off air, and getting in touch with your inner wild child. Then, of course, they want their grandchild near, but without the responsibility of actually looking after both of the girls.'

'*Girls?*'

'Oh, yes, Odessa has said so.'

Well, that was that it seemed. Odessa hath spoken, and the word was that they were female. It must be pretty exhausting being an oracle. I wondered what would happen if she was wrong. But then again, it seemed she never was. Or maybe like all oracles she screwed up occasionally but managed to turn it around to her own advantage.

We pootled around some more on the piano, Davey marvelling at my total inability to recognise any tune at all.

'Oh, yes,' I said proudly, 'I was asked to mime in all the singing classes at school.'

'I'm not surprised at all, dear,' Davey said acidly.

Wafts of food were hitting us, and my stomach rumbled. Davey glanced sympathetically at me and said, 'I'm starving too, how long do you think Alex will be?'

I immediately conjured up visions of a crashed car, mangled on the side of an icy road, or Claudia clinging to him at an airport, in a scene resembling *Casablanca*. I bit my lip with worry.

Davey laughed. 'Come on, I'll teach you "Chopsticks", that should take your mind off the missing fiancé.'

Good grief. Fiancé? I hooted with laughter. I was rather hoping that Alex might mean a lot to me, but fiancé hadn't even got in under the wire of my rather fevered imagination.

We were wrestling for chords, with Davey calling me really rather rude names indeed, when Odessa announced that lunch was ready.

'What about Alex?' I blurted out.

She smiled at me. 'Oh, he'm be here in about five minutes, I reckons.'

It never ceased to amaze me. But by now I didn't doubt her at all, and meekly went to wash my hands.

Jocasta had changed into a startling outfit of canary-yellow wool. It was not the best choice, as it made her look very sallow and tired. Even Davey, who normally could be counted on for good manners, told her that she looked like a bowl of exhausted custard.

'I know,' she said smugly, 'that's why I wore it. This way the family conference won't go on too long. You'll all hate looking at me so much that you'll want to get out as soon as possible, so you'll all agree with whatever I say!'

Davey and I laughed, and soon we were joined by Edward who looked disapprovingly at his wife. 'Always said that you could wear a potato sack and turn heads, not too sure about that, though,' he growled.

Tabitha wafted downstairs, keeping her eyes firmly on the ground, and just as we were all making our way into the Painted Parlour, I heard the very welcome sound of a car pulling up outside.

Alex burst into the hall and practically into song, he was so patently happy.

'Oh, my God! The relief – I can't tell you! Now, before *anyone* says *anything* about me behaving badly I can at last reveal to you all the sheer barminess of Claudia. We broke up, properly, about three months ago, but she begged me for another chance, and like a fool, I agreed. But I knew she wasn't pregnant because, well, I am acquainted with the facts of life and Claudia and I have not known each other in the biblical sense for many, many months. She then told me, at the airport if you please, that I had an Oedipus complex, and that she had been sleeping with a mutual friend of ours in Paris for six months! Heaven help the poor sod, that's all I can say.' He moved towards me and draped an arm around my shoulders. 'Even the dread of the family

341

conference now leaves me unmoved. Can I smell kedgeree? Then let's eat!'

I saw that the whole family were gazing at Alex, entranced. He was so full of energy and vitality it was impossible not to be drawn to him.

Even with the brooding question of Tabitha and the trust fund hanging over all of the Stantons, lunch was a very jolly affair indeed, with Edward forgetting that he was meant to be in a bad mood and uncorking far more wine than was probably good for us.

Chapter Twenty-three

Nietzsche said somewhere that life was a choice between boredom and suffering. What he didn't say was that there would be times when you had to cope with both at the same time.

The family conference started after lunch. Even I could have told them that this was *not* a good idea. Everyone (apart from Tabitha, of course) had had far too much wine, and all anybody wanted to do was have a snooze. It had been going on so long that I had developed jaw ache from clenching my jaw in an effort not to yawn.

Edward, who during lunch had been quite affable and benign, was now belligerent, and Jocasta was beady-eyed. Davey had the set stubborn look on his face that I knew only too well, Tabitha was fiddling her hair round and round her fingers, and Alex was leaning back in his chair with a not terribly pleasant expression on his face.

I had tried to extricate myself earlier, but had been told by all the family to 'sit down'. It had been like being given an order barked out by a group of army officers, and I had muttered 'Sir, yes sir' under my breath. So I copied Odessa and sat quietly, with my arms folded across my chest.

Davey was in full flow about some childhood incident. 'I have never recovered from the teddy-bear washing. I really think that it has marked me all my life . . .'

I made the mistake of looking enquiringly at him, so he explained.

'Well, when we were young, we all had teddy bears, in fact I was a *devoted* teddy-bear carer, *unlike* my brother here, who used them to man booby traps in the garden.' He shot Alex a scornful glance. 'Anyway, I decided that they were all dirty and could do with a wash. I filled the bath with water and gave them a good scrubbing. It didn't occur to me to wonder why the bath had practically emptied itself, before I'd pulled the plug out. The bears had absorbed it all. I suppose the stuffing was straw or something. I staggered down to the garden and very carefully pegged them by their ears to the washing line to dry overnight.'

He paused for full dramatic effect here. It was lost on the Stantons who had obviously heard this story many, many times, but I nodded encouragingly, and he continued.

'Well, when I went to the garden the following morning, the most *devastating* sight hit me. All that was left on the line was a row of ears! The weight of the water-logged bodies had been too much of a strain, and had simply pulled away from the pegs. But *imagine* my

344

horror. I cried for days, didn't I?' He appealed to Odessa.

I sniggered, and Alex guffawed.

'That's as maybe, master Davey, but it don't make no sense of what's goin' on now, do it?' Odessa said evenly.

Oh, Lord, we were off again. Voices were raised all round the table.

'Well, yes, it *does*, if you think about it, I mean to say, I was probably *traumatised*. That's why I really, really can't even *think* about helping to raise a baby in any way at all. Simply ridiculous—'

'Utterly impossible to talk to, even as a child! Really, Davey, I do think you *might* be a bit more help. If you knew what your father and I have gone through the past years. The worry and the *expense* of setting up the trust fund and the will—' Jocasta sounded exasperated.

'Oh, so expensive was it that you didn't manage a holiday last year?' Alex said sweetly. 'No, silly me, not one, but two trips to Egypt, wasn't it?'

Edward turned on him. 'How dare you take that tone with your mother! Apologise immediately. And Egypt was a business trip, well, a buying trip anyway. And what we do with our money is none of your damn business—'

'Now, now, Edward—'

'Don't now-now me, Jocasta. You know I can't bear it. Makes you sound like some namby-pamby nanny that wears support stockings—'

'*Support stockings!* I have never worn support stockings in all my life, though there was that time when I strained my elbow and had to wear a sling—'

Tabitha joined in the fray by shouting, 'I don't see what support stockings or slings have to do with the fact that I am quite capable of bringing up my own baby, and if I want to bring the baby up here, or travel with the workshop, it has nothing to do with anyone else.'

A general uproar greeted this, and Davey shouted, 'That's because you are nothing but a selfish silly little girl, who won't stay in one place long enough to bring up anything other than your lunch!'

Tabitha threw a cup of (cold, luckily) coffee over him and then promptly burst into tears.

Edward shouted at Davey, 'Now look what you've done! Upset her, really!'

Jocasta picked up a salt-cellar and threw the salt with a very bad aim over the coffee stain on his shirt. Most of it missed and caught Davey full in the face.

'Christ, blinded by salt! That's all I need,' Davey said, tears streaming down his face.

'That's boiling vinegar in a silver bowl, Shakespeare or the Bible,' Jocasta said helpfully. 'And *do* stop making a fuss. I suppose you can add this to your list of grievances, like the teddy bears,' she added nastily.

I was gazing at them all open-mouthed. I had never seen a family behave like this before. It was extraordinary. They were at each other's throats.

Alliances and affections changed every few seconds,

346

and it seemed that no grudge was too old to bring out and air. I felt a tap on my arm, and looked up to see Odessa beckoning me out of the room. I tiptoed behind her, relieved to get out, but also loath to miss any further revelations.

As I was closing the door I heard Davey accuse Alex of cheating in the last roof race, and saw, just before the door clicked shut, Alex turn an apoplectic red and demand an apology.

'Oh, dear,' I said to Odessa. 'Do you think this will go on much longer?'

'Hard to say. I'll let them mither on for a bit, it clears the air anyway,' she said matter-of-factly.

I followed her to the kitchen and we loaded the dishwasher, with me explaining to Odessa just what was required.

She eyed the machine distrustfully, but her doubt soon changed to downright gadget worship when she saw how sparkly everything was. I could see that soon every scrap of china was going to be immersed in the maw of the dishwasher. We made some tea and sat at the kitchen table, with me yawning my head off.

Odessa glanced at me and said, 'Take yourself off for a sleep, why don't you? I'll wake you when I've sorted them lot out.'

I nodded vaguely, too tired to enquire what her solution was going to be. I kissed her on her cheek, which seemed to please her immensely although she brushed me away, and climbed the stairs. I missed not having Jicky to cuddle. He had been like a living shawl,

347

and although the snow was nearly gone by now, it was still damn cold.

I flopped on to the bed and within seconds had fallen asleep. I only woke up because my feet were so cold, and I stayed awake just long enough to wrap myself, papoose-like, in the quilt.

The next time I opened my eyes it was dark outside. My God, they can't *still* be at it, I thought, trying to calculate how many hours the Stantons had been snapping at one another. I went to splash some water on my face, and was happy to see that someone, Davey probably, had carried my luggage, that Patrick had dropped off, into my room.

I surveyed myself in the looking-glass. So many things had happened to me since I first got on the train at Paddington, only a few days ago, that I was surprised I still looked the same. I brushed my hair, and tried to make it look as though Russell had just weaved his magic over me, but I can't say that I succeeded that well. Perhaps it was the sort of haircut that demanded the attentions of a very expensive London hairdresser every week. Damn.

I dabbled into the make-up bag that Jessy had given me, and rather inexpertly applied the gunge. That, at least, was an improvement. Mind you, anything that disguised the ravages of the icy cold weather, too much alcohol and a rich diet could only succeed in making me look better. I still had a certain glow about me, for all the blemishes. I put that firmly down to the ministrations of Alex.

I rummaged through my suitcase, trying to find something new to wear. In the end I dragged out the scarlet suede skirt that I'd worn on the train. (Sneakily hoping, of course, that it would jog Alex's memory and fuel him with lust.) I had just struggled to do the zip up – the amounts of cream and butter really had taken their toll – when there was a knock on my door.

Odessa walked in, looking amused.

'Odessa, what's happened? You're smiling!' I said, hoping that this was a good sign and that whatever the differences were downstairs they'd been resolved.

'Fair goin' at it still, they are! I've made 'em tea, then more coffee. Tabitha's fallen asleep, Davey an' Alex are shoutin' the odds, Edward keeps tryin' to waltz off into his study, but Jocasta's locked the door! I reckons it's better than anythin' you'd see on the telly. Right funny it is!' She was rocking on her feet, chortling to herself.

'But have they got any further?' I asked doggedly.

'No,' she said scornfully. 'I reckons it's about the right time for me to go and tell 'em what they'm got to do. That's why I've come to see you.'

I couldn't think what possible reason I could have to fit into all of this, but I sat down on the edge of the bed, prepared to listen. I did so hope that it didn't involve me *too* much, for as much as I loved them all, I felt that this had nothing whatsoever to do with me.

Odessa opened her mouth, about to talk to me, when there was an ominous groan from the ceiling. We both glanced upwards, and to our mutual horror saw that the ceiling was moving. There was a large bulge in it

349

that seemed to have a life of its own. We watched, fascinated. Then there was a loud crack, and we ran out of the room, pausing at the doorway.

The ceiling fell down, followed immediately by gushing water. Lath and plaster, wallpaper and rust streamed down on to the bed, followed by clouds of ancient dust. I leapt to life and ran back into the room, rescuing my suitcase. Thank God I hadn't unpacked. A large lump of ceiling was buried in the mattress, directly where I had been sitting!

We both stared at one another. Then we looked up again. The remaining ceiling rippled and bulged, and then the rest of it came tumbling down with a loud crack and bang. A joist or rafter hung down from the jagged hole and above that was sky.

I screamed, Odessa screamed and we both clutched each other and ran off down the corridor.

Alex and Davey were running up to meet us.

'What the hell was that noise?' Davey called out. 'Are you all right?'

'Christ, Claudia hasn't come back and shot you, has she?' Alex said, looking worried.

Jocasta and Edward weren't far behind them.

'Good God! What is it?' shouted Edward.

'Darlings, are you hurt?' Jocasta called out.

'Ceiling,' I spluttered. 'The ceiling has fallen down!'

Alex and Edward surveyed the damage, and we all jostled behind them.

'Is it safe?' I asked nervously. 'Shouldn't we all go downstairs?'

'It's OK,' Alex said gloomily. 'I think the weight of the snow, and then the thaw, has damaged the roof. Let's just hope it doesn't spread. Christ, imagine trying to get hold of a roofer at New Year, it's going to cost a fortune! But haven't you just had the roof done?' he asked Jocasta.

She looked very uncomfortable.

I remembered her telling me that she'd paid for the roof with the proceeds of flogging her diamond necklace.

'Well, *sort* of ... No, Edward, don't look at me like that. You were away at the time and, well, it seemed *so* expensive, so I just had the front half done, and then I bought myself the diamond necklace copy so you wouldn't know that I'd sold it! But now you do. Oh, dear.'

Half the roof done? *Half.* It seemed incredible to me that anyone, even Jocasta, could have half a roof fixed.

But Jocasta was burbling on: 'The man was ever so sweet, and he did say that I really should have the whole thing done as it was quite dangerous, but I thought, well, the children are grown up now, and they don't do the roof race any more, so I didn't think that it mattered. Had I *known* that it could fall in at any time ...' She paused, then added in an aside, 'I would have put Clara in there!'

I stifled a very unworthy laugh, and looked anxiously around to see the reactions of the rest of the family.

Edward was speechless, but Davey and Alex started to berate their mother.

351

'Honestly, Jocasta, what were you thinking of?' Davey said incredulously.

'Yes, really, Ma, half a roof finished!' Alex said, squeezing my hand.

Tabitha came running up the stairs to see what all the commotion was about. I noticed that she flew to Edward, then Odessa, like a bird returning to a safe nest in the middle of a storm. Odessa tucked her under her arm and soothed her.

'It's all right, 'tis only the old roof giving way. Nobody be hurt. But you'm not goin' to your room till the roof is fixed.'

Jocasta was still wailing her apologies, and trying to pacify Edward who was glaring at her in a way I wouldn't have thought possible.

Odessa guided Tabitha downstairs, and tucked her up on a sofa in the hall, close to the fire. She spread a rather moth-eaten tartan blanket over her, and went to make her some tea.

The rest of us trailed behind her. Davey and Alex were still questioning Jocasta about her dealings with the roofer.

'But if he *told* you it was dangerous, surely you must have realised that to only have *half* the sodding roof done—' Alex said unbelievingly.

'I know, I know. Oh, I am sorry! What can I say?' Jocasta was wringing her hands, and nervously pushing back into her hair the usual escaping hairpins.

'I think, Jocasta, that the best thing you can do is go

352

and change. I will not talk to you if you continue to wear that sick canary colour,' Edward said firmly.

'Is it safe to go upstairs?' I asked.

'Oh, yes. Luckily, my wife's bedroom is obviously under the *new* roof,' Edward said acidly.

'Oh, darling, I *hate* it when you glare at me so! And since when has it been *my* bedroom? It's always been *our* bedroom,' Jocasta said, placing a hand on Edward's shoulder, and looking beseechingly up at him.

I could see him soften, and he patted her reassuringly. She meekly trotted off upstairs to change, and Edward muttered, 'Copying her diamond necklace! I sometimes wonder about the sanity of your mother.' He glared accusingly at Davey and Alex and I could see that they were controlling their mirth.

The next couple of hours were very tedious indeed. We cleared the wreck of the Chinese room as best we could, and Alex pinned up sheets of polythene (well, cut-up rubbish bags) over the gaping hole that framed the night sky.

'Just pray that it doesn't rain,' he said gloomily.

A large rafter was jutting down from the roof, one end balanced on the bedroom floor. The whole thing looked exceedingly precarious, and I was very nervous about going in there.

Edward was mourning the loss of some tapestry and a beautiful Chinese scroll that had been in there, whilst Davey was trying to calculate an insurance claim on a piece of paper. This time it was Edward who looked very uncomfortable.

Davey glanced at his father, and slowly put the paper away.

Oh, dear. It seems that between them they had not only had half the roof completed, they had also failed to cover themselves with insurance.

The only good thing, as far as I was concerned, about the roof falling in was that it put an end to the seemingly interminable family conference. Well, for the time being anyway.

A very subdued Jocasta, along with Edward and Davey, decided to take a bottle of champagne down to the farm for Demelza and Tom, and to have a peek at the new baby, Bianca.

'Bianca *Poppy*,' I smugly reminded them.

Tabitha had made a nest for herself in front of the fire and was playing patience with a pack of very tatty old cards. Odessa had put a leg of lamb in the Aga oven, and was now buttoning herself up into her spaceman coat ready to walk home.

'Now then, Poppy, you'm take the meat and potatoes out in an hour and a half,' she warned me. 'And the veg is all done. I'll sort you lot all out in the mornin',' were her last ominous words.

Alex and I went into the kitchen and peered at the meat. A very tantalising smell wafted around the whole room.

'Agony, isn't it?' Alex asked.

I nodded. I was very hungry indeed, perhaps it was all the unaccustomed emotional turmoil.

'I know! We need something absorbing that will take

354

our minds off the hunger pangs,' Alex said, a wicked smile spreading over his face.

A shiver of delight snaked its way up my spine.

'No, Miss Greedy! I was thinking of chess, do you play?'

I instantly denied that I had been thinking about anything else at all, and unconvincingly said that I had in fact been the school chess champion.

We both laughed, and Alex cleared a space on the crowded kitchen table for the chessboard and lit some candles.

To say that he was a distracting chess partner would be a huge understatement, at the very least. He called his pawns 'prawns' and rewarded them by dunking them in a glass of wine. He had a special affection for the knights, and would encourage them by making giddy-up noises. He also kept up a running commentary on the whole game.

'Oh, brave little prawn, here, have a sip of this rather splendid Chablis. Oh, Poppy, your gee-gee is very lonely out there, isn't he? I'd better send someone out to deal with him, whoops, here we go!'

I was easily distracted, and he soon had a heap of my chess pieces by his side.

'Now who do you think that the new baby will look like? Melza or Tom? Though of course, as she now has your name, she'll grow up to be utterly divine.'

I glowed with pleasure at this compliment and he swooped down on my lonely knight, wiping it off the board.

'Now, Poppy, you're really going to have to concentrate, you know. Do you miss Jicky? Silly question, of course you do. Still, lovely funeral to look forward to tomorrow. You can borrow all of Jocasta's jet and look like a Russian princess in full mourning. I shall ravish you behind the gravestone in the garden, so do make sure you're not wearing any knickers. Oh, dear, looks like checkmate!'

I stared at the board, trying to wriggle out of his move, but found it impossible. I conceded the game, and we packed up.

'Tell me more about this will,' I said, hoping I'd learn more from him than I had done from Davey.

He sighed. 'Oh, it's so tedious really. Edward and Jocasta, for reasons best known to themselves, have made it so that the first one of us to have a child decides the fate of the Abbey. You know, does it stay a private house, become a hotel, or of course if Tab has her way a bloody commune or something equally daft like a retreat. None of us can sell it, even if we all agree to. So you see, Davey, though he does adore it here, would never actually want to live here, though he would hate to lose his say over it.'

'What about you?' I said, slowly polishing some glasses.

'Me? Well, I'd adore to live here, but . . .' his voice tailed off.

I knew what he meant. The Abbey was huge and rambling and undoubtedly possessed a great charm

356

and pull on the Stantons, but it was in a terrible state of disrepair and needed more than love to fix it.

I day-dreamed about what I would do with it. I suppose a glorified B and B would do, though it would end up more like Fawlty Towers than the Ritz.

'What's all this about the trust fund then?' I asked. Then added in a rush, 'Please don't answer if you think I'm being too nosy, it's just that I don't understand very well.'

'Not at all,' Alex said, dropping a kiss on the top of my head, which left me reeling. 'They set up a trust fund for all of us, which Davey and Tabitha have both dipped into rather heavily. It was meant to mature after their deaths, but it seems that Davey and Tab persuaded them to let them have access to it earlier. I had a bit too, I didn't even need it really, it was stupid of me. I only bought a car with it.'

It felt very odd to hear Alex talk of his inheritance, which obviously revolved around the death of his parents, so casually. Maybe that's what happened in rich families, I thought. I couldn't tell if the Stantons *were* rich, though. I mean, in comparison to my family they were, but then, a lot of people were. I thought about Jocasta's jewels, Edward's antiques, Davey's allowance, the Abbey, the extravagant lifestyle. And then there was the leaking roof, the lack of heating – it was impossible to tell. Perhaps they just had different priorities from other, more normal, people.

We heard them crash through the front door. They were obviously all in high spirits, as they were belting out a song. It seemed that visiting the baby had had the desired effect, because Edward and Jocasta were grinning at each other and Davey was positively wet-eyed.

'Oh, something smells good in here, is it nearly ready? I am starving!' Davey said. 'The new baby is so divine, I felt like becoming a father myself, till I realised what that would entail!'

Jocasta gave him a disapproving glance. 'It's the most glorious, mystical thing you can imagine. The joining of a man and a woman, wonderful, isn't it?'

Oh, my God, she was looking at me! I blushed and turned away, my face on fire.

'I don't think we need any unsolicited testimonials, darling!' Edward said, laughing.

'And I think it's a bit late for extolling the virtues of heterosexual love to Davey!' Alex said.

'Yes, indeed,' Davey said acidly, throwing me a glance.

Tabitha put her head around the door and said sleepily, 'What's all the noise about? Is supper nearly ready? I keep smelling it, and although I know I shouldn't eat meat, I think I will have to! The smell is making my mouth water!'

Chapter Twenty-four

We all consumed dinner very greedily, and I was astonished to see even Tabitha wolf down a large helping of nearly everything. Edward seemed to have forgiven Jocasta and all seemed well.

When the last piece of fruit had been swallowed, and coffee cups pushed aside, the conversation turned, as it inevitably did nowadays, towards Tabitha and the baby.

'I wish you'd all leave me alone,' Tab said, fiddling with her hair. 'If I want to have my babies *and* give all my money to the travelling workshop, that's up to me. It's such bad karma to interfere with other people's lives, if only you all knew! You're probably all setting yourselves back loads of reincarnations. Besides, there's nothing you can do about it,' she added defiantly.

'We'll see about that,' Edward was heard to mutter.

Jocasta stood up, pushing her chair away from the table, and hurled her napkin to the floor like a challenge. 'Well, I for one have heard *more* than enough for one day. I am retiring to bed, I shall see you all at

359

the funeral tomorrow, at eleven fifteen. That should give Alex and Davey lots of time to dig the grave.' She eyed us all challengingly around the table, and then swept out of the room, calling for Edward to follow her, and please would he bring her knitting with him.

Edward sighed, and wished us all good-night.

Davey, Alex, Tabitha and myself sat silently at the table. It seemed that a stalemate had been reached. I cleared my throat and timidly said, 'Tab, what is it *you* really want to do?'

She smiled at me, and was about to reply when Davey said, 'Oh, for Chrissake, don't answer! I am sick to *death* talking over and over this. I'm going to bed, too, armed with a good book and a hot-water bottle. I suggest we all do.'

He stood up and patted Tab on the shoulder and dropped a kiss on the top of my head. He glanced sideways at Alex and muttered, 'Cheating on the final roof race – ridiculous! Sleep well, o brother mine, if your conscience allows.' Tabitha left the room with him, and Alex and I faced one another over the debris of the meal.

'My God,' Alex said, 'I love my family, but they can seriously damage your health, can't they?'

I knew exactly what he meant.

'Well,' he continued, 'this is unusual, isn't it? No sick monkey, no glass in bottom, no mad Claudia, that leaves just us. Time for bed, I think, don't you?'

I controlled my blush with sheer willpower alone. I would have felt uncomfortable with waltzing off to bed with Alex, but as the Chinese room was uninhabitable, and no one had mentioned at all where I was going to sleep that night, I thought it would be OK.

Alex laughed. 'Don't worry, I think everyone expects you to sleep with me tonight. I warn you now, I like to have the left-hand side of the bed, and I do rather enjoy having a bedtime story read aloud to me.'

He stood up and held his hand out to me. I glanced doubtfully at the mess on the table. It would be frightfully rude just to walk away from it and leave it all to Odessa, but then, everyone else had.

'Oh, leave it. If you feel terribly guilty, we can always set the alarm and run down early in the morning to wash up. Though, I must point out, I don't expect you to be able to run with ease anywhere at all tomorrow,' Alex said, giving a comedy leer at me.

I laughed and took his hand. We walked upstairs, with the smell of the pine cones that had been burnt on the fire following us. I noticed that the Christmas tree had shed absolutely no needles at all, which just proves how bloody cold the Abbey is.

Alex lit some candles in his room, to stop me 'noticing the stains on the walls', he said. I thought the room was lovely, stains or not.

I was self-conscious about taking my clothes off for about five seconds. But as Alex flung his off and leapt into bed, shouting at the iciness of the sheets, it all felt so normal, that I found I didn't mind at all.

I really can't bring myself to tell you the details of

that night. Let's just say that it was beyond rapture, and left me very, *very* impressed.

Alex was hell to actually *sleep* with, though. Or perhaps it was just due to my not having shared my bed with anyone for so long. I was used to having a double mattress all to myself, and Alex sprawled diagonally across it, whilst throwing his arm over my face. He also snored, ground his teeth, mumbled and generally behaved like someone with St Vitus's dance.

I wouldn't have changed it for the world.

I watched dawn creep through the curtains, and made tentative moves to extricate myself from his arms. He merely tightened his grip on me, and started to snore again.

As I'd spent most of the night pinching myself to make sure this was real, I could afford to wallow in a bit of smugness, I thought. So I studied his sleeping face with great interest. Every line and stubble growth was now permanently filed in my memory.

I wriggled some more and finally got free of his clasp. As I did, his eyes immediately flew open. He looked startled for a moment, and then he smiled.

'My God, I thought I must be dreaming. But I really do have Poppy Hazleton in my bed. How very, *very* delightful. Good morning, did you sleep well?'

'Good morning,' I replied formally. Adding, 'No, I bloody didn't. You snore like a hog, *and* you grind your teeth! Not to mention the mumbling and groaning and, ow, ouch, no, Alex, stop it! I mean it, stop it—'

Needless to say, we didn't get up for quite a while.

362

When we finally did, Alex (I was delighted to see) had that swaggering 'cat that swallowed the cream' look on his face. He was even whistling when he came out of the bathroom.

'Why are you smiling?' he asked, pausing while putting his socks on.

'Because you look so very, very pleased with yourself,' I said.

He sniggered. 'Well, so would you if you were me. The woman of my dreams in my bed, and I have acquitted myself admirably, or so I thought?'

'Oh, yes, yes, indeed. But there's no need to make it sound like a school exam, you know. It *does* take two . . .' I said primly, brushing my hair in the looking-glass.

'Hmm, well. All I can say is, look out. I have warned you that I intend ravishing you behind the grave. So make absolutely sure you're not wearing knickers!' Alex said in a teasing voice.

'Really, Alex! In this weather – I don't think so!' I said, laughing.

We were still giggling as we ran down the stairs.

Davey had beaten us to the clearing of the Painted Parlour, and was loading the dishwasher.

'Well, there's no need to ask how you two are,' Davey said, looking at us through narrowed eyes. '*Do* try and stop radiating lust or love or whatever it is, it's far too early for it.'

I poked my tongue out at him, and he grinned back.

'Tea?' he asked. 'Or do love's *not* that young dream feel they deserve champagne?'

363

'Tea would be lovely,' I said primly.

Davey and Alex laughed, and I was quite glad to find that I had crossed the first hurdle of meeting another Stanton after spending the night with Alex. Of course, it *was* only Davey who, I thought, was genuinely very pleased for me. I mean, he was the one who'd made me come down here and practically ordered me to have some fun, wasn't he? Maybe his idea of fun hadn't quite stretched as far as to include his brother – but what the hell.

Despite the upcoming funeral I was in a careless, happy mood that nothing could deter.

We sipped our tea, and then Davey and Alex went off, grumbling, in search of spades to dig poor little Jicky's grave with. I was clearing away the breakfast tea cups and unloading the dishwasher when Odessa came in.

'Mornin', Poppy,' she said, giving me the once-over with her remarkably clear eyes. 'Well, well, well, if it ain't the girl who'm got 'er man, well done, my lover.'

I began to blush, much to her obvious amusement.

She laughed at my (admittedly rather smug) embarrassment and continued to talk to me.

'Right then, now we'm alone, I should tell you what's goin' to happen—'

'Oh, I know,' I interrupted. 'The funeral takes place at eleven fifteen, and Davey is going to play some music, although quite what he has in mind, I don't know, I've never heard of "Yellow Monkey Rag", have you? I could only think of "Hey Hey We're the Monkees", which, I have to say, I *loved* when I was a child. And then—'

'No, you daft bugger, you sound like Jocasta. I mean, what's goin' to happen in the future 'ere.'

'Oh. No, I mean, what?' I said with alarm.

She glanced sternly at me. ''Tis obvious to any fool. But it does depend on 'ow you'm feel about it.'

'Feel about *what*?' I said, beginning to panic.

As she outlined her plan to me, I had to sit down at the table and fiddle nervously with a large bowl of glass grapes that were on it. I listened agog to what she was saying. When she had finished talking, I sat, open-mouthed, staring at her.

She crossed her arms over her bosom and regarded me with a serious look, tinged with anxiety. That in itself was quite worrying, I had never seen Odessa look remotely anxious about *anything*.

'Well?' she demanded, staring at me.

'I'll think about it,' I promised her, standing up and leaving the kitchen. I heard her call my name, but I ignored it, and walked slowly upstairs. I met Jocasta at the top of the stairs, who was looking very excited. No doubt looking forward to dressing up for the funeral, I thought to myself.

'Poppy, Poppy, do come quickly, where are the boys? Oh, never mind, *do* come and look . . .'

She took my hand in hers and dragged me towards the Chinese room, still a scene of devastation. She was chattering away breathlessly, telling me what she and Edward had discovered. I had only half my mind on what she was saying, most of it was still in the kitchen with Odessa.

365

'. . . So you see, I said to Edward, if one has a dream like that, there could well be something in it, I mean I know that Freud – dreadful little man, believed that *everything* was connected to sex, which of course is absolute twaddle, but dreams are different, aren't they? So, anyway, here we are!'

She pushed me into the room, and pointed upwards. I saw that Edward was clambering about amongst the rafters, the clear sky visible through the shattered roof. It looked highly precarious.

'Oh, Edward, do be careful,' I called out.

'Don't worry, m'dear, I have a very good head for heights. Stay still, I'm going to drop some things to you,' Edward carolled down in a very happy voice.

I glanced apprehensively at Jocasta, but she was beaming with joy, and calling to Edward to hurry up.

A shower of what looked like coins soon fell around us. I bent to pick one up and examined it. It was black with age, and I rubbed at it to try and see what it was.

'A William the Conqueror silver penny, and oh, look, a groat, that one's Roman, and oh, do look, Poppy, lots and lots of sovereigns!'

Jocasta was hopping up and down with excitement, gathering the coins up as quickly as she could.

'I completely see the attraction of that woman, what was her name now? You know, the one that was seduced by horrible Zeus who had disguised himself as a shower of gold, *most* seductive, I quite see now! Oh, Edward, how many more are there? Lots and lots, I hope!'

Jocasta called to Tab and Odessa about the hoard and asked them to fetch a basket, and soon we were all scooping up coins. As fast as Edward scattered them down, we picked them up, Jocasta exclaiming with delight at every find.

'Do you think they are *very* valuable?' Tabitha said doubtfully, rubbing at a Roman coin and trying to hold her dressing-gown together at the same time.

Edward's voice boomed down from the roof, 'We'll have to look them up in Spinks, but not a bad haul, I should say!'

Davey and Alex appeared at the doorway. 'We saw Edward from the garden in the roof, what the—' Alex said.

'Oh, darlings, isn't it wonderful?' Jocasta said. 'I dreamt that there was something lodged in the rafters and made Edward climb up to see, and *look* what he found! A positive treasure trove! They must have been up there for years and years ...'

Davey examined closely one of the many coins, and then started to rifle through the basket. 'My God – what a find!' he said excitedly.

Exciting or not, it was damn cold in the room, and my mind was on the plan that Odessa had cooked up in the kitchen. I kept glancing at her, and she motioned for me to go with her. The rest of the Stantons were too busy with their treasure to notice us leaving.

We inevitably, as one somehow did at the Abbey, ended up in the kitchen. Odessa obviously wanted an answer from me, but I didn't feel qualified to give one.

To be honest, I didn't feel qualified to answer *anybody* about *anything* at the moment. Odessa's sharp eyes were boring into me, and she cleared her throat and said, 'Well?'

I tried to avoid answering her and decided to make some tea to play for time. As I was banging about with cups and saucers, I thought furiously to myself. Odessa had suggested (well, it was more like a command, to be honest) that the whole Tabitha problem would be easily solved if I stayed at the Abbey, *with* Alex, to look after her *and* her baby or babies. Leaving Tab free to float off where and when she liked.

I could see the logic in it, but I had far too many conflicting emotions in my mind to think clearly. I mean, supposing Alex was horrified by the idea? Supposing Edward and Jocasta were? Not to mention Davey ... Besides, did I want to be a glorified nurse-maid to the Stantons? Part of me jumped at the idea, and part of me rebelled. I could see that it wouldn't just be Tab and the baby I'd be looking after, Jocasta practically needed a full-time nanny herself. As much as I loved them all, I could well end up as a sort of scullery maid if I wasn't careful.

'Well?' Odessa said again.

I looked Odessa squarely in the eyes and said, 'I *really* don't think that would be a good idea—'

'What wouldn't be a good idea?' Alex said, making me jump. I hadn't heard him come into the kitchen at all.

'Oh, nothing ... Would you like some tea?' I said, blushing.

'No. I want to know what isn't a good idea,' Alex said determinedly.

Odessa told him.

I turned away so I wouldn't have to see his face, and clashed the tea cups together in my agitation.

Alex exploded with irritation. 'What? *What!* She's not some sort of bloody unpaid nurse! She's not staying here to look after Tab's bloody offspring, what a *ridiculous* idea! –'

Phew. Well, that was good. At least we were on the same wavelength.

'– The only way that Poppy is staying here is as my wife, and even that –'

His *what?* Oh, my God. No, I mean really – Oh. My. God.

A strange sound caught my ears and I swung round to look at Odessa. She had both of her hands clamped over her mouth, obviously trying very unsuccessfully to smother her laughter. She caught my eye, and gave up any attempt. I gazed in wonder at her, she'd done this thing on purpose! She'd actually manipulated the whole situation to make Alex, well, I suppose the word propose has to be used, although of course, he hadn't actually asked me or anything. I stared at her, open-mouthed. I could hardly believe it.

I swung round to look at Alex who was still stomping around the kitchen hurling abuse at Odessa. He had managed to work himself into a tantrum of historic proportions. He eventually ground to a halt when he saw the tears of laughter streaming down Odessa's cheeks.

'You are, without question, the most wicked woman in Cornwall, possibly Britain,' he said, standing in front of her. 'Luckily for you, I happen to love you, as I do this woman here. Now then Poppy, will you or won't you be my wife? Odessa here is a witness, so no wriggling out of anything.'

Of course, the whole family at that point burst in through the kitchen door carrying the loot that they'd found in the roof.

Alex had dropped to his knees in front of me, and was holding his hands out to silence the rest of his family. They, however, knew a romantic situation when they saw one and crowded around, exclaiming and offering advice.

'Oh, darling, you need a ring, really you do—'

'Never mind your mother, my boy, you go right ahead and pop the question, but don't take no for an answer—'

'Marriage is such bad karma, can't you both commit to each other with a fire ceremony on the beach or something?'

'Oh, Poppy, think of the fun, we'll be related or something, and don't forget, I can always give you away or write a fantastic speech or—'

'Take my ring, darling, she needs one.'

I felt overwhelmed and, it has to be said, slightly weepy and a bit claustrophobic. Suddenly above the voices of the Stantons were excited children's voices. I

370

looked up and saw Toby and Eve from the farm, with Demelza and Tom.

'We're here for the funeral,' Toby explained gravely, looking reproachfully at most people's happy faces. 'It's meant to be *sad*.'

We assured him that it was, and it would be, whilst Jocasta cooed over the new baby, Bianca Poppy.

'I shall talk to you later,' Alex whispered, giving me an amused look.

I nodded and followed Davey and the others from the room where we formed a procession out to the pet cemetery. Jocasta hastily threw a selection of black shawls and scarves over us all, I had a particularly dreadful bit of tatty Spanish lace over my head which Davey said made me resemble a punk Madonna.

She had made the most marvellous coffin, though, decorated with vines and palm leaves. To remind Jicky of his homeland, I thought. That's what I needed at the moment – a bit of home. I needed time to think. I could tell Alex was disappointed that I hadn't immediately swooned at his suggestion of marriage, but I was far too overwhelmed about everything to consider it seriously. Common sense alone told me that this was far too hasty. We had barely known each other for more than days, not even weeks or months. There really hadn't been time for me to consider marrying him. I wasn't even sure that he was serious about it. I felt very confused and knew that I needed some space away from the Stantons.

Davey was playing a ragtime tune on the piano,

371

which he informed us was Yellow Monkey rag, and Alex took it upon himself to be the pallbearer. Jocasta seemed to be chief mourner, and made us all follow her down the garden. Edward, I reflected, would willingly follow her anywhere down the garden path, but what about me? I knew that if I accepted marriage with Alex, I would be marrying the whole damn lot of them.

The grave was tiny, but even so, with the ground being so hard, it must have been tough work to dig it. Edward read a service out from a leatherbound book and solemnly entered Jicky's name and the date to a list of now long-dead Stanton pets. Toby and Eve laid a small untidy home-made wreath of holly and pine on the grave, and Jocasta gave me a poinsettia flower to place on the top. We all had a bit of a snivel, which did me the world of good, and hurried back to the Abbey to get out of the cold. I noticed that Odessa hung back behind us, and placed what looked like a bunch of twigs on the grave, making sure that it was pointing a particular way.

Davey was pounding out any tune that had monkey in the title on the piano (of which there were a surprising amount) whilst Jocasta and the children made up a poem about the sad demise of Jicky. Edward and Davey dispensed whisky in a businesslike way, but I turned my nose up.

'It's a proper funeral drink,' insisted Davey, plying me with some.

'But I hate it!' I wailed, refusing even to sip at it. Really, the whole day was proving to be too much for me, and I slipped upstairs, determined to find a bolthole where I could sit and think by myself for a while. I collapsed on to a sagging *chaise longue* in the library and stared around me. What *was* I going to do? Was Alex even serious? I just didn't know. I mean, I know that I had been day-dreaming about it, but the whole thing had been set up by Odessa. I wasn't sure that Alex even knew what he wanted.

I thought of all my options, and after dithering around for a while I came to a momentous decision. I *would* make my mind up, but I would make it up at home. It was time for me to leave the Abbey.

Chapter Twenty-five

This, of course, was easier said than done. It was, after all, New Year's Eve. It was mildly surprising to me that no mention of any arcane ceremony had been made by the Stantons. They seemed to have a game, or rule, or tradition for every other day, but not this one. Or maybe they all met on the roof at midnight and howled at the moon. It wouldn't surprise me.

I felt surprisingly calm as I made my way back to the funeral party and announced that I really had to go home, and would Davey please drive me to the station.

A flood of advice was hurled at me, and to my horror I saw Alex leave the room, run up the stairs and slam his bedroom door.

I felt like a fool, and promptly burst into tears. I realised that I had mistaken my feeling of calm for one of sorrow and panic. Sorrow, I suppose, because everything was changing far too quickly for my liking, and panic because, well, I suppose the panic was quite obvious.

Dear Davey kindly ushered me to the kitchen and made me drink some tea, whilst Odessa sliced a loaf of bread and made sandwiches for everyone. Funeral meats, I supposed, gloomily.

'Now then, Poppy, you do know that the trains, if there are any, will be *hell*?' Davey said.

I nodded. 'I know, Davey, but I can't explain, I just need to be at home. I've had the most amazing, fantastic time, but I need to be at home to make it all feel real. Can you understand?'

Odessa was packing up some food in a bag, and plonked it in front of me, saying, 'You'm need that for that nasty train. Now then, I won't say goodbye, my lover, 'cos you'm be back very soon. Don't you fret, it'll all be fine.' She moved regally out of the kitchen and Davey and I looked at one another.

'She is, I have to say, usually correct in every way. Maddening, isn't it?' Davey said, looking thoughtfully at her departing back.

'Mmm, I suppose so,' I said doubtfully.

'Come on then, let's go, if you insist,' he said gruffly.

I jumped to my feet and ran upstairs to gather my belongings together. To my surprise, Jocasta and Tabitha had packed for me, and were standing at the top of the stairs. Oh, my God, perhaps they were in a hurry to get rid of me?

'Now then, Poppy darling,' Jocasta said warmly, clutching my arm, 'don't think we want you to go, because we *don't*, not at *all*. But I do so understand that you need to make your mind up at home. I was *exactly* the same when Edward proposed. I had to bolt back home and think very *very* hard, it drove me mad, quite

375

mad, for days, but then of course Edward sent me the most *divine* diamond and I simply—'

'Sshh, Ma,' Tabitha interrupted, 'I think she just wants to go.' To my surprise, she hugged me hard and whispered in my ear, 'Oh, do come back, I promise you won't have to look after my babies, we'll sort something out, but do come back, won't you?'

I hugged her back and ran down the stairs.

I said a flurry of goodbyes to the children, Tom, Demelza and Edward. Alex hadn't reappeared, which disappointed me, and worried me greatly. As I got in the car with Davey, I looked back at the huge outline of the Abbey silhouetted against the cold winter sky and saw the crumbling dragons that were perched on the roof.

'Davey, do look! The dragons on the roof, maybe that's the meaning of the motto, you know, dragons guarding the hidden gold, all those coins just underneath the dragons! What do you think?'

Davey laughed and we roared away from the Abbey with the children running beside us till the drive became too steep for them. I waved wildly at everyone, still searching for Alex, but I couldn't see him anywhere. I was frantic with worry and felt that I should have tried to talk to him, rather than leaving so hastily. I had thought at the very least that he would want to say goodbye to me, and arrange to call me or see me. I hadn't expected such a violent reaction to my departure. The countryside flashed past us, and all too soon we were in the steep high street of Bodmin, heading towards the station.

I glanced at Davey, who was remarkably quiet. His profile was as familiar to me as my own, but I couldn't judge by his expression what he was thinking.

'Davey?' I said tentatively.

'Hmm?'

'Are you cross with me?'

He barked a laugh, and said, 'Good God, no. I was rather hoping that you would be my sister-in-law, think what fun we could have . . . But, well, even if you say no, and I do see that Alex is quite a handful, you'll stay on in the shop, won't you?'

I nodded and felt tears fill my eyes. Oh, God, the second someone was nice to me the waterworks appeared. We were heading past the sawmill now and turned right into the station road. Davey drew the car up outside the station, and turned the engine off.

'OK. Have you enough money for the journey? Good. Well . . . Oh, God, I am *hopeless* at this sort of thing . . . I think it's much better if we don't look at one another, by the way.'

I dutifully turned my head away from him and studied the cars parked on the other side of the road. I saw out of the corner of my eye that he was fiddling with his watch chain.

'As I was saying . . . Oh, Poppy, I would love to have you as part of the family, but what I'm *really* trying to say is, well, even if you decide *not* to marry Alex, I consider you part of the family anyway . . . So, get

377

yourself home, have a good long think and, well, make sure you make the right decision. Don't forget, we're all barking mad, so think what you're taking on!'

I leant over to kiss him, and saw that Davey was genuinely worried about me. Just as I was getting out of the car, I said, 'Davey, tell Alex that I will phone him, I do want to speak to him, I mean, we haven't even arranged to see one another or anything and—'

'Don't worry. He'll be in touch,' Davey said reassuringly, adding under his breath, 'even if I have to kill him!'

I watched the car disappear down the road and staggered across the footbridge with my luggage to wait for a train to London. The platform was nearly empty except for a group of fairly tipsy students and a few couples who were sitting resignedly on a bench. I joined them and asked when a train was due.

'Well, my handsome, they *say* there's one on his way from Penzance, but that could mean anything,' the man said wearily. ''Tis not the best day to travel, New Year's Eve.'

I know. It seems that I would never pick the right day to travel. It sounded like one of those Chinese fortune cookies: Tuesday is inauspicious for travel, or for killing chickens, your fortunes will change on Saturday.

I settled down to wait, cursing that I hadn't picked up one of Davey's many books to while away the time with. It goes without saying that absolutely nothing was open at the station. The few kiosks that were there were firmly battened closed. I looked around me, the station was set miles away from the town and winter trees lined the platforms. It was still cold, but the air was soft. I was in danger of feeling very sorry for myself indeed, I mean, I know that the man of my dreams, well, *fantasies*, had proposed – but had he? No, not really. It was a crazy idea to even think about marriage with a man I'd only known for a few days. And, to be honest, brutally honest, I felt outclassed. Outclassed and outnumbered by the Stantons. I loved all of them dearly but I felt so bland and just plain damn *normal* in comparison that I wasn't sure if I could cope with them, let alone cope with Alex. He was a Ferrari to my Fiesta, if you know what I mean. You know, I was the Shetland pony, and he was the Arab stallion – and he hadn't even said goodbye. Bastard.

I planned what I would do when I finally got home. I'd phone Jessy and see what she was doing, maybe I could go round there and tell her what had been going on – and return her lovely clothes. Of *course* not, fool! It was New Year's Eve and she would undoubtedly be going to some wonderful, trendy party. The sort of party where they were all in some sort of creative job and wore odd expensive clothes and sat on each other's laps whilst quaffing brightly coloured cocktails. Damn. I'd have to resort to the TV tonight, and we all know what that means, don't we? Bloody Trafalgar Square full of idiots throwing themselves into the fountains and belting out 'Auld Lang Syne' in a drunken slur, followed by a slushy film or highland revels. Oh, God. Maybe I should just get quietly drunk?

A few more people had arrived on the platform and were gazing hopefully down the line. Needless to say, everyone seemed to be part of a couple, which made me feel even sorrier for myself, if that were possible.

Stop it, I told myself firmly. You've been single for years and years, nothing's changed. You were perfectly happy as you were before you came to Cornwall and you can carry on being so.

Hmm.

Well, it was worth a try.

Anyway, Alex *will* call. Davey will make him.

I know, maybe the Troll was at home? She'd love to hear about the carry-on in Cornwall. No, she was bound to be out at some garage party where she could pogo away and get blasted on cider. I resolved to pick up some wine on my way home, the corner shop was always open, day or night, and if you spoke very nicely to Mr Singh he would always sell you some after-hours alcohol. I drew my jacket closer to me and shivered slightly.

There seemed to be a sort of general movement on the platform, and although no announcement had been made, and certainly no train noises were to be heard, a collective bush-telegraph system had prompted people to stand at the edge of the platform with their bags. Like a lemming joining other lemmings for mass suicide, I joined them.

The train pulled into the station and as I climbed inside I realised just how long I'd been sitting in the cold. It was deliciously warm inside, and not very full.

With a wealth of seats to choose from I settled myself down at an empty table, resolving not to strike up a conversation with *anyone*. Not even a nun.

A cheerful-looking family opposite me were trying to appease the whimperings of their young daughter, who was asking for a drink.

'I shouldn't think the buffet'll be open, but I'll go and check,' the father said.

The woman leant towards me and said, 'We only just caught this train in Penzance by the skin of our teeth! We didn't have time to pick up any food or anything.'

I smiled politely back at her and blessed Odessa for giving me a packed lunch. I desperately hoped that the buffet *would* be open, and then I wouldn't feel too guilty about scoffing all of the undoubtedly wonderful Abbey picnic in front of them. After about ten minutes the man came back carrying tins of drink and packets of crisps.

'That's all they've got,' he announced, throwing them on the table, 'so let's all share and we'll be OK.'

The woman smiled again at me and offered me a packet of crisps. Oh, God, why were people so nice? I immediately felt guilty and rummaged around for the sandwiches that I'd been given.

Soon we were all eating everything in sight, and I assured the children – names of Tim and Alice – that Odessa's wonderful mushroom pâté really wasn't squished-up horse pooh.

'Really,' their father, name of Bill, said with admiration, 'I don't know where they get it from, really I don't!'

We passed a huge sweep of forest, and I thought

381

longingly of the moors around the Abbey, and how I hadn't had a chance to explore properly. The snow had gone by now, but I heard from the Brooks family how their journey home to Reading had been delayed by the terrible weather.

I pretended that I was sleepy, so that I could move back to my own seat and make a cushion from my scarf. I was staring out of the window without actually seeing anything and letting thoughts drift in and out of my mind. Why hadn't Alex said goodbye? *Why?* Was I so unimportant that I didn't warrant a farewell? Or was he just angry that I hadn't joined in the light-hearted proposal? I couldn't decide.

What were they all doing now at the Abbey? Probably getting sloshed on whisky at the funeral wake, making up more poems with the children about a naughty monkey that had died in the snow ... Edward and Davey were probably poring over an old coin catalogue trying to work out how much their secret stash was worth ... Tabitha might be pouring her heart out to Odessa in the kitchen, making endless cups of tea ... Jocasta would be crying out that she couldn't find her knitting and would someone help her, which reminded her of a story *circa* 1956 ... and Alex? I just didn't know.

I closed my eyes and let the movements of the train lull me to, if not sleep, then a light doze. I woke up with a jerk as the train stopped. Oh no, not *again*! I looked out of the window and saw that the train had merely stopped at a station, and not in the middle of a field, as before on my eventful journey down.

We started up again, after much slamming of doors, and once again I closed my eyes. With every turn of the wheel I knew that I had left behind me all that I had ever truly loved. But I would *not* weaken. I wouldn't. Alex would have to ask me properly, if he wanted me. I smiled to myself, as I knew only too well that I would be phoning the Abbey by tomorrow at the very latest, despite my resolve not to. There probably wouldn't be any point really, as they never answered the damn phone anyway. Perhaps I wouldn't have to, perhaps he'll call me. Oh, God! Shut up, shut up. Just doze till London, *then* allow yourself to dwell on it, I told myself firmly.

I was drifting off when I heard the calls of the ticket inspector. I rummaged through my handbag, and pulled out all the tat that had accumulated there in search of the ticket. Hairbrush, make-up bag, a pamphlet from the monkey sanctuary, tissues, keys, pens, diary, a picture that Eve and Toby had drawn for me of Jicky, purse, bag of mints, lighter, and the pearls that Davey had given me spilt on to the table, but no ticket. I scrabbled through the back of my purse, finding several old Waitrose receipts, a book of stamps (empty), credit card (very nearly empty) and a fiver, but no ticket. The inspector, who was obviously very tired and desperately wanted to be at the Wheel Tappers and Shunters New Year's Eve bash rather than where he was, regarded me indifferently.

'Can you give me five minutes?' I begged. 'I know it's here somewhere . . .' I made a token effort of looking again in my bag.

'I'll do the end of the carriage and come back, love,' he said, moving off.

Oh, great. Supposing he shoved me off the train at the next station? Why hadn't I checked before I got on the train? Davey had asked me if I was OK for money . . . I went through all the rubbish again, knowing of course that it wasn't there. Maybe I could throw myself on the mercy of the nice family that I'd shared my sandwiches with? I was just plucking up courage to ask them, when the ticket inspector returned.

For some reason or other he was smiling broadly. Maybe he's had a nip of brandy up the other end of the train or something.

'The *gentleman*,' he said, gesturing somewhere behind him, 'has paid for your ticket and wants to know if you'd care to join him in the carriage belonging to the Grand Duke.'

What? *What!*

I craned my head round the seat and peered down the carriage. Alex was sitting in a window seat, grinning broadly at me. I jumped to my feet and rushed down to meet him.

'Alex! How on earth—'

He had stood up, and was holding his arms out to me.

'Easy really, I borrowed Tom's car and drove like the clappers to Penzance, where I picked up this train. I've been sitting there watching you for ages! I must say I'd make an extraordinarily good stalker ... Come here, give me a kiss.'

The ticket inspector and the Brooks family were watching goggle-eyed. What surprised me the most was that I didn't even blush. We stood in the train kissing until I thought my lips would give out. I could feel his stubble burning my face, and it was starting to sting.

I finally pushed him away, to the obvious disappointment of the children, and we sat down.

We both started talking at once, and then laughed.

'Did you really think I'd let you go without saying something?' Alex asked, his eyes searching my face.

I squirmed slightly, and then nodded.

'You fool. Of *course* I wouldn't.'

I looked away and stared out of the window. The train was rushing past a stretch of sea, and it seemed that the waves were practically lapping at the carriage. Alex followed my glance, and said, 'Dawlish. A very romantic place, I've always thought, the sort of place your future wife agrees to marry you.'

I stared at him, still confused. This man took everything so lightly, what was the right response? I wasn't sure, I wasn't even sure of my own responses. I didn't know. I continued to look out of the window.

'Oh, dear, I can see some nifty talking is called for. But first, have this.'

Alex handed me a small envelope of crumpled brown paper. I gingerly unwrapped it. A dull lump of glass lay in the centre of its wrinkled brown nest. I looked questioningly at Alex, whilst fingering the glass. It felt hard and unyielding in my hand and I tried to work out the significance of it. It wasn't very big, about the size of a broad bean.

Alex laughed again, and said, 'It's a diamond, an uncut diamond. It worked for Ma and Pa, so I thought it might work for me.'

My God, I was holding a diamond! What were they? A family of international jewel dealers? I looked at it again more closely. Honestly, if you saw it on the floor you'd chuck it away without a second's thought. I tried to imagine it polished and cut, but it was impossible.

'Look at the light through it,' Alex commanded.

I dutifully held it to the light and gasped. A thousand facets twinkled back at me.

Alex leant forwards and gripped my hands. He held them so tightly that I could feel the stone pressing uncomfortably in my palms. But I didn't move one muscle. Whatever he was going to say would make me decide, of that I was sure.

'Poppy, I know it's too soon to make your mind up now. But let's get a few things straight. About Patrick, for instance, I was wildly jealous which is why I behaved like an idiot about him, and no, before you ask I most definitely did not have an affair with his ex-wife, I just drove her to London before she went out of her mind with boredom from living with him.'

I glanced at him and saw him concentrating on his words.

'I know all about the overwhelming effect of my

family, and I know that I must seem to be part of them. Well, I won't lie to you, I am. But it doesn't mean that I am not my own person. I love you. We can sort everything out, you will *not* be a nanny to Tabitha's babies, nor will you be a companion to my mother or a shop assistant to my brother. You will *not* be Edward's secretary or Odessa's scullery maid. You will be my wife. We will build a separate, but parallel life. We don't have to live at the Abbey, we don't even have to live in Paris, or London. I can work wherever I like . . . though I must say, I would draw the line at Ipswich. You really have become a part of us all you know.' He paused for a moment and then added, 'So, will you at least think about it?'

I had been going through as many emotions as the diamond had shown prisms. His hands were gripping mine tightly.

I thought of the Abbey and all the people that it contained. My best friend Davey practically lived there; for all his London ties it was to the Abbey that he went back time and time again. Even Tabitha, with her terrible-sounding workshop, had gone there when she was in trouble. Then there were Jocasta and Edward, the hub or the heart of the Abbey, holding us all under their spell, and of course, the true witch of the place – Odessa.

I looked at Alex's face and I saw the laughter lines and the set of the eyes that had never known a refusal. Yes, I was pretty sure that he was a bit of a bounder, in Patrick's terms. But women have always had a soft spot for bounders, haven't they? He might make me very unhappy or, of course, he might make me delirious with joy. It was a gamble. But all partnerships were, weren't they?

'Again, I won't lie to you and Odessa has this mad plan that Tab will take one of the twins with her, and we'll have the other one – but we can sort all that out. We can sort anything out if we want to enough.'

The pressure on my hands now was unbearable, and I tried to wriggle them away.

'No, not till you have promised to think about it,' Alex said urgently.

I nodded.

'What?' Alex said. 'You have to say it out loud.'

'Yes, Alex. I promise to think about it,' I said softly, my heart nearly stopping with delight.

Alex whooped with joy and sent the diamond spinning across the table and on to the floor. We both dived under the table to rescue it.

'Thank God! Now follow me,' Alex said, taking me by the hand.

'Where are we going?' I asked.

'Sshh, you'll soon see. But I'm rather hoping it's something to help you make up your mind.'

Alex dragged me down the lurching train, passing through the now shuttered buffet, first-class carriages and a crowded aisle where people were jostling to get out of the train with luggage. I saw we were at Reading and I waved to the Brooks family as they left the train, and they wished me a Happy New Year.

'And to you!' I called back, grinning my head off.

Alex pushed open a door, and we were in a sleeping compartment. There were candles, a bottle of brandy and a very tatty green velvet throw over the sleeping platform.

I whirled round to look at Alex. 'How did you manage this?' I gasped.

'Fast thinking, a hefty bribe to the guard and a strong belief that you would say yes,' he said, pushing me gently down on the bed.

He continued: 'The train stops at Paddington, waits for three hours and then turns around and comes back to Penzance. It's the overnight sleeper, which by my reckoning gives us a good nine hours in the Grand Duke's carriage . . .'

Epilogue

I never did make it back to London.

Life with the Stantons was as exciting and maddening as I had anticipated, but the rewards were great. To feel truly part of a family was a wonderful experience for me.

I set up (with a great deal of prompting and general good-natured interference from Alex) a chocolate mail-order business under the Abbey name, and Jocasta designed the box with a sleeping dragon on it. These little blue-and-white boxes found their way into many a famous name's home, and soon we were deluged with orders. I even had a 'Jicky' special that involved chillies, which have become very popular.

Tabitha had her babies – Odessa was, of *course*, right. She gave birth to twins, a boy and a girl named (which made Alex and me giggle a bit) Cosmo and Cosima. Tabitha took the babies to a commune in the South of France, much to the general disgruntlement of the family, who dearly wanted to dandle the babies on their laps and keep them where they could see them. But I think she was right. The commune is a lovely place, with olive trees and the sparkling Mediterranean in the distance.

Edward and Jocasta spent nearly all the money they made from the coin find on the Abbey – a new roof *and* central heating were installed – but there was enough left over for a trip to Egypt for them both, where they indulged in rather a lot of superfluous antique buying. Edward came back complaining of malaria, but we all think it's an excuse for him to take it easy in his study most of the time. He spends most of his time in there, rewriting his will.

Davey surprised everyone, including himself, I think, by falling for a Thai man called Nang who he met over there last year on a buying trip for the shop. Nang is exquisitely beautiful, and eyes us all with delighted amusement, as well as showing Odessa some fabulous Thai cooking in the kitchen. He runs the shop, and Davey, in London with ruthless efficiency. They come down to the Abbey often, sometimes bringing Jessy with them, to the delight of Patrick who seems smitten.

Alex travels a lot, and when he does, I miss him desperately, but I have no time to wallow in loneliness, being surrounded as I am by such eccentric, exciting company. Tom and Demelza are just round the corner, and she and I have become firm friends.

Two years later, we still haven't set a date for our marriage, mainly because we can never agree on a location. Davey favours a beach setting in Asia, Edward the Nile, Jocasta rather fancies the top of the Eiffel Tower, and Alex wants somewhere dramatic like in the middle of a desert. I'd rather have the wedding at the Abbey.

Odessa? Well, she looks after us all, as well as teaching me how to prepare lotions and potions.

She is insisting that we marry in Cornwall, and if it's a battle of wills between Odessa and Alex, I know who my money goes on.

I know I am a different person from the shy, dithering woman who was seduced by Alex on a train two years ago. Sometimes I look back, and wonder what would have happened to me if I hadn't met the Stantons. I know one thing for sure, my life would be far emptier.

Sometimes I catch Odessa's eye when we are making chocolates in the kitchen, and Jocasta is trying to help by trailing through the room dropping hairpins and demanding that we all stop what we are doing to admire the afternoon sky, and Edward plays some jazz very loudly in his study, then Alex slams through the front door, kissing us all hello, and we smile together. Those are the times when I know that I am probably the happiest woman in the world.